A Single Spy

Also by William Christie

The Warriors of God

Mercy Mission

The Blood We Shed

Threat Level

The Enemy Inside

Darkness Under Heaven (As F. J. Chase)

Bargain with the Devil (As F. J. Chase)

A Single Spy

William Christie

Minotaur Books
New York

A SINGLE SPY. Copyright © 2017 by William Christie.
All rights reserved. Printed in the United States of
America. For information, address St. Martin's Press,
175 Fifth Avenue, New York, N.Y. 10010.

www.minotaurbooks.com

The Library of Congress Cataloging-in-Publication Data
is available upon request.

ISBN 978-1-250-08081-3 (hardcover)
ISBN 978-1-4668-9265-1 (e-book)

Our books may be purchased in bulk for promotional,
educational, or business use. Please contact your
local bookseller or the Macmillan Corporate and
Premium Sales Department at 1-800-221-7945,
extension 5442, or by e-mail at MacmillanSpecial
Markets@macmillan.com.

First Edition: April 2017

10 9 8 7 6 5 4 3 2 1

For Richard Curtis,
for never giving up

Acknowledgments

To my family and friends, for their constant support and encouragement.

There is always the one person who first says, *You can do this. Try.* So I must always single out my mother for the special praise she so richly deserves.

To Keith Kahla of Minotaur Books, for the best, most thorough, and most pleasurable editorial experience I've ever had. Thanks for putting in the work, Keith.

To my agent, Richard Curtis of Richard Curtis Associates, Inc. In each book I always write something along the lines of "Only Richard and I know what we went through." This novel he carried through fire and flood. I'll never be able to properly express my thanks. Richard, you deserve the dedication, and more.

Readers can reach me at christieauthor@yahoo.com, william christieauthor.com, or Author William Christie on Facebook.

PART I

The New
Soviet Man

1

THE COMPLAINT BEGAN TO RUMBLE DEEP DOWN IN THE mule's throat. Alexsi hopped up from the ground and rubbed her nose and ears before the sound could work its way out and erupt into a deafening bray that would ruin them all. She scuffed her front hooves in the sand, settled down, and kept silent. If you gave a mule something to think about other than what was annoying it at that particular moment, it tended to forget all about it. You really couldn't force a mule to do what it didn't want to. The other men would beat them, of course, but then people just liked beating things. Especially what couldn't beat them back. But all he had to do was offer the mules the occasional sugar beet and they would follow him like dogs.

The desert looked flat from a distance. But once you were inside it there were all kinds of subtle hills and valleys that could hide men and horses and a string of mules from plain sight. And a teenage boy.

Alexsi looked up at the progress of the moon and saw that it was past midnight but still at least three hours from sunrise. It was a half-moon. Any fuller made it easier to see at night, but also made it too easy to see them. From the stars he knew they were on course. It was cold, and now that the mule was quiet he stopped stroking her and stuck his hands back into the pockets of his lamb's fur coat. She nuzzled him, though he knew it wasn't out of love. She was looking for a treat.

He checked her load to make sure it wasn't rubbing on her. The two long rolls strapped to the yoke harness contained Mosin-Nagant rifles wrapped up in canvas like carpets. Rifles were one of the few things the Soviet Union produced that someone in another country would want to trade for. The other mules also carried rifles, and tins of rifle ammunition.

The border with Iran was up ahead. At this spot it was just a horse road patrolled by Russian border guards, but the talk was that soon there would be a tall wire fence and land mines. So everyone was rushing to make what money they could before that happened.

The men he was with were Shahsavan tribesmen, as were those they were waiting for. Nomads, Azeri-speaking, and the arbitrary Soviet-Iranian border had cut them off from their traditional pasture migrations from southern Azerbaijan to northern Iran and back. When Reza Pahlavi, the one-time sergeant who now called himself Shah, seized power in Iran in 1921, his first goal had been to bring all the independent tribes to heel. He defeated the Shahsavan in 1923 and exiled their chiefs. Some of the tribesmen moved to the city of Ardabil and settled down. The rest still ran their flocks of sheep, camels, and horses between pastureland according to the grass seasons and tried to keep a step ahead of the government. But fewer pastures meant having to fight for them. And smaller flocks and less powerful chiefs meant more raiding to stay alive. So they always needed guns.

On the other side of the border their Azeri cousins had taken one look at collective farms and Soviet power and gone into smuggling. Alexsi knew they were on borrowed time but he wasn't sure they did. They still talked about being free men.

They allowed an outsider to ride with them because Alexsi could do three things they could not. The first was read and write. He'd been living by his wits on the streets of Baku. Then one morning he bumped into four Shahsavan, looking much harder than the usual yokels from the hills, wandering about hopelessly lost looking for a smuggling contact. Though Alexsi hadn't known that at the time. Always on the hustle for a few kopecks, he'd offered to guide them and they'd accepted out of sheer desperation.

During the meeting he'd had to wait outside in the hall for his money, trying to look young and meek while a couple of enormous thugs stared him down. When it was over, the rubles the tribesmen paid him were obviously counterfeit. After he quietly passed that information along, the knives flashed out and an instant later the two thugs were left vainly trying to hold their cut throats together. It was even worse than slaughtering sheep, since sheep were tied up and didn't run around spraying blood everywhere once the killing cut was made. At that point Alexsi was thinking that leaving without his money might not be the worst thing in the world, but the Shahsavan, who took being cheated badly, kicked down the door in order to reopen negotiations with their contact.

Things only got worse. All the noise attracted attention, and with more thugs pounding up the stairs, Alexsi was presented with the choice of greeting them by himself in the hallway or running into the room where the fight was going on. Inside, and with no good options, he dove for the nearest neutral corner and tried to make himself as small as possible. It wasn't like a boys' fight: a live-or-die contest never lasted long. This one ended with the contact and four of his men spilling their guts on the floor and screaming their last breaths while the tribesmen fished the real money out of their pockets. The Shahsavan, he learned, only cut throats when they were in a hurry, wanted things kept quiet, or didn't feel the need to make a point. Having seen all he wanted to, Alexsi was the first one out as soon as a safe path to the door presented itself. He wasn't alone. The tribesmen thundered after him, either out of instinct or terror at the prospect of being lost in the big city again. Later the Shahsavan were enormously impressed that, rather than head down to the street where they might bump into more of the disemboweled criminal boss's henchmen, he'd led them up and over three adjoining rooftops, choosing to ignore the fact that he hadn't exactly been waving his arms and urging them to join him. As soon as they all were safe and laughing at their good luck, they offered him a job.

The second thing that kept him in their company was his ability with locks. During their escape he'd opened a locked rooftop door in a few seconds, and the tribesmen thought that was the most amazing thing they had ever seen. Urban life and its tools and ways were foreign to them, and they'd been used to kicking their way into and out of places. A confederate who could open locks was more in keeping with their stealthy desert instincts. Not to mention safer.

The third reason was that, incredibly enough considering their trade, he spoke Russian and Farsi and they didn't. You needed Russian for school, and growing up on a kolkhoz, a state farm near the Iranian border, meant you picked up a lot of Farsi. The Shahsavan only spoke Azeri and their tribal dialect, and with their nomad sense of superiority didn't feel the need to know anything else. Usually any stranger they bumped into during border crossings ended up being disposed of by the jackals, but they considered having someone who could translate very useful in emergencies.

Riding and shooting were second nature to the Shahsavan, and they taught him to do both better than he'd ever dreamed. They also taught him to live in the desert and scout without being seen. They insisted he become a Muslim, and to keep from ruining a good deal he agreed, praying when they did.

After a few trips he had more rubles hidden away than most party bosses in the Soviet Union, let alone sixteen-year-olds. He didn't even have to break into the state food stores to eat anymore. Though he still did occasionally to get the good stuff they kept locked away for themselves, and for the sheer thrill of burglary. It had been his routine since escaping from the state orphanage three years before. Whatever he didn't use himself he sold in the flea market in Baku. The market might not be Communist, but the authorities allowed it because things were so bad that if they didn't let people sell their possessions in order to buy food there might be a revolt. They kept a close watch, though, so Alexsi had learned it was better to get some old woman to sell your loot in exchange for a piece of it.

They were waiting there in the desert because the smugglers didn't bother keeping track of the Russian border guard patrols. They had a much simpler and more direct method. While they paused just short of the border, four tribesmen were sneaking up on the nearest border guard post a kilometer away. The guards were used to harassing rifle shots from angry tribesmen, but when these four opened fire with their brand-new Degtyarev light machine gun the post would panic and shoot off their emergency flares to summon all the roving patrols back to their aid. And the smugglers could then cross the border unmolested.

Sometimes the rifles would be exchanged for Iranian gold, which was best. Sometimes opium, when it was in season. But usually they drove back a flock of sheep, the tribe's main currency. Harder to manage, but food on the hoof outside the state system could always be turned into good money.

The rifles came from a Shahsavan sergeant in the local Red Army garrison, the Azerbaijan Division. Older weapons packed in grease and set aside for wartime mobilization. Replaced in their crates with broken rifles that were supposed to be disposed of. The crates were counted regularly but no one ever bothered to look inside. The same with the ammunition. The wooden crates were still stacked up in the armory, but the metal cans of bullets that had been inside them were long gone.

Sound carried a long way in the desert at night, and everyone heard the shooting start at the border guard post even though it was kilometers away. Usually the machine-gun fire was followed by a patter of frantic shots from the post, but this time there was a roar of return fire. It made the mules jump, and Alexsi had to go down the line to calm them.

The flares popped in the far distance, little pinheads of red and white light. Now everyone was counting down the time for the patrols to ride to the rescue.

A soft, low whistle spread through the air. The kind of muffled sound you hear for a brief instant at night and then dismiss that it ever happened. The tribesmen could make it carry a very long way. Without further command everyone silently slipped back onto their horses and the column of riders headed out. Even the mules got moving without complaint, probably because it was warmer to be walking.

With flankers on both sides of the column looking out for ambush, they crossed the border road into Iran. The Iranian border guards didn't even have to be paid off. They didn't patrol at night. It was too cold and too dangerous.

After a while they stopped, and following the usual routine Alexsi rode up to the head of the column.

Selim, the leader of the tribesmen, softly called out, "Anatoli, time to go."

It was a world of informers—Alexsi knew that only too well. So when the Shahsavan first asked his name, and names were of enormous importance to them, he had given that of his worst enemy back in the kolkhoz. If word ever got out of a Russian boy riding with a group of tribal smugglers, and it probably would, the authorities could go back to the farm and arrest Anatoli. Every time they called him that, Alexsi imagined Anatoli desperately trying to convince the police he wasn't a smuggler, and it was hard to keep the smile off his face.

It was his job to go out and meet with the scout for the Iranian group, and then bring them all together. This was much safer than two groups of armed men bumping into each other in the darkness. Everyone was always alert to the possibility of other raiders waiting in ambush to take their goods.

"There was a lot more shooting at the border guard post," Alexsi whispered.

"Don't worry," Selim replied. "They probably put more men in there since the last time."

Alexsi was worried anyway. It sounded like a lot more men. He slid down from his horse and handed the reins to Selim. "Rashid, let's go."

He and Rashid always went out together. One man wandering alone in the desert at night might never be seen again.

"I can't walk," Rashid replied. "I'm sick."

Rashid was his age. The Shahsavan considered a sixteen-year-old a man, and as a matter of practicality liked their scouts to be the fastest runners and smallest targets. Rashid had never been sick before. If he'd been sick, why had he come along in the first place?

Alexsi walked down to Rashid's horse. "What's wrong?"

"I'm sick to my stomach," Rashid said with a groan. "I can't walk."

Alexsi instantly knew that Rashid was lying. It wasn't even a good act.

"I'll send someone else with you," said Selim, who had heard everything.

"No, I'll go by myself," Alexsi said quickly.

There was a pause while Selim thought that over. "Are you sure?"

"I'll be all right," said Alexsi.

Selim thought it over some more. "If you get lost or there's any trouble, fire one shot and we'll be right there."

"I will," said Alexsi.

Selim leaned over his saddle and pointed out the small hump of a hill in the near distance. One desert hill in the dark of night was never the same as any other to the Shahsavan.

"I see it," Alexsi said.

Selim patted him on the back.

Alexsi left his rifle on his horse. It was too unwieldy at night. Ducking low to be out of sight, he unhooked the water bag from his saddle and slung it across his back. Straightening up, he reached under his coat and drew the Nagant revolver from the leather flap holster, the same as the secret police bluecaps wore. He looked back at Selim, who nodded, and trotted off into the darkness.

As soon as he was out of sight of the column, Alexsi squatted down on the sand to think things over. Something was definitely wrong. Rashid was obviously faking so he wouldn't have to go with him, so there was something more out there in the desert. Perhaps the tribesmen had decided to get rid of him, and Selim was a better actor than Rashid? No, they would have just cut his throat instead of putting on a big act. Probably Rashid together with his brothers had made a deal with someone and arranged an ambush to take the guns. Back there Alexsi had wanted to get on his horse and gallop off, but the Shahsavan would have ridden him down and killed him. In any event he wasn't about to go walking straight up to that hill.

Alexsi rose and headed off to his right to make a wide circle around the nearest high ground. He moved very slowly. The Shahsavan had taught him that the secret to quiet movement was just tamping down your natural impatience and going achingly slowly. He walked bent over, so as not to present a human profile on the desert horizon.

Alexsi stopped every few paces to turn his head about and listen carefully. And especially to smell. The clear desert air gave away many secrets. At that moment the wind shifted and he smelled cigarettes. Not someone smoking. The smell of it on their clothes. So there was someone out there, and not just up on the hill he was supposed to go to.

He dropped to the ground and began crawling on his stomach. Such a smell wouldn't carry very far. He moved into the wind so it could continue to bring him information.

There was a slight rise to his front, and Alexsi inched his way up toward it, feeling with his hand for any rocks his movement might dislodge. He stopped. Someone was up there. He could feel it. Then he heard the metal rasp of a water bottle being unscrewed. It puzzled him. Tribesmen used skin water bags, not canteens. As if to reward his patience, the breeze brought him more information. Rustling. Whispers. The wooden clunk of a rifle stock hitting a stone.

There were a lot of them, and they were all around. His column of Shahsavan seemed to be in the middle of a crescent of ambushers. But too noisy to be other tribesmen. Iranian soldiers? No. Iranian soldiers wouldn't come out at night. And these were more skilled than Iranian soldiers, though not as skilled as tribesmen. They had to be Russians. But why would Russians be inside Iran?

And then he realized. This meeting was the only sure place they would stop. Rashid must have been caught by the Russians and squealed to save his skin.

As always fear first announced itself in the pit of his stomach. Alexsi's finger caressed the curve of the revolver's smooth metal trigger, but he withdrew it. Firing a shot would be like shouting his presence to the world. And between the Russians and the Shahsavan was not the place to be once shooting started.

What to do? Running back to the Shahsavan meant dying with them. Trying to sneak through the line of Russians while they were ready for ambush would be next to impossible. Alexsi thought about finding a place to hide, and then making an escape after the battle. But even if he didn't get shot in the cross fire, the Russians might wait until daylight and then sweep the area for survivors. And he was on foot. How far could he get before being caught? The Russians had to be on horses. Horses.

Alexsi set his revolver on the sand and pushed the wooden toggle out of the loop to open the large lower pocket of his coat.

The Shahsavan lived by rifles. Machine guns were a wonderful modern novelty but frowned upon for the way they gobbled up scarce and expensive ammunition. And the crate of Model 1914

hand grenades from the Great War that turned up in one shipment they regarded only as exciting toys. With instruction provided by one tribesman, a deserter from the Red Army who left
immediately after castrating his Russian lieutenant for the unpar-
donable insult of striking him, they passed an enjoyable afternoon
throwing the grenades in the desert: exclaiming loudly at the
explosions and nearly blowing themselves up because they had
no tradition of throwing things and were barely able to get the
bombs far enough away to keep from being killed.

But Alexsi had kept his, thinking it might come in handy.

The grenade was shaped like a small bottle with a stick extending from the narrow end, except it was all made from sheet metal.
Remembering the huge explosions that came from those metal
sticks was making his hand shake. Alexsi put the grenade down
and flexed his finger to make it stop. He picked it back up, grasping the handle and depressing the spring-loaded priming lever.
There was a metal safety ring that went around the handle to
keep the lever from flying up and activating the fuse, and he made
sure that was between his third and fourth fingers. He armed the
grenade by turning the safety catch away from the hammer at
the end of the priming lever.

Quickly, before his hand could start shaking again, he reared
back, judging the distance, and hurled the grenade at the top of
the rise. As it left his hand the ring between his fingers slipped off
the handle and let the lever fly up, completing the firing sequence.

There was a loud pop from the grenade in midair as the primer
ignited the powder train, and someone up on the hill fired a nervous shot in response.

Alexsi hadn't been counting on that. The Shahsavan instantly
shot back, and the entire hillside around him erupted in muzzle
flashes. There had to be more than a hundred Russians.

This was bad. Russian bullets cracked overhead and Shahsavan bullets exploded into the ground all around him. Alexsi stuck
his nose into the desert sand and curled up into the smallest shape

possible. Bullets cracked like cart whips around him. Their passage was so close he could even feel the air move. The sound of so many guns was deafening. Now his hand was shaking so badly he was afraid he'd pull the revolver trigger without meaning to. So much time seemed to go by he thought he'd made a mistake with the grenade, and it was his only hope.

Then there was a huge bang followed by screaming atop the hill. That was it.

It seemed like the whole world was pressing down on him in an effort to keep him there against the ground. The last thing he wanted was to get up but he knew it was certain death to stay there as the Shahsavan found the range.

He lurched up, even though the usual strength had drained away from his legs. He scrambled up the hill, clawing the sand with his free hand while the other held the revolver. He could practically feel the flames from the Russian muzzle flashes. He definitely felt the Shahsavan bullets remorselessly lashing the air all around him.

Reaching the top, Alexsi ran into the billowing black smoke cloud from the grenade, which was the only place there wasn't any shooting going on. He stepped on a soft body that screamed in response, and as he recoiled away from it violently collided with someone running in from the opposite direction. The impact slammed him onto the ground and nearly knocked him senseless.

Alexsi struggled to both get his breath back and find his feet again. The other party loomed over him, wearing that silly Red Army *budionovka* felt hat with the high central peak that looked like he had a funnel on his head, and bellowed, "Watch where the fuck you're going!" Then looked down a little closer through the smoke and said, "Hey . . ."

Alexsi shoved the revolver in his face and pulled the trigger. The muzzle blast shocked him—he had never fired the pistol at night—and seemed to set the Russian on fire. The Russian fell backward over his legs. Alexsi frantically kicked him off so he could get up. As he did, he snatched up the *budionovka* hat with his free hand and swung the revolver around, ready to keep shooting.

But the noise of all the Russians on the hill firing their rifles was so deafening that his pistol shot had been swallowed up in it. As the grenade smoke thinned out, Russians were running around. They were probably screaming, but it was impossible to hear them.

Alexsi slapped his own lamb's fur *papak* hat off his head, replaced it with the dead Russian's hat, and came up off the ground right into a dead run. As he went over the top of the hill, someone close by shouted in Russian, "Come back here, coward!" A pistol shot zinged by him, but it only made him run faster.

He picked up speed going down the reverse slope, so fast that he nearly got ahead of his legs and fell on his face. He leaped over scrub bushes and was concentrating so hard on his footing in the dark he almost didn't see the Russian holding the six horses.

The Russian's rifle was slung so he could grasp all the reins. "What's going on?" he shouted to Alexsi in his Russian cap.

"Bring up the horses!" Alexsi yelled back in Russian, rapidly closing the distance between them.

"What?" the Russian called out, just as Alexsi slammed into him and smashed the butt of the revolver between his eyes.

The Russian crumpled to the ground, breaking Alexsi's fall. He dropped his pistol and lunged for the horses' reins before the startled animals could realize they were free and run off. One of them got away from him, but he had the other five. Then he frantically scrambled over the ground to reclaim his pistol. It seemed that every time he reached out his free hand the excited horses he was holding in the other would rear up and yank him back.

He was just about to abandon the effort when his hand touched metal in the darkness. Alexsi jammed the revolver back into his holster and swung up onto the saddle of the nearest horse. He spurred it into a gallop, pulling the rest of the animals along behind.

When he reached the nearest rise the desert lit up faintly as the Russians began firing flare pistols over the Shahsavan's heads. Alexsi could see the Russian muzzle flashes all around them, except for in the rear where they had ridden in, and he knew that the Shahsavan would be following their usual drill when in trouble and scattering to the four winds, only to rendezvous at a prearranged place later. He thought he might still be able to convince them that the first shot had been his and he'd tried to warn them.

As if to prove him both right and wrong, firing broke out at the rear of the Shahsavan column. But there were at least two Russian machine guns, and Alexsi was awed by the sight of them firing some kind of special bullets that made paths of light in the darkness, telling them where to aim. The spitting lines of light crisscrossed along the rear of the Shahsavan column, sealing off the only escape route.

Alexsi turned and spurred his horse even faster, knowing his smuggling days were over. There were no canteens on the Russian horses, though he had enough water in his own skin bag to make it. He thought briefly about a life in Iran, then turned the horses back toward Azerbaijan and what he knew.

He galloped his horse until it collapsed from exhaustion. He left it splayed out on the desert sand, blown, ribs heaving, and jumped onto the next one, which had had a much easier time running without a rider. When the third went down he kept the last two at a steady trot, alternating between them whenever one tired. As long as he stayed away from the roads, the Russians, with one man to a horse, could follow his tracks for as long as they liked but would never be able to catch up with him.

2

ALEXSI CROSSED KHAGANI STREET INTO THE SHADE FROM THE morning sun and didn't bother looking up at the statues of the poets in the stone arches above. At first he'd wondered what it took for anyone but a general or a ruler to have a statue carved in their image, so he made sure to find out their names and read their works. Some were good, and the others probably knew someone.

He trotted up the white stone stairs, as always feeling small against the sand-colored columns that towered up to the next floor and the glass skylight above. Turning right and through another door, he stopped and drew a breath. He loved the way libraries smelled. And the General Library was not only the biggest in Baku, but the biggest in all Azerbaijan.

They didn't let you take books home, but that was all right. At the lending libraries you had to give your name and show your papers, and he had no intention of ever doing either. At the General Library you found the books you wanted in the card files, then gave a list to one of the librarians in the reading rooms who went and fetched them. In this particular room there was a very pretty young librarian who was always friendly. If she was there today, and still friendly, he was going to ask her to lunch. He'd tell her he was older than he looked, and she would have to be impressed that he had the rubles to pay.

The reading room was always half full of pensioners this time of the morning. There were three long rows of plain wood desks and chairs, enough for about five hundred people. The ceilings were very high, and most of the light came from the outer wall that was all equally high arched windows. It reflected off the sand-colored walls, which glowed almost pink from the morning sun.

Ah, yes, his librarian was there behind the desk. She was speaking to one of the others, but when she looked up and saw him instead of the usual shy smile there was fear on her face.

Alexsi froze, just for an instant, then immediately whirled about and sprinted for the door. When he was only halfway there it crashed open and two burly men in suits, obviously cops, charged through to block his escape.

Alexsi skidded to a halt, grabbed an empty chair, and slung it at their legs to slow them down. He whirled about again and dashed toward the librarian's desk, the only other exit. A skinny middle-aged man in an even worse suit than the cops' stepped out into the aisle, his hands outstretched. He said, in that reasoning adult voice Alexsi always found so annoying, "Now, stop—"

Without even breaking stride, Alexsi punched him square in the nose.

With a cry of surprise and pain, the man crumpled to the floor. Alexsi ran right over him. Should have minded his own business.

He was almost to the librarian's desk when two more cops suddenly appeared around that.

Alexsi halted again, trapped. Another instant of indecision, then he grabbed an empty chair and ran toward the windows. He leaped onto a desk, trampling the newspaper of a bearded old man who looked up at him wide-eyed, and hurled the chair at the glass panels of the arched window.

But instead of going through the window and opening up a path to the outside ledge, as he'd planned, the chair only cracked the glass and bounced right back into his face. The chair hit before he could get his hands up, and he slipped on the slick wooden desktop and fell flat on his back. Now people were screaming loud enough to make his ears hurt. Before he could move again the end of a club rammed into his stomach just below his ribs. It forced all the air out of his lungs and folded him up into a tight ball.

Helpless, Alexsi gasped for breath but was unable to draw any in. A fist slammed into his ear and he was dragged off the desk and onto the floor. His arms were expertly pinned behind his back, which only made his breathing problem worse. Thinking he'd die of suffocation, he violently thrashed about, more to get some air than to break free. But before he could do either the club cracked into the back of his head and the world went black.

3

ALEXSI WOKE UP WITH HIS CHEEK PRESSED AGAINST A DAMP concrete floor. He tried to lift his head but it felt like it was tied to an anvil. He then tried to roll over but was halted by a crushing pain in his skull. His vision was fuzzy; he couldn't seem to focus his eyes. Unable to do anything else, he lay there waiting, hoping really, that some or all of that would change for the better. It had been a long time since he'd felt that way. Since he'd gotten free of his father. Until now a beating had just been a bad memory.

He knew he was in a prison cell—he didn't need a clear head to figure that out—but he had to concentrate hard to remember how he got there. Bit by bit, it came back to him.

The legs of a table were right in front of his face. There was a stool next to it. Those two things, and his body—which was not fully extended—took up the entire floor space of the cell. Not a cell, really. More a cubicle. No room to lie down straight. Definitely no room to move around. The walls were white. And when he was finally able to roll over, very slowly, he saw that the light, so brilliant it hurt his eyes, was coming from a bulb dangling from the ceiling inside a protective wire cage. It had to be at least 200 watts.

Since it was too painful to do anything else, Alexsi took stock of his pockets. His knife was gone, as was his money and his lock picks. His papers, too. The only thing they'd missed was the five hundred rubles he'd sewn into the lining of his coat. And the little folding knife in the pocket he'd sewn to his underwear right above his cock. That was another Shahsavan trick; the police always balked at searching you thoroughly down there.

After a great deal of effort he made it up to the stool, though it felt like being stabbed in the head over and over again. On the table was a metal plate with half a small loaf of black bread and an enamel mug of water. Alexsi forced himself to eat all the soggy bread and drink all the water. But as soon as he finished he had to piss, and there was no latrine bucket in the cell.

Alexsi pounded on the steel door, each blow echoing inside his head. He shouted, "Hey! I have to use the toilet!" He kept pounding until the metal flap covering the peephole in the door opened up. The glass of the peephole was set back in a little cone-shaped receptacle in the door, so you couldn't reach the glass and they could see the whole cell. The door had to be at least seven centimeters thick.

"Why are you banging?" an official voice demanded.

"I have to use the toilet," Alexsi replied into the peephole.

"Step away from the door," the voice ordered.

Alexsi complied, even though it only took two steps back to reach the opposite wall.

Two guards blocked the doorway. They wore the secret police red collar tabs with raspberry piping around the edges.

"If you bang on the door for any reason you will be punished," said the shorter of the two. "Remember this."

"I have to go to the toilet," Alexsi repeated.

"It is forbidden to shout," the guard replied dispassionately. He couldn't have been more bored, as if he gave this same speech all day, every day. "If you need to call someone, wait until the peephole opens and hold up your finger."

Alexsi held up one finger in front of them.

"A humorist," the guard stated. "You'll do well here. All the humorists do."

"Place your hands behind your back, and keep them there," ordered the junior guard. "Move."

They led him down the hall and shoved him into a tiled closet with a hole in the floor and iron foot stands. Water bubbled in the hole. Alexsi had been hoping for at least a tap where he could drink more water, but no such luck. Not wanting to waste an opportunity that might not come again for some time, he squatted over the hole and tried to shit. There was a scrape of metal, and the peephole in the door opened up. Alexsi sighed.

All he could manage was a small hard turd. He raised and buttoned his trousers carefully—this was not the time for the knife to come clattering out onto the floor.

They walked back, and a sergeant was by his open cell door, holding a folder full of papers. "Where have you been?" he demanded. "We're waiting for him."

"It was an emergency," the senior guard said. "He had to take the world's smallest shit."

The junior guard laughed loudly, but he was silenced by a hard look from the sergeant with the papers. "Move," he ordered Alexsi.

They walked down empty hallways, pausing at steel doors where women guards peered through peepholes and turned keys to let them through. Finally they came to a door that a guard opened to reveal bright sunlight.

Alexsi stopped short. One of the guards gave him a hard shove between the shoulder blades, and he stumbled through the doorway. Having to keep his hands behind his back made him fall flat on his face. He looked up, and there was a double row of rifle-carrying secret police lining the way to the open rear door of a gray van.

A hard kick encouraged him up off the ground, and a rifle butt to the kidney sent him into the back of the van.

So this was what the inside of a Black Maria looked like. There was a narrow center aisle with four steel cabinets on each side. A seat for a guard at the end of the aisle. One cabinet door nearest the end of the van was still open, and as Alexsi climbed up over the bumper another hard shove sent him into it.

He fell onto someone, who shoved him away. His head hit the back wall, and the cabinet door shut hard, ramming his feet inside.

It smelled like piss and puke. Alexsi felt his way in the darkness onto a metal bench seat. His eyes hadn't adjusted yet. One other person was in the cabinet with him, sitting opposite. The one who had shoved him away. The space was so small their knees were touching.

The Black Maria was moving now. It bounced so much you had to hold on to your seat or your head would keep hitting the roof.

Alexsi wasn't about to be the one who started any conversation. Being talkative just made people think you were afraid.

Though his eyes were now used to the darkness, all he could see was the black outline of the person opposite him. He heard him shift in his seat. Then a hand grabbed him by the throat. A raspy voice said, "Sit still and shut up, and you won't get hurt."

Alexsi didn't move. The man's other hand pawed at his pockets. Since he didn't resist, the hand at his throat relaxed a bit. The man's other hand moved down his trousers, then began to feel his shoes to see if they were worth taking.

Alexsi shot up out of his seat. The hand, without any leverage since its owner was bent over, came off his throat. Alexsi pinned the thief against the wall and punched the knife up under his ribs.

The thief let out a cry as the blade went in, and Alexsi twisted the knife. The thief didn't make another peep. It was just like the Shahsavan had said. If you wanted no noise and not a lot of blood, then up and into the heart, and twist.

Alexsi held him there against the wall until the body went limp and the raspy breathing stopped. He withdrew the knife and stuffed the thief's shirt into the hole to keep it from leaking all over the place. He arranged the body in the corner against the wall. He wiped his knife off on the dead man's clothes, folded the blade, and slipped it back into his underwear. That first shove when he'd entered the cabinet had alerted him for trouble, and while still bent over and fumbling for his seat he'd slipped his hand into the waistband of his trousers and retrieved the knife. Only a fool counted on anyone's goodwill.

Alexsi went through the thief's pockets. No knife. Well, if he was going to start something he should have had one. There was a pocket watch. And a fountain pen. Obviously stolen. Alexsi thought about keeping them to barter down the line, but decided to remain true to the tenets of socialism: Own nothing individually. And then no one can take anything away from you.

In another pocket was about five hundred grams of bread wrapped in a cloth. Someone else's bread, no doubt. Alexsi sniffed it. It seemed all right.

As the Black Maria bounced along, he propped his feet up on the dead man's lap to keep him from falling over, and leisurely ate his bread.

4

THE BLACK MARIA CAME TO AN ABRUPT STOP, BRAKES SQUEAL-ing, which slammed Alexsi into the steel wall. Good thing he still had his feet braced on the dead thief or the carcass would have fallen over onto him. The Maria turned about, then backed up quickly. An instant after it stopped, a flash of bright light through the cracks in the cabinet door indicated that the rear door was open. The inside guard began flinging open the cabinets, shout-ing, "Out! Out!"

Alexsi positioned himself next to the door. As soon as the lock clicked and the door came open he was out and over the bumper of the van.

The Black Maria had backed right up to the door of a railway car. A guard on each side filled in the narrow gap between the two vehicles, brandishing bayonets and yelling, "Move! Move!"

Alexsi took a quick look around as he grabbed the rail and pulled himself into the car. They weren't anywhere near a station. The prisoners were being loaded out in a railroad switching yard.

Inside the car he shouldered his way past other prisoners who were still blinking at the light and trying to get their bearings. If he upset the order there was always a chance they'd forget who had been in which cabinet.

From the outside it looked like a regular baggage car. Inside the compartments were separated from the central corridor by a grating of intersecting diagonal bars, so the guards could see in-side.

More shouting guards funneled them down the corridor and into an open compartment.

Alexsi quickly took stock. No windows, of course. There were no seats, just shelves. Two on top, a middle row that went all the way around the compartment except for a climbing space near the door, a bottom row, and the floor. One glance told him the dif-ference between the criminal and the political prisoners. The *blatnye*, the thieves, were on the middle row. The politicals were all soft, citizens yanked out of their homes, moist eyes searching about for someone to tell why it was all a mistake, they weren't supposed to be there. And the *blatnye* were hard and cold as iron, from the streets, marking out the weak and looking around to see who had anything worth taking.

Clearly that middle row was the most desirable place. Alexsi was sure they were going to pack them in asshole to navel, and he doubted that the trip would be short. But he also knew that if he wanted a space in the middle row he'd have to fight for it. And he didn't want to attract any more attention until he found out just how seriously they were going to take the body in the Maria.

Just then a whistle blew, and there was shouting in the corri-dor. The guards crashed into the compartment, clearing the pris-oners out of their way with truncheons.

The sergeant with the folder of papers strolled in behind them. "All right," he shouted. "Who likes to play with knives?"

Alexsi had already wormed his way into a corner behind a tall scarecrow of a political holding a suitcase out in front of him like a shield. If they didn't know, then all the better. Maybe some-one else had a knife and was feeling guilty about playing with it.

Silence reigned as the guards stared at the prisoners, and the prisoners tried hard not to look the guards in the face. This lasted until they brought the inside guard from the Black Maria into the compartment.

"Well?" the sergeant with the papers said to him harshly. "Are you going to tell me you don't know who was in your vehicle?"

Alexsi casually rested his hand over his mouth.

The guard looked them over, clearly uncomfortable because all the other guards were looking at him. And they were pleased they wouldn't be the ones held responsible.

"That's the one," he said finally, pointing at Alexsi.

As a last resort Alexsi tried the "What are you talking about, I'm just a kid?" expression, but the guards thrashed everyone out of their way, grabbed him, and dragged him out of the compartment. Alexsi knew his Russians, and his cops. They only cared about having someone to pin it on. And now that they had him in their hands they certainly weren't going to complicate their lives trying to figure out whether or not he'd actually done it.

They were about to drag him off the train when the sergeant with the papers said, "Wait."

Two guards slammed Alexsi face-first against the grating and held him there.

The sergeant thumbed through his folder. He found the page he wanted. "Turn him around."

The guards twirled Alexsi around and slammed his back into the grate.

The sergeant held a card with a photograph pinned to it up to Alexsi's face. He made a gesture, and they spun him around again and smashed his face back into the grate.

"You can't have him," the sergeant said.

"I have a dead man back in the van," said a voice behind them. "Regulations categorically state that prisoners committing additional crimes while in custody must be removed from transport and detained at the scene of the incident in question."

"I know all that," the sergeant said tiredly. "But look here." A rustling of paper. "We *have* to send him on, no delays permissible. They'll decide what to do with him there."

"But what am *I* going to do about this now?" the voice from behind demanded, quite upset.

"Complete the paperwork and forward it along," said the sergeant. "That's my advice to you."

"Fuck *me*," said the voice from behind.

"Put him in the punishment cell," the sergeant said. "And search him properly this time before he sticks one of us."

They frisked Alexsi again while he was up against the grate, and once again they missed the knife. They pushed him down the corridor.

The punishment cell. Thirty men to a compartment was a regular cell. Alexsi wasn't looking forward to the punishment cell.

Just before the corridor stopped at another grate that Alexsi guessed separated the prisoner from the guards area, they unlocked a barred sliding door.

"Take your shoes off," one of the guards ordered.

They'd probably guessed his knife was hidden in there, and were going to search them thoroughly. Once they were off, and while he was still bent over, they shoved him through the door.

Once Alexsi picked himself up off the floor, he saw he was in a narrow compartment with an upper and a lower berth. All to himself. Unbelievable. The prisoners in that other cell would have fought each other to death to be in here, if only they'd known.

The train began moving. An instant later the compartment door slid open with a clanging of steel and a guard threw Alexsi's shoes inside. The sole lining had been torn out, and one of the heels was detached. Alexsi looked at it in his hand. Not a bad idea. A little whittling and inside that heel might be a good place to hide his knife. Especially since they'd been kind enough to loosen the nails for him. But that could wait until dark.

A little while later the grate opened again and the guard passed him in a chunk of black bread, a cup of water, and a shiny piece of dark-colored fish. Alexsi gingerly touched his tongue to it. Smoked Caspian carp. Shit. And the salt would make him go mad from thirst. If this was all he'd be eating during the trip, no fish until he saw how much water they'd be dishing out.

Over the next day his judgment was confirmed. Only dry bread and fish, a few cups of water, and two trips to the toilet.

As the days passed, he tried to keep track, but there was no bulb in the compartment and the only light came from the corridor. They blended into frequent stops and constant thirst. Locomotives were switched; cars were coupled and uncoupled; they sat immobile for incredibly long periods.

Alexsi thought of what it must be like in the other cells and told himself to count his blessings. Knifing that thief had been incredible good luck.

5

1936 Somewhere in the Soviet Union

THEY TOOK HIM OFF THE TRAIN IN THE DEAD OF NIGHT. AND as they walked him down that central aisle to the door, Alexsi was astounded to see the other compartments empty through the grates. Every other prisoner had been removed along the way. His stomach tightened up. Where could they be that was just for him and no one else?

What he could see offered few clues. It was just another railroad switching yard. But it was enormous.

Expecting another Black Maria, or worse, Alexsi was again shocked to find himself pushed into the backseat of a regular automobile, pinned between two hulking plainclothes secret policemen. Of course they said nothing, and of course he knew better than to ask any questions.

In this first small space after the train he was immediately conscious of just how badly he smelled after so many days of not washing. His escorts acted impervious to it, though they both lit cigarettes almost in unison.

It was freezing cold, worse than the desert at night. They bounced across an untold number of train tracks and finally left the yard through a guarded gate in a fence. And then they were in a city that was all bright lights and huge buildings. Much bigger than Baku. With no idea in which direction the train had traveled, he was at a loss. He knew prisoners went to Siberia, so he thought over his geography lessons. Karaganda? Kras-noyarsk?

No, there was more city and more city, and they couldn't be traveling in circles. They went over a river, but it could have been any river. The buildings and street signs told him nothing, since he knew only the streets of Baku. Then the car took a turn around a corner and in the far skyline an image popped up before him that he had only ever seen in books. The onion domes of the Kremlin. They were in Moscow. Moscow. And in an automobile just for him?

Back in the train's punishment compartment he had been feeling prepared for whatever might occur. Now his stomach was swimming in a sea of fear.

October Twenty-fifth Street. He had heard of that. And a big yellow building. Another street sign, and another turn around the side of that building. Malaya Lubyanka Street. Lubyanka? Oh, no. Everyone in the Soviet Union knew the name of the central head-quarters of State Security.

The car stopped and they pushed him out. One of the plain-clothesmen pushed a button on the wall and a door opened from the inside. They turned him over to two State Security enlisted men in full uniform and gleaming boots, wearing pistols.

Alexsi was walked down a long straight corridor that was all white: walls, ceiling, and floors. It was lit by those same caged 200-watt bulbs they had in Baku. A white painted door stood open, and they shoved him inside. The room was all white tile, and otherwise completely bare.

"Undress," one of the uniforms ordered.

His little knife now was in his shoe heel. If these guards found it he was prepared for the beating. But if they didn't it might come in handy.

As he handed over his clothes they took razors and cut open the lining in his trousers and jacket. And immediately found his five hundred rubles.

"Why do you have money hidden in your jacket?" one demanded.

"There are thieves everywhere," Alexsi replied.

They just narrowed their eyes at him while he tried to look wide-eyed and innocent.

After that they went over his clothes inch by inch. Opened the lining of his shoes, but they didn't pull the heels off. Alexsi just stood there naked and stared at the wall, so they wouldn't catch him stealing glances over at his shoes.

"What is this?" they said, pointing to the homemade knife pocket in his underwear.

Alexsi shrugged. "I kept money there after my pocket was picked one day."

They cut all the metal buttons off his clothes and threw his belt to the other side of the room.

When they were finished they clicked on a battery torch and examined his hair and scalp. Then his nose and ears. One guard put on a pair of thick black rubber gloves.

"Open your mouth." He poked his gloved finger into every crevice of Alexsi's mouth, lifting up his tongue with thumb and forefinger like it was a curtain blocking his view.

"Hands against the wall, spread your feet apart." And at that Alexsi nearly puked all over the tile room. It took every last bit of willpower to choke it down. It wasn't the finger rammed up in his ass, searching for hidden contraband there. It was that the rubber glove sheathing the finger up his ass was the very same glove that had just been in his mouth. And while the guard had been considerate enough to check his mouth first, Alexsi was dead certain his mouth and ass were not the only ones that glove had ever been inside.

He was still trying to shake that thought out of his head when they handed him a piece of soap that had the consistency of a grinding wheel and told him to take a hot shower. If they'd been between him and the water he would have trampled them both, even if it meant getting shot. He rushed under the stream, soaped his fingers, and scrubbed out his mouth, in his haste totally oblivious to the pleasure of his first wash in a long time.

When he was finished, they told him to get dressed. No towel was offered. So Alexsi shook himself off like a dog and, still wet, climbed back into his now ripped and tattered clothing.

They led him out a door and across an open interior courtyard to another part of the building, and in his damp clothes he thought he might freeze to death. He was shivering uncontrollably once they were inside again.

They took his photograph and his fingerprints and put him in a dark gray cell with two other men. There were three iron beds, with mattresses, but no other furniture in the cell. His cell mates were sleeping, or trying to. Once every minute, the metal cover over the peephole rasped open to examine them. Steel doors constantly slammed like artillery fire down the corridor outside.

Alexsi took his shoes off, put them under his head, and draped his coat over his eyes as if to give some relief from the burning lightbulb. In a few minutes he had the knife out from the cavity in his heel, and back inside the pocket in his underwear.

It seemed as if the door opened every few minutes the rest of the night. His cell mates were taken out and new ones put in their place. This happened over and over again.

In the morning the cell door opened with the shout, "Get up!"

Alexsi shot up from the bed and the guard threw a broom at him. "Sweep out the cell and be quick about it."

Alexsi put his shoes on and stamped his feet to set the loose heel back into place.

When he was finished sweeping the guard marched them all down to the toilet and stood there shouting, "Hurry up! Hurry up!"

Back in the cell they received a soggy hunk of black bread and a mug of tea that might as well have been hot water. But at least it was hot.

That was the high point of the day. Alexsi sat in the cell while a parade of different prisoners was brought in and out. No one was allowed to sleep during the day and if a prisoner drifted off a guard came shouting in during one of his every-minute peephole checks and threatened them all with a beating.

For lunch they were given tripe soup. Based on the quality of their now-razored clothing it seemed like his two current cell mates had been important men. They were twice his age, in their thirties. One of them started crying out loud at just the sight of the soup in its dirty plate and dirty spoon. Alexsi only shook his head and shoveled it down. The crybaby should have waited until he tasted it to start bawling—now that was something to cry about. But at least it wasn't smoked carp. And the spoon might not have been clean, but he was fairly sure it hadn't been up some-one's ass.

In the afternoon the guard came in and pointed to Alexsi. "Out!"

Alexsi stepped out into the corridor and put his hands behind his back without being told. Two guards walked him down the corridor, through two doors, and into his very first electric eleva-tor. It went up, and the sensation when it began moving was so startling he nearly fell over.

The ride was much too short. Down another corridor, waiting for steel doors to be opened, and then another cell.

This one was bigger. It had a table and stools in addition to the beds. And he could instantly see there was going to be a problem. Because along with two cowering politicals were three thieves.

They were well muscled and wearing only their undershirts to display their lavish tattoos. The leader was short but with shoul-ders and arms like a gorilla, and a sneer that showed off two dull steel replacement teeth. No gold for the *blatnye*. Someone would only try to rip it out of your head.

As soon as the door was shut he sauntered up and thrust his hand with two extended fingers in front of Alexsi's face. The message was unmistakable: I'll gouge your eyes out. "Let's see if that coat fits me, little boy. Give it up and you won't get hurt."

Alexsi made a series of instant calculations. The *blatnye* didn't seem at all concerned about guards at peepholes. So it was up to him. He guessed what being their slave would mean.

Alexsi shoved his right hand down into his trousers.

The *blatnye* leader let out a harsh laugh. "Oh, he has something he wants to show me, eh?"

While everyone was staring at his crotch, Alexsi lunged with his left hand and snatched one of those outstretched fingers in his fist. The *blatnye*'s eyes went wide with surprise. Alexsi snapped his wrist forward and the finger broke with a loud crack. The *blatnye* screamed like an animal. Alexsi kicked him square in the balls and shoved him back into the other two.

That only slowed them down for an instant, but it was all Alexsi needed to get his knife out. They charged him. Alexsi took a quick step to the right that changed it from two men attacking him side by side to one slightly behind the other, putting himself close enough to the table to snatch up a stool to protect his weak side. As the nearest one threw a punch Alexsi, quicker, put the stool in the way of his fist and slashed him across the face with the knife. He was aiming for the eyes but missed and cut across the forehead just above the eyebrows. Which worked just as well because the blood gushed out in a flood and blinded the thief as if he'd cut the eyes out.

As soon as he saw the knife the thief who had been slightly behind quit the fight and leaped back to the far side of the cell, his open hands stretched out in front of him. But the leader came up from the floor fast and, compensating for the loss of his hands, aimed a savage kick. Alexsi sidestepped out of the way and as he went by slashed him across the side of the throat. Knowing he was hurt badly, the leader grabbed for his throat as the blood sprayed and Alexsi cracked him in the back of the head with the stool.

While all this was going on the two politicals were screaming their lungs out from under their beds. As Alexsi cautiously
advanced on the remaining thief to finish him, surrender or not,
he slipped on the blood on the floor and fell flat on his back. The
thief rushed out of his corner and leaped onto him, aiming to
crush him with his weight and pin the knife hand down.

Alexsi only had time to bring his knees up, and the thief hit
them first instead of landing straight onto his body. That gave
Alexsi just enough free space to punch the knife into the thief's
ribs. Alexsi kept stabbing, fending him off with his left arm as the
thief tried to get ahold of his throat. The lungs were unfortunately not a quick killing blow.

The cell door crashed open and many feet came pounding
in. As the thief was yanked off Alexsi left the knife in his ribs
and covered his head with his arms as the rubber truncheons
sailed in. The screaming inside the cell was deafening but it wasn't
coming from him. The blows rained down from all directions
until finally he was grabbed by the collar and dragged out into
the corridor.

6

1936 The Lubyanka, Moscow

ALEXSI DIDN'T RESIST. HE WOULD HAVE BEEN MORE THAN happy to get up on his own but they just kept dragging him along the floor.

The ride ended in a toilet where they tore all his clothes off, threw him naked up against a wall, and strip-searched him again. No shower this time. While he was still propped up against the wall, they threw buckets of ice-cold water on him and washed the thieves' blood off that way.

He never saw his own clothes again. While the other guards stood ready, patting their truncheons into the palms of their hands, one shoved a bundle of clothes at him. A pair of stiff canvas trousers and a jacket stuffed with what felt like cotton and stitched like a quilt to hold the padding in place. Instead of shoes, straw slippers and no socks. They screamed at him to hurry up and dress, and as soon as he did they handcuffed him with his right hand in front and his left hand behind his back, with the chain between his legs scraping his balls. It forced him to walk bent over like an ape.

A guard with his pistol drawn recited, "Prepare for interrogation. Do not move your head to either side. Do not move without being told. If you do not follow instructions to the letter it is our right under regulations to shoot you out of hand."

The way he was bent over Alexsi could barely even look to his front, but he wasn't about to argue over it.

He had his second elevator ride, but conditions made it impossible to savor it as much as the first. He hobbled along the passages while the lead guard banged his key against his belt buckle every time they passed a door as a warning to anyone inside that a prisoner was passing by. If there was a noise in return and a door opened, they pushed his face against the wall so he couldn't see who it was. They did the same if anyone else was coming down the corridor.

After a very long and tiring walk through the labyrinth of hallways they grabbed him by the collar and pushed him into a room. Alexsi's handcuffs were unlocked and he was pulled upright, back aching, to see two stone-faced State Security lieutenants standing before him. One stamped a receipt and handed it to the guard in exchange for his body. The other grabbed him by the upper arm in a steel grip, took him into an adjoining office, sat him down hard in a heavy wood chair, and left.

The office was both austere and elegant. Nothing on the walls but dark wood paneling and a portrait of Stalin. A huge and quite beautiful wooden desk, as dark as the walls and the chairs, everything arranged on the top in perfect order. Behind it sat a man in a black suit like an undertaker. His hair was streaked with gray, slicked back and plastered flat like a skullcap. Not one of the well-fed Chekists who seemed to populate the building. He was so gaunt, the flesh of his face under the cheekbones looked like it had been scooped out with a spoon. With shoulders slightly hunched Alexsi thought the man resembled nothing so much as a vulture poised to pick at his carcass.

A cigarette was burning in an ashtray. He held a Soviet internal passport in his hands and was thumbing through it intently.

He looked up from it and fixed Alexsi with piercing eyes that appeared jet-black in the shadows of the room. And an instant later stunned him by speaking not in Russian but fluent German. "Young man, your papers say that you are Anatoli Borisovich Bulgakov. I say you are Alexsi Ivanovich Smirnov. What do you say?"

Alexsi was so shocked he didn't say anything. They knew his name. They knew he spoke German.

"You've had a busy night," the man observed dispassionately, still speaking German. "Ordinarily I'd enjoy playing cat and mouse with you. But it has taken much longer than expected to bring us together and time is of the essence. So if you are not Alexsi Ivanovich Smirnov, and you do not speak German, then you are of no use to me and I will have you removed from this room and liquidated immediately."

Alexsi believed him. "I am Alexsi Ivanovich Smirnov," he said in German.

The gaunt man gave no sign whether he found Alexsi's German pleasing or displeasing. He tossed the internal passport onto the desk and took a contemplative drag on his cigarette. "This really is quite good. I assume you bought it from someone who issues the genuine article to Soviet citizens."

"That is correct, good sir," Alexsi said, still in German. No sense getting this fellow upset with him so early; he was scary enough just sitting there. Plus he was having to concentrate very hard since his German was rusty from disuse. It was harder to lie in a foreign language.

The gaunt man just stared at him as if he were memorizing every detail of his face. "Do you know where you are?"

"In Moscow," Alexsi said. "The Lubyanka."

"Are you familiar with the phrase: Abandon hope, who enter here?"

"It is from the book *Inferno* by the Italian poet Dante," Alexsi replied. "It is the sign on the gates of hell."

"Do you believe in hell?"

Alexsi just looked around the room.

The gaunt man's lips curled in the faintest and most fleeting of smiles. "Have you read the other books of the *Divine Comedy*?"

"I didn't finish them," Alexsi said.

"Why not?"

"Hell was much more interesting than heaven."

"Yes, it always is, isn't it?" said the gaunt man. "Do you know why I ask you these questions?"

"You knew I understood your German," Alexsi replied. "You wanted me to talk long enough to see how well I speak it."

"And what makes you think that?"

"Because the questions weren't about anything."

"They could have been to frighten you."

"I was already frightened," Alexsi said.

The gaunt man favored him with another brief smile that was really just a twitching of the lips. "Does any other reason occur to you?"

Alexsi thought about it. "You maybe wanted to see how stupid I am since I haven't been to school in years."

"Yes, but you have been a dedicated patron of our state libraries, have you not? I salute your commitment to knowledge, especially since libraries were the only place you could be found with any consistency. In order to make your acquaintance it was necessary for a team of men to wait patiently in every library in Baku. And what does all this tell you? Everything that has happened to you since that day in the library. Beware, now. Your answer is very important."

Alexsi let out a breath. "You want me for something."

The gaunt man clasped his hands together on the table. "Very good. You are meeting all my expectations. I would even say exceeding, but you are full of yourself quite enough already. As I said before, I do not have time to waste. The Main Directorate for State Security of the NKVD of the Union of Soviet Socialist Republics has decided to offer you the chance of joining us as a secret agent. We accept only volunteers for this vitally important work. If you agree, and prove your loyalty by perfectly executing your orders, in return State Security will help you in every way you could possibly imagine and grant you greater opportunities for your future than ordinary citizens. Your mission will be to actively help the Soviet government build a Communist society throughout the world. As such, you will have the chance to win the highest honors." He paused and gave Alexsi a piercing stare. "Do you accept?"

Alexsi was certain a refusal would mean his death. "I accept."

The gaunt man continued to examine him with those eerie eyes. He took another long drag on his cigarette and arranged it neatly back in the ashtray. "Do not imagine for a moment that I am ignorant of your thoughts. You agree now, gain your release, and then disappear at the earliest opportunity. I have no doubt that you could eventually accomplish this, despite our vigilance. And no doubt the *blatnye* would welcome you with open arms. The three you met tonight are down in the dispensary—well, actually one of them has left this world due to your efforts—and you impressed them deeply. They cannot stop talking about you. You could put on the tattoos and become a thief-in-law. You would go far. Until we caught you again. We catch everyone sooner or later. Then it would only be a matter of a quick death from a bullet or a slow one in the bottom of a mine in Kolyma. Whichever pleased us. Because we are absolutely merciless with anyone who betrays us. Now, I ask you again and for the final time. Do you accept?"

Alexsi stared back into those black eyes. As it happened, those had been his thoughts exactly. But better to live another day. "I accept."

The gaunt man once again gave no sign of either pleasure or displeasure. He passed a blank piece of paper and a fountain pen across the desk. "At the top write today's date, Moscow, and the word 'promise.' In Russian," he added.

Alexsi just shrugged.

"What?" the gaunt man demanded.

"The date, sir?" Alexsi said.

The man grunted in comprehension and flipped around his desk calendar so Alexsi could see it.

It had taken nearly two weeks to get from Baku to Moscow. Alexsi wrote as directed, then raised his head.

"Write exactly as I dictate," the gaunt man ordered. "This promise is given to the GUGB of the NKVD of the USSR in which I, Alexsi Ivanovich Smirnov, bind myself to execute and obey instantly all orders given me by the GUGB. I swear to report to the GUGB all anti-Soviet activities which come to my notice. I swear to talk to no one concerning my work for the GUGB. I shall sign all reports written by myself concerning my duties with the pseudonym . . ." He paused. "You will pick a name: person, animal, object, or number, by which you will be known to us."

Alexsi was first distracted by the fact that they seemed to have changed the name of the secret police. But maybe this was something different and even more secret? He hadn't the faintest idea what name he ought to pick for himself. He racked his brain until he saw the gaunt man becoming impatient, then said the only thing he could think of. "What about Dante?"

"Dante it is," the gaunt man replied. "Write it in." After Alexsi scratched it on the paper, he said, "Now sign your full name, and in brackets below: Dante."

When Alexsi was finished the gaunt man took the paper back, carefully slid it into a folder, then stood and offered his hand.

Alexsi stood and shook it. The man was taller than he had imagined.

"Very good," the gaunt man said. "My name is Grigory Petrovich Yakushev. From this moment on I am your chief, and your training will begin immediately. You will give it your full and complete attention, because only excellence is accepted in our work. Now memorize this telephone number: K-6-32-15."

"K-6-32-15," Alexsi repeated.

"You will be released immediately and taken to the place where you will live. You will call me at that number at one o'clock in the afternoon tomorrow exactly. Use a kiosk on the street, not the telephone in any residence whatsoever. You will ask for me and use only your pseudonym. Do you understand?"

"I understand," Alexsi said.

"I hope so," Comrade Yakushev said. "You have been warned once. You will not receive another. I look forward to our meeting tomorrow."

Not knowing what to say—thank you somehow seemed inappropriate—Alexsi gave a little bow that brought another faint smile to his new chief's face.

When he left the office the stone-faced lieutenants were now smiling at him. They escorted him down the elevator to the ground floor where it seemed that an assembly line had been set up just for him. A barber cut his shaggy hair and shaved the equally shaggy beard that had grown on the train ride. He took yet another hot shower, this time at his leisure and this time with a fluffy white towel at the end. No washing for over two weeks, and now everything from ice water to steam in one day. At each stop the now-amiable lieutenants watched over him and supervised everyone's work.

As soon as he was dry and combed, they presented him with a smart brown suit that fit him perhaps not perfectly but as well as any garment in the Soviet Union. A white shirt with a collar, cufflinks, a tie, and shined leather shoes. A Kirov wristwatch on a leather band. After he admired himself in the mirror, he was brought to another little room with a table and a chair. And waiting for him on the table was a pot of borscht, a thick pork chop, fried potatoes, and half a loaf of sliced white bread with butter. There was even red wine in a crystal carafe. Alexsi tasted it suspiciously, thought it terrible, and timidly asked if he could have some tea. A lady in a white coat had been standing by. The lieutenants only had to give her a look and she brought him some instantly.

Alexsi told himself to go slow, since he knew what all this rich food would do to him after so many days of bread and water and smoked fish. His stomach had shrunk and he had to force himself to leave food on his plate and not stuff it into his mouth regardless. Or into the pockets of his new suit.

One of the lieutenants actually asked him politely if he was done instead of throwing him out of the room. Down the hall and they slipped a thick wool winter suit coat over his shoulders, a scarf for his neck, gloves for his hands, and a fur hat placed on his head like a crown. There wasn't another mirror, but Alexsi looked down at the clothes as if he'd transformed into someone else. It was like the Frog Prince in the Brothers Grimm tales, except instead of a princess, Comrade Stalin was the one who had thrown him against a wall and changed him from a frog into a prince.

He must have chuckled out loud, because one of the lieutenants said, "What's the joke, comrade?"

Saying what was in his head would have been a guaranteed bullet to the back of it. Instead Alexsi replied, "I was just remarking over my good fortune. Long live Comrade Stalin."

In response everyone in earshot shouted out loud enough to nearly make him jump out of his new clothes. "Long live Comrade Stalin!"

Seemingly out of nowhere, and obviously for him, appeared a young man of about twenty, also wearing a suit. He held out his hand. "Call me Sergei."

Alexsi shook it, but hesitated. "What name shall I use?"

Sergei smiled. "Use your pseudonym only in communication. I will call you Alexsi."

Everyone was smiling now. Though Alexsi knew that all it would take was a simple change in orders and everyone who was smiling now would be tearing him to pieces.

A uniformed sergeant unlocked a steel door and opened it to reveal the Moscow night. *"Dosvidanie,"* he said. I'll be seeing you again

He was smiling, too.

7

1936 Moscow

SOMEHOW THE AIR OUTSIDE THE LUBYANKA DIDN'T FEEL AS cold as it had before. Alexsi didn't think it was just the warm clothes he was wearing. He wasn't about to call it free air, but at least it was open air. And a new lease on life. The stars were beautiful, fading slightly in the faintest hint of approaching dawn.

As they emerged from the side street into Dzerzhinsky Square, his eye was immediately caught by a sign on a building that said: CHILDREN'S WORLD. "What is that?" he asked Sergei.

"That? The toy store?"

"An entire store just for toys?" Alexsi said, amazed.

"That's right."

They crossed the square and entered a building on the south side. "You'll enjoy this," said Sergei, pointing to a sign over some stairs that seemed to lead belowground. "It's brand-new; only opened this year."

It said: DZERZHINSKY STATION. Down the stairs and Sergei stopped him in front of the bust of a man in the vestibule. "This is the founder of our great service, Comrade Felix Dzerzhinsky."

Alexsi paused respectfully in front of the bust, pretending to be suitably impressed. He looked like any other man. But that wasn't surprising. He'd come to learn that all cruel men looked like every other man.

Sergei paid fifty kopecks for a ticket for each of them, and they continued belowground and onto a platform in the middle of what looked like a tube with strikingly patterned black marble walls and electric lights overhead. Below the platform there were train tracks. A train that ran underneath a city. Moscow was just a continuous series of marvels.

"The first trains of the morning are just starting up," said Sergei. "We might have to wait a bit."

"Do people go mad from being underneath the ground like this?" he asked.

Sergei laughed. "Some. But most are so astounded by Comrade Stalin's great socialist achievement that they forget to be afraid. And then they get used to it."

There was a rumbling, and then a light appeared down the tunnel and a train thundered in with a great rush of air. The doors actually opened by themselves with another blast of air, and they both stepped into the car.

Sergei stood and held the shiny metal rail that went up into the ceiling. Alexsi copied him. Alexsi was surprised that the sensation of traveling through the tube was the same as riding a train in the open air.

They remained in the car through two stops and got out at the third. The station sign said: PALACE OF THE SOVIETS.

"This is even more beautiful," Alexsi said. The station floor was covered with squares of red and gray granite, and as you walked, there were rows of columns in marble blending into white that seemed to have their own light coming from inside.

"It is the gateway to the Palace of the Soviets," Sergei replied. "So it must be suitable."

"What is the Palace of the Soviets?" It seemed a harmless way to see if questions were going to work.

"You did not follow the architectural design contest?" Sergei said, amazed. "It was news throughout the world."

"The news sometimes arrived a little slower to my part of Baku," Alexsi replied. "Forgive my ignorance."

"It will be the wonder of the world," Sergei exclaimed. "The congress hall and administrative center of the entire Soviet Union. Built on the land of the demolished bourgeois cathedral for the glory of the proletariat. The tallest building in the world."

"Will it be right in front of us as we leave the station?" Alexsi asked. He thought the moving electric stairs they were on were quite wondrous enough.

"Oh, it is not yet constructed. But it will be."

The vestibule where the train riders entered and exited was a huge circular arch supported by columns. More people were coming in than leaving. Sergei took him by the arm. "You can always tell the new riders. They cannot stop looking up, and they bump into everyone."

They walked south down streets that were just waking up. Alexsi had no idea how he was going to find his way anywhere without a guide.

Turning onto a side street, Sergei led him up some stairs into a stone building. They went up another flight of stairs, down a hallway, and Sergei unlocked a door. With a flourish of his hand, he said, "This is your apartment."

The first thing Alexsi noticed was that, unlike every other Soviet apartment, there wasn't anyone else living there. Which was unprecedented in his experience. There were freshly painted walls and thick blue curtains. A sofa, chairs, a table. Spare and severe furniture, in the Soviet style, but to his eyes unbelievably luxurious. A gas stove and a refrigerator instead of an icebox. He opened it up and was greeted by a gust of cool air and shelves filled with food. Milk, sour cream, butter, cheese. If they were trying to impress him, it was working.

Sergei indicated some papers on the table. "Here is a street map of Moscow and a map of the metro. You may carry them with you, but guard them well. Maps are restricted items, and it would not do for our enemies to learn the plans of our streets." He reached into his pocket and set a great deal of money on the table.

"Comrade Yakushev has directed that your five hundred rubles be returned to you, along with a fifteen-hundred-ruble advance on your first month's salary. You will sign this receipt."

Alexsi took the offered pen and signed. It was almost as much money as he'd made in a good smuggling month. An unskilled factory worker made maybe 150 rubles a month. You could buy five kilos of sugar for 50 rubles. If you could ever find a shop that had five kilos of sugar for sale, that is.

Sergei handed him keys. "This apartment is yours. You may use it however you wish. The linen will be washed and replaced, and the rooms will be cleaned without you bothering yourself about it. Leave a list of foodstuffs you require on the table and they will be provided without any deductions to your salary. Ordinarily you would have the right to shop in government stores, but for reasons that will be made clear to you this is not possible now."

Alexsi knew government stores. They were stocked with food and goods that were not available to regular people. Government stores had been his favorite places to break into and steal from.

He couldn't bring himself to feel happy about all this luxury. He knew in his soul that he would have to pay for all of it one way or another. All that money had to be bait, to dare him to try to run away.

"I will let you get some rest now," Sergei said. "You remember your orders?"

Alexsi nodded. "Any advice?"

Sergei's smile dropped away. "Carry them out to the letter. Every time, without exception or deviation. Only then will your future be bright." He turned to go, then placed something on the table. It was Alexsi's little folding knife. "Comrade Yakushev wanted you to have this. For luck. And he cautions you not to let it find its way into anyone."

"It won't," said Alexsi, picking it up.

Sergei closed the door behind him. Alexsi put the knife in his pocket and looked around the apartment that was all his. Another room of his own, and the best yet. Sergei hadn't needed to say "for now."

8

1936 Moscow

ALEXSI HAD TO BUY A COPY OF *PRAVDA* IN ORDER TO GET COINS
for his phone call. It occurred to him that another reason they had
given him so much cash was to see if he would go crazy buying
things and attract all sorts of attention to himself. So the money
would remain tucked in his underwear.

Every Soviet clock he saw told a different time. And he didn't
think it wise to trust his life to his Soviet wristwatch. At the phone
kiosk he dialed the operator and asked her. Two minutes before
1:00. He counted down the seconds and dialed K-6-32-15.

A man's voice answered with just "Yes?"

Alexsi said, "Comrade Yakushev, please."

"Who is calling?"

Alexsi almost said his name, then remembered. "Dante."

"Hold the line."

A few seconds later Yakushev's voice came over the phone.
Speaking German again. "I assume you are near your place of
residence?"

"That is correct," Alexsi replied, also in German.

"In precisely forty-five minutes you will walk north on Petrovka Street past the Bolshoi Theatre. When you see me, give no
sign of recognition. You will receive instructions on where we
will meet. Do you understand?"

"I understand," said Alexsi.

The line clicked dead.

Alexsi rushed to the Palace of the Soviets metro station and made his first blunder by taking a train south instead of north. Realizing what he had done, he got out at the next stop and ran to the opposite platform. He was practically jumping out of his skin waiting for the next train. But there seemed to be one every couple of minutes.

He had the city and metro maps tucked away inside his newspaper. If maps were secret items, then it wouldn't do to be walking the streets clutching them in his fist. Failure here wouldn't end in a regretful handshake and a train ticket back to Baku, but a bullet. They wouldn't allow someone who had seen even a little part of their world to live.

Fortunately they were making this first test easy. He would be getting off in Dzerzhinsky Square, the same place they boarded the train that morning.

Alexsi waited just south of the Bolshoi until it was 1:45. It was so cold his face was numb, though there was no snow on the ground yet. Electric streetcars clattered past, followed at safe intervals by horse-drawn wagons moving goods around the city. Almost no automobiles, but then they were only for officials.

There was a smell of wood and coal smoke in the air, frying onions, burning tobacco, and unwashed people and clothes, though tamped down by the cold.

He folded his newspaper up and began walking north. Just to be sure, he tipped his hat to a middle-aged woman about to pass him and pointed to the beautiful building with the eight towering columns holding up the entrance. "Excuse me, Comrade, but is that the Bolshoi?"

"It is," she replied gruffly, not slowing her progress in the slightest.

The cobblestone street was very wide, but the sidewalks were narrow. In front of the theater was a little park with trees and bushes that were now nothing but brown skeletons standing against the cold. Alexsi saw Comrade Yakushev appear out of the park. Something told him to stop, so he did and gazed up in appreciation. It looked like pictures from books of Rome and Greece. The statue atop the entrance peak was someone in a chariot pulled by four rearing horses.

Someone brushed against him on their way by, and Alexsi felt a hand slip into his suit coat pocket. As good as a very good pick-pocket.

He kept walking north until he found another bench. Only after he sat down did he slip the paper out of his pocket and into the newspaper so he could read it without being seen reading it. An address, an apartment number, and "two o'clock."

It took some hard looking at the map, but the address was farther north and two streets over. At two o'clock Alexsi trudged up the stairs. The apartment door was slightly open, so he took that as a signal and walked in without knocking.

Comrade Yakushev was sitting on the sofa. "Close the door, take off your coat and hat, pour yourself some tea, and sit down."

He was definitely exact in his instructions. Alexsi followed them, pouring a glass from the samovar on the side table and adding a spoonful of sugar.

"Why did you stop?" Comrade Yakushev said without preamble.

"In case you were going to whisper instructions to me," said Alexsi. "If I stopped while I was walking it would be as if I recognized you, and that was contrary to your orders."

Yakushev had a way of silently staring at him before speaking that was incredibly unnerving. "You were correct. What we did in this case is called a brush contact. An agent passes information to another without recognition."

"I understand," said Alexsi.

"Speaking of surveillance, did you notice anyone during your journey?"

"Yes," Alexsi replied. "Two men as I left my apartment, one

following from behind and one in front. Then two different men as I left the Dzerzhinsky Station, using the same procedure."

"How did you know they were following you?"

"I'm not sure how to describe it."

"Do so nonetheless," Yakushev ordered.

Alexsi fought for the right words. "People do what they do, convincingly. But someone who is watching you has to pretend to do something else. It's not convincing. If you watch *them* closely, you can tell."

Yakushev lit a cigarette. "This is not the first time I have concluded that your previous experiences prepared you well for our work." He offered his open cigarette case. "Would you care for one?"

"No, thank you. I do not smoke."

"That is very uncommon. Why not?"

Alexsi remembered the little street boys in Baku smoking moss when they couldn't scratch up some tobacco. And then coughing up blood. "I have seen men get sick, even go mad when they could not obtain tobacco."

"So you are always prepared for everything to be taken away from you?"

Alexsi shrugged. "At least things that would make me go mad."

"What about alcohol? Its absence does not induce bad effects." Yakushev made another twitching of the mouth in lieu of a smile. "Unless you drink the way many Russians do. Do you abstain because you are Muslim?"

That, as Alexsi had come to recognize, was another one of those innocent sounding but potentially fatal questions. "No, I am not Muslim. At first I did not drink because I was beaten whenever someone was drunk. Later I avoided much misfortune when others were drunk and I was not."

Apparently Yakushev found his answers satisfactory because he abruptly changed tack. "Did you purposely take the wrong train in order to lose the first two who were following you?"

He did know everything, didn't he? "No, I took the wrong train by accident," Alexsi admitted.

"That is good. If you do detect that you are under surveillance, you must do nothing about it. Because if this surveillance is only routine due to your position, or because you are only under suspicion, then to elude it will serve to confirm to your enemies that you are, in fact, a trained agent. So you must always be aware if you are under surveillance, but take no further action. The only exception is when meeting a contact. Then you must make absolutely certain you are free from all surveillance, or cancel the meeting. Mark my words on this."

"I do," said Alexsi.

"Actually, you were followed by more than four men. The others were out of sight, ready to reinforce those you saw. We are training them at the same time we are training you. I will teach you the technique of establishing a vantage point, where you will be able to always detect surveillance without seeming to do so. It is not like the cinema where you look for reflections in store windows or turn around suddenly. Our methods are much simpler but one hundred percent effective."

Alexsi nodded and sipped his tea, which was getting cold.

"We will spend our mornings on this," said Yakushev. "The rest of the day I have an urgent task for you. It has come to our attention that a group of students at Moscow State University, traitors despite all the advantages our socialist system has offered them, are engaged in a conspiracy against the life of our dear leader, Comrade Stalin. It will be your mission to infiltrate this conspiracy."

Alexsi just took some more tea.

"Excellent," said Yakushev. "You are afraid your face will reveal your thoughts, so you drink and therefore give absolutely nothing away. Well done. Only by first achieving power over yourself will you be able to achieve power over others. You will now tell me what your thoughts are exactly."

Alexsi put down his glass. "These plotters are doing something that means death if discovered. Will they invite a total stranger into their midst?"

Yakushev looked down the tube of his cigarette at him. "Given many months, no doubt you would succeed in worming your way into their confidence. But by then it would be too late." He reached into the briefcase that was open next to his feet and extracted a photograph. He handed it to Alexsi. "As it happens, I believe you know this person."

The photograph had been taken on the street, obviously without the subject's knowledge. This time Alexsi knew his face had given him away. "I do."

"Her name?"

"I knew her as Aida."

9

THE ORPHANAGE HAD ONCE BEEN A MANSION. IT WAS THE most incredible thing the thirteen-year-old Alexsi had ever seen. A wall painted with blue flying birds. Even though it was cracked and peeling, it was still miraculous.

The gray-haired woman with a face like a hawk was wearing a dress that was nicer than any he had ever seen. Comrade Stalin looked down at him sternly from a wall, but he was always there. The woman was reading the stamped documents of his life. She looked up at him and said, "Alexsi Ivanovich?" as if the papers might have been lying.

Alexsi nodded warily.

She addressed him in Russian. "Welcome to Special Orphanage Number 27."

Alexsi wondered what was special about it.

"Do you understand Russian, child?"

"Yes, mistress."

"You do not use that term here, Alexsi Ivanovich. We are Communists here, not bourgeois reactionaries. My name is Anna Rahimovna Aliyev. I am in charge of this place. You will call me Comrade Director."

"Yes, Comrade Director."

"I trust you had a pleasant trip here, and have been treated well so far."

It wasn't a question, so Alexsi didn't bother answering it.

"You have noticed this place we are in?" she said.

Alexsi nodded again.

"This huge house was built for one family," she said with exaggerated disgust. "But the capitalist exploiters are gone, and the state has taken over this place to build Communism through the next generation."

She was looking at him as if she expected him to say something. Alexsi had no idea what that might be. It would be stupid to say the first thing on his mind, which was that it seemed to be good luck for her.

"You!" she blurted out, as if filling in a question she had never asked. "You are the next generation, and we will teach you to build Communism here." Her tone softened a bit. "Circumstances have required that the state take charge of you. The other children here are the same as you. I know this is difficult; all change is difficult. But you will soon find a home and a happy new life here."

Her tone was the same as the men back on the kolkhoz when they were trying to sell something for more than it was worth.

"Do you have any questions?"

Many, but if experience had taught him anything, it was that it wasn't smart to ask questions. "No, Comrade Director."

She looked down at her papers, then back up at him. "Alexsi Ivanovich, we have both boys and girls living here. You have experience with girls?"

Well, the questions were getting tougher, but he was getting used to not understanding what anyone meant. "There were girls at my school, Comrade Director. And on the farm . . ." Out of ideas for possible answers, he stopped.

For some reason she sighed and looked down at her papers again. "Because we have both boys and girls living here, it is important that your relations with girls be correct, yes?"

Alexsi still had no idea what she was talking about, but it was clear what was expected so he nodded dutifully anyway.

She sighed again. "Alexsi Ivanovich, do you know what a penis is?"

Alexsi had no earthly idea what that had to do with what they were talking about. "Y-yes, Comrade Director."

She brightened up a bit, as if she now had something to work with. "Good. Under no circumstances will you let one of the girls here touch your penis. Do you understand?"

No, not at all. "Yes, Comrade Director."

"Good. If you do, your health will fail. You will sicken. There will be nothing we can do for you. Do you understand?"

Not in the slightest. "Yes, Comrade Director."

"Excellent." Now that she had fulfilled her socialist duty to the health of his penis, she gave the papers on her desk a little pat, as if putting his history to bed. Rising from her chair, she said, "It is time for you to meet everyone."

There were close to a hundred children of various ages lined up in a big room filled with tables, waiting to receive their lunch. The boys were all dressed the same as him, brown trousers and pullover shirt, so it was like a school uniform. The girls wore plaid dresses with sailor collars. The Comrade Director stopped the serving, which set off an undertone of angry grumbling. Then she made him stand beside her with her hand clamped on his shoulder, so he couldn't run away even if he had been thinking of it, while she made a speech ordering everyone to make him feel welcome. Before she was done the children started banging their trays. At first she pretended that it wasn't even happening. Then, when it was on the verge of getting out of hand, she concluded her remarks with a forced smile and blithely walked off, leaving him there.

The children all stared at him as if he were naked, and then nearly in unison turned their backs toward the lunch line, erupting in a roar of conversation.

Alexsi fell in at the end, picking up a tray and a dish and a mug and a spoon. The meal was kasha with milk and a scoop of sugar, a quarter-kilo chunk of black bread, a pat of butter, and tea. The women servers looked like illustrations of witches from the Brothers Grimm, and they kept snapping at the children to move faster through the line. By the time Alexsi got there the kasha was nearly gone, and as he stood there gazing down into his not-full bowl one of the witches threw an extra chunk of bread onto his tray and barked at him to move along.

As he came off the line the children were looking at him again as they crammed the food into their mouths. Alexsi instinctively realized that if they thought he was afraid he was finished, so as he walked across the room he stared back at them until they looked away.

He picked the far end of the table at the far end of the dining room, and sat by himself. He ate his food and was still hungry when he was finished.

When the meal was over he carefully watched what everyone else did. So he put his dirty dishes into the metal tubs with all the others, and followed the children as they filed out.

Going down the hallway the crowd in front of him stopped suddenly and parted, and Alexsi knew something was going to happen. He stuck his hand into his pocket and quickly opened the drawstring on the pouch he'd smuggled in.

Blocking his way were three of the bigger boys, maybe fourteen or fifteen. Everyone else was a safe distance back, watching.

The one in the center, the leader, said, "Got anything good? Hand it over or you'll get hurt."

"That's right, turn out your pockets," said the one to his right.

Back on the farm, there was a boy named Anatoli who hated him. The first few fights Anatoli had started, Alexsi had no trouble beating him. Then Anatoli put a gang together. Alexsi was still carrying his solution to that: an old cast-iron nut, heavy but small enough to fit in his palm, salvaged from the farm scrap pile. And a length of heavy twine tied to it.

The leader was smirking in anticipation of some fun. Alexsi knew what he was thinking: give the new kid a good thrashing to put him in his place, and keep everyone else in their place, too. At first, his stomach started hurting but that feeling was replaced by one of grim determination. If he didn't fight back now his life here would be a nightmare.

Alexsi jerked his hand out of his pocket and threw the nut into that smirking face as hard as he could. It hit the boy right in the eye; he screamed and threw his hands up to his face.

If there were just one, Alexsi would have kicked him in the balls then. But there were two more to deal with. For the moment they were frozen in place by the unexpected turn of events, but he knew that wouldn't last long. Alexsi jerked his hand back. One end of the twine was tied to the nut, the other looped around his hand. Alexsi swung his hand over his head and the nut made a loud buzzing sound as it picked up speed circling behind his back. He had practiced enough that the nut went exactly where he wanted it to go.

It hit the loudmouth on the right just above the ear, and at a most excellent speed. His eyes rolled back in his head and he crumpled to the floor.

Now the third enemy had seen enough and turned to run. But Alexsi leaped onto his back and brought him down to the floor, his forefinger through the hole in the middle of the nut, smashing it into the boy's head with all his might. After only a few blows the boy stopped yelling and was still.

Alexsi rolled off him and jumped up on his feet. He turned his attention back to the leader, who was down on his knees, holding his eye and still screaming. Alexsi tossed the nut out behind him. It hit the floor, still tethered to him by the twine. He swung his arm forward as if he were using a whip; the nut hummed past his ear and struck the leader on the back of the head with a sound like a ripe melon dropped to the ground. The leader pitched face-first onto the floor and didn't make any more noise.

Alexsi stood there panting, all three enemies scattered about like rag dolls on the floor. The other children were gaping at him like a circus audience who had just seen the bear eat the trainer— totally unexpected, but an even better show.

A girl broke out of the pack and dashed up to him: his age, pale and pretty with huge blue eyes that were shining with excitement. "Give it to me!"

Without thinking, Alexsi yanked the pouch from his pocket, stuffed the nut and the twine inside, and stretched out his hand to her.

She snatched the pouch from his grasp and stuffed it under her skirt. Without a pause, she'd skipped back into the crowd of kids and disappeared.

Behind him there was shouting and the pounding of heavy feet on the wood floor. The audience scattered and two male attendants ran up and grabbed him by the arms.

ALEXSI THOUGHT it would be a beating, but it turned out like his old school, where the principal had to yell at him first before the thrashing with a stick. They locked him up until the Comrade Director was ready to shout at him.

"Three boys in hospital with fractured skulls!" was how she began. "One in a coma! Well? What do you have to say for yourself?"

Experience had taught Alexsi that the louder people were shouting the more repentant he had to be. Head hanging low, he finally said, "Comrade Director, it was not *my* choice to fight with three boys on my first day here."

Her face was red, though he noticed that she was gripping the edge of her desk so hard her hands were white. "That they were three troublemakers is beside the point."

"Why is that, Comrade Director?" he asked mildly.

"Enough from you!" she shouted, coming up half out of her

chair. Her eyes searched the top of her desk as if she was looking for something sharp but not particularly valuable to throw at him. Then another thought came to her. "It is said you used a weapon. Where is it?"

So the informers were already at work. Good to know. Alexsi held his open hands out from his body in an expression of total innocence.

The Comrade Director looked over his head at the attendants standing behind him. Alexsi could practically feel them shake their heads, and he worked hard to keep that smug feeling off his face.

The Comrade Director knocked her knuckles on the desk. "Still, we cannot let this pass without punishment. We must be stern with you." She nodded as if to confirm the decision her knuckles had already brought her to.

One of the attendants grabbed him by the shoulder and pulled him out of the office.

They locked him in a small room. It had a cot, a jug of water on a little table, a mug, and an enameled chamber pot with a cover sitting in one corner.

He sat down on the cot and waited for the punishment, but nothing else happened. He couldn't believe it. That was it? Being locked in a room? Alexsi nearly laughed out loud with relief.

When they let him out the next morning, everything was different. The attendants eyed him warily. The witches serving breakfast didn't shout at him the way they did the other kids. And when he sat down at the end of a table like before, a bunch of kids moved over to sit all around him. He ignored them, but one of the smaller boys tugged on his sleeve and said, "Do you want my bread?"

Alexsi almost took it and crammed it into his mouth, thinking the kid was full. Then he realized that no one there was full—everyone had to be as hungry as he was. The kid was offering his bread for *protection*.

Something told him to think that over carefully. He pictured himself being the boss of all the kids in the orphanage. No. It would be good for a while, until a few boys eventually decided he wasn't that tough and got him when he wasn't paying attention. Or someone new like him came along one day and cracked his skull open. And then all the kids who did what he said would just go to the next one who was stronger, as if he'd never existed.

"Keep your bread," he said to the boy, who looked crestfallen. But then he added, "You don't have to give your stuff to anyone if you don't want to."

"Really?" the little boy said.

Alexsi just nodded.

It worked out even better than he'd hoped. The news of what he said spread like fire. He wasn't making anyone do anything, so no one resented him. But anyone thinking about offering protection was afraid of what he might do, so no one tried to push anyone around. And he didn't have to fight. A couple of boys approached him with offers to form a gang, but he brushed them off.

Though he did miss that little room of his own. He slept in a huge room full of boys, with barely enough space to walk between their iron beds. The house certainly hadn't been designed to hold that many, let alone children, and trying to get to a lavatory to do your business was a nightmare in itself. Every now and again they found a pile of shit in a corner when some kid hadn't been able or willing to wait, and the attendants went mad. There weren't enough taps or sinks, so in the morning it was cold washes above the waist from basins. They had to take turns on housework duty, which meant cleaning and carrying in the morning water and washing dishes in the kitchen and cleaning up the occasional pile of shit. Once a week they got a full wash in the *banya,* the steam bath, and were given a change of underwear after that.

After wash and breakfast there was school. The teachers

couldn't care less if anyone learned anything. Alexsi didn't mind. He'd always been able to learn from books, so who needed teachers?

Of course there was always political instruction. As far as he was concerned, if they told you the sky was yellow and your eyes said it was blue, and you could get into trouble saying it was blue, then why bother? Just tell them what they wanted to hear, nod your head at the right time, clap your hands along with everyone else, and sing their stupid songs.

Food was the main problem. It was mainly kasha and macaroni and soup and tea. Sometimes some meat, but not very often. And sometimes cocoa or milky coffee. Always black bread. He was constantly hungry. While on duty washing dishes he'd scouted where the pantries were, but they were locked up tight.

He tried to get his pouch back from the girl who had hidden it, but every time he approached her she ran away. She was in his classes, but she sat away from him and it wasn't something that could be discussed openly.

Then one day he was outside reading while the rest were playing. After the fight everyone treated him like a dangerous animal whose attention you didn't want to draw. And that was fine with him.

Out of the blue the girl dashed up to him and whispered in his ear. "Meet me in the back stairway an hour after they turn the lights out."

That was it. She sprinted back to a giggling ball of girls who were all whispering to each other and stealing looks at him. And she was acting like they had dared her to speak to him.

ALEXSI HAD already clocked the schedule of the attendants who walked the floors at night. The girl was wise, because an hour after lights out was when they relaxed their vigilance and went off to play cards with each other.

His bed was at the end of the room near a wall anyway, so it was a simple matter to wait until everyone's breathing told that they were asleep and form his sheets and the pillow into a mound under the blanket and slip away.

He was wary of waiting in the stairway in case it was a trap for some of the other boys to attack him. But the girl was already there. She raised a finger to her lips and Alexsi nodded approvingly.

She led him up the stairs to the top floor where the Comrade Director and all the bosses had their offices. Alexsi approved of that, too. It was forbidden for the children to be there, and there was nothing of interest besides offices, so it probably wasn't patrolled with the same vigilance as the rest of the house.

They tiptoed down the hall, and at the far end the girl opened a small door. It was a closet where brooms and dustpans and the cleaning materials for the floor were kept. This girl was clever; no one would be looking in there after dark.

She closed the door behind them and clicked on a chain to light a dim bulb. "If we keep our voices soft, no one can hear us."

Alexsi nodded and leaned against the wall, ready to run or fight if necessary.

The girl's hair was as black as night, even blacker against a face so pale it seemed to shine on its own. Her eyes were huge in her small face, the same blue as the birds on the first wallpaper he'd ever seen. She looked up at him strangely, as if she were waiting for him to say something. When he didn't after a while, she reached under her dress and brought out his pouch. She opened it and shook out what was inside into her hand.

She placed his pocketknife on the floor, along with the nut and twine, which still had dried blood on it. She held the rest out to him. "What are these?"

"Nothing," he said. "Give them to me." He reached out his hand, but she pulled hers back to her breast.

"If you don't tell me I won't give them to you," she said.

"Give them to me or else," Alexsi warned, looming over her.

She didn't seem at all concerned. "If you hit me I'll tell on you."

Alexsi knew he was checkmated. They would always believe a girl. "They're picks."

"Picks? What kind of picks?" she demanded.

Well, she wasn't going to be put off easily, that was for sure. "Lock picks," Alexsi said finally.

"I thought so," she breathed, looking down in her hand. "Where did you get them?"

"I made them."

"Made them? How?"

"From pieces of metal. And a file."

She had been turning them over in her hands, and now she looked back up into his eyes. "Do they work?"

"I wouldn't have them if they didn't work," said Alexsi. Stupid question.

"How did you learn how to use them?"

"I took locks apart to see how they worked," said Alexsi.

She was searching his eyes with hers, and finally asked, "Are you hungry?"

"Of course I'm hungry," Alexsi replied. Everyone was hungry.

"Are you willing to take a risk for some food?"

Alexsi eyed her suspiciously. "I'm not going to be the only one taking a risk."

"I'll go with you the whole way," she said.

Alexsi thought it over. She wasn't stupid, and she obviously knew her way around. And she'd kept his stuff safe and hadn't squealed to the authorities. "You're talking about getting into the kitchen?"

The girl nodded solemnly.

"Then you know that the locks aren't the main problem. It's the attendants sitting in the dining room in front of the kitchen door, playing chess all night. And all the other doors not only have locks, they're barred." The attendants knew that sneaking into the kitchen was every kid's dream; they weren't totally stupid.

"I know a way," she said. "But I need someone who knows how to pick locks."

"How?"

"It will take too long to tell you," she said. "We must do it now, to have time before the cooks come in early to start making the breakfast. Just follow me."

Alexsi didn't care for that. How could he know if her plan was sound? But then again, if they got caught, what would happen? Get locked in the room by himself again? Fine.

"All right," he said. "Give me my stuff."

Now she handed it all over. They left the closet and she led him farther down the hallway. Turning a corner, she stopped, and it took him a moment to see what she was standing next to in the darkness. It practically blended into the wood paneling. A sliding wooden door about waist high on the wall, a meter wide and half a meter high, with a single brass knob that almost couldn't be seen, it was so dark with tarnish.

The girl grabbed the knob and pushed the door up until it locked. Inside was like a wooden box, open in front, with two thick ropes off to one side.

"It's a dumbwaiter that goes down into the kitchen," she whispered in his ear.

Alexsi had no idea what she was talking about. But he watched as she climbed into the box and pulled up and down on the ropes to move the box up and down. That was really something. He'd read about elevators before, but nothing like this.

"I'll send it back up after I get down," she whispered. She handed him a chunk of wood. "After you get in, close the door and put this under it so we can get back out."

The girl seemed to have thought things through. She pulled on the rope and the box slid downward. Once the top disappeared from view, Alexsi stuck his head into the hole. Even in the darkness he could see how the box was lowered by the ropes and a pulley. He lightly touched the rope as it moved. It seemed to be in pretty good shape, but he could also see what a misfortune it would be if it broke while he was in the box. Well, the girl had done it.

The rope stopped, and a moment later it began to move in the opposite direction. Soon the empty box was in front of him.

Staring into it, he almost lost his nerve. What if he got stuck on the way down? Wavering, the only thing that moved him was that the girl had done it, and she'd surely call him a coward.

He sighed and began folding himself into the box. He had to rearrange his body twice until he was all the way in and able to grip the ropes properly. When he slid the door down with the chunk of wood holding it slightly open, he was in total darkness and started sweating as if it were summer, and it suddenly became very hard to breathe.

After pulling on the rope for what seemed forever, faint cracks of light began to show through the bottom. Then he was in another opening, and the girl's head was right in front of him.

It was the kitchen. There were no lights on, but moonlight came through the high windows on the back wall and reflected off the wall tile. And brighter light from the frosted glass panel above the door to the dining room.

Alexsi wanted to leap from the box, but he forced himself to slip out as quietly as possible. His shirt felt like a wet rag. As soon as he was back on his feet, the girl took his arm and whispered in his ear, "Don't worry. I felt like that the first time."

And with those few words of sympathy she completely won him over.

There was more than enough light to see by, and they could hear the voices of the attendants playing chess through the dining-room door. Alexsi turned around and looked at the open hole he'd come through, and realized it wasn't meant for people. The rich had used it to send food from the kitchen to the upper floors, without someone having to walk it all the way up the stairs. Dumb-waiter. Now he understood.

She led him away from the pantries where they stored the food to a door around a corner that was protected with a stout new silver padlock. During kitchen duty Alexsi had been where they kept the food, always escorted by a cook who watched his every move and made him carry everything, no matter how heavy. But he'd never seen anyone go in this door.

He held his hands up in a questioning motion, but the girl emphatically pointed to the door and pantomimed opening the padlock.

Alexsi shrugged and hoped she knew what she was doing. He didn't need light to open the padlock; it was all about feeling the pins with the pick. He had it unlocked in less than a minute. The door was easier. The keyhole lock below the knob was very old and only a matter of pressing in the large pins and circling the lock. He opened the door very slowly so it wouldn't squeak. The girl was practically jumping up and down with excitement.

They both slipped inside, and the girl took hold of the light chain and motioned for him to close the door before she turned it on.

He did. The chain rasped, the switch clicked, and the bulb popped on.

It was just like the story of Aladdin's cave. There was food he had never seen served in the house, some food he had never even seen before in his life. Loaves of white bread on the counter. *White* bread! They never had white bread, only black bread. There were two delicious-looking cakes under things that looked like big glass jars over serving plates. Shelves full of jars of jam and tins of exotic food. The bastards. They'd been keeping it all for themselves. No wonder all the kids were always hungry, and all the grown-ups had fat bellies.

The girl had been rummaging through the shelves, and now she gave off a muted squeal and held up a big paper-wrapped bar. She was about to tear the paper off when Alexsi lunged over and snatched it from her hands. "Don't open it!" he whispered fiercely.

She put her hands on her hips and did everything but stamp her foot. "But it's *chocolate*," she whispered back plaintively.

Alexsi leaned in close to her ear and made his case. "If we want to come back again, we have to make it look like nothing happened. There's only four bars of chocolate here—they'll know someone stole it."

She still looked longingly at the bar and whispered, "But it's *chocolate*."

Alexsi carefully replaced it on the shelf exactly where it had been. He motioned for her to hold up her skirt to make a carrying basket. He took a loaf of white bread and rearranged all the others so there was no gap on the counter. There were two loaves that had been cut—he left those alone. He took a jar of jam and restacked the shelf to make the row symmetrical. And chose a fat tin of fruit. That was enough. Even if the grown-ups did notice what was missing, they'd think one of *them* filched it.

After a last careful turn around the storage room to make sure they'd left nothing out of place, he clicked off the light and practically pushed her out. She was still gazing longingly at those chocolate bars.

He lifted her back into the box, a necessary act with all the food wrapped up in her skirt. As soon as she disappeared out of sight he dashed back and relocked the door and the padlock. There was still a steady hum of conversation coming from the dining room.

The rope stopped moving, and he waited patiently. Then there was a loud clunk, like a metal tin being dropped on wood. It echoed down the dumbwaiter shaft like a cannon shot.

Alexsi hoped it hadn't actually been as loud as it sounded to him, but the conversation in the dining room had stopped and he knew he was in trouble. As soon as the weight was off the rope he pulled it hard hand over hand to get the dumbwaiter down.

The voices were talking in the dining room again, but the pitch had changed. He heard the squeak of chair legs on the wood floor and the groan that adults always made when they stood up.

A key was inserted into the kitchen door lock. Alexsi frantically worked the ropes. The key turned and the dumbwaiter slid down in front of him. He leaped into it and pushed the wooden door shut just as the kitchen door opened.

Alexsi could see the kitchen light snap on through the cracks in the dumbwaiter door. If he tried to pull himself up, it would be heard.

He could hear leather soles tapping on the tile floor. The footsteps circled the kitchen, rattling doors to make sure they were locked. As they came closer the dumbwaiter rope went taut. The girl was impatient, trying to pull him up. Alexsi locked his hands on the rope so the dumbwaiter wouldn't move, praying the girl wouldn't make any more noise.

The footsteps stopped right in front of him. Alexsi was sweating again; he even tried to breathe quietly. He waited for that moment when the dumbwaiter door would be thrown open and he would be dragged out for punishment. It seemed that both he and whoever was in the kitchen were both waiting in limbo for an eternity.

Then the footsteps started up again, and the kitchen light snapped off. The door was shut and the lock was locked. Alexsi heard it all with crystal clarity. He wanted nothing more than to yank at the rope and take himself out of there, but he forced himself to wait long enough for them to sit back down and resume their game. Only then, very slowly, did he pull himself up.

The girl was waiting at the open door upstairs, and she seemed furious that he'd taken so long. Alexsi just held up a finger to his lips. He climbed out and sent the dumbwaiter back to the kitchen. He'd seen that there was a line marked on the rope that told when it was in the right spot.

"You were down there forever," she said, as soon as they were back inside the closet.

"They heard you drop that can," Alexsi said. "They came in to check."

Her hand flew up to her mouth. "I'm sorry."

Alexsi just shrugged as he sliced the loaf of bread in half and then in pieces with his pocketknife, making two even piles. Stabbing the blade into the tin of fruit, he cut a rough X at the top and pushed the four flaps down to open the tin.

She took the knife from him and began spreading jam on the bread. She'd taken off her cap after the exertion of the thievery and the wisps of black hair dangled over her face. She really was pretty, with those big blue eyes.

Watching her, he asked, "What is your name?"

"Aida," she said.

"I've never known anyone with a name like that."

"It's from an opera."

Alexsi digested that. "I've read about operas. It's a play where they sing instead of talk, right?"

She looked up from the bread and brushed the hair from her eyes. "You never heard an opera?"

Alexsi snorted. "Operas don't come to farms."

"Not even on the radio?"

"Who has a radio?"

"There wasn't even a radio on your farm?"

"Well, on the kolkhoz where I lived, there was a radio at the community center that people listened to at night. But if you ever said you wanted to listen to an opera they'd beat you up and throw you out the door."

"You're funny," she said, handing him a slice of bread. "Your name is Alexsi, isn't it?"

Alexsi just nodded. The bread was light and fluffy. Not like the black bread they always got, which sometimes tasted like it had sawdust mixed into it. And it was fig jam, almost the best thing he had ever tasted.

"Why are you eating so fast?" she asked.

Alexsi paused for a moment to swallow. "So if someone pushes that door in and takes this food away from us, at least I have something in my stomach."

"You are the funniest boy I ever met," she declared. And then, "I can't tell you the rest of my name. It's secret."

Alexsi took up another piece of bread from his pile.

She went back to spreading jam, to try to keep ahead of him. "Don't you want to know?"

"You just said you couldn't tell me because it was a secret."

"You're so funny. I can't tell you because my papa was very important. He knew Stalin himself."

Alexsi went on eating.

"Don't you believe me?" she asked.

"If you say so."

"It's true. Papa called him Koba. They knew each other from before the Revolution. Stalin killed him."

Alexsi didn't want to say he was sorry, because maybe she felt like he did. He'd be overjoyed if he heard that Stalin killed his father.

"Papa said that Stalin was waiting patiently until he had enough power. And Papa said that when Stalin thought the time was ripe he would kill everyone who could ever challenge him. And everyone who knew him before, when he was weak."

She talked really fast, the way most girls did. The words spilled out like they were afraid you were going to run away before they were finished. Aida passed him another piece of bread. She'd spread the jam on thick. With a whole jar to use on one loaf, it was the first time in his life he'd ever had enough. Alexsi thought but didn't say that it sounded like Papa had talked a lot. No wonder he was dead.

Aida scooted over until she was leaning back against him, reaching into the tin for a slice of fruit. "Open your mouth."

When she fed it to him Alexsi's stomach felt like when Anastasia back at his old school used to put her hand on his leg. And it was a preserved pear in sugar syrup. Maybe the best thing ever.

"You said you lived on a kolkhoz?" she said.

"That's right."

"You got out just in time. It's going to get bad there."

"It's already bad," Alexsi told her.

"Papa said it was impossible to turn twenty million farms into a quarter of a million collectives in just four years. People would starve."

It sounded crazy to him. Maybe her papa was crazy. "Then why do it?"

"Because Papa said that the peasants were always the key to power in Russia. That when they stopped supporting the Tsar, the Tsar fell. He said that the peasants didn't care about Communism, so they had to be kept under control until they did. And the only way to control the countryside was for the state to be in charge of the farms. So Stalin ordered it done no matter what. Starving wasn't part of the plan. But there weren't enough tractors and things, the crops spoiled before they could be picked up, and soon there wasn't enough food for everyone in the country. They didn't mind, though. The party is never wrong, and Stalin would never admit he was wrong—his enemies might attack him."

It occurred to Alexsi that being Stalin was a lot like being the boss of kids in an orphanage. But then he'd always seen for himself that no matter what kind of shit they talked, the bosses always made sure *they* had enough. "That's why you have to look out for yourself."

Aida stretched her head back to look up at him. "Papa said the worst thing about famine was that the first to die were always the simple people who did what they were told. The ones who would never steal food, lie, or break the law. He said the new Soviet man who would be created by these conditions would be terrifying." She fed him another pear slice. "Like you."

"I'm not the only thief here," Alexsi said defensively.

"No, you're not. But we're full, aren't we."

"For the first time in a long while." He looked down at her. "You remember everything your papa said?"

"I remember everything everyone says."

"I'm a nice fellow," Alexsi said. Though he wasn't sure who he was saying it to. "Just don't push me around. Or hurt my friends."

She looked up at him again. "Am I your friend?"

Alexsi only shrugged.

She twisted around so she was up on her knees and they were face to face. "Allow me to thank you for the food." She put her arms around his neck, leaned in, and kissed him.

Alexsi was frozen in the fear of both not knowing what to do and the terrible prospect of making an embarrassing mistake.

Aida seemed to sense that. "You can put your arms around me. And just move your lips with mine."

His whole body seemed to be humming, but it wasn't like the trembling when he thought he was going to die. Though he was just as scared. The burglary had been easy—this was hard. She was so slender and so soft. They kissed some more. She tasted of pears.

"That's better," she whispered. "Now open your mouth and just touch tongues. It's so much better than ramming your tongue down someone's throat—that's terrible. Oh, that's nice. You're so gentle," she said, marveling.

Clearly she had kissed boys before, but Alexsi was just glad someone knew what they were doing. His cock was hard as a tree branch, and he tried to move so it wasn't touching her. Who knew what she might do?

But she was on to him instantly. "Oh, what's that?" She touched him through his trousers. "Let me see."

She pushed him, and as he fell back he caught himself on his elbows. She unbuttoned his trousers and pulled his underwear out and away without touching him. And he was staring at her staring at his penis, which was literally pulsing back and forth under her gaze every time his heart beat. And his heart was beating very fast.

She reached out and touched the shaft with the fingertips of both hands. Her touch was so light he felt like he was going out of his mind. And then her hands closed around it without really closing around it. She was touching him as if he were made of thin breakable glass.

When she pushed his foreskin down and ran her fingertips up and over the head Alexsi groaned, "Aaah." His hips bucked and he shot past her startled eyes; his come hit the closet wall and he felt as if all his insides had been pulled out through his cock. His right leg just shook back and forth without him doing anything about it.

When he regained his senses he looked up quickly to see if he had offended her. But she was smiling at him. "It's still hard," she whispered. She kept sliding her hands up and down, and each time her palm rolled over the head it felt so incredible he could barely stand it. He was holding his breath to keep from making too much noise, and each time he had to breathe it came out in a half groan, half squeak that made her giggle every time.

Alexsi wasn't sure which was better: her touch, or the way she was looking at his cock as she stroked it, biting her lip in concentration. Soon he couldn't take it anymore. "Again!" he gasped.

She giggled and ducked out of the way, and again it came out like a pistol shot. Aida patted his cock as if she were giving a dog a "good boy" pat, and jumped up to get a cleaning rag off the pile and clean his come off the inside of the closet. More than a little embarrassed by that, Alexsi pushed it back into his trousers and buttoned up.

"Oh, you hid it away," she said when she was finished. "I like to look at it."

Alexsi felt his face burning red.

"Would you like to touch *me*?" she asked.

Alexsi managed to get out, "Very much."

Aida put her hands up under her skirt and slid her underwear down, primly stepping out of them. She sat back down and pressed her back against his chest. Then she took his right hand and licked his fingers.

Alexsi was glad he had already come twice because otherwise he would have again, just from that.

"Go ahead," she said. "Just touch as gently as you kissed me."

Alexsi put his hand under her skirt and slid his hand up her leg to guide him to where he needed to go.

Aida moaned and leaned back hard against him. "Oh, that's nice."

Alexsi took the hint and slid his hand back and forth along the inside of her thighs. He was watching her carefully; she had her chin down on her chest, and her eyes closed. He tried to touch her the same way she did him, as if she were made of brittle glass. He wouldn't have touched himself the same way, but how she had done it was a thousand times better.

Finally he pressed the palm of his hand against her, just to get a sense of the unfamiliar geography. Aida bucked her hips up and whispered, "Yes, just hold your hand right there."

He did, with a little more pressure until she seemed to tire of it. Then he explored very carefully with his fingertips. He had never touched a girl's parts before, and there were so many folds and ridges. She was squirming all over the place, so he supposed he was doing it right. With his arms around her his face was in her neck and he kissed her there because she seemed to like it.

Without meaning to, his finger slipped inside her, and she cried out. "Sssh," he said in her ear. With her eyes still closed she grimaced and nodded. She was holding on tight to both his forearms, not to stop him but just for something to hold on to.

He left his finger where it was, because that was definitely working. It was very wet and sticky there, and he could see why she'd licked his hands to make them slick. As he continued exploring his thumb brushed a little knob of flesh and she practically leaped onto his shoulders. He thought he was going to have to put his hand over her mouth.

She grabbed his hand and rubbed it back and forth over that knob, as if he were washing a spot off a window but much lighter. He understood instantly that he had to follow the way she was thrusting her hips and then go progressively faster. It seemed that girls were the same as boys in that regard, though they took so much longer.

Finally she grabbed his arms even harder and her hips came up off the floor. He felt the cry beginning in her throat and he clamped his hand over her mouth. Just as well because she practically screamed behind his closed hand. Her body seemed to close in around his finger inside her, and pulse back and forth in a little spurt of wetness. Absolutely amazing. A whole new world.

When she calmed down, she said weakly, "Please take your hand away. It's very sensitive now."

"Let me see," said Alexsi.

"Promise you won't touch it again."

"I promise." He twirled her around on her bottom so she was facing him, and lifted her skirt up so he could see in the dim light of the closet. Amazing. The fine little wisps of hair were wet and matted, and the rest was like the petals of a flower. It seemed that girls pissed from the hole the cock went in the same way boys came though the piss hole.

"It's ugly, isn't it?" she said.

"No, it's beautiful," Alexsi replied truthfully.

"I think yours is prettier."

Alexsi shook his head.

Footsteps came down the hall.

Aida rushed to put her underwear on, but Alexsi held her firm. He knew she wouldn't make any noise so he didn't put his hand over her mouth. His arms were wrapped around her, and she had her hand over his.

The footsteps passed by their door, turned the corner, and could be heard taking the stairs down.

"We should go," Aida said. "If they find our beds empty they'll search the whole house and then lie in wait for us to come back."

Alexsi nodded. He handed her the tin of fruit and they took turns drinking the sugar syrup until it was all gone. While she put on her underwear, he took a dustpan and carefully brushed up all the crumbs they'd left on the floor. He emptied them onto the rag she'd used to wipe up his come and crushed the empty tin flat onto it. The empty jam jar he placed on top, and he tied the rag around it like a package.

"Why did you do all that?" Aida asked.

"If the cleaners find anything in here they'll know something is wrong," Alexsi whispered. "Even if they don't think anything is gone from the kitchen. You can't just take things, you have to cover your tracks. I'll get rid of all this stuff in the bottom of the trash bins. No one will ever find it."

Her eyes were shining with excitement. "When will we do this again? Tomorrow night?"

Alexsi shook his head. "At least a week."

"That long?" she said, pouting prettily.

"If they realize something is missing from the kitchen, they'll set a trap for the thief. But if we wait long enough, they'll get tired and think they were mistaken."

She hugged him hard around the neck. "I knew I was right about you."

"You go first," he said. "I'll follow right behind. Straight back to bed." He wanted to check the closet one more time before he left.

She kissed him, and her tongue teased its way into his mouth. He felt himself getting hard again.

Aida giggled, rubbed herself against his crotch, and slipped out of the closet.

Alexsi was glad the whole house was asleep because all the

rich food made him have to shit over and over again. It seemed like he spent half the night on the toilet.

Later, back in his bed amid the thunder of snoring boys, getting hard each time he thought about Aida, Alexsi reflected that he should have known they were lying about *that*, too. Having a girl touch your penis was the greatest thing in the world.

10

"THIS GIRL AIDA GAVE YOU NO OTHER NAME?" COMRADE Yakushev demanded.

"She said she could not tell me," Alexsi replied. "That it was secret."

"Why?"

"Because her father had known Comrade Stalin."

"And the father?"

"She said," Alexsi replied, putting emphasis on those first two words, "that Comrade Stalin had killed him."

"She did."

"Yes. I know nothing else about him."

Yakushev exhaled a great puff of smoke. "Now we see the origins of the conspiracy. Her father was a well-known enemy of the people, despite his high position. Yet Comrade Stalin has given orders that children should not be held liable for the crimes of their parents. This girl was taken in by the state, as you were."

At that Alexsi shifted uncomfortably in his seat.

It didn't escape Yakushev's attention. "You took a misguided path, due to lack of attention on the part of those who were responsible for you. This girl, on the other hand, was nurtured by the state. Given every opportunity. Brought from the farthest edge of the republics to Moscow State University itself. And this is how she repays our great nation and our great leader."

There was an edge to his voice that restored the cold, clench-

ing grip of fear to Alexsi's stomach. He had run into many officials, before and after his time with the Shahsavan. A man on the
make would do whatever he was ordered, but not one thing more,
for fear of blundering. And if offered a bribe he would happily
help himself. But a fanatic like this couldn't be bought, dodged, or
intimidated.

"Her name is Aida Rudenko," said Yakushev, "and she will be
your entry into this group of terrorists. Now, the most important
aspect of secret work is the creation of what we call a legend. It is
almost exactly like an actor preparing to play a role. You are Ham-
let, Prince of Denmark. A man has killed your father the king and
taken his place. This murderer has married your mother the queen,
and is perhaps preparing your death also. Your every action as
this character is in accordance with these principles. So, pour
yourself some more tea. Visit the toilet if you must. And think
carefully and tell me who you will become and what story you
will tell in order to reacquaint yourself with this girl. I caution
you that every legend must be grounded in reality. You cannot
present yourself as a circus juggler unless if called upon you are
able to actually juggle."

Alexsi sat in the toilet for a good long time because he doubted
he could think properly with Yakushev staring at him.

Then he retook his seat.

Yakushev lit another cigarette. "You neglected to flush the
toilet."

Alexsi was fairly certain that was a joke, and marked its appearance. He was not counting on many more. "I do not think
I can be a student. How would I reach university in Moscow after
running away from an orphanage in Baku? And how do I simply
appear one day with no one ever seeing me before? Also, if I
posed as a student, they might ask me about subjects I know
nothing of."

"I agree," said Yakushev. "And now your solution."

"I am a thief," Alexsi said. "Newly successful. You can tell me what the main rackets in Moscow are. Food? Petrol? Alcohol? Perhaps all of them. I bribed an official for my apartment in the Arbat. I have money. I have resources. I am outside the law already, and the forbidden is always attractive."

Yakushev finished his cigarette and stubbed it out. "Go over to the table and write me out your story in detail."

11

AS THE GIRL CAME OUT OF THE STATE BAKERY, SHE TURNED and faced the door in order to shut it against the stiff wind. The queue for bread wound around the inside of the store but everyone had packed themselves in tightly so they wouldn't have to stand outside in the cold. Like every Russian Alexsi couldn't look at a line without making the calculation. At least an hour's wait, if they didn't run out of bread before you reached the counter. Of course, they would always have some hidden away in the back. That's why it was better to steal it.

Timing it carefully, he leaped up the steps to intercept her.

When she closed the latch and turned she collided with his chest.

Alexsi lightly grasped her upper arms to keep them both from falling down the steps. "Your pardon, Comrade."

"Excuse *me*," she replied.

Still holding her arms, he said, "Do I know you?"

She kept her eyes down and said, "I'm certain you don't."

"I'm certain I do," Alexsi said.

Since he was going to be persistent, she finally raised her gaze to brush him off. But instead they went wide. "Wait." She examined his face minutely. "I can't believe it." And then she pressed her gloved hand against his chest, as if to confirm that he was actually real. "Alexsi?"

"I would know those eyes anywhere, Aida," he said, smiling.

They were so very blue. She was wearing her black hair long and straight, which based on what he had seen was not the current style. Though it suited her.

"Alexsi! My goodness . . ." She threw her arms around his neck.

There was now a crowd of people waiting to get in to the bakery, and being Russians they were getting angry, so with her still wrapped around his neck he lifted her by the waist and carried her down the stairs and out of the way.

When he set her down they were both laughing. Aida drew back and touched his face fondly. "How did you get here? How did you get to Moscow?" She brushed her hand across the wool of his coat. "In your very nice clothes."

Alexsi thought she was even more beautiful as a woman. Taller, and both her face and body had filled out nicely. "I should ask you the same thing."

"I'm a student at the state university," she exclaimed.

"That's wonderful," he said. "But don't they feed you there? You come away from the bakery empty-handed."

"Oh," she said, holding up her empty shopping bag. "It's my girlfriend's birthday, and I so wanted to give her a cake. I was going to bake it, but finding all the ingredients was impossible. Now it seems I've been to every bakery in Moscow, but no cakes."

Alexsi took her by the arm. "Perhaps I can help. I wouldn't want a friend of yours to have an unhappy birthday."

"And how are you going to arrange that?" she said, smiling at him.

"There," he said, pointing up ahead. "Let's take that streetcar."

"Are you kidnapping me?" she asked, still smiling.

"It's not kidnapping if you come with me willingly," he replied.

"I suppose I have to," she said. "I can't let you go. I have several thousand questions for you."

They dashed out into the street as the tram started moving, the conductor ignoring them both. Alexsi grabbed the rail and helped her up the steps.

They exited at Arbatskaya Square and crossed over it. "Let's try in here," Alexsi said, gesturing toward the wedge-shaped building on the corner.

Aida pulled back on his arm. "Alexsi, no! Not the Praga. That restaurant is too expensive."

"Really?" he said. "I've never been inside. But I have walked by and seen people eating cake. So let's go in."

They took a table. It was easy to see how rich the place had been, though like all the prerevolutionary buildings of Moscow you could also see how it had been beaten down for lack of maintenance. Still, the walls and ceilings were ivory with carved wooden columns in every corner and flanking the doors. All the paneled details were outlined in gold. There were crystal chandeliers, and dark velvet drapes hung in the windows. Carved statues looked down on the diners from the walls as if they didn't care that their fingers and toes were chipped. Alexsi ordered cake and tea for two.

"No one can afford to eat here," Aida said, holding the menu over her mouth to muffle her words.

"Yet there are people eating here," Alexsi replied.

"I mean regular people."

"I'm sure it will all work out," Alexsi said.

Aida made a gesture of resignation that was uniquely Russian. "I hope you know what you're doing."

"Now please tell me what you study," Alexsi said, as if he hadn't heard her.

"I study to be an artist," Aida told him.

"You must have great talent, to bring it all the way to Moscow."

"I did win a scholarship contest," she admitted. "It was very competitive."

"I congratulate you."

The waitress, a middle-aged babushka with a perpetually scowling face like a troll, set down their plates of cake.

"Thank you, Comrade," Alexsi said.

The waitress just walked away.

"That's the one thing I can't get used to in Moscow," Aida said. "How rude everyone is."

"Perhaps our pleasant manner will inspire her to change hers," Alexsi said.

Aida snorted out her laughter and then quickly clapped a hand over her mouth, embarrassed. When she blushed her pale skin seemed to spring to life. "Do you remember I said you were the funniest boy I ever met?"

"Yes, but you were the only person who ever thought that of me. I'm sure you now have a much wider sample to make comparison."

She giggled and shook her head in fond reproach. Then she reached across the table and put her hand over his. "You have been very careful on the tram ride to ask me every question and avoid every one of mine. Please, what became of you after the orphanage? One day you were gone, and they said you had run away."

12

ALEXSI DREAMED HE WAS BEING CRUSHED. THEN HE WOKE UP and realized he really was being crushed. The blanket was over his head and someone had it and was using it to pin him down in the bed. He couldn't move his arms but he lashed out with his legs and twisted his body, frantically trying to escape. It had to be more than one, because one boy couldn't hold him down like that.

"Hold still, you little shit," a strained adult voice said.

Alexsi recognized it as Maxim's, an attendant. He knew he couldn't fight them, so he relaxed and stayed still. The pressure on the blankets let up a bit, and he managed to slide his hand up under his pillow and get ahold of his pocketknife and tuck it under his armpit. Otherwise he knew he'd never see it again, and they were impossible to come by.

The blankets flew off and his arms were grabbed. There were three attendants, just for him. Maxim, Stanislav, and Yuri. They dragged him off the bed and stood him up, dressed only in his underwear. Every boy in the room was awake and up on one elbow watching him.

Alexsi had his fists clenched as if he were holding something. They pried his hands open only to find nothing. After that he dropped his hands to his sides and bent his arm a bit to let the pocketknife drop from his armpit into his cupped hand. When they pulled his hands up over his head to frisk him, he had the pocket-knife back in his fist. He'd practiced it until he could do it without looking. Just like the disappearing coin trick: look over here, so you don't see me doing something else.

They frisked him and shook out his clothes. And they took the bed apart. They found the nut and the twine, but nothing else.

"Get dressed," they ordered.

He slipped the knife back in his trouser pocket without anyone the wiser.

All the staff seemed to be running around the house. It was still dark, so Alexsi didn't know if they were up late or early.

The Comrade Director's clothes were wrinkled and she had too much makeup on, as if she'd applied it hastily.

"You have been stealing food from the kitchen," she informed him coldly. It was not a question.

Alexsi knew that in this case keeping silent would be the same thing as admitting guilt. "Comrade Director, when they give us an extra piece of bread for working hard in the kitchen, that's not stealing. Is it?"

She leaned back in her chair a bit, as if awed by his answer. But her voice was hard. "You have broken into the kitchen at night and stolen food."

The tone of her voice told Alexsi that she was convinced it was him. He knew he was in a tight spot, and it was getting tighter. But convinced wasn't proof. "But the kitchen is locked at night, Comrade Director. How could I break in?"

She took a different tack. "If you tell us where you have hidden the food, we will go easy on you."

That made him feel a little better. "I'm sorry, Comrade Director, but I don't know what you are talking about."

Now she leaned forward in her chair as if she were lunging at him with fangs bared. "You came down into the kitchen on the dumbwaiter. You picked the locks and you stole food. Where are your lock picks?"

Alexsi took that statement like one of his father's punches to the head. He wondered what his face looked like. He still wasn't going to give in. "I don't know what you're talking about, Comrade Director."

She tossed his nut and twine onto the top of her desk. "You said you didn't have a weapon, either. Yet here it is."

Well, the time had passed for meekness, and he wasn't about to beg for mercy. Alexsi just looked her defiantly in the eye and said, "If you remember, Comrade Director, I never said I didn't have a weapon."

She looked past him to the attendants standing behind and said, "Take him away."

They locked him in another little room. Not the same one as before, but similar. Yuri sneered at him. "You think you're tough. You'll find out in prison."

As soon as they locked the door, Alexsi rushed over and put his ear to it. He heard Yuri say to Maxim, "You think anyone will listen to him?"

"A thief?" Maxim replied. "No. We might have an inspection because of it, but that's no problem."

Alexsi sat down on the bed and looked at his hands. He should have known.

After two months of weekly trips down to the kitchen, one night he and Aida came upon two padlocks on the secret pantry door instead of one. So the staff had figured out they were being robbed. Alexsi knew if the two of them kept on, it would only be a matter of time before someone would be waiting in the dark to catch the thief. He'd wanted to give it up then, but Aida showed him the attic. It was a huge space full of boxes and old furniture and hiding places. A hiding place had always been the problem, with so many kids and prying eyes in the house. She wanted to do it once more, taking as much food as they could and hiding it in the attic.

And it worked. They loaded up the dumbwaiter with tins of

food and jars of jam until he was afraid the rope would break. After all the trips back and forth up to the attic he could barely move his arms. When they were finished he'd left the pantry door open, the padlocks hanging from their hasps, and the back door of the kitchen unbarred and ajar so they'd think someone had run off with the stuff. And she finally got her chocolate.

Aida was the only one in the world who knew about his lock picks. He hadn't told her he'd hidden them up in the attic, realizing that if anyone ever found them in his possession he'd be fingered as the thief for sure.

His first thought back in the Comrade Director's office was that she'd been caught doing something and had to tell on him to save herself. But that only showed how stupid he was. Now with the food hidden up in the attic she didn't need him to pick locks. Or share the food.

He should have known. He should have known when she told him that she was the one who had informed on her papa. Now she'd be playing with someone else's cock when she needed something.

Alexsi reached in his pocket and took out the knife. He unfolded the blade and tested the edge with his thumb.

MAXIM THE attendant flipped through the mass of keys on the ring until he found the one to the room. "Keep your eyes open in case he tries to run past us," he said to Yuri.

"I'll open it," Yuri said, snatching the ring from him. "You keep watch."

He had to go through the ring all over again to find the key. Maxim just watched him and shook his head.

Yuri inserted the key into the lock. "Ready?"

Maxim took a short wood truncheon out of his back pocket. "I swear if the little bastard throws something at me I'll break his head."

"You ought to do it anyway," said Yuri.

"Yes, *I* ought to do it," Maxim replied contemptuously. "Just open the door."

"Ready?" said Yuri, turning the key.

"Just open the fucking door," Maxim muttered.

Yuri swung it open, and they both stepped up to block the doorway. Nothing happened. They waited there for a moment, balanced and ready for action, then in unison they both leaned their heads inside to look.

The room was empty.

13

1936 Restaurant Praga, Moscow

"I HAD TO RUN AWAY," ALEXSI SAID. "THEY WERE GOING TO send me to prison. So no one would ever find out that they stole the food—"

"Before we stole it from them," Aida said, gripping his hand tightly.

"One of those little rats must have seen me bringing it up to the attic and squealed," Alexsi said. "That's the only thing I can think of. I was working so hard that night I must have been careless."

"They never caught me," Aida said.

"I'm glad," he said, putting his other hand over hers. "So it had to have been one of the bastards who slept in the same room I did. They must have seen me get up and sneak out."

"So you didn't tell them about me after they got you."

"Them? Of course not. I told them nothing."

"And you ran away."

"I wasn't waiting around to see what they had in store for me."

"I'm so sorry. We were so young then. It must have been very hard for you."

"Just as well," Alexsi said brusquely. "Instead of having to sit there and listen to their shit for a few more years I got out in the world and learned what was what. Apologies for my language."

"It doesn't upset me," she said, still holding his hand. She looked like she was about to cry.

"This cake is good, isn't it?" he said. "Be honest, since I don't have the most refined tastes."

"It's excellent," Aida said.

Alexsi gestured for the waitress, who ignored him.

"As I said," Aida muttered.

"We needed to finish our tea anyway," Alexsi said.

When Aida was done with hers, Alexsi gestured to the waitress again, who this time sauntered over slowly.

Alexsi said, "Comrade, I would like to purchase a whole cake. In a box, please, for me to take away."

"It's only sold by the portion," the waitress informed him gruffly. "Those are the rules, young fellow."

She slapped their bill down on the table. Alexsi caught her hand and pinned it to the tabletop. Alarmed, the waitress tried to pull away but he held her fixed. She opened her mouth but before she could draw breath, Alexsi said quietly, "You would be wise not to make a sound."

She froze. Aida was staring in shock.

Alexsi turned the waitress's hand over and placed some money in her palm. "This is for the number of portions that make a whole cake." He added some more rubles to the pile. "This is for your trouble." And then some more, finally closing her fingers on the money. "And this is for anyone in the kitchen who needs to be taken care of. So go back there and box one up. Right now."

The waitress opened her hand slightly, glanced down, and riffled through the notes with her thumb. "Meet me at the kitchen door. It's in the alley."

She went to step back, and Alexsi caught her wrist this time. "The *best* cake, you understand? If I knock at that door and no one shows up I'll come back and see you again. And if you were thinking about calling for the police and keeping the money that way, just let that dream pass, because then my friends would come find you. And they're not as well mannered as I. Right, Comrade?"

Now the waitress was shaking. "Yes, sir."

Alexsi let her go, and she rushed into the kitchen. He counted money onto the table to pay their bill. "Shall we go pick up your cake?"

"Forget her, you frightened *me*," Aida said as he helped her put on her coat.

"Yes, but she's much more polite now, isn't she?" Alexsi said.

They walked around the corner to the alley and Alexsi knocked on the iron door. It opened almost instantly, and the waitress handed him a box.

She went to close the door but Alexsi easily hooked her arm with his free hand. "Just a moment, Comrade." He passed the box over to Aida. "Take a look inside and make sure there's a cake in there."

Aida set the box on a garbage bin and untied the string holding it closed.

Alexsi kept his eyes on the waitress, and his hand on her arm, smiling pleasantly all the time.

A cook stuck his head in the open doorway. "What's going on here?"

"Fuck off if you know what's good for you," Alexsi told him.

The cook vanished.

"There's a cake inside," Aida announced. She looked up at the terrified waitress and added, "It's very nice."

"Excellent," Alexsi said. He released the waitress and told her, "Thank you for everything, Auntie. Good fortune to you."

She gave him a quick jerky bow of the head and slammed the iron door shut.

Alexsi took the cake from Aida and offered her his other arm. "There, we got you a cake. And had a chance to sit and talk."

Aida was examining his face in much the same way Yakushev had. "You must have a very important job."

Alexsi stopped in his tracks and turned to her. "*Job?* Jobs are for suckers. Did you think I'd ever work for *them?*"

"I don't know what to think," she said. "But I do know it's wonderful to see you again." She took his hand and looked at the time on his wristwatch, pausing briefly to admire it. "I have a class. But you must come to my friend's party tonight. After all, you bought the cake. And I thank you for that."

Alexsi reached into his coat and passed her a pocket notebook and a fountain pen. "Please write the address for me. I've been working hard to learn the streets, but much of Moscow is still a mystery."

She wrote it down and slipped the pen and notebook back into his coat herself. Then she threw her arms around his neck again and kissed him hard on the mouth. "When I look at your face I think back on so many things."

"It has been a long road from Baku, hasn't it?" Alexsi said.

Aida took the cake from him, kissed her gloved finger, and touched it to his lips. "I'll see you tonight."

"Tonight," Alexsi said.

He watched her sway away from him, winter coat snug against her hips. Then he checked the time on his wristwatch. The first Soviet watch they'd given him had broken a day later. This one was very fancy. Someone had left it behind when they entered the Lubyanka.

14

FALLING SNOW BROUGHT AN INDELIBLE SILENCE TO MOSCOW'S streets. Even the incessant metal clattering of the streetcars was muted. The clopping of the horses' hoofs was muffled, and the animals strained their way through the streets with heads bowed under the weight of the ice on their traces.

It occasionally snowed in Baku when the winter Khazari winds blew in, but it was always gone after a day or two. Nothing like this. Half a meter of snow. Alexsi couldn't stop reaching down to touch it, soft and fleetingly pure white before it was soiled by the dirt of the city. The snow even seemed to make the frigid air feel a bit warmer.

Though that may have been because he was finally learning how to dress against the Moscow weather. He had never worn wool long underwear before, but at least now he didn't feel like the progress of every journey was marked by the number of shops he had to step into to keep from freezing to death.

He checked the number of the student dormitory against his written directions and went inside. There was a sort of little hall that ran perpendicular to the entrance. The inlaid wooden floor looked like someone had been racing horses over it. Black iron chandeliers hung from a fancy tile ceiling but half the bulbs were out of order. Propaganda posters hung from the walls. Stalin steering the wheel of the ship of state. Lenin pointing in front of a factory smokestack like he was demanding that a bus stop for him. And Alexsi's favorite: determined peasants marching like soldiers behind their tractor, rakes propped over their shoulders like rifles.

There was a woman at a desk in front of the stairs, obviously a gatekeeper to keep track of everyone.

"Name?" she demanded.

Alexsi smiled at her. Every middle-aged Russian woman he encountered in an official job looked like they belonged on the wicked side of a fairy tale. "Anatoli Romanov." Still sticking it to Anatoli, but it wouldn't do to present the same false name someone might know from Baku.

"Who are you visiting?"

"I don't know, Comrade. I was invited to a birthday party."

"Room number?"

He told her. She wrote it all down carefully in her logbook. "May I pass, Comrade?"

Still writing, as if it were a torturous effort, she didn't bother to look up but only nodded.

Alexsi went up the stairs. The place was a thunder of voices and many, many different kinds of music being played loudly and from all directions. And many pretty girls passing and smiling. Very nice. As he stepped off on the correct floor, it looked like a portion of the wall had either flaked away or been pried off, the exposed white brick staring out at him.

He confirmed the room number one more time before knocking, but based on the volume, that had to be the place. There was a wooden mailbox hanging on the door, which looked like it had been beaten with a wagon whip.

A pretty blond girl with green eyes answered his knock, laughing at something from behind her. When she saw his stranger's face and his suit she became serious and looked him up and down carefully. Then, hesitantly, "Are you Alexsi?"

"I am," he said, smiling. "Do I wish happy birthday to you?"

She embraced him and kissed him on both cheeks. "You do. I am Nadia. Thank you so much for my cake. Come in, come in."

He handed her a small package. "I am a terrible poet. So please accept this instead of a birthday poem."

"But you already gave me a cake," she said.

"That was from Aida," he said.

Nadia took his arm and called out, "Aida! He's here!"

They were in a little alcove, with the doors to two other rooms open. They were packed with people and fogged with cigarette smoke. Four beds that everyone was sitting on hugged every wall, with desks crammed into the only space between them. A boy was playing a guitar and a few people were singing along. The song wasn't familiar, but then he didn't know much about music.

Aida pushed her way through the crowd and kissed him again. She and another girl helped him off with his coat and hat.

"I'm so glad you came," Aida said.

"I brought some vodka," Alexsi said, handing her the cloth shopping bag full of bottles.

"I'm not going to say you shouldn't have," she told him. "Because we were about to start rationing what we had left by the sip."

Nadia rushed up behind him and hugged him hard. "Look at this beautiful silk scarf he gave me," she said, showing it to Aida.

Aida examined it and gave him a wry look. "It seems you will have a harem before the night is over."

"Aida!" Nadia said.

"It was all a clever ploy of mine to avoid having to sing or write a poem," Alexsi said. "There would absolutely be no harem then."

Both girls giggled.

"Let us introduce you around," said Nadia.

He met Larissa and Raya, another blonde and a redhead. They all wore their hair short and curled, in the current style. Unlike Aida. "These are my special girlfriends," Aida said.

Nadia showed them the scarf, and they gave Alexsi appraising looks.

"Are all the girls in this university so pretty?" Alexsi asked Nadia. "Or just your friends?"

"Harem, definitely," Aida remarked.

Dmitri was the one playing the guitar. Alexsi marked him as the typical intellectual. Thin and frail, with a wispy moustache he definitely should not have tried to grow. And he played the guitar because he was almost too shy to talk.

"And this is Yuri," Aida said of a burly fellow holding court with two girls. Yuri had a thick head of dark hair he obviously spent a great deal of time combing back so it would lay correctly. His shirt was open to show off his mat of chest hair. Alexsi instantly dismissed him. The guy who looked tough only because he always made sure to never enter a room where there was anyone who looked tougher. "Yuri, this is my friend Alexsi."

Yuri stuck out his hand. "Aida made you sound like Al Capone."

"He's fat," Alexsi said blandly.

Yuri was trying to give him a hard handshake and make him pull back. Alexsi returned it until Yuri dropped his hand like he'd touched a hot radiator. Yuri sat back down. The big man with the girls, Alexsi thought.

The girlfriend Raya came up with a tray full of glasses. "Here you go, everyone. Alexsi brought a lot of vodka, so we can keep drinking."

Aida raised her glass and looked straight at him. "I've already toasted the birthday girl, so this one is to friends returning from long journeys."

"To friends," everyone repeated.

Alexsi touched glasses, then he just touched his lips to the vodka without draining the glass like everyone else.

Yuri wasn't about to miss that. "You're not drinking, Al Capone?"

"I don't drink," Alexsi said.

"You don't say. Stomach trouble?"

"No, I just don't drink."

Yuri said, "I don't trust a man who doesn't drink."

"Yuri!" the girls said in reproach.

"Then don't," Alexsi replied, as if he could care less. "It's a good policy these days. As a matter of fact, you have the look of a stool pigeon to me."

Yuri came up off his chair with his fists up. "I'm no informer!"

"That's what they all say," Alexsi replied calmly. "And then they act upset when you put the finger on them."

"Apologize!" Yuri shouted.

"Don't excite yourself," Alexsi advised. "You might fall on your knife."

Yuri was enjoying working himself up to make a scene, but that cut him off like lifting the needle from a gramophone. "I don't have a knife."

"I do," Alexsi said.

"Enough, you two," said Aida, taking Alexsi's arm.

Alexsi allowed himself to be led across the room. "Interesting fellow. I don't want to spoil Nadia's birthday, but if he keeps poking at me something bad will happen."

"He's always like this when he's drunk," Aida said.

Now Yuri sat back down and pouted some more, shaking off the two girls who tried to comfort him.

"We saved you a piece of the cake," Nadia said to Alexsi.

"Oh, please, everyone get their fork and have another bite," Alexsi said. "I already had my cake today with Aida."

At that moment Dmitri with the guitar spoke for the first time. "Aida told us the story of the cake."

"Did she?" said Alexsi, as if he didn't care for that at all.

"She did," said Dmitri. "My question is, why would you take such a risk?"

Aida said, "Dmitri . . ."

Ah, so he wasn't the shy one after all, Alexsi thought. "I wanted a cake."

"No," said Dmitri. "I mean—"

"I know what you mean," Alexsi said. "I ran into a friend I hadn't seen in years. I wanted a cake to make Aida happy, so I got one. I do what I please, but I know what I'm doing. I know every waitress in a place like that is an informer for the bluecaps. So I scared her so she'd only call them after we left. And even so she probably thought twice because she'd have to turn over the money."

"And what if someone here should denounce you?" said Dmitri, as the girls tried to shush him.

"Who cares?" Alexsi retorted. "You see, my friend, the Chekists would still have to find me. And they won't."

"What if they do?" Dmitri asked.

Alexsi just snorted through his nose. "If I hear their boots on the stairs I won't be hiding under the bed praying they go to someone else's door. And I won't accept it as my Russian fate and open up with my hands out for their cuffs. I'll go out the window and I'll turn up in Leningrad or Yekaterinburg with another name. And if one day they do get me I'll tell everyone I had a great time and I lived well and I said what I pleased and did what I pleased. And I'll be in the exact same place as the sucker who kept his mouth shut and ate shit and did what he was told and got the knock on the door at midnight anyway."

"So if I asked you your full name?" said Dmitri.

"Don't concern yourself because I'm sure you don't know my family."

"And if I asked what you did for a living?"

"I would say, without anger, that it's none of your business."

"And if I asked if you could get me a wristwatch like yours?"

"I would say sure. But, no offense, I doubt you could afford it. And not having the money, I also doubt you'd take the risk to get it another way."

"I must have another drink," Dmitri said. "If I keep talking with you any longer I will have no principles left."

"Yes, please," Nadia said nervously. The discussion was taking place in her room, after all. "More vodka for everyone."

"Except Alexsi who doesn't drink," said Dmitri. "I see it now. A man needs a clear head if he's going to be leaping from windows."

As the vodka dwindled again everyone began falling asleep on the beds. Alexsi had been sitting there like a scientist observing a laboratory experiment.

Aida had disappeared one of the times he was in the toilet, and he assumed she'd left to see a boy. But the door opened and there she was with a tray of glasses she'd washed. "We seem to be the only survivors."

"Walk you home?" said Alexsi.

"That would be nice."

As they crossed the courtyard outside with arms linked, they both gave each other a tug in the opposite direction. "I live over there," Aida said, pointing.

"I didn't mean *your* home," Alexsi said.

She took her hand out of the crook of his arm and looked up at him with a searching expression.

Alexsi just held his arm out to her.

Aida took it.

SHE GASPED as he opened the door of his apartment. "Look at this! I live in a wardrobe in comparison. With another girl."

Regardless of passion, Russians didn't go tearing each other's clothes off. Clothes were too hard to come by. Aida stood naked before Alexsi and said, "Have I changed much from the little girl you used to know?"

"You're much more beautiful now," Alexsi said truthfully. The lithe little girl now had a woman's breasts and hips, though the same wisp of jet-black pubic hair. And a puckered appendix scar that he found incredibly sexy. He was fully erect and, looking down, said, "You see you still have that same effect on me."

She also looked down, and bit her lip the same way, and it was like being back in that closet again. He embraced her and they tumbled onto the bed.

He had been with other girls in Baku, girls attracted by the delicacies he stole from the special food stores. They ate what he brought and then lay back on the bed, spread their legs, and paid for their dinner.

This was something completely different. Aida was on him like a wildcat. Biting his neck between kisses. Biting his shoulders. She was moving so fast he could barely get ahold of her to caress her. And urging him on like the manager of a sports team. "Yes, yes, put your mouth on my nipple." And in case he had suddenly gone deaf grabbed his hair at the back of his head and pulled him onto her breast. "Yes, suck gently like that. Now harder. Yes!"

In the midst of all the thrashing he finally managed to get his hand between her legs. And then things became even crazier. After only a few moments she grabbed him by the shoulders and pushed him onto the bed on his back. With one hand on his cock she threw her leg over him like she was mounting a pony and plunged herself onto him.

Alexsi moaned, half in pleasure and half in amazement. No girl had ever done *that* to him.

Aida just rocked herself front to back and side to side. It made his thrusts when he had been the one on top seem embarrassingly inexpert. And then she began lifting herself up and letting herself fall back down on his cock. When she rose up until her pussy lips were just brushing the head of his cock, and it was in danger of falling out, and then slid back down excruciatingly slowly it was all too much—he tried to hold back but he came.

"Oh, no," he said out loud. He could feel his face burning red. Humiliated, he went to pull himself out but Aida clapped her hands on his face and was actually holding on to his ears with both hands like the wheel of an automobile.

"That's all right," she said, gasping. "That's all right. Just do what you used to do with your hand."

"While you're there?" he said helplessly. Meaning, while she was still mounted on top of him.

"Yes, yes," she said. "While you're still inside me. Hurry. Yes, that's right. Like that. Faster, now. Yes."

She was so urgent he was half afraid she might tear his ears off. Because of the strange angle he ended up using his thumb and the palm of his hand. And he worked so hard his wrist nearly cramped up. But it must have been all right because she bucked and moaned and came with a scream that he was afraid would bring the Chekists watching him crashing through the door.

And all her thrashing while he was still inside her got him hard again—it must have been a month since he'd been with a girl—and she felt it and went back to riding him. All he could do was hold on to the sheets as she spun around like she was doing gymnastics. He didn't come fast this time but she did again, clutching at him so tightly he was afraid his cock would tear off. But he was still hard so she kept going relentlessly and came once again. When he finally came this time there was no hope of rousing him, and she collapsed atop him, panting hard, her face in his neck. Alexsi's one thought was that his jailhouse knife fight had actually been less strenuous.

He awoke to the smell of toasting bread. Aida was in the kitchen poaching eggs wearing only her slip, and a pot of tea was on the table.

Alexsi poured himself a glass, added extra sugar, and smiled ruefully at her.

She waved the cooking spoon down her body. "Your apartment is a dream. My heat is so bad I have to cook in my winter coat."

"I know you want to ask," said Alexsi.

"You don't have to tell me."

"The Chekists are out hunting the poor starving guy who siphoned the petrol from his boss's automobile and traded it for some eggs. I'm taking truckloads. I got a big shot everything he needed for his dacha in the country. Better stuff than all his circle, and he didn't have to wait for it like the rest. He's got plenty of *blat*." The all-encompassing Soviet word meaning connections, influence. "He pulled some strings and got me this place. It was the least he could do."

"I nearly fainted when I saw what was in your refrigerator," Aida said.

"Take whatever you like with you."

"I couldn't," she said.

"Think about it," he said. "I want to see you again. But now that you know a few things about me, it could be dangerous for you."

"How could I stay away when you already decided you trust me?" she said.

"What do you mean?"

"You brought me here. You took a chance on hearing boots on your stairs."

"It was a chance worth taking," he said.

They ate the eggs and the toasted white bread with butter. "I feel like a princess," Aida said.

Alexsi quickly brought his glass of tea up to his mouth, because he wasn't sure that he wasn't looking sad. "Ah, fairy tales."

Knowing that every Russian girl had a shopping bag folded up in her purse in case she happened to pass a store that actually had something available for purchase, he filled hers up with the contents of his refrigerator.

"When my girlfriends see this, you'll definitely have a harem," she said.

"That would be much too tiring," he replied with genuine feeling.

Aida just laughed. "I see you have a telephone. Is it permitted to call you?"

He wrote down his number for her. "And how may I get in touch with you?"

"That would be a maddening process for you of calling my dormitory, speaking to the witch at the desk, and her refusing to walk up the stairs and fetch me. Would a woman calling a man outrage you?"

"I'm very modern."

"Then I will," she said.

He went to put on his coat. "What are you doing?" she said.

"I'm going to walk you back to the university."

She thumped him on the chest with her fist. "No, you won't. It's not far."

"Are you sure?"

"I'm sure," she said. She kissed him very tenderly. "I'll be seeing you."

"I hope I'll be seeing you," Alexsi replied.

As she walked down his stairs, he was remembering the last time she kissed him, in that closet.

15

1936 Moscow

ALEXSI HAD HOPED THAT HIS LONG NIGHT AND LATE MORNING would grant him a reprieve from his morning spy classes. No such luck. His telephone rang with a summons literally the moment Aida left his apartment.

The exercises were actually quite interesting. But the worst part was the writing. It always followed the same routine. Yakushev would provide the instruction, there would be a practical application, and then he would have to write a report on everything that had taken place. Today they met at that same apartment north of the Bolshoi, and he had to write down everything that had happened the night before.

"Unacceptable," Yakushev said, shaking the papers in his fist as if he were trying to make them confess. "Your report is unacceptable. Insufficient detail. A thorough physical description of this cake waitress who has forgotten her socialist duty and become a capitalist, if you please. Also, if you would be so good as to provide a complete physical description of everyone at this birthday party to accompany their names."

Alexsi had learned that when Yakushev framed orders in the form of polite requests he was only being sarcastic. And after the brutal tongue-lashing he received one day after trying to defend himself—something he was foolish enough to do only once—the only thing to do was sit quietly and take it.

"Your operational work so far is good," Yakushev conceded,

the calm after the storm. "The improvisation with the cake? Inspired. Did you know that Comrade Stalin's bodyguards use that restaurant as a canteen?"

Alexsi shook his head, waiting to hear what trouble he was in now.

But Yakushev also shook his head, his eyes on the report. "Heads will roll."

Yet Alexsi thought he didn't seem very upset about it. Some kind of Chekist office politics, perhaps.

Now Yakushev looked over his reading glasses at him like a dissatisfied schoolmaster. "No matter how good the work, if it is not properly set down in a report, it is as if it never happened. And why is there nothing here of the girl Aida Rudenko's visit to your apartment? Are you afflicted with bourgeois sensitivity?"

"I only thought to save some time," Alexsi said. "I assumed there were listening devices in my rooms."

Yakushev's glare was icy enough to freeze him solid. "When I tell you to write a report with every detail included, you will write a report with every detail included. Is that understood?"

"Yes, Comrade," Alexsi replied dutifully.

"Do not trifle with me, boy. No one is indispensable." He crumpled up the report. "Write it again."

Alexsi took up the pen, which felt like a stick full of thorns in his aching hand. But it did seem that he was fairly indispensable. They still spoke in German, so this thing with Aida wasn't what he was being trained for. And now he knew they really were listening to everything in his apartment, in addition to watching his every move outside.

After what seemed like hours of writing, Yakushev took up the report again. "Better." His eyes still on the paper, he said, "I am relieved to see that you said nothing derogatory toward Comrade Stalin or Marxist-Leninist theory."

The tone was conversational, but Alexsi realized with a start that he had just dodged a bullet to the brain. In truth, at the party he had been tempted to use his license to say what no Russian could say. Only Soviet instinct had held him back.

Yakushev made no comment on the fact that Alexsi had obstinately included every pornographic detail, instead honing in on one aspect. "You actually told the girl Aida Rudenko that she should not see you again?"

"Yes, Comrade," Alexsi replied.

"Since that is categorically contrary to your instructions, what possible reason could you have?"

"She had already decided to come to my apartment. I thought telling her it would be dangerous to see me again would ensure that she would want to."

Yakushev took off his reading glasses and set them on the desk. "Clearly, despite your years, you have learned something of women." He filed the report in his briefcase. "There will be those who will say you should be more aggressive in your approach. I do not agree. Every real intelligence operation is like a seduction, and men who only use whores know nothing of seduction."

That gave Alexsi the impression such a criticism had already taken place.

"Hopefully you are understanding something important here," Yakushev said. "Real espionage is not about stealing blueprints and strangling guards with wire. It is about placing yourself in the position, and creating the proper conditions, where people willingly provide you information. Clear?"

"Clear, Comrade," Alexsi replied. He'd understood that from the start. Using the exact same tricks as the criminal, except not as a way to stay out of jail. Now you were a confidence man for the state.

"Good, said Yakushev. "Since you have redone this report adequately, from memory you will rewrite your report from yesterday's exercise in how to follow in a busy area. Remember that unlike physical strength, which has finite limits, the capacity of the human memory, if properly trained, is limitless."

Alexsi knew the number of times he was going to hear that would probably be limitless, too. And if there were any discrepancies between the two reports, there would be more abuse.

Late that afternoon, when he was back in his apartment soaking his writing hand in a bowl full of snow, his telephone rang. Alexsi just groaned, positive it was another unannounced exercise. He lifted the speaker off the hook with his left hand; with the right cramped from writing he was doing many more things with the left hand these days.

But it was Aida. "Do you like my modern ways?"

"Very much," Alexsi said. "Are you free tonight?"

"As a matter of fact, I was calling to invite you out. How modern is that?"

"Scandalously modern," said Alexsi. "Shall I play hard to get?"

She was laughing across the line. "If you like. It's a full moon tonight, and we're all going skating at the Hermitage Garden."

"Ice-skating?" Alexsi said. "You're inviting the boy from Azerbaijan ice-skating."

"I know, I know," she said, still laughing. "That's what I was thinking also. Or is this just you playing hard to get?"

"No, this is me picturing myself ice-skating."

"You could tell everyone you were the champion figure skater of Baku, and no one would be the wiser."

"They'd know as soon as I fell on my arse. What about a nice, warm cinema instead?"

"I already promised I'd go. And everyone asked for you. . . ."

Alexsi groaned over the phone. "All right. I'll go. Just don't be crushed if I don't skate."

"I will prepare myself for the disappointment."

"Shall I pick you up?" he asked.

"No. Meet us there. At nine."

"All right," he said. "Until then."

"Until then."

Alexsi hung up the phone and groaned again. Night, outdoors.

He would have to wear every piece of clothing he owned just to survive until morning.

RIGHT BEFORE nine he stepped off the Petrovka Street tram and followed the streetlights down the shoveled path through the gardens, the snow heaped up as high as his head on both sides. The Hermitage Theater was invitingly lit up, but he honed in on the outdoor lighting to the area of the park they'd made into a skating rink. Of course, that was the thing about winter in Moscow. All you had to do was dump some water on the ground and you had a skating rink. Young people were skating and laughing and passing around vodka and huddling around fires burning in barrels to warm up. Next to the rink there was a shack to rent skates.

He circled around the rink to find his party, and his newly trained eye noticed their surveillance before he noticed them. It was definitely *their* surveillance, because his was still strung out behind him. The sheer number of watchers, watching but pretending not to watch, was enough to make up a full side for the secret police football team.

So he followed the watchers' eyes to the bench where everyone was sitting. Aida, Dmitri, Nadia, Larissa, and, unfortunately, Yuri.

As he walked up, Aida saw him first and started laughing. "Is that you under there, Alexsi?"

He was wearing a heavy wool greatcoat that came down below his knees and was wonderfully warm. *Sapogi* leather boots with hobnailed soles that gripped the snow and ice. He had only been able to find a pair in a size too large, which turned out to be a blessing in disguise since that left room for three pairs of stockings. And a scarf wrapped around his face in addition to his neck. "Yes."

Aida said, "Well, a man who doesn't drink vodka has to keep warm somehow."

"My blood wasn't thick enough to start with," Alexsi said, his voice muffled through the scarf. "But I'm quite comfortable, thank you for asking."

He leaned over to kiss the girls on both cheeks and shake hands with Dmitri.

Larissa elbowed Yuri, and he stood up to offer his hand. "I wish to apologize for the way I acted at the party."

"Don't worry about it," Alexsi said, taking his hand. "I apologize for nearly cutting your throat."

Yuri's face told that he wasn't sure whether Alexsi was joking or not.

"Sit, sit," Dmitri said, and they all scooted over to make him a space in the middle of the bench.

Alexsi looked down and said, "I don't see any skates."

There was silence for a moment, then Aida said, "I confess, we brought you here with ulterior motives."

"Oh?" Alexsi said.

Silence again, except for the excited undertone of the skaters and the trees crackling in the frost. Then Dmitri said, "You're a direct fellow, so may I ask you a direct question?"

"Go ahead," Alexsi said.

More silence. Then Dmitri said, "Can you get me a handgun?"

Now it was Alexsi's turn to offer them some silence. "No."

"So you can't get a gun," said Dmitri.

"Of course I *can* get you a gun," Alexsi replied. "I *won't* get you a gun."

"If I had enough money, why not?" Dmitri demanded.

"Because, serious fellow that you are, if I get you a gun, you'll use it," said Alexsi. "And, first thing, you'll be sitting in some interrogator's chair coughing up my name. Then I'll have to leave town. And I like Moscow. So nothing personal. What you could pay me isn't worth the risk."

"What if I told you I'd use the gun to change the world?" said Dmitri.

"Well, now that's different," said Alexsi. "Actually, no it's not. I was just joking."

"I'm not," Dmitri said angrily.

"I know," Alexsi replied. "That's exactly why I won't get you a gun."

Dmitri turned to Aida. She said, "Alexsi, please hear us out."

"I'm listening," Alexsi said. "Just out of politeness, you understand."

Aida said, "Dmitri."

Dmitri took a long breath and said, "We're going to kill a tyrant."

"That's a long list these days," Alexsi said.

"We're going to kill Stalin," Dmitri said.

Alexsi was disgusted. If you could be that stupid and go to university, then he certainly wasn't missing anything. If you want to kill Stalin, then go kill Stalin. Don't put together a party to hold hands and have discussions and give you the courage you didn't have in the first place. What he said out loud was "Wonderful. I knew something like this was going to happen. Now my head is on the block whether I get you a gun or not, just for sitting here listening to you. Thank you all very much." He shot an accusing look at Aida, who turned away.

"That knock on the door you like to joke about?" Dmitri said angrily. "Every one of us has lost someone we love to that knock. And we're going to kill the man responsible."

"Why?" said Alexsi. "It won't bring them back. It certainly won't change anything."

"Of course it will change things," said Larissa.

"The Romans didn't ask 'why bother' when they killed the dictator Caesar," Yuri blurted out.

"You could have picked a better example," Alexsi said dryly. "I only went to the university of public libraries, but I still know that after they stabbed Caesar there were another four hundred years of Caesars after him."

"With him dead there might be a chance for the old ideals to come back," said Dmitri. "What part of Communism from Marx and Engels do you see today?"

Alexsi knew if that got started he would be sitting out there in the cold until dawn. "Politics aside, if you don't mind me asking, just how do you intend to kill Stalin with a handgun? Knock on the Kremlin door one night and when he answers in his night-shirt shoot him in the head? You'll never get near him."

"We have it all planned out," said Dmitri. "Stalin drives past the Arbat regularly on the way to his dacha in Kuntsevo. We'll shoot him as he goes by."

"You'll shoot his steel-plated automobile with a pistol?" said Alexsi. "That's quite a plan."

"Well, get me a machine gun then," Dmitri said angrily.

"And you'll hide that under your coat?" Alexsi retorted. "Look, as I said before you've screwed me but good. So no matter what, I have to get out of town and I'll need money to set up someplace new. I'll get you a few hand grenades. You can be standing on a street corner and roll them under his car when it slows down to take the turn. Now what will you pay me?"

"We have one thousand rubles," said Dmitri. "But we hoped you would believe in our cause."

A thousand rubles, Alexsi thought. It was enough to make you weep. "I believe in *my* cause. Any of you know someone who has some *blat*? A relative that runs a warehouse? Know the timetable of any shipments?" He stood up. "Think about it. I'm going to make a circuit around this place to get some feeling back in my legs and make sure no one is watching us."

He trudged through the crowd at the rink, oblivious to the good cheer all around. Even before his spy training he would have been able to smell the secret police in a circle around them, hovering like carrion birds. Those fools, with all their advantages. Couldn't wait to rush to their doom and drag as many as possible down with them. And the Judas among them was . . . ? Alexsi had his own ideas.

"Well?" he said, sitting back down on the bench.

"Is anyone watching us?" Yuri asked anxiously.

"If they were we never would have seen him again," Aida said quickly.

"Clever girl," Alexsi said. "So?"

"The university cafeteria gets its food shipment on Monday afternoon," Larissa said. "Two trucks. No one wants to stay late and unload them, so they sit there until Tuesday morning."

"Now you're talking," said Alexsi. "The food, the trucks, the petrol in the trucks, and the thousand rubles should just about cover it."

"You're still going to take our money?" Yuri demanded.

"You're damned right I am," Alexsi replied. "If you don't like it, shop for arms someplace else."

"When will we get the grenades?" Dmitri asked.

"Wednesday, noon, right here at this bench," Alexsi replied. "When you hear about the two trucks being stolen, you'll know. But Aida comes alone. No one else. Do we have a deal?"

"We have a deal," Dmitri said.

Alexsi stood to take his leave of them.

Aida caught his arm. "Will I see you?"

"You'll see me here on Wednesday," Alexsi said, pulling away from her.

16

"I WISH TO BE SURE I UNDERSTAND YOU CORRECTLY," YAKUSHEV said over his cigarette. "You told this man Dmitri Kursky that you would *not* get him a gun."

Alexsi almost shouted at him then. Between the exercises and the reports and having to do this work also, he was only getting a few hours of sleep a night. He had a constant headache from the memorization and the pressure of having to do everything correctly or catch a bullet in the brain. But no matter how much he wanted to, he didn't shout. Yakushev took meticulous note of his every word, his every move, his every gesture. And expected him to be a sphinx like his instructor at all times. So Alexsi drew a breath and gathered himself before answering, "Of course I told him that." And then without waiting for the next tongue-lashing, "You wanted me to be a thief. And a thief would say, 'Fuck your mother; what's in it for me?' While every Chekist would say, 'Of course I'll get you a gun; I'll bring it tomorrow; you don't even have to pay me.' And even a group like this would know enough to run away as fast as their legs could carry them."

"No, *you* wanted to be a thief," Yakushev countered. That deadly expression had left his face, though only someone who spent every day with him would have been able to tell. "Yet I see you are right. I was the one who told you that an agent has to live his legend, and you did exactly that. I should not fault you. And, yes, our people who work within our borders can be blunt instruments. I should commend your subtlety." He shuffled the papers of the report. "You worried me for a moment."

Alexsi made his own Russian translation from that. Any show of humanity and they would rub him out along with these poor fools. "Will you arrange for the food trucks to be removed from the university cafeteria, or shall I do it?"

"No, this task will be accomplished by others," said Yakushev.

"I am also not sure if I was correct to cut off relations with Aida Rudenko. It seemed to be what a thief angry about being deceived would do."

"I believe this was also in character with your legend," Yakushev said, after more careful deliberation. "In the future you should beware a break with any valuable source. But women are tempestuous, and therefore they tend to understand and forgive tempestuousness in others more so than men. Now indulge my curiosity. Why hand grenades and not a pistol?"

"I doubt any of them would know one end of a revolver from another," Alexsi replied. "But even so, if you gave them one without a firing pin or cartridges with no gunpowder they might still notice. Or go out in the woods for some target practice first. I didn't think you'd give them a working pistol to shoot at Comrade Stalin's automobile. And even a lunatic wouldn't try to pry a hand grenade open to see if there was real explosive inside."

Yakushev offered up another of his long pauses. "Again, I cannot fault your reasoning. You will be provided with deactivated hand grenades."

"Must I stand on the street with them and throw these grenades at some passing automobile?" Alexsi asked.

"No, in accordance with the statement you have already made to these terrorists you will hand over the bombs and then disappear. And your work in this affair will be finished."

Terrorists, Alexsi thought.

"Now on to today's exercise," Yakushev said. "You have learned how to follow in both busy and not busy areas. How to blend in, how to take a vantage point, how to change appearance and disappear, and how to calculate distance and time in relation to foot travel. Now you will learn how to use that same methodology to determine whether or not you yourself are under surveillance and what to do about it. An agent must know when he is being followed, and even more important, be absolutely certain when he is not."

17

1936 Moscow

AT NOON THERE WERE LITTLE CHILDREN AND THEIR MOTHERS
skating at Hermitage Gardens instead of drunken teenagers.

In keeping with his new training, Alexsi was late in order to let
his contact arrive first. This way he could check the entire area
for any surveillance before committing to the meeting. If you were
sitting somewhere waiting for a contact to arrive, and they showed
up with the police, then you were trapped.

Aida was all alone. She looked so small and vulnerable sitting
there on the bench—it made a man want to rush to her side and
help her. As he sat down he wondered how she did that.

"Are you terribly angry with me?" she asked.

Her face was as pale as the new snow, framed by that dark hair
and those eyebrows. The inferior Soviet lipstick always rubbed
away; women spent their days constantly reapplying it. But even
lipstick couldn't secure the redness of her lips against the Moscow
cold. "No, as a matter of fact, I'm not angry at all."

She was obviously surprised by his tone, and said, "I'm glad.
It's only because what we're doing is so important. In just a few
days—"

He held up a hand to cut her off. Then he dropped it to tap his
finger on the shopping bag he'd set down between them. "These
are the new issue RGD-33 grenades. The fuses are already inside,
so don't go knocking them about."

"We won't," she said, subdued.

"They're very simple. Move the thumb safety on the handle to the left, exposing the red dot. Then all you have to do is throw it. The motion of the handle sliding activates the mechanism, and four seconds later it explodes. Can you remember that?"

"I will," she said.

Alexsi exhaled his breath, and the cloud of condensation drifted away like smoke in the freezing air. "I know you will. You remember everything that everyone says."

"What are you talking about?"

"You told me that once, long ago."

Now her face hardened against him. "If you say so. Here is your money."

He took it from her hand and put it right in his pocket.

"Won't you count it?"

"No. I know it's correct."

"I heard about the food trucks. You'll disappear along with them now?"

"I'm not going to be throwing grenades at Stalin, if that's what you mean. By the way, I've always known who turned me in back at the orphanage."

She had been peeking at the grenades inside the shopping bag, and now those dark lashes rose up and the blue eyes flashed back to his face. "Really? When I first saw you at the bakery I thought you had come to kill me. And I thought you still might after the birthday party."

"Then you were brave to come with me."

"Your fate is your fate. You must accept it."

Fate his ass. She always loved the danger, and was confident she could do anything, including fucking all thoughts of murder right out of him. "I don't believe in fate. Fate is for operas."

She was looking at him intently, as if trying to reason something out. "I never asked if you had seen *Aida.*"

"I listened to a recording in a library in Baku. But I fear I will never be an opera lover."

"Well, it is Italian after all."

"I read the translation. I didn't think much of the plot. An Egyptian slave girl, secretly an Ethiopian princess, in love with Pharaoh's captain of the guard."

"You found it outlandish?"

"Not the secrets part. Or the betrayal."

"Then the ending?"

"That Aida would die for love? Well, let's not go into that. And Radames, the captain of the guard, was a sucker if you ask me."

"I'm frankly amazed to hear you say that," she replied.

"You shouldn't. Lately I've become convinced that if I hadn't had to run away from the orphanage, I still would have ended up on this park bench, or at least another one just like it. But I would not have learned as many things as I did."

"I thought you didn't believe in fate."

"I don't. I'd rather be a Russian realist than a Russian fatalist."

"Alexsi, I feel like you're trying to tell me something, and I have no idea what it is."

"It's not a good feeling, is it? That you might not be as smart as you think you are?"

Aida was still looking at him, but her face changed and he felt her turn away as she decided that whatever it was, it wasn't worth the bother. She half rose, leaning over to grasp the shopping bag, and gave a little cluck of pity. "Poor Alexsi. I'm always getting you into trouble, aren't I?"

Then she kissed him exactly the way she kissed him that very first time. She walked away, then turned as if she was expecting to see something happen. It didn't. And then she turned away again and was gone.

18

THE APARTMENT WAS SO QUIET ALEXSI WAS CERTAIN HE COULD hear his wristwatch ticking. He wondered if that would be part of his training, to learn how to sit still and stare at someone for an indefinite amount of time. There was nothing to do but match the silence until the judge returned his verdict.

Yakushev said, "You will now tell me how you discovered that Aida Rudenko is also a secret agent."

Alexsi could have begun by saying that it would have been easier for an addict to give up opium than for the Aida he knew to give up being an informer. That it was now clear to him that the only reason their orphanage existed in the first place was to funnel children into State Security. That when he pulled his little act with the waitress at the restaurant any Russian girl who wasn't a stool pigeon would have run screaming for the nearest policeman to keep from doing ten years. That she was the only one of the group of conspirators who never had any surveillance about. That at every moment she was the perfect agent provocateur, staying in the background but very quietly nudging everyone forward. That she probably fucked the idea of killing Stalin right into Dmitri's head, and he never even realized it. He could have said all of that but he was feeling obstinate, like a trained animal who after countless performances balks at doing his trick. "I just knew it. Don't ask me how."

But rather than erupt in anger, as he was expecting, Yakushev only looked satisfied. "I knew it also. This is why I always choose the man who was poor. And I always choose the man who was beaten as a child. There are always plentiful candidates in our country, but harder to find the one who hasn't grown up to become a bully himself. Those have other uses, but not as secret agents. And do you know why?"

This time Alexsi didn't have to act out his bewilderment.

"Because to be oblivious is a luxury of privilege. This is why you see everything and miss nothing. Because the beaten child learns to enter every room and read everyone in it like a book, in order to discover who will and who will not raise their hand against him. It is a skill almost impossible to teach in any reasonable amount of time. And no finer preparation for an agent. You have spent your life preparing to become that agent."

Alexsi felt a flash of resentment, perhaps because he knew it was true.

"You were very subtle, of course," Yakushev continued. "I read your report alongside the girl's. They match almost exactly, but she is still mystified as to your motives. I see you toying with her, and she knowing something is wrong but still having no idea what." He chuckled, which was more disturbing than reassuring coming from him. "She even warns that the grenades may be booby-trapped, and should be examined carefully. And you should be arrested immediately because of your skills at escape."

Alexsi remembered that last time she had been standing there, just before she left, waiting for the bluecaps to swarm him and drag him away.

And now came one of those rare Yakushev smiles, there and gone in a flash, that was also less than reassuring. "I don't begrudge you your moment of triumph, but only as a learning experience. Unlike in melodramas, there is no moment when a secret agent can reveal or even allude to his true identity to anyone not already aware of it. It is inevitably fatal, and regardless of the circumstance there is always a way out if you keep your wits. Do you heed me?"

"I do," Alexsi said.

"Good. So be clever but not too clever. Risk is thrilling, but always have the discipline to minimize it. It is fatal for an agent to indulge his passions."

"I understand," said Alexsi, acting but not feeling suitably chastened.

"Good. Except for those reservations I cannot fault your performance. Do you wish to hear the reviews?"

Alexsi knew he'd be hearing them no matter what. "If it is permissible."

Yakushev described what happened clinically, as if he were reading from another dry report by someone whose hand was aching and just wanted to be done with it. But Alexsi saw it much more vividly in his mind's eye. The five teenagers standing on a street corner in the Arbat district, traditional home of intellectuals and artists. Not far from his own apartment, actually. Dmitri quivering with excitement, ready to take his place as one of the heroes of song and story. Yuri uncharacteristically silent because he was shitting his pants from fear. Aida probably standing beside him to keep him from running away before the final act. The other two girls shaking in their boots but determinedly carrying the grenades in their bags.

Three automobiles speed down the street, and of course it's Stalin's motorcade because they are the finest American luxury automobiles so who else's would they be? They slow to take the corner and everyone throws their grenade. Or not. Perhaps fear freezes them in place; perhaps Yuri drops his at his feet. If they had any sense at all they would run, but they want to watch the explosions and themselves making history. But of course there are no explosions, just Chekists pouring from the vehicles and the buildings and possibly the snowdrifts also. Screaming from the girls as they all are kicked and punched and handcuffed and thrown into the Black Maria that arrives on cue. Then in the Lubyanka Aida laughing and having a congratulatory glass of cognac and basking in the admiration of her fellow Chekists while her dear friends are taking the rubber hose down in the interrogation rooms. Not because there is anything more to learn, really, but for daring to raise their hands against the Soviet colossus. Perhaps the entire drama in the streets was filmed with cinema cameras, and Stalin will watch it later, with the secret police high command anxiously awaiting his reaction. And he stares impassively at the screen, bangs the ashes from his pipe, and says it's about time you did your jobs correctly.

And then there was Yakushev in the very same voice saying, "The men Dmitri and Yuri, and the women Nadia and Larissa have been interrogated and shot. Those of their friends who should have reported their suspicious actions have received the appropriate sentence of twenty-five years at hard labor."

Twenty-five years for attending a birthday party, Alexsi thought. There's a present for you. His reaction was an inward shrug. It all would have happened even if he had never been there.

"The girl Aida Rudenko is a member of the NKVD city and province of Moscow section," Yakushev said. "Considering your past history, my old second section of internal counterintelligence requested your participation, since there was no reason the Moscow section should gain full credit for uncovering this plot. I regarded it as an excellent training opportunity. Everyone involved has been rewarded for their work." Yakushev passed an identity book across the desk. "You are now granted the right to shop in special government stores. And you may regard the one thousand rubles the girl gave you as part of your reward."

Alexsi glanced at the book. It was State Security Identification with his photograph.

"You have a question," said Yakushev. "I can tell."

"I was only wondering why they weren't arrested at the beginning," said Alexsi. "I can't see the difference between them wanting to kill Comrade Stalin in the first place and all the trouble it took to get them standing out on a street corner with hand grenades."

"Listen to me, boy. I am your master, and you work to please me. Correct?"

"Of course, Comrade," Alexsi replied.

"We all have masters to please. Will you say that there are no enemies of Communism? And that these enemies are not only in the capitalist world, but here in our own country also?"

Alexsi shook his head. He couldn't argue with that.

"Comrade Stalin knows that the enemies of Communism are tireless in pursuing their plots against him. If you tell him there are no plots then he will naturally think you are either incompetent or one of those doing the plotting. Well, here we have a plot. Comrade Stalin is satisfied we are doing our jobs. The Organs receive more resources to accomplish our vital work as the sword and shield of the state. Do you see?"

Alexsi nodded. And the competition between the Moscow section and this second section. Just as he thought before: Chekist office politics. Yakushev's man wins. Medals for everyone. It really was like an opera. And these were people who would think nothing of annihilating four students like they were insects underfoot in order to gain a promotion. Not just them, but untold numbers every day. Because how else would the many thousands of guardians of State Security occupy their hours? If Stalin wasn't a madman already, he would be after hearing about all the plots. The whole country is trying to kill you, Comrade Stalin. Well, then I'd better kill them all first. No, don't even think about that, Alexsi told himself. It might come out on your face.

Yakushev said, "Now that you have proved you can be trusted, the time has come for you to learn the ultimate objective of your training."

Just like the little pieces of their exercises coming together in a greater whole, Alexsi could now see their purpose in inserting him into this conspiracy. It had all been a test, but with real human lives. They wanted to be certain he would follow their orders, no matter what; no hesitations, no refusals. They wanted him as ruthless and unprincipled as they were. They wanted to see if he would flinch from having blood on his hands. Well, as long as they were satisfied, then they could think whatever they wanted. Alexsi knew in his bones that if his and Aida's reports hadn't matched perfectly he'd be facedown in a ditch somewhere instead of a thousand rubles richer.

Yakushev said, "You of course recall Friedrich Shultz, the boy you grew up with. And his family."

"I do," Alexsi replied. And then as if to mock all his previous thoughts: oh please, oh please, if somehow they are free don't tell me I have to betray them now. If nothing else they did broke him, this would. Because everything he had done, everything, had been for them.

19

1932 Soviet Azerbaijan

"OH, NO," EMMA SHULTZ SAID DESPAIRINGLY AT HER FIRST sight of Alexsi crossing her threshold. But she composed herself quickly. "Friedrich!" she snapped at her son. "Bring me a basin of water."

Freddi had been supporting his battered and bleeding friend. "Yes, Mama."

Emma turned to Alexsi and visibly softened. "Sit down at the table, dear, and let me look at you." Then to her daughter, who was hovering behind, not wanting to miss a second of what was going on, "Gerdi, watch the supper."

Gerde was a flaxen-haired miniature of her mother, and at nine was three years younger than Freddi. "Yes, Mama."

When Freddi brought the basin Emma Shultz briskly produced a small sheet of rough cotton wool, not one of her good towels, and a medicine bottle half filled with a thick, alarmingly orange-colored fluid.

"Be still, dear," she said softly, cradling Alexsi's chin in one hand while she toweled away the rest of the blood and ooze with the other.

Her hand was so cool, and her touch so gentle that Alexsi closed his eyes and rested the weight of his head in her palm.

"Were you fighting again?" she demanded, a little more sternly.

"No, Aunt Emma," he replied in German.

They had been speaking Russian up to that point, and she

shook her head in pleased amazement. "Your accent is better every time." She paused, and then, "So it was your father?"

He nodded against her palm. Her blond hair was mostly gray now, and she wore it in a pair of braids. Work and worry had scored her forehead and the corners of her eyes, and weighed down the skin of her face, but she had the kindest blue eyes Alexsi had ever seen.

Emma Shultz let out a sharp blast of breath that conveyed disgust far more effectively than mere words. She tore off a piece of the cotton, placed it over the neck of the medicine bottle, and shook it. "I'm afraid this will hurt you even more, my dear, but we cannot allow the cut to become infected. Especially so near your eye." She stopped, and said in Russian, "Did you understand what I just said?"

"Yes, Auntie," he replied in German. "I'm ready for the medicine."

Watching her the boy close his eyes and tense up his body, Emma Shultz's face took on an expression of utter sadness.

When it was over Alexsi helped Freddi with the water, fetched wood for the stove, and swept the floor before supper. The Shultz home was like the rest in the kolkhoz: too small for all the people in it, rough wood, the ground floor a living area and kitchen and table and stove and chairs. Above a half loft, where the adults slept. But in many other ways it was so much different from his. There was a hand-laid wooden floor instead of a dirt floor. It was so much cleaner that he liked to sweep it just to see it clean, not even to make himself welcome. There was a cabinet with old and amazing porcelain objects and dishes, not to mention a beautiful wooden box filled with silver knives, forks, and spoons with amazingly intricate handles that Freddi had secretly shown him once. He said they were carved from the tusks of elephants. And even more amazingly, another cabinet filled with books. Just like the library. Aunt Emma even let him look at them as long as he was careful and washed his hands first.

And she made exotic German meals. Her cabbage was laced with vinegar and spices. Alexsi thought her potato soup was the most delicious thing ever. It was enough to make you forget how rotten the potatoes were.

After supper the women washed the dishes. He and Freddi fetched more wood and water. Otto Shultz sat with his pipe, reading a book. Alexsi didn't want to go home to get his school text so he sat at the kitchen table practicing his exercises from Freddi's.

"I will make you a bed," Emma Shultz announced.

Otto clicked his pipe against his teeth, but Alexsi was grateful for the reprieve. Emma hovered over him while he washed himself and scrubbed his teeth with a finger dipped in salt.

His pallet was on the floor, next to Freddi and Gerdi's bed. When he heard from Freddi and Gerdi's breathing that they were asleep, Alexsi quietly put his clothes back on against the night chill and tiptoed over to the bookcase. He removed a thick volume and, clasping it in his arms to keep from dropping it, inched his way through the darkness of the room to the stove. He opened the firebox door a millimeter at a time to keep it from squeaking and carefully placed a piece of wood on the dying coals to give himself enough light to read by.

With his back against the warmth of the stove, Alexsi ran his fingers over the soft embossed leather binding and gently turned the pages to the story he had been reading last. He was delayed, as always, by the beautiful engravings that demanded to be looked at. They called the Brothers Grimm fairy tales, but to him they were not so far from the way people acted every day. From the first time Aunt Emma read him "Hansel and Gretel," translating as she went into Russian, he knew he had to learn German so he could read them himself. It had been a word-for-word struggle at first, and he had exasperated Freddi with questions, but now he could read them easily. Save a word or two to ask Aunt Emma in the morning. He didn't want to make her angry, the way everyone else was when he asked them questions, but she always seemed happy when he did.

Alexsi heard whispering from up in the loft, and stopped turning pages so he could hear.

Otto was saying in German, "We barely have enough to give our own children. We cannot afford to feed that boy so often."

"Then what will happen whenever his father beats him and throws him out of the house?" Emma demanded. "He will go hungry. Or worse, steal food."

"He probably does that anyway," said Otto. "They say there isn't a lock in the kolkhoz that can keep him out. He is probably listening to us right now."

At that Alexsi felt a twinge. He would have rushed back to bed, except he was afraid of making a noise and giving himself away.

"He has a good heart," Emma insisted. "And he is so bright. You hear how he speaks German, to please us? Just by listening and asking me questions."

"Intelligent and no morals is an evil combination," said Otto.

"Where is he to learn them, except from us?" Emma demanded again. "What am I to say when Freddi brings him home and insists we give him supper?"

"Freddi has too big a heart," said Otto.

"Would you rather him be heartless like everyone else in this place? I am proud of our son. He loves Alexsi, and Alexsi loves him. Freddi is a good influence on him."

"And what kind of influence is he on Freddi?" said Otto. "He will get Freddi into trouble, and then *we* will be in trouble."

"Alexsi will not risk his place with us."

"Boys do not think of things like that."

"I will not turn him away," said Emma. "His mother dead, his father a brute?"

"Dear," said Otto. "Our situation is precarious enough as it is."

"We came to Russia to build Communism," said Emma. "You were wounded fighting for the Bolsheviks in the Civil War."

"The Russians think I am a German first, and then perhaps a Communist," said Otto. "And always suspect because of it."

Alexsi knew the Shultzes had moved to the kolkhoz from Helenendorf. It wasn't far. He had been there once when Pyotr went trading. A strange place, a farm settlement built by Germans who came a long time ago to escape the wars of Napoleon. A little German village in the midst of Azerbaijan. Freddi said that they moved because they were Communists, which was good, and the other Germans were bourgeois, which was bad.

"Chauvinism," said Emma, a bit louder as her voice rose. "If only Lenin had lived. This group are nothing but gangsters. Camorra, not Communist."

"Ssssh," Otto whispered. "Dear, one of the children could innocently repeat something you say, at school, and that would be the end of us."

"This is exactly what I am saying," Emma continued, just as loud. "Once a party member was on the political vanguard. Now you must be a cow. Waiting to be poked with a stick to tell you where to go."

Otto said patiently, "Dear . . ."

Emma said fiercely, "Our children will see the Revolution succeed."

"Now about the boy," said Otto, unmistakably desperate to change the subject.

"I will not sit back and watch him become an ignorant bully like his father. I will not. With his brain he could be a scientist, an engineer. He could go to Moscow and be a credit to the party."

Alexsi heard Otto sigh in the darkness, his way of reconciling himself to the familiar sensation of being unable to move his wife.

The stove behind Alexsi's back was beginning to cool. He didn't understand words like "chauvinism" or "Camorra," but he understood enough. He would have to think of a way to add food to the Shultz larder. And think of how to do it so Aunt Emma would not refuse. The light from the firebox had died to where he could not make out the printing of the book. Rather than use any more of the Shultz's firewood he carefully closed the door, replaced the book, and crept off to bed. He would have to find them more wood, too.

Just like the stories in the book. He had been wrong not to repay the kindness of the good.

20

"DO YOU RECALL THE FATHER OF THIS FAMILY?" YAKUSHEV asked.

"I do," Alexsi said, fighting to mask his dread.

"What was his name?"

Was? Not is. "Otto."

"Very good. This Otto Shultz has a brother who lives in Munich, Germany. His name is Hans Shultz. Did you ever hear anything of him?"

"I knew Otto had a brother in Germany," Alexsi said. "And that he was a capitalist. Because of this, the family did not speak of him. I know nothing more."

"I see," said Yakushev. "This Hans Shultz is a high official of the German Foreign Ministry. He is an early member of the German Nazi Party. Recently he has lost both his wife and his only child, a son, to a motor vehicle accident. He writes to his brother Otto's son Friedrich in the Soviet Union and asks if he would like to join the now sadly smaller Shultz family in Germany."

Alexsi had lain awake nights wondering why Soviet State Security had gone to such pains to hunt him down and bring him to Moscow. Now he finally knew.

"I believe that the members of your kolkhoz called you and Friedrich Shultz 'the twins,'" Yakushev said. "This Hans Shultz has never seen anything more than a baby photograph of his nephew. No one alive knows the Shultz family of Azerbaijan better than you. Your German is near fluent and you have a gift for accents. Therefore we propose to send you to Germany as Friedrich Shultz."

So even if his friends weren't already dead, they would never, ever, be set free. He should have known, Alexsi told himself.

21

ALEXSI HAD HIS PLAN ALL READY. THE SACK OF FLOUR WAS heavy on his back. He knew if he brought it directly to Emma Shultz she would order him to take it back to where he had stolen it. Even though he hadn't stolen it. He had stolen alcohol. Men never paid attention to a boy when they were drinking and playing cards. Hearing that some in the next kolkhoz were selling samogon from a still hidden up in the hills, he had missed his supper and walked the whole way there, waiting in the cold darkness outside one of their houses and following the man up into the hills later. Then returned to the spot later when the batch was done and the distillers gone, helping himself to a single jug. With only one missing the men would each think that one of the others had stolen or drunk it.

Stealing food from the storehouses was too dangerous. Stealing illegal alcohol and trading it for food the authorities had stolen themselves was much safer.

His plan was inspired by the Grimm tales. He would let himself into the Shultz house when no one was there and fill the flour bin with none the wiser. As if it were a reward from a magical person for being kind to him.

He had skipped school, so he knew Freddi and Gerdi were still there. Otto would be working in the fields. And Aunt Emma in the cowshed.

He knew exactly where to watch. A house near the Shultzes',

which like many of them had no foundation. The unpainted wood frame sitting on a pile of stones or brick. Alexsi stashed the sack of flour in the space underneath and, pushing a stick before him to drive out any snakes or wasps, crawled in deeper until he reached the other side. With his head back in the darkness he could over-see the Shultz house without being seen himself.

But instead of an empty house, what Alexsi saw brought that familiar feeling of cold compression back to his stomach. A man was standing in the yard. An official man, because who else would be wearing a suit? His hair was wet with grease and combed back over his skull, and he was smoking a cigarette. Parked in the yard was a long steel-gray van with four wheels and dimples in the metal sides where windows ordinarily would have been.

A shrieking sound came from inside the Shultz house, and then the entire family spilled out the front door. They were surrounded by three men in green uniforms and shiny black boots, carrying rifles. The tops of their green caps were blue, with red bands around the crowns. The afternoon sun glinted off the red metal star of Soviet power on the front of one of the caps.

The shrieking was coming from Gerdi, who was clinging tightly to her mother's skirts. Otto Shultz was carrying two small suitcases. He looked dazed, shuffling like a man about to drop after working too long in the fields without water. Alexsi had seen Emma Shultz smiling and angry, and happy and sad. But he had never seen her totally without expression before. Freddi was on the other side of his sister, trying to quiet her.

The official man threw his cigarette down on the ground and stepped on it. The ones with rifles pushed the Shultzes through the open door into the back of the van. One of the bluecaps followed them in after shouting some orders that Alexsi could not hear clearly, and the other two locked the door behind him and went up front to the driver's side. The official man climbed into the passenger side. The engine started roughly with a gust of blue exhaust that was darker than the men's caps. In a few moments they were gone, with only the dust trail from their wheels hanging in the air like morning mist.

That was the Black Maria, Alexsi thought. The children were always threatened with it. If you are bad the Black Maria will come to take you away.

He didn't cry. They hit you, and then if you cried they hit you again for that. So to keep from being hit twice you learned not to cry. It was as simple as that. You could learn anything.

He just felt hollow, as if everything inside him had been roughly scooped out. His one thought was to get inside the house for the Brothers Grimm book.

But he also knew he couldn't do it now. The Black Maria had made everyone on the kolkhoz vanish from sight. But they would all be watching. In the daytime there were always women's eyes watching everything. He would have to wait until dusk at the earliest, when everyone was eating supper.

So he made himself comfortable in the dirt, the cool musty shade of the house looming over him.

But the stillness did not last long. Farm carts suddenly clattered down the tracks from different directions, all stopping at the Shultz house. His father and maybe half of the dozen men in his father's work brigade.

They gathered together for a bit in the yard, smoking and talking until the kolkhoz manager arrived riding on his mule. But he didn't order them all to go home. The official men had put a red seal on the lock of the Shultz door. They didn't touch it but instead unscrewed the doorknob, also one of Alexsi's favorite tricks, and they all went inside.

In a few minutes they came out the door carrying the Shultzes' furniture, which they loaded into the carts.

None of these men seemed to be afraid of the secret police and their red seal. Nor were they afraid of the prying eyes of the kolkhoz. And there was the manager holding his mule's bridle and laughing along with them, though of course doing no work. So they either had permission from the secret police to loot the Shultz home, or the secret police would be paid off once the Shultzes' belongings were sold. Instead of working in the fields they had all arrived within an hour of the Shultz family's arrest. And if the arrest was no surprise, then the Shultzes had been denounced by some or all of the men he was watching. Alexsi tested his proof and could find no errors.

The china cabinet came out now, and what had to be the piles of dishes wrapped in blankets. Then armloads of books, which, unlike the china, they tossed into the cart like so much trash. With that Alexsi knew the Grimm book was gone forever. He wouldn't be able to steal it back without being caught—everyone knew how close he'd been to the Shultzes, and a pretty book in German was too distinctive. Even trying to trade his now-useless bags of flour for it would raise too many questions. Why do you want it, Alexsi? Are you going to make trouble for us?

The men cleaned out the rest of the house, closing the door and screwing the knob back on. One of the men, Semyen, clapped his father on the back and said something that made them all laugh, the devils.

Alexsi carefully marked each of their faces, though he knew that there was no one he could call upon for justice. No one but himself.

22

ALEXSI WAS EXHAUSTED. HIS DAYS WERE NOW SPENT AT A RED Army school for wireless technicians. It wasn't just learning Morse code, but repairing and even building radios. He could see what they intended by that. The school would have been hard enough, with death the penalty for a failing grade. Not to mention putting on a uniform every morning and going by yet another false name and legend, watched by more informers, and death again if he slipped up on anything. But as soon as the school day was over, there were more exercises.

That afternoon they had driven him to a factory and walked him through its entirety. Then immediately shoved him back into the vehicle, returned him to Yakushev's training apartment, and set him to work creating from memory a detailed diagram of the plant he had seen only once. There was no question that in the days to come the instant he relaxed he would be called upon to diagram that stupid factory over and over again. And every version he presented had better be identical.

Always watching. Every second they examined him for the slightest sign of irritation, the briefest hesitation in answering a question, the most fleeting loss of concentration due to fatigue. How he moved, how he held his hands, how he crossed his legs. Any error would be criticized at length until there were no more errors. The pain in his head was a constant companion, and all he wanted was to let his mind rest for a little while. These days he could only sleep if he had a glass of vodka first. He still hated the stuff, but swallowed it down like medicine. It made his dreams terrible. Always being chased—but either he could only move in slow motion, no matter how hard he strained, or he was paralyzed, unable to move at all.

But even after all his labors that day he wasn't released to sleep and dream. Yakushev brought him to supper at a government canteen and of course carefully watched him eat. It seemed that the man took all his nourishment from tea and cigarettes. After previous meals where his table manners had been brutally corrected, Alexsi no longer ate as if someone might snatch his food away at any moment but treated each forkful as if the contents were made from nitroglycerin and would detonate if not handled with proper care.

BACK AT the training apartment a man he had never seen before was waiting for them. In his midtwenties, blond, handsome, with the unconcealed arrogance of the handsome man who knows it. Alexsi immediately disliked him.

Yakushev acted as if the man was not there. "Now we will discuss a subject of the utmost importance to the espionage agent," he announced. "Women."

Despite his throbbing headache Alexsi perked up. At least this subject had the prospect of being both easier and more interesting than learning high-frequency antenna theory.

"Being denied access to the normal levers of power in society," Yakushev began, "women offer what men desire in order to obtain what they desire themselves. What they offer is sex. And most women are clever enough not to provide what they offer until they have already received what they desire. Despite their commonly supposed susceptibility to romanticism they are in general far more realistic about such matters than men. One must not dismiss romantic love, of course, but one must also not overemphasize it. As a physical and emotional manifestation of biological attraction it is a much more common feeling of one person for another rather than two people for each other. Which brings us in a complete circle back to my original point."

Alexsi was convinced that Yakushev talked this way just to make it difficult to write reports on his classes.

"A man may be in love with a woman," said Yakushev, "while she may only be in love with how he meets her goals. A woman may be in love with a man, and he in love only with the use of her body. Do you follow me?"

"Yes, Comrade," Alexsi replied dutifully.

"Unlike in our country," said Yakushev, "in the West it is customary for men to solicit the advice of their wives in matters both small and great. Therefore women may exercise power over organizations or even nations out of all proportion to their actual position. Also in the West there are a great many exclusively female social groups that wield influence over national affairs. Their directors are correspondingly influential. All these women I have described are, in general, older and of substantial means. They cannot be bought. However, they can be interested and influenced by a virile young lover. And such a lover would gain access to circles of power and information that he could not otherwise." He paused. "If you had different inclinations we would train you to attract homosexuals. There are many in the West who occupy important positions, and for the most part they live hidden and sexually frustrating lives. Since their behavior is considered criminal, they can easily be blackmailed into helping us, though they are much more unstable than women and must be handled with greater care. But you need concern yourself only with women."

Always testing. Where would you hesitate? What would you refuse? Alexsi kept his face fixed. Everyone in the Soviet Union was just a means to an end. Yet they always talked about how workers in the capitalist world were treated as nothing more than gears in the factory machinery.

"Also," said Yakushev, "even women who are not influential are important to the work of an agent. Through them you can access subjects of interest and their circles much more naturally than by any other method. They may also help you in influencing those subjects without having any knowledge of your ultimate goals. However," he added with emphasis, "convince a woman that you want her, that you love her, commit yourself, and then fail her sexually, and all your careful work is undone."

Though all this was probably a regular part of their spy training, Alexsi couldn't help wondering if somehow Aida had managed to have the last word on him.

"But," Yakushev went on, "be completely successful in satisfying her beyond all her expectations and you bind her to you. To achieve this goal I turn you over to Comrade Orlov."

Until now the blond man had been sprawled across the divan. Now he sprang up and sauntered over to an easel he had set up before them. He flipped over the cover to reveal an anatomy chart of a woman. "Young comrade, I am going to teach you to bring a woman to climax and satisfy her completely. Even one that does not excite you in the slightest. I will also teach you techniques whereby you can accomplish this repeatedly and over great duration without being the worse for wear yourself."

Orlov didn't speak German. It was the first time Alexsi had heard Russian in the training apartment.

Using a small wooden pointer, Orlov tapped the chart for emphasis. "Now, we begin by discussing female anatomy, paying particular attention to the major nerve branches and how they relate to what we will call primary and secondary zones of arousal."

The lecture went on for most of the night. Alexsi had to use a trick he had learned to keep from falling asleep: tighten the muscles of your eyes as if you were trying to read fine print and continuously move them back and forth to keep from glazing over. Once again Communism had achieved the impossible. They had managed to make sex boring.

Finally Orlov reached the end of his charts. "There," he announced. "Now your task is to prepare a report on this instruction. Present it to me tomorrow and if I am satisfied with your comprehension we will proceed to practical application."

So much for sleep.

23

1936 Moscow

THEIR CHEKIST DRIVER KEPT HIS FOOT DOWN ON THE ACCEL-
erator of the GAZ-A sedan as if he were driving down a racetrack
instead of slushy Moscow streets. The wind screamed through the
seams in the fabric top, loud enough to drown out the passengers
if they felt inclined to do the same. He handled the steering wheel
with all the delicacy of an interrogation club and at every turn the
automobile skidded nearly across the road. The cold made the finest quality Soviet rubber windscreen wipers so hard they might
as well have been wood for all the good they did against the light
snow that was falling. No one said a word to the driver. There
were vast numbers of mathematicians and concert musicians in
the Soviet Union but few automobiles, and those who knew how
to drive them were a rare species. It wouldn't do to upset him.
Alexsi was watching Orlov and saw that he wasn't the only one
relieved when the ride was over. There was something to be said
for streetcars.

The house was well guarded, but not obviously so. Now
there was a job for you, Alexsi thought, guarding a secret police
brothel in the middle of winter. Perhaps that was where they sent
the spy school failures they didn't shoot.

During his time on the streets of Baku Alexsi had learned
that all the whores who managed to stay out of jail for any length
of time were secret police informers, and for that reason he had

kept away from them. His headache had lifted but was replaced by that hard knot in the pit of his stomach.

Orlov took him into a room. Perhaps from too much reading Alexsi was expecting erotic portraits on the walls and a general color scheme of red. But there was nothing on these walls, not even a clock. The barren room was furnished only with a divan and two armchairs. The room was clean and smelled strongly of stale cigarettes with a faint but unmistakable background odor of sex.

"Sit down, watch, and pay attention," Orlov ordered.

Alexsi took his place in one of the armchairs. His stomach was bouncing all about his insides.

Orlov took off all his clothes. Alexsi hadn't been ready for that. He fervently hoped Yakushev hadn't been lying about the homosexual part.

Orlov walked naked over to a door and pressed a button on the wall beside it. The door opened and out came a chubby girl, painfully plain, who wore her dress as if it was the first one she'd ever had. She didn't speak a word, but stared at Orlov as if she had never seen a naked man before. Alexsi thought that it must be *her* first night, too. The whole awkward scene made his heart go out to her. She wasn't ugly. She was just a poor plain peasant girl who no one had ever taken the time to show anything, and was now about to be used like toilet paper.

Speaking to Alexsi as if the girl wasn't even there, Orlov said, "As you can see, she is nothing to look it. But I will take care of her nonetheless."

Smiling warmly, Orlov took the girl's hands and led her over to the divan. He undressed her, and Alexsi could see she was shaking with fear.

Once she was naked also, Orlov said, again as if she didn't exist, "As you can see, I am not aroused by her in the slightest. To do so, I press myself to her body to make physical contact and look only in her eyes. You will note that the eyes of every woman are beautiful, even if she is not. In a case like this where there is no

attraction you must think of the most satisfying sexual experience you have ever had. In an opposite case where a woman deeply
attracts you, in order to achieve longevity you must think of
something that repels you."

Now Orlov stopped talking. Rubbing his body gently against
the girl on the divan, he gazed into her eyes and became erect.

Alexsi sat there like a theatergoer watching a play he did not
really want to see.

Orlov began making love to the girl, using the primary and
secondary zones of arousal and all the tricks he had lectured
about, which Alexsi had also dutifully recounted in his paper. At
least the girl had stopped shaking, but otherwise she didn't seem
to be responding at all.

Orlov entered her, and the intercourse continued for such a
long time that Alexsi had to force himself not to time it, just out
of curiosity. Then the girl suddenly gripped Orlov's shoulders,
arched her back, and let out that unmistakable cry of ecstasy. But
Orlov didn't slacken. He continued apace, and after a few minutes
more the girl cried out again. Alexsi wouldn't have believed it if
he hadn't been sitting there, and he would be willing to swear her
climax had been genuine.

Orlov pulled out, and the girl actually hugged him. He gave
her a little tap and gesture, and she dressed and left the room.

Standing there before him, Orlov said, "As you can see, the
proper state of mind is vitally important. But as we have discussed previously, once you have achieved arousal your points
are breathing, recognizing the moment of impending ejaculation
and retreating before you reach it, and muscle control. And this
muscle is . . . ?"

"The one that stops the flow during urination," Alexsi repeated
dutifully. He couldn't say much for the experience of being lectured by a naked and fully erect man, though it did make it easy
to keep your attention fixed upon his face.

"Good," said Orlov. "As you have seen, if you have done your

work properly in bringing her to the proper level of arousal before penetration, and then sustain your erection, her climax is assured. And without ejaculation on your part, your endurance can
be indefinite."

Alexsi thought that the class must be over, but Orlov pushed
the button by the door again. And proceeded to have five more
girls over the next five hours.

The demonstration was undeniably impressive, but Alexsi would
be hard-pressed to say whether torture would have been preferable to sitting in a chair and watching someone else fucking for
five hours.

Orlov finally put on his clothes, and Alexsi's relief was inde-
scribable.

"Now, the student," Orlov said, taking his place in the other
armchair and lighting a cigarette.

As Alexsi had feared, Orlov was going to be sitting there. He
dutifully took off his clothes, and his stomach felt like it had
shrunk down to a hard little nut in the center of his gut. Never
mind the first girl, he had to concentrate to keep his legs from
shaking.

He pushed the button, expecting the worst.

But the girl who emerged through the door was extremely beautiful. A redhead with pale green eyes and skin like cream. She
looked at him boldly and smiled. Normally that would have been
more than enough to get him as hard as a rock, but no such luck
with the feeling of Orlov's eyes burning into his back.

Alexsi led her over to the divan and began to undress her, telling himself: slowly, slowly, slowly, and feeling like a schoolboy
reciting in front of the chalkboard. Her body was gorgeous, with
pert breasts, nipples like puffy buttons, and a warm flame of pubic
hair between her legs.

He stroked her face and her neck and her shoulders and her
arms. He slowly circled her breasts until he reached the nipples
that he ever so lightly held with his thumb and forefinger.

And, following his lessons, letting her breathing tell him when it was time to move on.

He touched the very tip of her nipple with the tip of his tongue, lightly circling across the surface as if the end of his tongue was the finest abrasive. He teased it as slowly as he could, until she grabbed his shoulders and tried to pull his mouth onto her breast. He let her, taking the nipple into his mouth with gentle sucking pressure while still teasing it with his tongue.

By the time he worked his way down to her pussy the girl was throbbing like an engine. But he was still as limp as a shoelace. Between following his steps as if he were taking a test, and Orlov sitting there staring at him, there was no hope. No matter what he thought of didn't work.

He caught the girl looking around him to Orlov, and then as if at a signal she pushed him back a bit with a hand on his chest, bobbed her head down, and took him into her mouth.

No girl had *ever* done that before. She forced herself down onto him like a sword-swallower and sucked him in like a vacuum pump. He forgot Orlov, the room, the house, everything—and he was hard now.

While she was sucking him she swirled her tongue around the head of his cock just like he had done to her nipples, and all the detailed instruction and muscle control sailed away on a tide of pleasure. Her mission accomplished, the girl drew her head back while still sucking, and when he came out of her mouth with a pop he came all over her face.

Alexsi was mortified. He held his breath and waited for the girl to shriek in disgust. Her eyes widened with surprise, and then she began to giggle loudly.

Alexsi had no idea what to do. His first impulse was to grab a piece of clothing and clean off her face. But before he could do anything Orlov was suddenly between them, pushing him out of the way and violently beating the girl with his fists.

She screamed in terror and he knocked her off the divan onto the floor. Now that she was out of range of punches he kicked her toward the door as she scrambled wildly on her hands and knees to get away from him.

She went through the doorway like a soldier under fire diving for cover. Orlov aimed a final kick as she disappeared, and still in a towering rage grabbed up her clothes and heaved them through the doorway, finally slamming the door shut hard enough to take it off the hinges.

He turned to face Alexsi and his face was white with rage. "I'll teach that little pig to laugh at a Soviet officer!" And then that rage flowed down to the only remaining target. "And you! Pathetic! Everything that you were taught, forgotten! Fucking dogs take longer to come than you. All the technique in the world is useless, *useless* without self-discipline!"

Alexsi just stood there naked and at attention. Face burning like it was afire, limp as a boiled noodle once again.

"Even if you *could* get it up again tonight, it would only be because you're seventeen, not because you learned anything," Orlov said contemptuously. "Any further training now would be a waste of time. Put on your clothes and get out of here. Practice on yourself so there won't be a repeat of this disaster. Well? *Get out!*"

In the car the driver was looking at Alexsi in the rearview mirror. "Didn't go so well?"

The last thing in the world Alexsi wanted was to talk about it. But here was someone else who would be reporting on his every expression. "No," he muttered.

The driver leaned over the seat. He was an older man, with a gray moustache that was a duplicate of Stalin's. "Don't worry about it, son. You're not the only one I've seen go in there, and the first time almost always ends badly. But when they're done with you, you'll be able to do it in Red Square at noon. Atop Lenin's tomb. On May Day."

Now that was something to look forward to, Alexsi thought.

24

"YOUR TRAINING IS NOW COMPLETE," YAKUSHEV SAID. "THE time has come for you to be operational."

"Yes, Comrade," Alexsi replied. If the entire point of their training was to make him happy to go out into the unknown, then it had worked. He felt like he hadn't slept in a week after surviving all their final examinations. Chased by dogs, interrogated by policemen, pounding out Morse code in total darkness and up to his ass in freezing water, having sex with an audience watching. Yakushev assured him that it would be harder than the actual spying. He had better be right. At least he would be free of this bloodless vulture of a man. Now would come his final orders, all practicality. No emotional parting, no sentimental Russian kisses on the cheek from this one.

"There are a few things I should like to tell you now," said Yakushev, as always lighting another cigarette. "We almost never send an agent as young as yourself into the field, mainly for reasons of maturity. But, as you know, in this case the legend and the operational situation demands it. I have complete confidence in you."

"Thank you, Comrade."

"You have no frame of reference, so perhaps you think your preparation has been identical to every other agent's. I assure you this is not the case. We send thousands of secret agents outside our borders every year. In most cases they are trained to a certain level, and our expectations for them are at a certain level also. If they fail it is no great loss. We supply them with equipment that is necessary to their work, but if discovered will mark them as a spy and ensure their violent interrogation and eventual execution. They operate in networks that, if one betrays, others fall. You, however, will be different. You will take nothing with you but your wits, your memory, and your training. Normally an agent in your category would be teamed with another who would act as your radio and cipher operator. But not knowing the course of your future life, how could anyone remain alongside you? This level of security is unprecedented, and a mark of how much we value your potential as a penetration agent in one of our main adversary nations. It will be up to you to fulfill that potential."

Alexsi would have been disappointed if there had been no threat.

"You know nothing about me," said Yakushev. "I will tell you this. I have spent my career catching spies. Not like that pathetic little group of revanchists you were sent to infiltrate, but dangerous professionals from France, Germany, Japan, and England. All dedicated to overthrowing the Communist Revolution. Have you ever heard of Sidney Reilly, whose real name was Rosenblum?"

Alexsi shook his head.

"No matter. Suffice it to say that he and the others like him are dead, their missions failed. And every mistake they made has been stored away." He tapped his forehead. "I have used this knowledge to make you uncatchable. It is why you were never sent to any of our special schools. I will never leave the Soviet Union. You cannot be betrayed. If you fail it will be because of yourself alone."

Alexsi unfortunately recognized the import of that statement. If he was caught and the Germans began pulling out his fingernails, he could give them nothing. No identities of other spies he had gone through training school with. No secrets, except perhaps how the Soviets train a spy. He had only ever been in the Lubyanka as a prisoner. Apartments, streets, parks, factories, houses—he hadn't the faintest idea what a secret police building looked like on the inside. It was very clever of them.

"Your legend is perfect," said Yakushev. "You have no idea. Nothing is more difficult than for a Russian to impersonate a native German among Germans—just as difficult for a German, no matter how perfect their training, to come into this country and pose convincingly as a native Russian. You will be posing as a frightened, German-speaking Russian teenager who is traveling to a strange land for the very first time. In reality you *are* that Russian teenager. With good luck and your natural talents it should be possible for you to eventually rise to a position in Germany where you will be able to uncover their greatest secrets. Perhaps even personally bring about the inevitable victory of Communism in that country. Do not think I exaggerate. We gather information by many means, but a single spy in the right place and at the right moment may change the course of history. This will require years of patient effort on your part. Rest assured that we will always be with you to take care of everything you need. If you succeed you will join the greatest heroes of the Revolution and the highest honors will be yours. Complete your mission and you will never have a worry in your life."

Now comes the stick, Alexsi thought.

"Open the album on the table beside you," Yakushev ordered.

It was like a scrapbook. Full of dead men and women. Clippings of news articles, photographs of violent death. Shooting, strangling, poisoning, road accidents, bomb blasts. Germany, France, Switzerland, England, Holland, Sweden, Turkey, Egypt, Mexico, America. It went on and on.

"As you can see, our arm reaches everywhere," said Yakushev. "You recall I once said that we are merciless toward anyone who betrays us? There is no escaping Soviet justice. Only two entities know you are a Soviet secret agent. Yourself and the Organs of State Security. So you can only be trapped by the Germans if you blunder. If, however, after some time in the West you begin to feel that you are beyond the reach of the Soviet government and therefore free to abandon your work, well, recall that many have made that mistake, and it is always their last. If we choose not to deal with you ourselves, it would be a simple matter for a German agent in this country, under our control, to discover and pass along the fact that you are in the service of the Soviet Union. And then your fate, rather than your reward, would be assured."

Alexsi didn't say a word.

"Your loyalty is not in question," said Yakushev.

Everyone's loyalty is always in question, Alexsi thought. It should be the national motto.

"It is just that the life of an agent has highs and lows. It is during the low moments that one can become weak. One final point. Never forget that those you will live among are our most bitter enemies. You are a Soviet fighter in plainclothes, and you must be merciless toward them."

"Yes, Comrade," Alexsi said dutifully. And then parroted what was expected: "I serve the Soviet Union!"

"I am not worried," Yakushev said, patting the folder on his desk as if it were a puppy. "When I first read your file I told myself: this is a boy who has no mercy in him. And now I see I was correct."

More fool you, then, Alexsi thought. He didn't care a fig for Stalin or Communism or world revolution. He worked for them because he had to—he'd always done what he had to. They thought he was one of them; they'd put him in their special orphanage because he'd denounced his father and everyone who destroyed the Shultz family to the secret police. But he'd only done that because he wasn't strong enough to kill them himself.

"Your pseudonym of Dante is now obsolete," said Yakushev. "You will require a new one, to be used in all your communication and identification procedures."

Wonderful, Alexsi thought. Now I have to think up something else.

"I have taken the liberty of choosing one for you," said Yakushev, looking distinctly pleased with himself. "Your new pseud-onym will be David."

Alexsi just stared at him blankly. He supposed one name was as good as any other.

Yakushev looked disappointed. "You have never heard of the Bible story, of the boy who with only a rock and sling killed a giant?"

"No, Comrade." A Bible in a Soviet library? If he *had* ever come across one, he'd think it was a trap so they could see who tried to read it.

PART II

The Sling
and the Stone

25

1937 Munich, Germany

ALEXSI STEPPED OUT ONTO THE ROOFED BUT OPEN-AIR PLATform of Munich's Central Station. His breath and that of his fellow passengers condensed into a thick gusting cloud as they jostled together in their rush to free themselves from the train, but it was barely freezing—balmy compared to Moscow. It was still winter, though spring was near enough for hopeful anticipation. The air smelled of cigars and roasted chestnuts.

Most of the Germans knew where they were going. They put their heads down, squared their shoulders, and strode off as if they were pulling plows. Others, bewildered, looked about for signs or directions.

The Russian boy stood there as if anchored to the concrete, watching. Waiting. The wind shrieked around the metal roof like a soul in torment. They had taken away his sharp Moscow suit and cleverly picked out traveling clothes for him. A threadbare suit, typical Russian quality, seams coming apart, two sizes too large. It made him look small and helpless. During the trip older women had clucked over him and offered the food they'd packed for their own journeys.

There was no need for him to act tired and forlorn and bedraggled. The trip had actually been only slightly shorter and marginally more comfortable than the prison train from Baku to Moscow, except that at least there was food and drink and he could go to the toilet whenever he wanted.

No Russian, or German for that matter, could cross Poland now in safety, even by train, so he had traveled from Moscow to Leningrad to Finland. Then Sweden and down to Denmark into Germany. Train and ferry. At each border crossing he and his small battered case containing only a change of clothing, toilet articles, and a few books in German for the journey had been examined like bacteria under a microscope.

Alexsi was carrying a laissez-passer issued by the German embassy in Moscow, travel documents good only for a one-way trip. His name was Friedrich Shultz. The Russians didn't just issue passports and open their gates to any of their citizens who wanted to leave. Anyone bearing a Soviet passport other than a Soviet diplomat might just as well wear a sign that said SPY. So perhaps even while they were hunting him in Baku the NKVD had let the German embassy fight with the Soviet Foreign Ministry to let Friedrich Shultz leave the country. Perhaps they had even made the Germans pay for him; Alexsi didn't know.

The little traveling money he had left in his pocket were German marks. Just like a German, the Russians had all exclaimed, laughing, when it arrived from the embassy along with his papers. Just enough, not too much, until the capitalist had a good look at what he bought, they said. As always Alexsi had been silent, though based on his smuggling experience it was clear that no one anywhere else in the world would offer up anything they had, even a single ripe apple, for a Soviet ruble. And these Hitler Reichsmarks actually had value, unlike the Weimar marks that required a wheelbarrow full to buy a loaf of bread.

As he was watching, a man was watching him. Tall, over two meters. Handsome in a rough way, with that pale but ruddy German skin, pouched circles under his eyes, and deep age lines like saber cuts running from the bottom of his nose to the corners of his mouth. Around fifty, distinguished but worn. His hat was in his hand, revealing thinning white hair swept back on his head, with two valleys where it had retreated back from the central peak. A thick white regimental moustache concealed his entire upper lip. Wearing a beautiful gray suit coat with a fur collar that only revealed the trousers of a dark pinstriped suit.

The man seemed to make up his mind and strode up to him with military bearing. As he approached a slight double chin gave away the middle-aged girth his tailored clothes concealed, and even closer a pair of brilliant blue eyes that were like something apart from his weary face.

The man marched up to him. Alexsi had to look up to meet his eye.

The man said, "Friedrich?"

Alexsi replied, "Uncle Hans?"

Hans Shultz stood there almost at attention, and looked him up and down as if he were conducting a military inspection. Then, as if he had come to another decision, presented his hand.

Alexsi took it, and felt his own enveloped in the hugeness of that paw. But he was ready, and as the grip bore down on him he matched it and returned it. The hand was smooth but very strong.

The blue eyes locked onto his. Not pleasure, not suspicion. Just an armed neutrality for now. "I am pleased to finally make your acquaintance, nephew."

Alexsi wasn't at all surprised. Every German he had met so far had been just as formal and reserved. Except when they were drunk. "And I yours, Uncle." The only thing that surprised him was that his uncle was alone. Somehow he had always pictured him waiting for the train with an entourage.

"You must resemble your mother," Hans Shultz observed matter-of-factly. "I never met her."

Every word that came out of him, however pleasant, was like a bear growling. Alexsi didn't think he could help it—that was his voice. "They have always told me so, Uncle."

"Your German is quite excellent. I credit that to your mother, also."

"We spoke it every night at supper," Alexsi said.

"Did you?" Now those blue eyes were far away. "I would not have guessed." And with a faint turn of the head and crisp blink the eyes were back on him. "You must be exhausted and hungry, and I make you stand here in the cold. Come, let me take you home."

He reached down to take the battered case, but Alexsi picked it up first. "I will carry it, Uncle. You should not have to."

The eyes were now amused, though the voice came rumbling out, "Please yourself. Now how shall I call you?"

Alexsi said, "Everyone usually calls me Freddi, sir."

Another examination, a brief consideration, and then a decision. "You are a man, now. I will call you Friedrich."

"Yes, sir."

And then he was off, and Alexsi had to walk quickly to catch up.

Once they were up the stairs and inside it must have taken them a full ten minutes to walk across the interior of the station. Alexsi thought it was big enough to fly planes inside. Though of course he couldn't run a drill to confirm it, he felt they were being followed. It struck him that in Germany he would always be left wondering which side might be doing it.

26

1937 Munich

"TYPHOID. MY GOD," HANS SHULTZ MUTTERED. HE PUSHED his wineglass aside and said to the maid, "Susan, bring me a brandy."

They had eaten in silence because Hans Shultz had announced as they took their seats that when he was eating he preferred to eat, and when he was speaking he preferred to speak, and had to do both so often in his work that he preferred not to mix the two in his home. Alexsi had been quite relieved, though he didn't say so, that he wouldn't have to think about what he was saying. And could just tuck into his *schweinshaxe,* the braised pork leg crunchy with a brown crust on the outside and moist and juicy inside. With gravy and potato dumplings. It was absolutely delicious.

But then there was that moment after the *prinzregententorte,* the cake of six thin layers with chocolate buttercream in between—now officially the best thing he had ever eaten—that he had to set his utensils down and say what Yakushev had ordered him to say. That Otto and Aunt Emma and Gerde were dead. As soon as he heard, he had known that of all the lies they'd told him, this was not one.

"Your face is wounded," Hans Shultz said, after gulping down the brandy and sending the girl off for another. "I knew the news would be bad. You were dreading it as soon as I asked." He sighed and put those large pink hands palm down on the tablecloth.

"This is why I don't like to eat and talk. At least when bad news comes the food isn't spoiled." He raised his head, with a question.

"I was not there, Uncle. I was in Baku, working. They were in quarantine and gone before I could reach them."

"Ah." The Germans had a way of saying that to convey an emotion they otherwise declined to express. "Come," Hans Shultz said. "Let us take our drinks and sit down. There is much to speak of." He eyed Alexsi's wineglass. "Though it seems you do not drink. I hope this is not for me."

"I never found a taste for alcohol, Uncle."

"Ah. Just as well, perhaps. If you don't like to drink, then don't drink. And if you can't drink then absolutely don't drink, I say. You just become the foolish one in the room, then." And, as if an afterthought, "Your father was also abstemious." Hans Shultz motioned to the hovering maid, in her black dress and white apron. "Coffee for my nephew."

In the sitting room. Leather chairs and leather-covered books and dark wood. Portraits of long-dead German ancestors in armor staring critically down from the walls at them.

Prompted by his uncle, Alexsi told the story of the Communist Shultz family. The tidy little home amid the squalor of the kolkhoz. It was the first time he had ever been able to tell anyone of his love for those people, and for the first time in his life the words rushed out of him. After a while he excused himself and went to his suitcase. It had been thoroughly gone through, most likely when he was washing up. Alexsi wasn't surprised. He had probably made Uncle suspicious when he wouldn't let him carry it. He retrieved the photograph that Yakushev had given him, pressed in a book to keep it safe. The book was another Yakushev parting gift, a lovely leather-bound edition of the Brothers Grimm, in German. The devil's way of letting him know that *he* knew everything. The photo was a portrait of the Shultz family when Freddi was just starting school and Gerdi a toddler. Alexsi had no idea where they'd gotten it.

"This is all I have, Uncle. I took it with me to Baku. During the epidemic the people were ignorant and burned everything."

Hans Shultz only nodded. He stared at the photograph for a very long time. "Your mother was quite beautiful."

"She was a beautiful person, also, Uncle."

"If a boy does not say that about his mother, then there is something wrong." He continued staring at the picture. "And you were working? Not in school?"

"They would never send a German whose parents were not high party officials to university, Uncle."

"So you yourself were not a member of the Communist Party?"

"I know what you are asking, Uncle. I am not a Communist. If I was they would not have let me out. And I would not have wanted to go."

"Then why do you think they let you?"

"Because I was of no importance to them. And I assume they made you pay money for me."

His uncle was noncommittal.

"I will never forget it," Alexsi said fiercely.

Hans Shultz seemed to relax for the first time since meeting the train. "Think nothing of it, my boy. Would you care for a cigar?"

"I've never smoked one, Uncle."

"A cigarette, then."

"Tobacco was always too expensive," Alexsi said with a shrug. "So I never developed the habit. But with your permission, I will try a cigar with you."

Pleased, his uncle selected two cigars from the heavy wood humidor. He took Alexsi through the process: removing the wrapper; clipping, never biting off the end. Lighting with a match, never a lighter. Spreading the flame throughout.

"You must never breathe the smoke into your lungs," Hans Shultz counseled. "Close off your windpipe as you draw. Keep the smoke in your mouth."

Alexsi quickly mastered the technique, including holding the cigar curled over his forefinger as his uncle did.

"You have it," Hans Schultz said. "What do you think?"

"Quite good, Uncle." It really wasn't bad at all. And it seemed now that smoking one yourself was the only effective form of self-defense against the odor in a closed room.

Hans Shultz watched him with open amusement. "Enjoy them in private. But I advise you to avoid smoking them in public until . . . until you acquire some age on your face."

"I would look ridiculous, wouldn't I?" Alexsi said with a smile. "Like a child in a top hat."

Hans Schultz laughed, seemingly in spite of himself. He called for another brandy.

They sat back and smoked in silence for some time. It occurred to Alexsi that Hans Shultz was quite drunk. While the strong coffee had made him forget his fatigue and the heavy meal.

Finally Hans Shultz said, "My brother and I were quite close. But as we became men he was always much more the idealist. I did not share his politics. I knew the old ways would not survive the Great War, but I felt that Communism would wipe out everything that was good in Germany. We were never able to reconcile this. We reached the point where I was embarrassed to have a brother who was a Communist, and he was embarrassed to have a brother who was not. We were too young to put away our politics and meet each other on a personal level. And so I never met your mother. When war broke out, I went into the army and he left Germany. I did not know he went to Russia until later. I have always heard it said that Germans make the best Communists—I have never been able to understand whether this was a compliment or not. When Russia became Bolshevik after the war, contact was impossible." He paused, as if trying to find a way to word it. "You have told me of great hardships . . . I hope my brother was able to keep his ideals."

Alexsi knew that Aunt Emma was still a Communist even

when they were carrying her away in the Black Maria. He wasn't so sure about Otto. "Uncle, I . . . I think it is easier to be a Communist as long as you are free to not be a Communist whenever you wish."

Those blue eyes were looking at him down that cigar like a rifle barrel. Almost the exact same way Yakushev used to sight in on him over his cigarette. "That was very well said, nephew. Very well said. I will be sure to remember it." Another pause. "My poor brother. And you. Were you a disappointment when you did not feel the same as they did?"

"I never mentioned this to anyone, Uncle. In the Soviet Union people disappear for much less. As far as my family, I wanted to please them, but . . ."

"But?"

"Some people believe what they're told, Uncle. I believe what I see."

"Yes. And your parents?"

"They believed what they wished to be. In the end, I think, they were disappointed."

Hans Shultz rolled his cigar between his fingers, contemplating it. "This is the curse of belief. Given enough time, almost inevitably you will be disappointed." He looked up at his nephew. "It is a difficult thing when you become old enough to realize that your parents, who you love and idolize, are just people with feet of clay after all. You think you are alone in this, but it is a passage everyone makes."

"Thank you, Uncle."

"I remember when I lost my parents. And then . . ."

"We are both bereaved, Uncle."

"Yes. My wife was the most terrible driver. I ordered my son to always take the wheel when our chauffeur was not available, but on that particular day he defied me in this. As he did in most things." Another look down at the cigar. "But you cannot allow life to defeat you, nephew. You must carry on."

"I agree, Uncle. You may not be able to get over what has happened to you. But you can always get past it."

"You have an old soul, nephew. I imagine we have Stalin to thank for that."

27

1937 Munich

THE PARK BENCH HAD ARYAN PRINTED ON THE BACK RAILS, IN Gothic letters. Alexsi hadn't seen any benches marked JEW, so obviously Jews were not permitted to sit down. It was the first thing he noticed as he began finding his way around Munich. The Nazis were absolutely mad on the subject of Jews. Not that the Russians liked them overmuch, but this was something else entirely.

All the public accommodations were separately marked Aryan and Jew. People said the Nazis had gotten the idea from how Negroes were treated in America. Pasted on the windows of some stores were professionally printed signs that said: GERMANS BEWARE! DO NOT BUY FROM JEWS. And a brown-uniformed Stormtrooper with gleaming boots and a red, white, and black swastika armband standing by the door glowering at everyone who went inside. Though Alexsi noticed that some people still went in. It was going to take him some time to understand that. If Hitler didn't want people buying in Jewish stores, then why not nail them shut? Perhaps the Nazis didn't feel powerful enough to do that.

He had started reading the Nazi newspapers, particularly *Der Angriff* and *Völkischer Beobachter*. Just like the Soviet newspapers, if you understood how they lied, you could always find a doorway, open just a crack, to what was really going on. They condemned what they were most afraid of. They praised what was going badly. They were so much alike he wondered if Hitler had been taking lessons from Stalin.

The Nazis, it seemed, believed that Jews ran the world and were keeping Germans down. Alexsi thought that if that were really the case, then all the park benches would say JEW and Jews would be standing with their arms folded in front of German stores. And the Nazis seemed to associate Jews with Communism, which they also hated. Alexsi had to concede that there were plenty of Jews among the old Bolsheviks. But Trotsky was in exile, and based on the stories of the purge trials Stalin had pretty much killed the rest of them off.

Alexsi had a paper dish of sausages from the beer garden, and he ate them lovingly as he walked. Munich white sausages with sweet mustard. So good. And unlike Russian sausages you didn't have to take care biting into them in case some bone chips had fallen in the mix.

The English Garden was a park in the center of Munich. And the beer garden was large enough to feed a regiment inside. The park was designed by an Englishman in the late seventeen hundreds. The Germans were happy to tell him about it. Alexsi strolled around with his sausages until he was certain the entire area was clear. Especially since sitting on one of the Aryan benches near a funny-looking wooden structure they called the Chinese Tower was Sergei from that first night in the Lubyanka.

In the end he had to hand it to Yakushev. There was absolutely no difference in running countersurveillance drills in Moscow, where you knew you'd be shot if you failed the course, and doing the same thing in Munich, where you knew the Germans would hang you.

Alexsi took a seat next to Sergei on the bench and pointed with a sausage in his hand. "Tell me, does that look like a pagoda to you?"

"It looks like a German's idea of a pagoda," Sergei replied in

German. "I have a dentist appointment at noon. Would you be so good as to tell me the time?"

"I'm sorry, I don't have a watch," Alexsi replied.

"It's good to see you, David," Sergei said.

"I'm surprised to see you again," said Alexsi.

"Back to the embassy and out of the country by tomorrow," Sergei said. "I lost my Gestapo followers, but I doubt we have more than a few minutes. You are well?"

"Yes."

"Any problems on the trip?"

"None." Alexsi dropped his eyes to the newspaper he had set down on the bench between them. "My report is inside."

"Good," said Sergei. "We watched you the entire way. But it is good practice."

Alexsi knew that was a lie. They wanted him to think they were omnipotent.

Sergei said, "How are relations with your uncle?"

"Good so far. I'm not sure if he has made up his mind about me yet, or if he is just as reserved as every other German."

"We hope for the best," Sergei said pointedly. "He has given you some fine clothes."

"He had the maid burn my Russian suit," Alexsi replied, ignoring the threat. "Would you care for a sausage?"

"Thank you, no. You seem to be adjusting well. At first I thought you were a German as you approached."

"This is what you wanted," Alexsi said pointedly.

"Any homesickness?"

Alexsi's initial reaction to that was, what the hell are you talking about? He had never felt homesick in his life. Maybe because every place he had gone to, however shitty, was always better than the last place he had been. The friends that weren't dead had betrayed him, and it wasn't as if he missed his family. And, however strange, Germany was so unimaginably rich compared to

Russia that it didn't even bear comparison. But it wasn't hard to recognize one of Yakushev's pointed questions—always pointed enough to kill you if you weren't careful—so what he said was "Thank everyone for their concern, but I am fine."

At that moment a uniform was bearing down on them from the walk, and a harsh voice called out, "Stop right there!"

Sergei was getting ready to launch himself out of his seat, preparing to run. Alexsi reached behind the bench so his arm couldn't be seen and grabbed him by the belt, so he bounced up and came back down on the bench.

A burly German, squeezed into his blue uniform like one of the sausages, hat held down securely with the strap under his chin digging into the flesh. Pointing a huge finger that actually seemed larger than one of the sausages. "Trying to get away from me, eh?"

Alexsi could feel Sergei stiffen up next to him. "What do you mean, Comrade?"

"What do you think you're doing there?" the German demanded.

"Having a snack," Alexsi replied calmly. "Want some?"

"You promised to have a beer with me," the German said.

"You were playing," said Alexsi. "And I was hungry. You didn't tell me you'd have another break so soon."

"Another twenty minutes," said the German.

"No problem," said Alexsi. "Let me finish these and I'll meet you over there. You can tell me more about Munich."

"Don't forget," the German said, pointing that huge finger again.

"I won't," said Alexsi.

When he left, Sergei was practically shaking. "Mother of God," he breathed, in the heat of the moment forgetting Communism entirely and lapsing back to the church. "What was that, for fuck's sake?"

"He was playing in the band in the beer garden over there," Alexsi said. "Where I bought these sausages."

"That was a *bandsman*?" Sergei said incredulously.

"Of course," said Alexsi.

"What a fucking country," said Sergei, his voice deflated. "Even the musicians wear uniforms like police, and look like they can't wait to arrest you."

"The Germans do love their uniforms," Alexsi said. When he began doing his countersurveillance drills he'd been continually startled. If it wasn't Stormtroopers with faces like losing boxers strutting along like Olympians, it was boys in the Hitler Youth uniform of brown shirt, black shorts, and that same swastika armband practicing ordering each other about on the way to school. There were so many uniforms it was actually hard to pick out the Order Police in their eagle shako hats, green greatcoats, and pistol belts. "I know what you're thinking. But wherever I'm at I ask the Germans questions about Munich. Since I'm obviously a stranger, they all want to know where I come from, and I put the question back to them to see what my accent sounds like. They say everything from East Prussia to the Bavarian Alps to Sudeten German from Czechoslovakia. So at least I sound like a German to the Germans."

"They're drinking beer and it isn't even noon?" Sergei said.

"The Germans even drink it for breakfast sometimes," Alexsi replied. "They like beer almost as much as uniforms." And you thought the Russians were bad with vodka, he almost said. Almost.

"And what was that 'comrade' about?" Sergei was almost whispering now.

"Oh, the Germans use it all the time, like we do," said Alexsi. "But not the same way. It's like fellowship, not ideological. Are you feeling better now?" It pleased him that Sergei had been a lot more confident and arrogant in Moscow than he was here in the lair of the fascist beast.

"Not really," said Sergei. He took a deep breath, and got back to business as if everything he was supposed to say was also part of a drill. Which it probably was. "Comrade Yakushev salutes you."

"I return his salute," Alexsi said.

"Good. There is money in the bag." Sergei was referring to the paper sack between them. "For everything you might need." He checked his watch. "I must go. Unless you have an emergency, this will be both the first and the last face-to-face meeting."

"Tell everyone not to worry," said Alexsi. "I'm fine."

"I will. Good luck, Comrade."

He said that unconsciously, which made Alexsi smile.

Sergei left, taking Alexsi's newspaper with him.

Alexsi didn't linger so that no one the Gestapo questioned later would associate him with that bench. He ate the last sausage and threw the plate away. And in the public toilet transferred the neat bundles of German Reichsmarks to his underwear and threw away the sack in case anyone remembered seeing Sergei carrying it. As he emerged from the toilet, he noticed two pairs of what had to be Gestapo men sweeping through the area, trying to pick up Sergei's trail. This was why Yakushev hated face-to-face meetings.

28

1937 Munich

"HOW ARE YOU GETTING ALONG?" HANS SHULTZ INQUIRED.

"Very well, Uncle," Alexsi replied. "I am learning my way around the city. But with your permission, I would like to find a job. I should not be idle."

Though neither was smoking, the study smelled as if a century's worth of cigars had been absorbed into the woodwork. Whereas the sitting room was dominated by the portraits of the Shultz family ancestors, the study displayed the heads and pelts of various animals Hans Shultz had dispatched during his various diplomatic assignments. Alexsi couldn't imagine getting any work done with the glass eyes of the lion rug staring accusingly up at you from the floor in front of the fireplace. And the huge wild boar in the corner looked simply furious at being stuffed. An elephant's foot was the ashtray, which always struck Alexsi as a sadly undignified end.

Hans Shultz said, "When almost the first thing you did after you arrived was try to return the money left over from your travel, I said to myself, Here is a boy who is more German than Russian. Here is a boy who has been raised properly. And now you insist on working. My own son would have lain about this house until he was gray. I am proud of you."

"There is nothing to be proud of, Uncle. A man must earn his way." Actually, Alexsi had always enjoyed stealing and smuggling better, but no matter.

"You say that because you have had to work for everything. Still." Hans Schulz paused. "Now we must speak of serious matters."

"Yes, Uncle?"

"I hope you did not mind being examined by Monsignor George. I needed to determine your level of schooling."

"Not at all, Uncle."

"I confide in you that I had a priest do this because I needed someone who could keep his mouth shut."

"I understand, Uncle."

"No doubt he could not resist trying to force some religion into you. You were not offended?"

"Not at all, Uncle. I have read of Roman Catholicism."

"You don't say. From what I understand Stalin insists on being treated as a god."

"Yes, Uncle. I am ignorant of God, but I do know that if you offend Stalin, he will most definitely reach out his hand and destroy you."

At that Hans Shultz laughed so hard he had a coughing fit. Alexsi got up and poured him a glass of water from the carafe on the side table, next to the brandy. He handed over the glass and Hans drank deeply and sat back weakly. He took out a handkerchief and wiped his eyes.

Alexsi had been completely serious. But then you never knew what people were going to find funny, especially Germans. "I hope I didn't give offense."

"No, nephew. Actually, that was the first I have laughed in quite some time." He set the glass back down. "I lost my faith in the trenches at Verdun, but we are an old Catholic family and I still observe the forms for the sake of tradition. Make up your own mind. Just never tell a priest your private business, you understand. They are still men."

"Yes, Uncle."

"Tell them about your sex. They always like that. Your penance for that can cover everything else."

"I understand."

"Returning to the matter at hand. Monsignor George judges your mind to be first class. At university level. Certain gaps in higher mathematics and the sciences such as chemistry are understandable since you did not receive a German education. But he was quite impressed. And it is hard to impress a Jesuit. Clearly you would be wasted as a laborer."

"But that is all I have done, Uncle. It does not bother me."

"And that is to your credit. Allow me to be frank. Your Russian school certificates are the next thing to worthless here in Germany. Along with that, despite your heritage and your excellent German, the authorities will regard you as first a Russian, then a Communist, and therefore always worthy of suspicion. And ordinarily this would doom you to a less than bright future."

"I understand, Uncle. The Russians regarded me as a German."

"Hear me out. I am your uncle, and I am responsible to your parents for your future. There is a way around this. You have . . . or should I say had, a cousin, Walter. The son of my sister Lily in Hamburg. A . . . peculiar boy. There was some business with . . . well, let us just say how it ended. A suicide."

If Alexsi had learned anything, it was to be still.

"You say you have read of the Catholic Church. Well, in addition to being the act of a coward, suicide is a mortal sin. A suicide cannot receive the last rites of the Church, or be buried in consecrated ground. When Walter took his own life the family was shamed. Because of this the facts of his death were not handled in the usual open manner."

There was not a sound in the house except the footsteps of the maid dusting upstairs.

Hans Schultz continued. "I propose that we make a simple change. Friedrich Shultz of Azerbaijan becomes Walter Shultz of Hamburg. With Walter's name you can have the proper papers, and with them you can make your own way in German society without any difficulties from the authorities. And your natural talents can be put to good use."

Ironically enough, it was at that moment Alexsi recognized his Russian soul. Born of suspicious people, suckled on suspicious milk, raised on suspicion and intrigue and betrayal. He saw that Hans Shultz could not carry a Russian nephew along in his world, and, after all his pains, if there was war be forced to say, Here, take my nephew to a concentration camp. Alexsi saw all this, but still wondered if there was something more that he could not see. Because here was the key to his legend as a penetration agent creating another, even more perfect legend for him. "I trust you to do whatever is best for me, Uncle."

Hans Shultz rose up from his chair, leaned over, and slapped Alexsi on the knee. "Good. Good. This will make things much easier." He took his water glass over to the side table and exchanged it for a snifter of brandy.

Alexsi thought there was such finality to the way a German said "good."

Hans Shultz savored his brandy and his nephew's agreement for a moment, then went on. "In combination with this, I have made a transfer to the Foreign Ministry in Berlin. Which will require a move. You are in accord?"

"Of course, Uncle." A change of city along with a change in identity. Hans Schultz was thorough. He couldn't have people in Munich who knew him saying, What about that nephew of yours? Especially since he was the Foreign Ministry representative to Brown House, the Nazi Party headquarters in Munich. He would certainly have the connections to arrange a new assignment in Berlin. And, obviously, a change in official documents. Or perhaps a disappearance of certain documents. Knowing a little something about that particular subject, Alexsi was sure someone would have to be bribed.

"I have been looking over the curriculum at the University of Berlin. Something that would be appropriate to both your interests and future prospects. There is always literature, of course, as preparation for a career in law. But Monsignor George felt that your language skills might be more extensive than you admitted."

"It seemed something I should not reveal without consulting you first, Uncle."

"And that shows good judgment. Have you other languages besides German and Russian, nephew?"

"I can read English, Uncle, and write it somewhat less well. I barely speak it, though, and my ear is not nearly quick enough to converse. But I grew up with Azeri, which is almost identical to Turkish. And I speak Persian fluently."

"Most impressive. Such would be the envy of any diplomat. What would you say to a course in Oriental Studies at the University of Berlin?"

"Whatever you think best, Uncle. Would admission be difficult?"

Hans Shultz waved that obstacle away. "I have some influence. Let that be my problem. And despite his other difficulties with a normal life, Walter's grades in school were actually quite good."

29

1938 Berlin

ALEXSI KNEW IT WAS PAST MIDNIGHT, BUT HE DIDN'T WANT TO look at his watch until he finished the assignment. The other students at the University of Berlin moaned about the work, but it was a holiday compared to Yakushev's spy school. He barely knew what to do with all the free time. He'd built himself a radio but the NKVD ordered it cached unless war severed his links with the Soviet embassy. As soon as Uncle Hans settled them in Berlin, he'd set up what the Russians called a *taynik* to pass along his reports. He wrote one a week on what his uncle talked about from the Foreign Ministry, and any interesting documents from his uncle's briefcase. Those were the only secrets he knew, so the Russians could ask for nothing else. It was a grand, easy life.

His professor wanted the poems of Hafiz compared to the work they inspired, Goethe's *West-Eastern Divan*. Of course they had to bring a German into it. Alexsi didn't think it would go over well if he actually put down what he thought, that the classical Iranians wrote poetry with a feather while the Germans used a hammer and chisel. Except the West insisted on calling them Persians. Which would be news to everyone who lived there and had called themselves ēran-ians for a millennium. Not that it would matter in the least to a European.

He finished the last paragraph and made sure he had all his footnotes written down correctly. He'd type it up in the morning at home. The library typewriter room was crowded at all hours, and the racket was enough to drive you mad.

Otherwise the Berlin University library was wonderful. The Nazis only banned a fraction of the books the Soviets did, and as always they were mostly concerned with Jewish and anti-Nazi writers. Alexsi always had to fight off the urge to wander the stacks and pluck out interesting-looking titles instead of sitting down to his coursework. And when he needed some air, he could step outside, walk down the Unter den Linden, through the Brandenburg Gate, and be right in the urban forest of the Tiergarten, where the Electors of Brandenburg had hunted animals right in the city. It was a wonderful place to take lunch by yourself. It was also the location of his *taynik*. The Germans, he had been told, called it a dead letter box. A hiding place where you could pass documents back and forth without personal contact. His was a waterproof piece of pipe with a screw-on top, driven into the ground next to a prominent tree beside one of the little ponds. He placed his reports in the drop and another NKVD agent, who had no idea who he was, acted as postman and sent it along to Moscow.

Alexsi was gathering up his homework when someone began shouting at the other end of the floor, near the stairs. People were hissing, "Silence!" but the shouting kept on. Alexsi stood up so he could look over the top of his carrel and see what the disturbance was about.

Elizabeth, who had the next carrel, said, "What do you think is happening, Walter?"

Alexsi shrugged.

The person who was yelling was running down the length of the floor, but Alexsi couldn't make out what he was saying. An overtired and fed up scholar finally shouted back, "Why don't you shut up?"

Then finally it was close enough to hear. "They're rioting against the Jews!"

People were coming out of the stacks into the central aisle. "Who's rioting?" someone demanded.

"Everyone" came the reply. "The SA. The SS."

"Then it's official?" someone else asked.

Alexsi hid his smile away. Only a German would ask if a riot was officially authorized.

"I knew this would happen," someone said.

"I heard on the radio," said another voice. "Vom Rath died tonight."

Two days before a Jew in Paris had shot a German diplomat. Yesterday the German government had stripped the Jews of their rights as citizens.

"Let's go see," a student said. And at that everyone began moving toward the stairs.

"Do you want to go, Walter?" said Ernst, who along with Elizabeth was also in the Oriental Studies program.

"I want to go see," Elizabeth chimed in. She made no secret about the fact that she was at university to find a university husband. All of which made Alexsi careful to keep her at arm's length. Though he would have advised her, as a hausfrau to be, that she ought to go easy on the potatoes until after the wedding. "You know there's no stadium seating for a riot," he said. "You're right on the field."

"I'm not afraid," Ernst declared.

That's just because you're too stupid to realize you ought to be, Alexsi thought. Ernst was the classic blond-haired, blue-eyed German boy. A good little Hitler Youth, except he was constantly torn, to Alexsi's constant amusement, between his love of American big bands and obedience to the Nazi line that considered it degenerate Jewish and Negro music. "Let's go up to the roof and see what we're getting into first."

"Yes, that's a good idea," said Ernst.

Alexsi stacked his books and notebooks up in the corner of the carrel.

"You're not taking your books?" Elizabeth said.

"No, I'm not walking into the middle of a riot with my hands full of books," Alexsi replied.

"Another good idea," Ernst decided.

Alexsi just rolled his eyes.

They went up the stairs, and the door to the roof had a prominent sign mounted on it: ACCESS FORBIDDEN. But it wasn't locked. Alexsi pushed it open.

"But it's forbidden," Ernst said.

"I can read," Alexsi replied. "If you like, you can *imagine* what's going on outside while you wait here for someone to give you permission."

Elizabeth followed him through the door. Then Ernst.

The air smelled of fire. There were scattered pillars of smoke and flame throughout the city, but nothing like wholesale devastation. The streets seemed full of people, especially for after midnight on a Thursday. But no one was running about. It didn't seem like any riot Alexsi had ever heard of. Not that he had any experience with riots. The Soviets had learned from the mistakes of the Tsarists, and everyone knew they would instantly machine-gun anyone who even looked like the thought of rioting had crossed their minds.

Ernst pointed to the north, where there was much more smoke. "A lot of Jews live there."

Elizabeth was tugging at Alexsi's arm. "Do you think we can go see, Walter?"

Alexsi knew that his uncle, not to mention everyone else he served, would want a report of what was really happening. "All right. Just understand that anything can happen."

But no one was listening to him. They were watching the fires and their eyes were shining with excitement.

They joined a group spilling out of the library and turned north on the Artilleriestrasse. The moon was just past full, and as they crossed the Ebert Bridge over the River Spree it shone white on the rippling black water.

The smoke was thicker as they walked up Artillery Street. Soon their feet were crunching on broken glass. The sidewalk was carpeted with it. A crowd was gathered before a storefront with a gaping hole where the glass display window had been. A group of men were inside chopping everything to pieces with axes. They were wearing civilian clothes but their brawler faces had the unmistakable look of Stormtroopers.

To Alexsi it was the strangest thing. The crowd was watching without a sound. All you could hear was the sound of chopping and breaking inside.

"What a waste," an old man standing next to Alexsi said.

"What do you mean, sir?" Alexsi asked, genuinely curious.

"Just look," the old man said, waving toward the empty shop window and the glass on the ground. "They can't leave it like this. Someone will have to clean it up and put new glass in the window. Everything broken. That's good money wasted, young man. Who will pay for it? We will."

"Yes, that's right," someone nearby muttered. A few others added to the chorus of agreement. But no one said a word to the Stormtroopers with axes.

Alexsi continued up the street, by now not really paying attention to whether Elizabeth and Ernst were still with him.

He ran into another crowd, but instead of being silent this one was jeering loudly. People were holding up their children so they could see. They were shouting, "Hit him!" And, "See! That's what you get!" "Dirty Jew!" "That'll teach you!" "Serves you right!"

Alexsi pushed through so he could see. A man was sitting on the curb, hands clasped to his head with blood streaming through his hands. A Stormtrooper was standing over him with a club. A woman in a nightgown was sobbing, holding a baby in her arms and hunched over the child as if trying to completely cover it from the world. And a dark-haired little boy was standing next to the bleeding man, grasping his sleeve with a white-knuckled grip, shivering uncontrollably. Alexsi knew what that was about, and it wasn't the chill of the November night air.

There was a crack from above that made everyone look up. A piano came sailing out a second-story window. The crowd surged backward, people stumbling over each other. The piano landed in the street with a crash, splintering into pieces.

"What a shame," said a voice next to Alexsi.

He turned his head. It was Elizabeth. She was looking up at him, shaking her head. "It's not the piano's fault who plays it, is it?"

Alexsi just kept pushing through the crowd. He didn't care about anything else, but he didn't want to have to look at that shivering, terrified little boy any longer.

He passed more glassless storefronts. The Germans were amazing. Anywhere else there would be a stream of people helping themselves to what was inside. But here no one even seemed to be thinking about it. Of course, it wasn't as if the streets had been emptied of authority. Now and then you saw a policeman calmly walking about as if to make sure the rioting remained orderly.

At the next intersection he followed the commotion and turned right on Oranienburgerstrasse. There was a big crowd gathered in front of the Jewish synagogue there, the big one with the Moorish domes.

A bonfire was burning on the sidewalk right in front of the synagogue doors. Now and then men came out of the building and threw something onto it. Broken furniture. Books. Alexsi recognized the distinctive Jewish candelabra. And there were some big paper scrolls blazing away. Perhaps that was the Jewish holy book.

A truck from the Berlin fire brigade was parked across the street. The firemen were just sprawled in their seats, casually watching. But being German they still had their helmets on.

Alexsi walked over to one of the firemen who was leaning against the side of the truck, smoking a cigarette. "What's going on, Comrade?"

"We're standing by to make sure the fire doesn't spread to anything German," the fireman replied.

Granted, it was Germany, but Alexsi still thought it was all pretty well organized for a riot.

Young boys were throwing rocks up at the synagogue windows, then looking around quickly to see if anyone was going to stop them. When they saw they were free to continue, they went running off, shouting excitedly, and returned with armfuls of stones.

The crowd was shouting, "Burn it! Burn it all!"

Alexsi heard a stern German female *tsk* beside him. It came from an elegant-looking gray-haired lady whose face was grave in the firelight.

"What's wrong, madame?" he asked.

"If they can do this, the Catholic church will be next," she said with finality. And then when he turned back an instant later, she was gone.

The crowd at the eastern end of the street seemed to buck and heave. An Order Policeman in a shako and greatcoat and pistol belt broke through the mob of onlookers. He took one look at the fire and rushed through the synagogue doors.

"What's all that about?" someone asked.

A minute later Stormtroopers in civilian clothes carrying axes and crowbars began to spill out the front door. The policeman brought up the rear, pushing them out.

"What's going on here?" a voice from back in the crowd inquired plaintively, as if they were watching a motion picture and there had been a plot twist no one understood.

As soon as the Stormtroopers were out the door they suddenly turned about and began screaming at the policeman, who shouted back.

Alexsi edged forward carefully, trying to find the right balance between close enough to hear and far enough away not to get pulled in if some real violence suddenly broke out.

"Go back to your station!" the leader of the Stormtroopers screamed at the policeman. Alexsi knew he was the leader because he was pointing with his finger while all the rest were brandishing axes and tools. "It's all arranged! We have our orders!"

"This building is a protected historical landmark!" the policeman shouted back.

"Get lost!" the Stormtroopers screamed back. "You're in for trouble."

The crowd had now fallen totally silent in the face of this spectacle. Alexsi recognized their instinct. No one wanted to be on the wrong side of whoever won the argument. Just like at the shop before—be on the side of the ones doing the beating and you're safe; be on the side of the ones being beaten and you risked a beating yourself.

Some of the Stormtroopers took a few steps forward with their axes raised, trying to intimidate the cop into retreating.

Instead the policeman drew his pistol. At that there was a sharp gasp from the crowd, and people began backing up. The Stormtroopers did, too.

"I will uphold the law requiring this building's protection!" the policeman shouted. "You have been warned! Now get out of here before I open fire!"

Alexsi wasn't completely surprised when the Stormtroopers began slinking off like bullies who had been punched in the mouth.

The policeman blew a shrill blast on his whistle, waving over the fire brigade. Like good Germans, they hopped on their truck and motored across the street, following the policeman's orders and putting out the bonfire before it could spread inside the synagogue.

Once the fire was extinguished in a sooty, wet hiss, the crowd also began to slink away. A loud muttering rose up as everyone debated the pros and cons of the policeman's actions. If he had orders then he had to follow them, was the general consensus.

Alexsi was certain he didn't have orders. On a night when everything Jewish was being destroyed, and the fire brigade standing by to make sure only the right things burned, he doubted there were orders for one cop to defy the SA and protect the biggest synagogue in Berlin. That fellow, he thought, was going to have an interesting future.

Elizabeth and Ernst were gone, lost in the crowds. Depending on where you were walking, the streets were either full or deserted. If Jews were being abused there was a crowd watching it. And everyone who lived nearby was awake and standing out on their stoops to make sure what was happening didn't spread to their building. Most of the people standing in front of their homes had little booklets in their hands. It didn't register on Alexsi until he'd seen them over and over again. Everyone was keeping their *Ahnenpass* handy to prove they weren't a Jew. The Nazi document traced your lineage back four generations and proved you were an Aryan. It was full of the signatures and official stamps that both the Nazis and the Soviets loved so much.

When he first received Walter Shultz's little red booklet, Alexsi secretly found it hilarious. The Iranians of course called themselves Aryans, while the Germans seemed to associate it with Nordics and considered the brown people of the world racially inferior. At his uncle Hans's parties people would compliment him on his fine Aryan nephew. They weren't aware they were clucking over a subhuman Slav.

Yes, wave your little booklet at them, Alexsi thought. Maybe that will save your house from being burned, your furniture chopped up, your family beaten, and you dragged off to a camp. Tonight. On another night you'll be holding the wrong book and it won't save you. And the thieves of the world, who own nothing, will laugh at you as they slip away free into the darkness. Or take away the last of your precious things in prison.

At one elegant-looking mansion the iron gates were thrown open and a truck was parked in front of the entrance. Alexsi watched black-uniformed SS loading silver and paintings into it. So someone was making out, he thought.

He was just walking west now, in the rough direction of his uncle's house. There must not be anything Jewish around here, because the streets were deserted.

Echoing noise as a group of teenage boys ran by, right down the center of the street. All pent up and howling out their freedom on this night. Then the one out in front stopped suddenly, and the others followed suit. They held a little conference and the leader, walking now, circled back toward the sidewalk Alexsi was coming down.

Alexsi still had his knife from Russia. It had actually provoked considerable debate in Moscow, with all kinds of talk about border searches and creating suspicions. Yakushev finally shut them down by declaring that a boy who could smuggle a blade into the Lubyanka undetected would certainly manage to get it into Germany without any problems. But here in Berlin his uncle's maid was bound to go running to him about any sheaths sewn into underwear. Alexsi slid his hand into his pocket and cupped the knife in his palm, the blade still folded away.

They walked up to him. Alexsi's first thought was that, just like at the orphanage, and the Lubyanka, there was always three. For some reason it took that many to make them feel confident. They were a year or two older than him, dressed like workingmen, out of school.

There was no one else on the street. Even though there were lights in some windows, Alexsi wasn't expecting any help from the good citizens of Berlin

The leader said, "Look, a Jew."

The other two slid around to cut off his retreat.

"I'm not a Jew," Alexsi said calmly.

"Then what are you?" the leader asked, taking a step closer.

"A student," Alexsi said.

The leader took another step forward and shoved him in the chest with both hands. Alexsi passively let the shove take him a few steps back, and prepared to be grabbed from behind.

"I hate students almost as much as I hate Jews," the leader announced.

The pair behind laughed. Alexsi silently thanked them for pinpointing their location for him. He just smiled broadly.

At that the leader's face twisted up. "I'll wipe that smile off your face," he hissed, aiming another shove.

But as it came in Alexsi lunged forward, knocked both those hands up with his left arm, and punched the blade up under the rib cage. He briefly enjoyed the look on the little bastard's face before twisting his wrist to cut what hadn't already been cut and loosen the blade for extraction.

One of the pair behind him grabbed him around the neck. Alexsi leaned back into him to loosen the grip, spun half around, and quickly stabbed him in the guts. There was a startled "What?" and the hands around his neck loosened. Alexsi turned inside him, got a good grip on his jacket, and drove the knife up between his hands right into the center of the throat. A wide-eyed look, a gargled sound, another quick twist, and a sidestep as it came out to keep from being sprayed with blood.

A look of sheer horror from the third one at what had just happened and he was off and running now. Alexsi was after him, and the adrenaline was making their feet fly.

The shit was screaming, "Help! Help!"

Alexsi was briefly alarmed, and knew if anyone showed up he'd be the one who'd end up being chased. Then he realized that on this particular night absolutely no one in Germany would be coming to the assistance of anyone running through the streets screaming for help.

They ran for blocks, Alexsi close enough to hear the other boy heaving and crying in panic. Then, making a last-second decision to cut over onto a side street, the boy stumbled when it changed from pavement to cobblestone.

Alexsi was on him. He jumped onto the boy's back and let his weight drive him into the ground. With his knees on the boy's back, Alexsi grabbed his hair and pulled his head back.

"Please don't kill me," the boy blurted out, just before Alexsi passed the blade under his throat and made the killing cut.

"I don't like bullies," Alexsi told him, getting to his feet as the boy on the ground twitched and bled to death with no sound but a faint whistle of air through his cut windpipe.

He wanted to run, but made himself walk quickly away from the body. All the good Germans who had watched from their windows and done nothing would now be venturing out their doors with battery torches in their hands, calling for policemen and being helpful good citizens.

Now the feeling of pounding excitement and genuine pleasure at paying those three off gave way to familiar cold fear. This wasn't Russia, where they only cared about political crimes and you only got caught if someone squealed or if they were specifically hunting you.

But Alexsi shrugged that off a moment later. It was the knife or a beating, and his days of being beaten were over. As he walked he wiped the knife off with a handkerchief. The wise move would be to throw it away so it wouldn't be found on his person, but it was lucky and he couldn't give it up. He rubbed the blood from it and his hands with the handkerchief, which did go into a trash receptacle.

Under a streetlight he examined his clothing for signs of blood but didn't see any.

Alexsi briefly filtered himself through a crowd watching a stand-alone Jewish house burn to the ground. A streetcar arrived right in the midst of it with utter punctuality, and he climbed aboard.

HANS SHULTZ was in the sitting room when he came through the front door. "I've been listening to the radio," he said. "If they say it's bad it must be even worse."

Alexsi realized it was his uncle's German way of giving voice to those things he would never say, such as "Are you all right?" and "I've been worried." "Give me a moment for the toilet, Uncle, and I'll tell you all about it."

In the light of the bath he made a much more detailed check of his clothing. With clinical detachment he noted that his shirt cuff and jacket sleeve were stained black with dried blood. The maid would lose her mind if he threw them into the laundry bin. He ran water in the sink and set them to soak. There was blood under his fingernails, and the creases of his hands. In the closed room it was clear just how much he smelled of smoke. And who knew if there were any other droplets of blood, perhaps on his hair in the back, that he couldn't see? He'd been careless enough already. Alexsi filled the tub and bathed quickly but thoroughly, scrubbing himself all over with a brush. He went downstairs in his pajamas and robe.

Hans Schultz listened intently to Alexsi's account of what was going on in the streets. Minus the three killings, of course.

He lit a cigarette. "Of course there is nothing spontaneous about this, nephew, as you correctly surmised. The party has been waiting for a chance to confiscate Jewish money and property, and this assassination is merely a convenient pretext. The Jew in Paris, well, it seems that his parents were among the Polish Jews living in Germany that Hitler expelled last month. And then Poland would not accept them so they are trapped in no-man's-land on the border. So he decides to shoot someone at the German embassy, in protest. And randomly chooses my unfortunate fellow diplomat vom Rath, who I happen to know was under investigation by the Gestapo for pro-Jewish sympathies. Whatever this young man hoped to accomplish, he has now single-handedly disenfranchised all the Jews in Germany." He shook his head. "Too many ironies. No one would believe it."

"I can believe it, Uncle," Alexsi replied.

"This puts an end, it would seem, to the legend about Jews being smart," said Hans Shultz. "I have no sympathy. Any Jew who stayed in Germany after the Nuremberg Laws were passed deserves to have his house burned down for sheer stupidity alone. They must have thought Hitler couldn't last." He shook his head. "Foolish."

"Excuse me, Uncle, but in Russia they hate the Jews, too. But I don't understand it as the basis of a political movement."

Hans Shultz gave him a wry look. "Whatever is popular succeeds politically, nephew. Jew hatred is as old as the written word in Germany. Why, even Luther wrote almost as much about hating Jews as he did about reforming the Church. But as far as National Socialism, let us look at it this way. One can say that Germany lost the Great War because it foolishly insisted on fighting the entire world, and the home front fell apart in 1918 because everyone knew we couldn't win, was sick of war, and tired of being hungry. Or one can say that the home front fell apart in 1918 because Jewish Communists betrayed the nation and the undefeated fighting men. And that Jews caused the inflation later that made the money worthless and everyone poor."

"Which do you believe, Uncle?" Alexsi asked mildly.

Hans Shultz gave him another look. "Nephew, at various times during the war I personally fought the French, Serbs, Romanians, and Italians. So give me credit for not being an idiot, please. Still, it would be more pleasant to believe in the latter, wouldn't it? Everything that happened, happened to you. You are not at fault." He was standing at the window, and he pushed the drape back with his hand and peered out as if he was searching for a sign of the dawn. "Now when the Jews are pushed down, the ignorant are getting rid of someone they hate. The intelligent are getting rid of a business or intellectual competitor. And the party will be gaining a great deal of money, which confidentially they were almost out of." Now he turned back to Alexsi. "It's hard to explain how bad things were in the twenties, nephew. Not as bad as what you've described to me of Russia, but bad for Germany. We couldn't go on as we had. Democracy had failed—people were sick of it. They wanted one man to take control and give them orders. Hitler was an inevitability. Hindenburg was too old to resist him any longer. The businessmen backed him. People wanted bread and work. As far as his Jew mania, most people agreed with him. The rest didn't care and still don't. So you make your accommodation or get out. I am a German. And a German who is too old to start a new career."

Alexsi sat there silently. Germans didn't make confessions, they made statements. And this statement just happened to be extremely important. Because, as he'd learned in Russia, you couldn't bargain with an ideological zealot. But an opportunist was always open to negotiation.

Then Hans Shultz said, "The main question, of course, is what happens now? I have always been a pupil of the great Bismarck, in that it is far better to try to anticipate and alter events rather than simply react to them." He plopped himself back down in his chair and rubbed his chin. "The world will be outraged at this pogrom, of course. I see Goebbels's hand in the excesses of it, the destruction. He was on the outs with Hitler, and this is his attempt to reingratiate himself. And it will probably work. When the reaction from abroad comes in, Hitler will feel both besieged and confirmed in his worst instincts about the rest of the world. And when Hitler feels besieged he always lashes out." Hans Shultz looked up. "There will be war. It was always inevitable, but this will accelerate the process. Hitler will begin pushing at the world, and we shall see how much the world is willing to take. I think it would be best if you put your studies aside for the time being, nephew. And joined the army."

"Do you really think so, Uncle?" Alexsi asked. The Soviets at least would be pleased about it.

Hans Shultz nodded. "If you are going into the water no matter what, it is always best to dive in rather than be pushed. At least one can control where one lands."

30

1940 Berlin

ALEXSI STRAINED HIS NECK TO LOOK DOWN THE LINE OF FIELD gray uniforms arrayed along the walk on Tirpitzufer, then checked his wristwatch. His orders said to enter through Tirpitzufer 72–76, the four-story sandstone building up ahead that housed the Navy High Command. The problem was, everyone who worked there was lined up to do the same damned thing. If the queue didn't move any faster he would be late on his first day. This would not do.

A curious thing. He didn't see any enlisted men. Not that he blamed them, thinking back to his days as a sergeant officer candidate. He'd have gone a kilometer out of his way to keep from having to salute this many officers. It was bad enough being a first lieutenant with all the senior officers in Berlin.

Uncle Hans had gotten him posted to the Third Infantry Division, a Prussian Berlin unit. He'd emerged from training just in time to join it for the invasion of Czechoslovakia. Which was more like a training march through Czechoslovakia, really. The Czechs surrendered so completely that the only gunfire Alexsi experienced was one night when a drunken captain shot himself trying to get his Luger back into the holster.

Alexsi didn't think there was much of interest about an infantry company garrisoning a Czech town, though Yakushev always emphasized that you never knew what would be of value. There were no NKVD to pass along information with a *taynik,* so he mailed the occasional report to a box in a Berlin post office covered by Soviet agents. Invisible writing between the lines of an anonymous love letter with a false return to sender. Two and a half grams of aspirin dissolved in four hundred grams of water was his ink. Aspirin was always available. It was a German invention, after all. Since one of his duties was censoring his company's mail, the risk was negligible. His goal was to keep everyone happy with him, both Russian and German, while staying happily alive himself.

One thing that Yakushev always hammered into him was fighting the urge to confide. Alexsi never had the urge to confide in anyone. He made friends. People liked him, and he liked them. But when he moved on he never missed anyone, and never felt the urge everyone else had to stay in touch. He always had to turn homesick soldiers over to a sympathetic sergeant because when they whined they felt he looked at them as if they were crazy.

Upon the division's return to Germany everyone got a campaign medal and there were rumors the Third would be turned into a mechanized unit. Before that could happen, Uncle Hans sat the new lieutenant down after dinner and made another one of his proposals. Alexsi had been prepared for the glory or death speech, but Hans surprised him by pointing out that he was the only survivor of his officer training class in the Great War, and with his languages perhaps his nephew would be happier in Abwehr, the German military intelligence service.

It was so perfect Alexsi couldn't help being suspicious, but the Russians were overjoyed. Hans pulled some more strings and Alexsi began his second spy school, not unhappy to have missed the invasions of Poland and France, where a great many more infantry lieutenants were killed than in Czechoslovakia.

Now he just had to get into the building. Based on his experience enlisted men might not be smarter than officers, but they were certainly more clever. Alexsi gave up his place in line and walked briskly back down the tree-lined street, circling around behind the next building. Ah, there they all were. The enlisted going in the back door. Alexsi picked out his man, a mild-looking young sergeant wearing wire eyeglasses and the blue piping of support troops. A clerk.

"Sergeant!" he called out.

The sergeant whirled about and saluted. "Sergeant Dormer, sir!"

Alexsi returned it casually and flipped open the box of Memphis cigarettes he always carried but never used.

Surprised, the sergeant took one and Alexsi lit him up. "I'm Lieutenant Shultz. Listen, Sergeant Dormer, I need your help. I have an appointment with Admiral Canaris and with the line out front I'm going to be late. How do I get into the damned building?"

The sergeant looked him up and down, the white infantry piping on his shoulder boards, the single pip of a first lieutenant, the Sudetenland ribbon, and the diving eagle parachutist badge he'd gotten in training. German paratroopers were air force, not army, so it marked you as Abwehr to anyone who knew what to look for. "You can't be late for the admiral, sir. Follow me."

They went in a side door that was completely unguarded. Alexsi could just imagine trying to enter the Lubyanka that way. You'd get a hundred bullet holes in you just for *knocking* on the wrong door.

It wasn't an office building, it was a mansion that was being used as an office building. And if Sergeant Dormer hadn't been leading him, Alexsi might have been walking the halls lost until lunch.

Up the stairs and a few turns, and the sergeant waved him toward a massive oak door. "Here you are, sir."

Alexsi offered his hand. "Sergeant Dormer, if you ever need a favor, I'm at your service."

The sergeant returned a shy, limp handshake, then popped his heels and saluted. "Good morning, sir."

Alexsi just shook his head once the sergeant turned his back. Germans.

HE HAD been warned. Not the Hitler salute. A military one. Alexsi cracked his heels together and held the knife hand to the brim of his service cap, ignoring the snuffling sounds coming from the vicinity of his boots. "Lieutenant Shultz reporting for duty, Admiral."

The white-haired man behind the desk had only looked up from his papers when Alexsi came marching into his office. At first with an expression of mildly annoyed surprise, as if wondering how this person had ever gotten past the two Cerberus-like secretaries who guarded his door. Since, unlike Alexsi, he was both bareheaded and wearing a civilian suit, he only nodded instead of returning the salute. After Alexsi dropped his arm he said, "You may remove your cap and take a seat, Shultz."

"Thank you, Admiral." Alexsi whipped off his cap and tucked it away under his left arm before sitting down.

After peering at him intently for a moment, the white-haired man plucked a few papers from the untidy mountain on his desk and flipped through them, pen poised for signature. Behind him on a clothes stand hung a German naval uniform so shabby that any ensign daring to wear it would have been court-martialed. The office was spartan. Apart from the desk there was a sofa, a few filing cabinets, and a neatly made cot tucked against a wall. Behind him closed glass doors indicated a balcony. On the walls were a large map of the world, inscribed photographs of no one Alexsi recognized save the Spanish dictator Franco, and a Japanese painting of what looked like some sort of devil.

Recognizing that the silent treatment was a test of his composure, Alexsi tried to look relaxed but not bored. A light pressure on his boot caught his attention, and he looked down. Two bright-eyed dachshunds had their forepaws on his legs, staring up at him expectantly. Alexsi reached down and lifted them both up into his lap. Now they were trying to climb up his chest and lick his face. A little stroking and chest rubbing and soon they were each sitting poised on his thighs, gazing up at him with dreamy expressions while he played with their ears.

When Alexsi turned his attention from the dogs he saw the head of the German intelligence service smiling at him. "You make me jealous, eh?" said Wilhelm Canaris. He was speaking to the dogs. At the sound of him opening a desk drawer both dachshunds stiffened up and whirled about. He held up two biscuits and they shot off Alexsi's lap like a pair of stubby-legged blurs.

The admiral made them beg and then gave in. "Now be good," he told the dogs indulgently. "We have business to do."

He now gave Alexsi his full attention. "I don't trust a man who doesn't like dogs," he said. "And I trust the judgment of mine. You would be surprised. They take one look at a man and hide under my desk."

Alexsi kept his face blank and nodded politely. He sensed that his mission was accomplished, and telling the admiral how wonderful his dogs were would only mark him as a sycophant.

Canaris flipped open a file. "So, Shultz. Training completed. Honor graduate. Highest marks. Great aptitude. Well done." He looked up at him again, blue eyes punching through incredibly bushy white eyebrows. "More to the point, I see that when you received orders to join us, your division commander, General Lichel, was absolutely furious, and tried everything possible in order to keep you. It speaks well of you. Many commanders try to gift us their unwanted officers who happen to have another language. All in all, excellent. However, your application to join Abwehr I East is denied."

"Yes, Admiral," Alexsi replied politely. He knew the Russians would want him in the department working against Russia.

"I have enough Russian speakers," Canaris stated. "But a promising young officer who speaks Persian and Turkish is another matter. You have been to the region?"

Alexsi reminded himself to be on his toes. This scrupulously polite old grandfather had single-handedly escaped from Chile during the Great War when his cruiser was interned after the Falkland Islands battles. Including passing right through enemy Britain in order to get back home to blockaded Germany. After that even the military could appreciate that he was suited to intelligence work. "Unfortunately, no, Admiral. It has always been a dream of mine."

"Then it will be fulfilled. Allow me to give you some background. Our efforts in Iran to date have been admittedly spotty. Despite being the source of Britain's petroleum, our attention has been on France and then England herself. But there are conditions that can be exploited if done properly. As in every area of British influence, local feeling runs against them. However, our intelligence officers there have been working under diplomatic cover, unfortunately to no good effect. Recently Captain Leverkuehn, posing as the German consul in Tabriz, had his identity accidentally revealed under embarrassing circumstances."

At that moment the admiral startled Alexsi by letting out exactly the same German exhalation of disapproval that Emma Shultz had often used back in Azerbaijan when he was a boy. "The German minister in Iran, Mr. Ettel, has risen from clerk to SS brigadier in the past eight years."

Canaris seemed to feel this was explanation enough. "I propose to send a man into Iran under commercial cover, specifically as the representative of a Swiss textile firm we have a hidden controlling interest in. Persian carpets, you understand."

"Yes, Admiral," Alexsi replied. This was like being briefed for a mission by Beria himself. Impossible in the Soviet Union. But he had already heard that Canaris did not like to delegate anything.

Officers in Abwehr complained that it was chaos whenever he forgot an order he had given, or failed to file the papers.

"This man's mission," Canaris went on, "will be to take possession of a radio that will be cached by the German embassy. But otherwise to remain aloof from the embassy. And begin establishing agent networks. With a secondary mission of preparing sabotage actions. Do you follow me?"

From his training Alexsi knew that German army officers were focused on how to defeat the enemy on the hill in front of them. Rather than how to win the war, which was not necessarily the same thing. And German intelligence was a military service. Because of this they regarded spying as sending an officer out in a tweed jacket with a camera and a Michelin guide to see if the roads would bear the weight of tanks, or counting how many aircraft were on an airfield and how many troops were massed in a given sector. Or blowing up an ammunition dump, an arms factory, or a bridge. Not so much developing spies who would report on the enemy's counsels from within his own camp. With that in mind, he decided to take a risk. "No, Admiral," he replied.

Now Canaris looked surprised. "No? How have I lost you, Shultz?"

"Sabotage what, Admiral?"

Canaris seemed to give him a second glance full of new appreciation. "You keep your countenance well, Shultz. I don't think you are stupid, so I think you invite me to say more than I wish. Instead, why don't you ask *me* questions?"

At that moment the intercom buzzed. Canaris punched down the button. "No disturbances." Then, "Go ahead, Shultz."

"My question was about the mission, Admiral. What exactly will I prepare to sabotage, and why? The British oil operation in southern Iran? Iranian military installations? Transportation?"

"You will not sabotage the British petroleum wells, pipelines, or particularly the Abadan refinery without specific orders," Canaris stated. "Or the Trans-Iranian railway network."

Alexsi sat silently.

"Good," said Canaris, tapping his mouth with both index fingers. "What does this tell you?"

Now he reminded Alexsi of no one so much as his old professor Yakushev. "That we intend to take them," he said. "Though I don't see how."

"You don't? Rommel has been consistently victorious in the desert."

"If Afrika Korps takes Egypt," said Alexsi, "they still have to cross the Suez Canal. Then Sinai, Palestine, Transjordan, and Iraq. Even with heavy reinforcement our supply lines will grow longer, and the British will be able to move forces by sea from India and Africa. An attack from the Levant? The mountains are not tank country, and a defensive infantry fight there is to the British advantage. Will the Vichy French in Syria fight for us, and if they do, will the same soldiers who lost France make any difference? A revolt in Iraq? A revolt in Iran?" He only raised an eyebrow at that. "You did not ask me to prepare the ground in Iran for a revolt against the Shah."

"I didn't, did I? Excellent, Shultz. It seems these days our officer schools are teaching a strategic appreciation our generals seem to lack. So allow me to turn the tables and ask you a question now. What do you see as Germany's next strategic move in this war?"

"Invade Britain. Finish them off. If the British Empire falls, then the Middle East all the way to India is ours without a fight; the Far East to India will belong to Japan. If America ever enters the war, it would be impossible for them to invade Europe from across the Atlantic."

"I confide in you with no small regret that the Führer has no confidence in the ability of the German navy to move the army across the English Channel. There will be no invasion of England."

Alexsi went cold. After crushing Poland in less than a month, and France in just a little while longer, they weren't going to try to cross the thirty-four kilometers of water that would leave them masters of half the world? Then Hitler was going to gamble on the two-front war that had doomed Germany the last time. Like Napoleon he was going to invade Russia. Stalin had sat on his hands and made it possible for Hitler to win all those victories, to take Europe. And Alexsi knew why. It was pure Marxism-Leninism: let the capitalist world bleed itself. But now Hitler saw Stalin as the old crocodile waiting beneath the water with just its eyes visible, regarding him coldly for the right moment. And Hitler intended to strike first. "I understand, Admiral."

"Do you? Then enlighten me. What is it exactly that you understand?"

"That I will prepare for sabotage actions to thwart any British invasion north into Iran, or Russian invasion south into Iran."

Canaris said, "You know, Shultz, I was a bit worried about this as a first operation for an officer so young. Now I am worried no longer. You understand that since you are going behind the lines, so to speak, for reasons of security any further information over and above your operational assignment will be withheld from you."

"I understand, Admiral." That didn't mean a thing. This wasn't like the Lubyanka, where every door was locked and an officer in one section was shot if he as much as exchanged some friendly gossip with someone in another. Here once you were on the inside all you had to do was walk about and listen.

"You will remain here in Berlin for a few more months to receive briefings on the area and begin planning your mission. Then on to Abwehr Vienna, which is responsible for the Balkans and Middle East. From there to Switzerland, where you will assemble the final details of your cover identity and learn all you can about the textile business in what will be a regrettably short time."

"Yes, Admiral." Neutral Switzerland? Well, he remembered Yakushev's album. The NKVD could shoot him in the face just as easily there.

Canaris stood up and offered his hand. "May I say that you have made my morning unusually pleasant, Shultz. One becomes tired of having to explain everything in detail. I wish you luck."

Alexsi shook the hand, which seemed as mild as the man. He took a step back, slapped his cap back on his head, popped his heels, and saluted once again. "Good morning, Admiral."

But Canaris was already head down back in his papers. "Good morning, Shultz," he replied without looking up. But then, "Oh, Shultz?"

Alexsi turned on his heels. "Yes, Admiral?"

"Be so good as to remember me to your uncle, will you?"

"Of course, Admiral."

The dachshunds tried to follow Alexsi out the door, and Canaris had to whistle them back.

31

1940 Berlin

IN THE PRIVACY OF HIS BEDROOM, WITH THE DOOR LOCKED, Alexsi began his report to Moscow. After all these years he finally had a great secret for them.

On a single sheet of paper, and on the glass top of the desk to leave no impression, he wrote it out, beginning, as had been drilled into him, with the most important information: PERSONAL INTERVIEW WITH CANARIS. NO GERMAN INVASION OF ENGLAND. GERMAN INVASION OF SOVIET UNION PLANNED FOR SUMMER OF 1941.

He did several drafts, cutting it down until it was as short and succinct as possible. Now he had to encrypt it. Yakushev had insisted he do so in English, because with an intercepted message originating from Berlin any cryptanalyst trying to break the code would be expecting German or Russian. He made a straddling checkerboard using the mnemonic ASINTOER, which were the eight most common letters in English, and the remaining letters of the alphabet after:

    0 1 2 3 4 5 6 7 8 9
    A S I N T O E R
    4 B C D F G H J K L M
    9 P Q U V W X Y Z . /

Both he and the cipher clerks in Moscow used the same agreed-upon 4–9 gap. The period was used to end sentences, and numbers were written as themselves twice and straddled on either side with the slash. In converting a letter to a number he read across from the number on the left of the checkerboard and then up.

So INVASION 1941 would be encrypted as:

I=2 N=3 V=93 A=0 S=1 I=2 O=6 N=3 /=99 1=11 9=99
4=44 1=11 /=99
239301263991199441199

Next Alexsi went to the book he had been instructed to purchase upon arrival in Germany, an almanac of European industrial statistics. He flipped it open to a random page and picked out a number that happened to be for British coal production in 1930: 243,876,427 tons. He simply repeated it to the length he needed, and added it to his first group of numbers without carrying the tens digit:

  239301263991199441199
 +243876427024387642702
 =472177680915476083891

The continuous line of numbers that made up the message were broken down into five-number groups with zeros to fill out any empty spaces at the end. So the final encrypted message INVASION 1941 would be written as:

  47217 76809 15476 08389 1000

The coal statistic had come from page 147, line 3, column 7 of the almanac. That five-number group was the key to the entire message: 14737. He would add that number to the fourth group from the beginning of his message, and the fourth group from the end. And that resulting indicator group would be placed at the very beginning of the message.

With the indicator key and the identical almanac the cipher clerk in Moscow would be able to reverse his steps and decode his report. No one else could. Yakushev had assured him that the code was unbreakable. It had been adapted by Soviet intelligence from one used by the Nihilists, one of the many leftist groups, like the Anarchists, that the Bolsheviks had destroyed as they consolidated power after the 1917 Revolution.

As soon as he was finished, Alexsi brought the original report and all the paper used in coding to the toilet and burned it in the basin, carefully washing the ashes down the drain. Why not wait to throw them in the fireplace or the coal furnace? No, destroy them at once! Yakushev's voice still haunted him even in Germany.

Now that the message was in code, it had to be sent. Alexsi couldn't take the risk of it being fouled up by whoever cleared his *taynik*. Yakushev's orders were explicit in such a case. A war warning would have to be radioed direct to Moscow.

Which was in itself amusing because Yakushev categorically hated the use of radio. It was the best way to catch a spy. Amateur radio enthusiasts were all licensed, so whenever an unknown station began transmitting both the Nazis and Soviets immediately began using direction finding to try to locate it.

To reduce the risk you followed Yakushev's rules. You could never transmit from where you lived. You could never hide your radio, or anything else incriminating, where you lived. If you transmitted from the same place every time they would eventually catch you. And if you always transmitted on the same day and at the same time they would catch you quicker.

The temptation was to drag your radio to some quiet lonely place, but instead it was much safer to transmit from a busy location where many people lived, to confront a direction-finding team with a daunting number of choices if they managed to narrow down your general location.

Yakushev always emphasized that any method used before

was useless, simply because it was known. You had to come up with your own solution. Alexsi had one rule of his own, one that Aida had taught him well. Have no accomplices to betray you. Which precluded renting a room.

He folded up his message and placed it in his green packet of Memphis cigarettes. The sort of thing that attracted no notice if it had to be thrown away quickly.

After supper he left his uncle's house in the diplomatic quarter just west of Potsdamer Platz with nothing in his hands. In uniform, of course. In wartime Berlin uniforms were a guarantee of anonymity.

On the crowded evening streets any surveillance would have to be close. Whenever Alexsi turned a corner he would step into a shop and examine the window display from the inside, really watching for anyone coming down the street quickly and trying to catch sight of him. He was clear.

Three kilometers northeast of the Brandenburg Gate was the Protestant cemetery of the Sophienkirche, the Sophie Church. Alexsi went over the brick wall where a tree cast its shadow from the streetlights. There was a light breeze and overcast. Rain was threatening.

The cemetery gate was locked at night, and the grounds deserted. Alexsi still did two more drills, carefully circling his destination. No watchers. Other than the wind blowing the leaves, it was quiet. He wasn't afraid of the dead, only the living.

There was a line of large stone tombs on a path. Like little houses for the dead. Rich families who buried their dead aboveground and indoors. Some had the entrances bricked up. Others had old iron doors. Alexsi had picked one where he was sure the family had died out. A slender white birch had grown up in front of the entrance. The outside was carved like a Gothic church with a big cross in the center of the spires.

He had planned carefully for this day, making his own door key and carefully oiling the hinges to keep from waking the dead and anyone else nearby. It only creaked slightly as he opened it, and he closed it again as soon as he was inside.

Alexsi ignited the cigarette lighter for illumination and set it burning down on a stone slab that covered some fellow's coffin. Tucked away in a corner was a suitcase and a metal toolbox. He stripped off his uniform and donned a workman's boiler suit and a leather eye patch.

Yakushev would have dismissed it as impossibly melodramatic, but it was the perfect disguise. A missing eye was the only way to account for an otherwise able-bodied young man in civilian clothes these days. And no one would ever remember anything but that patch. What did the fellow look like? He had an eye patch, Herr Wachtmeister. Height? Hair color? He had an eye patch, Herr Wachtmeister. . . .

32

1940 Berlin

THE YOUNG MAN WITH THE EYE PATCH SHOULDERED HIS WAY through some bellboys having their smoke break at the service entrance at the back of the Hotel Adlon, the most luxurious in Berlin. All the film stars stayed there. They paid him no mind because he was wearing the dark blue service cap with red piping, and over his workman's clothes the blue armband with the gold swastika-bearing eagle of the Deutsche Reichspost, the German post office. He was carrying a metal toolbox.

He was inside and heading for the service elevator when an authoritative voice said, "Hold on, there."

Alexsi turned. "Yes?"

It was a watchman. Aggressive enough looking, if he hadn't been fat and middle-aged, with a blunt rounded head like a pistol bullet. "What are you doing here?"

"Telephone problem," Alexsi replied gruffly, as if to say, What do you think I'm doing here?

"The repairman just left," the watchman said. "What are *you* doing here?"

That was a shock. But as Yakushev said, you couldn't run, and you couldn't just stand there with your mouth open. "I know that," Alexsi said impatiently. "There's still a problem. I have to check the lines coming in from the street."

The watchman was looking him up and down. "I'll have to see about this."

"Your name?" Alexsi demanded crisply.

As a question he was most likely used to asking, that startled the watchman. "What?"

"If I don't get this fixed tonight, and the hotel complains," Alexsi said, "I'm not being blamed."

"All right, all right," the watchman grumbled. "Do you know where you're going?"

"I've worked here before," Alexsi said over his shoulder, already moving.

As he went past the kitchen his eyes flashed to the chalkboard list of rooms, for the room-service orders. He pressed the call button for the service elevator.

The elevator operator opened the door. A very old man, creaking like the door, whom they probably didn't want on the guest elevators anymore. "Floor?"

Alexsi had never been stopped before in a hotel, let alone questioned. He knew he should just go to the lobby and get the hell out of there. "Five."

"Now that's the job right there," the elevator operator said, closing the swinging grate. "Fixing telephones."

"As soon as I finish up here I have to go down into the sewers," Alexsi said. "I'll take your job tonight."

"The sewers?" the elevator operator said. "No, thanks."

When they reached the floor, Alexsi peeked out the door before getting off. No more Hollywood stars in wartime. The top floors were reserved for foreign dignitaries and Nazi Party big shots who took rooms on the weekends to do some whoring away from their wives. But it was a weekday. And if any of either were about there would be security men, a sign for him to get back in the elevator and go home. The hallway was deserted, and the room-service board had given Alexsi a good idea which rooms were empty. He knocked on the door and put his ear to it. No answer, no sound from inside. Hotel room locks were easy. He opened it up and peeked inside.

The room was clearly unoccupied. Alexsi wedged a triangle of wood under the door to keep it shut no matter what. He opened the glass door a crack and checked the balcony.

Once he was sure he was alone, he unpacked his toolbox onto the room's writing desk. The radio took less than ten minutes to set up. The receiver was a regular shortwave that, once removed from its bulky cabinet and speakers, was just a thirty-centimeter sheet of Bakelite with the tubes and mechanism mounted on it. The transmitter was more complex and completely homemade. The frequency coils were automobile copper tubing wrapped around cardboard toilet paper cylinders, the vacuum tubes of the best German quality. It looked like a pile of junk wired together in a shallow wooden tray, but it worked.

Alexsi connected the two units and strung the copper strand antenna wire across the room. He hooked it from picture frame to picture frame, small glass medicine bottles serving as insulators.

He was very proud of his idea. Germans submitted unquestioningly to anything official, so a telephone repairman could go anywhere. Transmit from an unoccupied hotel room for an hour or less, and then leave. A different hotel every time, the slow weekdays when they weren't full, people always coming and going. Even Yakushev would approve.

Alexsi plugged his power cord into the outlet and donned the hard Bakelite headphones. With the transmitter powered up and working, he tapped out D7Y continuously on his Morse key. This was his Soviet call sign.

Moscow was reading him weak and broken, and he had to reposition his antenna wires. Finally they gave him the go-ahead. He began sending his coded message. At the Red Army school they considered him a very fast operator, but it still took time to send out the numbered groups.

He thought he heard something over the static in his earphones and the clicking of the Morse key. Alexsi paused and pushed the headphones back. It sounded like a door nearby. And then a key being slid into the lock of his room, very quietly.

Alexsi quickly tapped out DAVID, to end the message and signal it was genuine. In one smooth motion he crammed the message paper into his shirt, scooped the receiver, transmitter and toolbox up into his arms, tearing out the power and antenna wires in the process, dashed across the room, kicked open the balcony door, and hurled everything out into the night.

The door unlocked but hung up on the wood wedge he'd driven underneath it. Someone gave it a hard kick but it didn't open.

The balcony ran all the way around the fifth floor, with only a low iron fence protecting the outside and the border of each room. Alexsi leaped up, grabbed the edge of the roof, and pulled himself up just as the door crashed open.

The edge was only about fifteen centimeters wide, and the roof sloped too sharply for climbing, especially with a light rain falling. Alexsi hesitated for an instant, but falling off would be preferable to being caught. He fixed his eyes on the far end of the roof, never once looking down at his feet, and ran flat out.

Everything was fine until he reached the end of the roof and tried to stop. The leather soles of his shoes gave him no traction. He slid forward, stomach-wrenchingly out of control. Fortunately a tall metal grate separated the last of the balcony from the building next door. The top of it came up to his knees. Still sliding, Alexsi stuck out a foot to try to stop himself. It hit the top of the grate, but the other foot slipped out from under him. He fell onto his ass and nearly off the roof. Only one hand grasping the grate for dear life and a single buttock on the edge of the roof were keeping him on. With the strength of sheer terror, Alexsi gave a great heave and pulled himself up. Now on his knees and both hands on the grate, he yanked himself upright, stepped on top of the grate, and leaped out onto the roof of the next building. Landing hard and rolling back to his feet, he dashed across that roof to the other side, pulled himself up to the edge, and stepped off onto the roof of the next adjoining building.

The joined buildings, all at roughly the same height, made it faster than running down the street. A diagonal walk across and he was on the other side of the block. Now he paused to check his back. No one was chasing behind him. Either they'd thought he'd run along the balcony and ducked into another room, or the Gestapo didn't have anyone dedicated enough to follow him across wet rooftops. He quickly peeked over the edge. There was a long gray radio-direction-finding van, with its distinctive circular roof antennas, parked at either end of the street. They must have been cruising the area, lucked upon his transmission, and that damned watchman and elevator operator tipped them off.

The roof door was locked. Alexsi gave it a sharp kick, but it only bounced back. He could tell from the resistance that the door wasn't just locked but barred. It was always something. He took a quick look around but there was no other roof exit, not even a maintenance hatch. Time was running short. The Gestapo and police had probably surrounded the hotel but soon would spread out all over the neighborhood. Alexsi circled around the edge until he found it. The fire escape was an iron ladder attached to the side of the building, following the rain gutter down to the street. Before going over the side Alexsi discarded his eye patch and Reichspost armband.

Leaning down over the edge of the building, he grabbed the top rung and swung himself over onto the ladder. Just his weight made it sway like a stalk of wheat in the wind. No sense wasting time, then. He clamped the sides of his shoes on the outside of the vertical rails of the ladder, got a good grip with his gloved hands, and slid down instead of climbing. Just as he used to slide down the silo ladder at the farm.

The ladder shook, and creaked, but at least gravity was doing most of the work for him. Gaining confidence, Alexsi lightened his grip and let himself slide down faster. It was going well, but what he couldn't see in the darkness was that whoever had installed it had bolted a few sections of ladder practically touching the large tubular metal rain gutter.

As he sped down, the ladder took an exciting swerve to the right and Alexsi's foot slid into the ever-narrowing space between the ladder and gutter and jammed tight. Alexsi yelped in pain as his right foot stopped. The rest of him, however, kept going down. He lost his grip on the ladder with his right hand, then his left, then he was upside down. By the time he was able to grab a rung he was facedown, his right leg was bent up around his buttocks, and it felt like his foot was about to snap completely off.

He couldn't move. His foot was stuck tight. So this was how it was going to end. Trapped by his own hand and dangling upside down from the side of a building, like a bat.

But after that moment of despair Alexsi gathered himself and with all his weight on his hands pushed two rungs back up the ladder and kicked up. But he couldn't dislodge his foot. The blood was rushing to his head. He locked his arms against the ladder and tried to push the right foot out with his left. Still stuck. Losing patience, he kicked brutally at the stuck foot with his left one, and it popped out.

Alexsi let his legs drop until he was right side up again. His vision grayed out as the blood redistributed itself from his head. As soon as he was sure he was going to remain conscious, he tested his right foot on the ladder to see if it was broken. It hurt when he put his weight on it, but it didn't seem broken.

He was running out of time. He let himself slide again, but slower now.

The ladder stopped about four meters from the ground. Alexsi hung from the last rung, and let go. He dropped to the sidewalk, trying to land mainly on his good left foot. A man carrying a briefcase was looking at him with his mouth open. "Is there a fire up there?"

"Yes, there is," Alexsi said quickly. "You go that way and find a fire alarm," he added, pointing. "I'll go this way."

The man dashed off. Alexsi popped his collar up around his ears and quickly blended himself into the pedestrian foot traffic. He was limping, but his right foot felt better the more he used it. Across the street, and then the next one. And he was finally clear of the search box and could relax a bit. That would have made quite the heroic obituary. Died due to a poorly installed fire escape while fulfilling his internationalist duty.

He walked steadily for two kilometers, zigzagging through the streets, and only then stopped at a café for some tea, a buttered roll, and a new vantage point. Making a much-needed visit to the toilet, he realized with horror that he still had the coded message stuffed in his shirt. He tore it up and flushed it.

When his nerves finally settled down, he took stock. They could sweep the pieces of his radio off the street, but they already knew there was a radio and they already knew the frequency. Any fingerprints would not have survived the rain. They had his cap, but all that would tell them was his hat size. Fingerprints from the room? How many different people's fingerprints were in a hotel room? And he'd worn gloves except when he was transmitting. He should be all right, though it had been close.

It had to have been pure chance. Or they were already in the area looking for another transmitting radio. Bad luck.

All thanks to Yakushev, though. Alexsi knew that without the old bastard's training he would have been standing there frozen when the hotel door opened, wondering how they'd gotten him.

He seemed to be free and clear, so he paid his bill and began a circuitous route back to the cemetery.

But on the next block over a car was creeping along slowly, floating surveillance searching the streets at random. Alexsi might not have on his postal cap and eye patch, but he was still wearing the same clothing.

Not letting the beaters goad him into running, he ducked into the first shop he came across. It was a pharmacy in the American style, with bright signs and a chrome and marble counter serving ice cream and sweet drinks along with prescriptions. Full of customers and chattering teenagers. He tried to push his way through them.

"What are you doing?" someone demanded.

Alexsi doubled over. "Going to be sick. So sorry. Have to vomit."

Like magic the crowd parted. Someone grabbed his arm and pulled him past the counter. Alexsi held his hand over his mouth, still bent over. "Sick, have to vomit."

In an instant he was in the back room. It was like the children's game of being slung hand to hand on the run. The only thing they wanted less than you sicking up all over the toilet they had to clean was you sicking up all over the floor they had to clean.

Seconds later he was pushed through a door and out in the alley behind the store. With a loud retching sound, Alexsi leaned over the nearest trash bin, waving them away. Which was fine, because they didn't want to watch it anyway. The door slammed shut.

That sound was like a starting gun going off. Ignoring the pain in his right foot, Alexsi sprinted down the alley and over a fence that blocked one end.

His luck held, because he emerged from the other side just as a streetcar was passing by. He ran for it and jumped aboard.

"You're not supposed to do that when it's moving," the German woman ticket taker lectured him sternly.

"I know," Alexsi said, offering her his warmest smile along with the fare. "I'm sorry. I'm just so late."

But having delivered her lecture, she was done with him.

Alexsi rode the streetcar until everyone who had been on it got off. He changed lines twice, and once more gradually made his way back to the cemetery and his uniform.

His uncle was still up when he came in, drinking by the fire.

"A filthy night out there," Hans Shultz observed. "You look the worse for wear."

"I feel the worse for wear, Uncle," Alexsi replied. "I really should stay home on weeknights."

"Nonsense, my boy. You only live once."

33

1940 Berlin

THAT NEXT MORNING AT ABWEHR HEADQUARTERS ALEXSI reflected on the truth of it. You had to have training in order to act normal. Otherwise after his close shave he'd be searching every face he came across, wondering if they suspected him. He wondered how many spies went mad from paranoia.

Amid the clacking of typewriters and the cigarette smoke and the coughing and humming and talking on the telephones, he wedged himself into the small corner desk he'd been given, of course the one nobody else wanted, and read through the stacks of messages and reports from Iran. What was amazing to him was that the Abwehr people inside the country seemed to have absolutely no idea at all about the country.

Typical Europeans. They drank in the European clubs with other Europeans, and played tennis with other Europeans and Westernized Iranians. The agents they recruited were either those same Iranian government officials who spoke their language and were happy to take their money in exchange for the latest palace gossip, or cab drivers and servants probably recruited by their own drivers and servants. Most likely relatives of their drivers and servants, Alexsi thought, knowing how it was done.

The office din was broken by a harsh voice demanding, "Shultz?"

Alexsi rolled his chair around slowly. Standing in the doorway was a captain with the twin lightning bolt runes of the SS on the right collar of his gray uniform jacket, and the diamond SD patch of the SS Security Service on his lower left sleeve. At his side was a ferocious-looking Alsatian dog. Incredibly enough, he had a whip, an actual stock whip looped around his left wrist.

Alexsi took a deep breath and fought the urge to launch himself out the nearest window. He'd learned his lesson from the library in Baku—this time he was certain his chair was heavy enough to break it. "Yes?"

"I need you at once." The Hauptsturmführer tapped one boot against the other, and the dog growled as if on cue.

The female clerk next to Alexsi was practically standing on her desk. But Alexsi felt much better now that he'd mastered that first artillery shot of panic. If he was going to be arrested it wouldn't be by a single SS man, even with a dog. And there would be a drawn pistol, not a whip. He whistled lightly through his teeth, and the dog's ears perked up. He stared into the dog's eyes, looked away for a moment, then stared again. He pointed his finger between the dog's eyes; the dog visibly relaxed, and his ears twitched. Alexsi pointed his finger down at his feet and the dog walked up slowly, nearly stampeding everyone else in the office who was in his path, sniffed Alexsi's hand, and sat down placidly.

Alexsi slipped a hand under the dog's chin and then rubbed his ears. Nothing compared to the half-wild farm dogs on the kolkhoz, not to mention the animals the Shahsavan kept for killing jackals threatening their stock. "Who's a sweet boy, then?" he asked the shepherd.

The SD man gave Alexsi an adversarial smile and tapped the whip against his leg as if he'd like nothing better than to use it. "I'm Captain Ressler."

Alexsi was still petting the dog. Who was now rolled on the floor getting his belly rubbed. "You said something about needing me?"

"I understand you speak Russian?"

"I do," Alexsi replied.

"I need an immediate translation of an important document."

"What you're saying is, you'd like me to interrupt my work and take a look at your document, as a personal favor."

Alexsi watched as the SS man considered all his options before finally replying, ever so grudgingly, "Yes."

"Fine. Let's see it."

"Come to my office."

Alexsi decided to give him that victory. He stood up and followed the captain out the door, whistling for the dog, who fell in at his heels. "A fine animal," he said, as they walked down the hallway.

Captain Ressler just glanced back at the dog with the same expression he would give a traitor to the Fatherland.

They ended up in the wing housing Abwehr III, Counterespionage. Which put Alexsi even more on his guard than he had been already. And made him regret humiliating the captain. Slightly.

In the office were two obvious Gestapo men, in civilian clothes. And an army captain and a major. As he came through the door they all looked at him with the suspicious eyes of policemen.

Captain Ressler handed Alexsi a document in a clear acetate sleeve.

"Why didn't you have the Eastern section translate it for you?" Alexsi asked.

"They claim they're too busy," Ressler said.

Preparing for the invasion, Alexsi thought. Perhaps he could use this somehow as an excuse to drop in on them. There would probably be maps up on their walls. He looked down at the paper in the sleeve. It was handwritten, in the Cyrillic alphabet. And the paper was stained and crumpled, as if it had been fished from the garbage. "It's a shopping list," he said. And then, with all of them looking over his shoulder, he pointed to each line. "Sausage. Margarine. Bread. Meat, with a question mark. Vegetables, canned, and another question mark. Soap. Laundry soap. Toilet paper. And then on the right, next to each item, what looks like the number of ration allowances this person has available to use. That's it, I'm afraid."

"What do you make of it?" Captain Ressler asked, quite mildly Alexsi thought.

"It doesn't seem like any kind of code to me," Alexsi said. "Though I'm certainly not as experienced as you gentlemen."

"We don't think it's code, either," Captain Ressler said. "Anything else off the top of your head?"

"Did this come from Berlin?" Alexsi asked.

They all looked at each other, as if they weren't sure whether or not to answer. Then one of the Gestapo men said, grudgingly, "Yes."

"I would say it's from someone more comfortable thinking in Russian than German," said Alexsi. Now there was a lesson for you. "So the question, it would seem, is whether the person who wrote it admits to being Russian, or claims not to be?"

They all looked at each other again. Finally Captain Ressler said, "His papers say he is not."

"Then that's certainly a counterespionage matter," said Alexsi.

Captain Ressler sat down atop the edge of a desk and tapped the handle of his whip against the wood. "What would *you* do next, Lieutenant Shultz? If you were us, that is."

Alexsi ignored the little mocking smile. "If you have this, you're already suspicious. I'm assuming it came from his trash. So you must be following him."

"Should we search his apartment?" said Ressler.

"You might as well arrest him and then search his apartment," Alexsi replied. "Otherwise, if he has any brains at all as soon as he comes home and sees the neighbors' faces he'll be off and running like a rabbit."

"How would you like to come work with us?" Ressler said. "I can arrange it."

"Thanks, but no," said Alexsi. "I'll stick to Abwehr I."

"What does Canaris have you doing?" Ressler asked.

Alexsi just stared back at him.

Ressler laughed. "Well what do you know?" he said to the others. "There is one person in this building who has some respect for security."

"Anything else I can do for you?" said Alexsi, handing back the acetate.

"At least let us offer you a coffee," said Ressler. "You'd think us ungrateful swine otherwise."

Alexsi made a gesture of acquiescence.

Without moving from the desk, Ressler bellowed through the open door, loud enough to wake the dead, "Six coffees!"

A secretary who looked like she was bearing burdens more heavy than a tray of cups came through the door.

"How do you take yours, Shultz?" Ressler asked.

"Black," said Alexsi.

When they were all sitting back with their cups, Ressler said, "So how did you come to learn Russian?"

Alexsi heard Yakushev's voice in his head. *There is no such thing as an innocent question.* "I had a Russian nanny when I was a child."

"Ah," said Ressler. "They say it's easier to learn a language when you're young. And you kept up with it."

"My uncle is a diplomat," said Alexsi. "He always encouraged me to learn languages."

"Nice to have such advantages," said Ressler. "No doubt you will have a bright career in diplomacy after the war."

Alexsi ignored the jab. "Who can say? Some people pick up languages easily."

"Ah, yes, I hear it's all in the ear," said Ressler. "Like music. Alas, I have no musical ability. And nothing but poor schoolboy French."

"I shouldn't worry about it," said Alexsi. "I'm sure the French will all be speaking German soon."

Everyone in the room laughed at that. Except Ressler.

"And you come from the Third Infantry Division, eh?" said Ressler. "I hear they're going mechanized."

"My apologies," said Alexsi. "I know nothing about you."

"Oh, just another former policeman," said Ressler, waving expansively to take in the others in the room.

Alexsi sipped his coffee.

"I like this fellow," Ressler announced. "He listens to everything but doesn't run off at the mouth. You push him and he doesn't get angry, he just pushes back. Even Gunnar tried to give him the business"—he gestured toward the Alsatian snoring under a nearby desk—"and now he's practically his slave."

Alexsi finished his coffee and set the cup and saucer down. "I'm glad I was able to help out," he said, standing. "But I have to get back to work."

"A cup of coffee seems like such poor thanks," said Ressler. "Come out on the town tonight. As my guest."

"That's really not necessary," Alexsi replied, warning sirens screaming in his brain.

"Please," said Ressler, in a tone that was not really a request. "It would be a comradely gesture."

Instinct told Alexsi not to push back too hard at that. "Very well."

"Excellent," said Ressler, smiling now. "I will collect you at the end of the day."

34

THE TWO NAKED GIRLS GRAPPLED EACH OTHER WITH practiced efficiency. Smeared with sticky brown mud, you could hardly tell they were naked. Which for Alexsi would have been the whole point. But for the rest of the men in the audience it seemed to be the mud and the combat. They were roaring as if it were the Roman arena and they expected to see only the winner survive. The girls, on the other hand, were like professional dancers who were being careful not to crush each other's toes.

The walls were the scarlet he'd been waiting a long time to see. The band in the corner had faces only slightly less red, and looked as if they were about to burst from their threadbare tuxedos. He had yet to see a thin German musician. The girls were conducting their business in a swirling shallow tank of viscous mud in the center of the room, with the tables arranged all around it. They had been preceded by the world's worst comedian, his face actually in white greasepaint like a clown, as if to signal that you really ought to laugh. At least it hid the sweat of desperation, Alexsi thought. The comedian had been preceded by the world's worst magician, who was still running around the periphery of the club trying to net one of his white doves who had made a mad break for freedom. Now *that* had actually been funny. It was all so appalling he couldn't wait to see what came next.

The waitress came in and set down the tray of beer mugs. Stacking up the empties, she shot a sideways glance at Alexsi's mug, down only an inch of beer, and then went over to him. He subtly shook his head, and she took away the full one that would have been his.

"A sparrow drinks more than you," Captain Ressler said contemptuously.

Alexsi had spent the afternoon listening to the women Abwehr clerks speculate that the whip and the dog and the strutting walk and the baby face and the Hitler moustache all had to belong to the owner of the world's smallest penis. They all said, Come out with us tonight, Walter, not with that bastard. You wouldn't think so after Aida, and the way the NKVD had taught him to use them, but Alexsi liked women so much more than men. After all that, he had to work to keep the grin off his face whenever he looked at Ressler. "Life is all about your perspective, my friend," he replied. "Just think of all the beer you haven't had to buy, and be cheerful."

"A philosopher lieutenant," Ressler grumbled, turning his attention back to the action.

A female hand came to rest on Alexsi's shoulder. Another club employee, a table girl. She had her blond hair in two large braids, and she was wearing the traditional German dirndl dress. For some reason it was like an aphrodisiac for German men, though Alexsi had to bite his tongue to keep from laughing every time he saw one. Here it was more of a naughty housewife thing. This girl's dress had a lace-up bodice that was very loosely laced up over quite a bodice.

"This isn't to your interest, is it?" she asked him.

"How could you tell?" Alexsi replied.

She laughed. "Would you like to buy me a glass of champagne?"

Alexsi smiled back, though he didn't see the point in paying a girl to pretend that she really wanted to fuck him. A whore was just like the girls in the Baku who flopped on their backs and let you fuck them because you had food for them to eat. No need for that with all the women around Berlin, and the men off in the army. "I'd love to, dear, but I'm just a poor lieutenant. You'll have much better luck with one of these wealthier fellows."

Her mask fell away for a moment, and she said, quietly enough so only the two of them could hear, "They get all excited and just want to tear something apart."

"A hard living," Alexsi said, placing a sympathetic hand over the one on his shoulder.

She examined his face and then just plopped down on his lap. "I have a few minutes to persuade you until they call me away. Do you mind?"

"Not at all," Alexsi said. "We can talk about the first thing that comes up."

That made her laugh uproariously and, Alexsi thought, genuinely. As if a reward for his wit, she gave a little squirm in his lap. "What's your name?"

"Walter," Alexsi said.

She said, "I'm Heidi."

Now it was Alexsi's turn to laugh loudly.

"What's wrong?" she demanded, still smiling at him.

"Nothing," Alexsi replied, resting one hand on her hip. "Let's both pretend that's really it."

She laughed again and flipped a braid the size of a cable back over her shoulder. If Alexsi hadn't ducked he might have been concussed. While they had been talking the audience had grown increasingly dissatisfied with the desultory action from the wrestlers. "I've had enough of this shit," Captain Ressler announced.

He stamped toward the ring, and the pimp who was playing the part of the fight manager grew visibly concerned at the sight of an SS officer bearing down on him. Ressler handed him some cash, and punctuated his orders with an outstretched finger stabbed into the pimp's chest. The man dipped his head submissively, and when Ressler was done held up the money and barked something at the girls in the ring.

One of them saw him before the other, and understood immediately. She stuck her heel behind the leg of the other girl and
pushed hard, sending her backward into the mud. The girl hit
with a splat, and the front-row tables had to duck as the mud
sprayed up at them.

The mud boiled and heaved, and the girl who had gone under
popped up with a look of surprise and anger on her brown face.
But her opponent wasn't about to relinquish her advantage. She
leaped on her, driving her back under the mud.

The crowd was on its feet. Captain Ressler was shouting, "That's
it! That's it!"

Two hands shot out of the mud, one grabbing the dominant
girl by the throat and the other by the hair. A good hard yank
pulled her off.

"Does this happen often?" Alexsi asked Heidi-in-his-lap.

"Sometimes," she said enigmatically.

"I believe it's about to turn ugly," he said.

"Now there'll be bad blood in the dressing room for a week,"
she said, sighing.

But this time the wrestling had degenerated into kicking and
scratching and mud throwing. The audience was going mad. Captain Ressler was standing on his chair.

"I have to go," Heidi said.

Alexsi looked over. A massive lesbian in a suit, who ran the
table girls and with whom he wouldn't have dreamed of arguing without a knife handy, was gesturing angrily in their direction.

"Do you have a pen?" Heidi asked.

Alexsi reached into his jacket and handed it over.

Heidi wrote something on a napkin, then folded it and handed
it back along with the fountain pen. She kissed his cheek and was
gone.

It had finally gone too far in the ring. Two of the pimp referees
were prying the girls apart and dragging them away to neutral

corners before there was real bloodshed. The audience was screaming abuse at them for ruining the fun.

Captain Ressler jumped down from his chair. "Wonderful!" he
exclaimed. "Just wonderful!" Then he looked at Alexsi intently.
"Shultz, you have lipstick on your cheek."

"Do I?" said Alexsi, wiping it away with the napkin.

"Did that slut give you her telephone number?" Ressler demanded.

Alexsi unfolded the napkin, took a look at it, smiled, and tucked
it away in his jacket. "It would seem so."

"I can't believe it," Ressler said. "You didn't pay a single mark
for her time, and she wants to fuck you for free."

Still smiling, Alexsi said, "Did I thank you for bringing me
here?"

Ressler grabbed his beer mug and drained it. "Another
round!" he bellowed into the air, slamming the mug onto the
table. "And let's get some more action going! What are we paying
you for?"

A few more matches and a few more rounds of beer, and
Ressler's head was dropping onto his chest. Alexsi seriously considered leaving him there, but decided that would just create
more problems than the fleeting satisfaction was worth.

Ressler came back to life in the cold air of the autumn night.
He was able to walk fairly well while gripping Alexsi's shoulder.
"You're a fine fellow, Shultz," he slurred. "You don't drink worth a
damn, and you're more snotty than any lieutenant has a right to
be, but all in all you're a fine fellow."

"Thanks, so are you," Alexsi said, humoring him. The last
thing he wanted to finish off the night was an SD man vomiting
on his boots. At least they'd been sitting far enough away that he
didn't have any mud on his uniform.

"I have to piss," Ressler stated. "Where can I piss, Shultz?"

"Hang on," Alexsi said. "There's an alley up ahead."

He stood guard at the entrance while Ressler leaned against

the brick wall. It took an agonizingly long time, but Alexsi wasn't about to urge him to hurry.

Ressler finally staggered into view. "I feel much better," he announced. "I should have gotten one of those girls. Shultz, let's go back and get a girl."

"I'm afraid the club's closed by now," Alexsi lied.

"Shit," Ressler muttered. "Let's go find a house."

"All right," Alexsi said, humoring him again. He was positive that any use of the word "no" would cause open hostilities to be declared. He'd get Ressler to his rooms, and then if he wanted to crawl out on his hands and knees looking for brothels that was his business.

They staggered down the street. As they closed on the next intersection, a little boy came running blindly around the corner and crashed into their legs.

"What's this?" Ressler demanded. Then, showing more dexterity than Alexsi would have given him credit for in his condition, he bent over and grabbed the boy by the shoulders. The child gave a little squeak of terror. He seemed to Alexsi about seven years old.

"Look at you," Ressler said warmly. "You look just like my son." He picked the boy up bodily and gave him a long, emotional hug. "My little Petie is in Hamburg," he said into the boy's ear. "I miss him so much. And when I see a fine German boy like you it makes me miss him even more. Here, let me show you." He set the boy down and went hunting in his jacket for his billfold.

The force of Ressler's embrace had opened the boy's jacket. Alexsi saw the point of a yellow star poking out. Now he knew why the boy's legs were shaking in terror. It was past the Jew curfew, and he must have borrowed a jacket to hide the yellow star, which the law said had to be worn so it could be seen at all times, in order to get home without being arrested. And there he was staring up at the *totenkopf*, the death's head skull badge mounted to the front of an SS officer cap.

Alexsi leaned over and buttoned the jacket up tight. He put a finger to his lips, and the boy, nearly paralyzed by fear, was able to nod.

By now Ressler had his billfold out and produced a photograph. "See, Shultz," he said, holding it up next to the boy's face. "He looks just like my little Petie."

"He does," Alexsi agreed.

Ressler turned the photo around so the boy could see. "You look just like my little son."

The boy, in his terror, was able to nod.

"He must be late for home," Alexsi said.

"Yes?" said Ressler, as if realizing the time. "Out late. Mother will be worried." He wagged a finger at the boy, then pinched his cheek roughly. "But boys will be boys." He put the photo back into his billfold and took out some money, slipping it into the boy's pocket. "Here is a present. You make me miss my boy. Now run on home, like a good boy."

The child dashed away from them as if he'd been shot from a cannon.

"A good boy," said Ressler, struggling to get the billfold back into his jacket.

"A good boy," Alexsi agreed. He helped Ressler get the billfold back into the inside pocket, and straightened his jacket.

"Now, a woman," Ressler said.

Alexsi had been afraid he'd remember that. But if he got Ressler home before he sobered up any more, it wouldn't be an issue.

They continued their march. And at the next street over, just south of the Tiergarten, a figure loomed out at them from out of a darkened doorway.

Alexsi almost went for his knife before he realized it was a woman. The tallest woman he had ever seen. She had to be over 180 centimeters, a towering German blonde wearing a long black leather coat, cinched at the waist with a wide leather belt and a shiny buckle to accentuate her jutting bust. And high black leather lace-up boots. More severe than pretty. Another woman he'd think twice about taking on without a weapon in hand. She looked them both over and said, "Who's been a bad boy tonight?"

Ressler immediately came to life. "I have," he announced.

Alexsi turned his attention from the streetwalker to the SS captain and said, only, "Are you sure you want to do this?"

Ressler shoved him away with one hand. "You have your slut's number. This one is mine."

The Amazon glared at Alexsi, as if daring him to interfere with the transaction. Alexsi made a surrendering gesture of "all yours," and turned on his heels.

Ressler had gone out without his whip tonight, but she probably had a collection of them. The Nazis had moved all the whores off the streets and into brothels, and sent the ones who resisted organization to concentration camps. But there were always a few die-hard independents in every trade.

His uncle had sat him down and told him about the signals the girls used. Not, as Alexsi thought at first, to order him off. Hans Shultz just didn't want his nephew getting into any trouble. So along with a present of a box of condoms came a few well-chosen words of advice about Berlin's ladies of the evening. Black boots meant you were going to get your buttocks cropped. At least. Which was good to know, because Alexsi didn't see anything sexy about getting his ass whipped. He'd had an entire childhood of it, and no one was ever going to do it to him again without a fight to the death.

As he walked home, thankfully alone now, Alexsi pondered the mystery of the Germans. If Ressler had caught sight of the yellow Jew star on the boy he embraced so warmly, he probably would have smashed the child's head into the nearest wall. Alexsi wouldn't credit a particular German love of brutality, since in his experience all people loved brutality. But the Germans were unique in other ways. It could have just been naked girls wrestling, but no—it had to be in the mud because they were scrupulously clean but fantasized about filth. They wrapped themselves in rules but longed for anarchy. They worshiped order but dreamed of riot. It was the way they denied themselves what they really wanted.

Alexsi stopped walking and stood stock-still as he realized for the first time that Hitler understood his countrymen perfectly. Hitler understood that war would unleash them. And they would be capable of anything. They would be terrible.

He shivered in the darkness of Berlin.

35

1940 Berlin

ALEXSI CHECKED HIS WATCH. IT WAS A FEW MINUTES BEFORE 6:15 in the morning. Moving the tuning dial a millimeter at a time, he tried to sharpen up the reception. It was the best radio he could find in a German shop, a Telefunken. In addition to the local broadcast radio it could also pick up long-distance shortwave. It was amazingly compact—just slightly bigger than a bread box. And at 295 marks it was a good thing the Russians had given him enough money to buy it. There were no radios in Russian shops, no matter how many rubles you had, while German shops were full of radios but you had to have the Reichsmarks to buy them.

He tapped the dial just a hair, and the clear stream of Morse code flooded in from Moscow. Alexsi adjusted the volume, but with the earphones plugged in only he could hear the station. No worries on this. He was only listening, not transmitting, so no one could find him.

The dots and dashes just kept rattling on. Messages to other agents, dummy traffic to confuse anyone monitoring the frequency, he had no idea. Finally he picked out the call sign D7Y, D7Y. That was him. After repeating that a few times to let him get ready, the numbers came in, Alexsi copied them onto the ready sheet of paper in the usual five-number groups. Finally the call sign repeated, and the message came in again. Alexsi checked it against his original work to make sure he'd gotten it down right. When the message repeated for the third time, he switched the radio off.

Alexsi opened his industrial almanac to the page, line, and column indicated by the five-number key group in the message. French steel production in 1929 was 10,428,286 metric tons. Alexsi subtracted 10428286 from his numbers groups, then used the staggered checkerboard system to convert the numbers into letters. The decoded message gave a reference date to his report on a German invasion of the Soviet Union. It read: YOUR CONCLUSIONS ARE RIDICULOUS. CONFINE YOUR REPORTING TO FACTUAL MATTERS.

Alexsi couldn't believe it. He'd risked his life for this? He hadn't necessarily been expecting praise—that wasn't how his countrymen went about their business. He had been expecting demands for more information, not to be told that he was an idiot. The only hope the Russians had to avoid the fate of the Poles, the Norwegians, the French, the Belgians, and the Dutch was to be ready for what was coming.

He was sorely tempted to leave it at that. He didn't think the Germans could conquer the Soviet Union. First of all, Stalin would have no qualms about sending everyone in the country off to their deaths. There were a great many more Russians than Germans, and unlike the Tsar's armies, which fell apart in the Great War, the NKVD would be holding machine guns right behind them to make sure they fought like heroes. But mainly the Germans had no idea of the vastness, the kind of space that swallowed up entire armies. And it wasn't like France, where they could drive their lorries down paved roads and fill the panzers up at the service stations when they ran out of petrol. When it rained you couldn't even walk a horse down a Russian road without the animal sinking half out of sight. And then there was the winter. It had nearly killed him, and he'd been living in a nice warm apartment, not a trench.

His problem was, it might be like Napoleon who had taken

Moscow in 1812 only to be run out again. The Germans getting just far enough in to capture the NKVD files with his name on them and put him up against a wall.

And if the Germans didn't win, he knew the NKVD. They wouldn't blame themselves for ignoring his warnings and telling him to fuck off—they'd blame him for not working harder to convince them. And that kind of blame would come in the form of a bullet.

Alexsi kept looking at the message and trying to figure out a plan. The best thing for him would be if the Germans were stopped right at the beginning, and everyone settled down in the trenches for a nice long war, like 1914. And he was safely out of the way recruiting spies in Iran.

Somehow he would have to obtain the kind of detailed information that would convince the Russians.

36

"SHULTZ!"

Each time it happened poor little Dagmar, the clerk at the desk next to his, still stiffened up in terror. Alexsi said, "Ah, Captain. Good to see you. Where's Gunnar?"

Captain Ressler was without both dog and whip this particular day. He acted as if he hadn't heard a word. "I need you."

"Again?"

"Yes."

Alexsi sighed. "Then I have to lock up these documents. Meet you at your office?"

"I'll wait."

Alexsi moved all the files on his desk to his shelf in the office safe. He made a point not to hurry.

In the hall outside he said, "What's going on?"

Ressler said, "I require your Russian again. You'll find this interesting."

"I'm sure," Alexsi replied, not very earnestly.

He followed Ressler down the stairs, carefully observing him for a limp or other signs of rough usage. But this time they were headed out a side door. "Where are we going?" Alexsi asked.

"Prinz-Albrecht-Strasse."

Ressler turned as he said it, as if he wanted to see Lieutenant Shultz's reaction. Alexsi gave him no satisfaction. "The air force main photo branch?"

"No."

There was an automobile waiting outside, though it was only about six blocks to the west, on the other side of the rail station.

Even in light sandstone, Alexsi thought, those old mansions from the Kaiser's time all looked like they were standing over you with clenched fists. Though with age, and time, and grime, that Berlin sandstone wasn't as light as it had been. They drove just past the building to the beginning of a multicolored-stone-block wall. A wooden gate stood between two pillars of pale brick. The driver used his horn. The gate opened and an armed guard checked all their identification before admitting them to the courtyard inside.

As they exited the automobile, Alexsi looked up at the Gestapo headquarters.

They had to show their papers one more time to gain admittance, and the guard meticulously entered their names into his ledger along with the time. Another waiting guard took them through a steel door onto the ground floor. Alexsi didn't hesitate, though; like the Lubyanka the lower levels of such places were like the lower levels of hell: where you never wanted to end up.

The walls were whitewashed brick. At each steel door their escort would unlock it from his ring of keys, and lock it again on the other side once they were through.

They passed rows of cells. Finally the escort knocked at one of the doors near the end of the hallway. A flap opened up and a pair of eyes examined them through a barred grate. The door was unlocked and they were inside some sort of anteroom with two desks and some chairs. Behind one desk sat a female secretary with a face like a straight razor. She made Ressler's Amazon streetwalker look as innocent as a schoolgirl. She was wearing earphones and operating a stenotype machine. An obvious Gestapo officer in civilian dress, but only his shirtsleeves, was smoking a cigarette and looking them over. He had a policeman's face and forearms like logs.

Ressler said, "Lieutenant Walter Shultz, Kriminalkommissar Gerhard."

The Gestapo equivalent of an army captain. Alexsi was used to being outranked. He gave the Hitler salute. *"Heil Hitler!"*

"Heil Hitler!" Captain Gerhard replied, returning the salute. "So. My friend Ressler's Russian linguist. I've heard of you."

Alexsi only gave a half smile in response. Everyone in the room seemed to be waiting for him to say something, but he didn't indulge them.

Finally Gerhard said, "Perhaps you can help us out."

"Happy to," Alexsi replied. "But no one has told me with what."

"Ah, I see now," said Gerhard. "My friend Ressler being discreet as always. Here's the story. We've caught ourselves a spy. The fellow who wrote the shopping list you were good enough to translate on the fly."

"So he is a Russian spy?" Alexsi said.

"I should think so," Gerhard replied. "He had a Russian wireless transmitter in his rooms. But according to him he doesn't speak Russian."

Alexsi's first thought was, This was the radio they were looking for when they found him in the hotel. And the fool had kept his under his bed. Now he absolutely knew why Yakushev hated radio. "You need me to translate something?"

"No," said Gerhard. "He had nothing besides a list of frequencies and transmission times. No codebook, no coding materials whatsoever. No documents of any kind."

"Then you have me at a loss," Alexsi said.

"He's already been through standard interrogation," said Gerhard. "Now he's having enhanced interrogation. We'd like you to go in and speak to him in Russian. See what happens; maybe you can jar him awake."

"I warn you, interrogation isn't my line," Alexsi said. "I'm fresh out of training. I don't want to spoil whatever you're doing."

"Not to worry," Gerhard said.

"Then what should I say?" Alexsi asked.

"Just tell him the game is up, that he needs to start talking," said Gerhard. "I want to see his reaction."

"As you like," Alexsi said.

Gerhard gestured to the stenographer to be ready. "Leave your cap on the desk," he told Alexsi.

Alexsi set down his dress cap. Gerhard unlocked a door on the far wall and ushered them through.

The room was the same pale brick as the pillars of the gatepost outside. The entire foundation of the building must have been made from it.

The first thing was the smell. All jails smelled of fear and piss and disinfectant, but this room assaulted you with it. A rough heavy wooden table took up the center, with grim rows of iron rings bolted along the sides. As he came through the doorway, Alexsi had to turn to see the naked man hanging in the corner. His arms were handcuffed behind his back, and a hook through the handcuff chain suspended him from a rope pulley attached to the ceiling. Hanging from just his wrists behind his back. Alexsi was sure the fellow's shoulders had dislocated long ago. There was a small pool of blood on the concrete floor below him, understandable because his toenails had been removed. Probably with pincers. Another Gestapo man in his shirtsleeves, smoking a cigarette, was standing beside the hanging man, whispering to him. This one didn't have the usual pug policeman's face. He was as young as Alexsi and quite handsome. Alexsi couldn't see the hanging man's face—his head was dropped down to his chest.

Gerhard made another gesture and the handsome young man ground out his cigarette on the hanging man's neck. The hanging man cried out. Then Gerhard motioned Alexsi forward.

Alexsi walked up, flanked on either side by Gerhard and Ressler. The handsome Gestapo man yanked his victim's head back so he was nearly eye to eye with Alexsi.

The fellow's face was swollen up from beating and caked with scabbed blood, so Alexsi couldn't tell how old he was. Just that he wasn't old. He looked back at Alexsi blankly.

"Listen, Comrade," Alexsi said in Russian, careful not to be *too* fluent. "You're good and caught. I'm sure back in Moscow they told you fine stories about all the heroes who wouldn't talk. Let me tell you something: They were lying. Everyone talks. You will too, sooner or later. And no one will ever hear the glorious tale of how long you held out. What's more, they won't care. So you might as well spare yourself and get it over with now."

The two bloody eyes contemplated him, and Alexsi knew exactly what was coming next. He took a quick step back, dodged to his right, and the wad of spittle aimed at him hit Ressler square in the face.

Ressler stood there in shock for an instant. Then he screamed in rage and punched the hanging man square in the testicles. A much louder scream rose up in reply, and Ressler, having completely lost control, showered the hanging man with a rain of furious punches. Alexsi retreated far back to the neutral corner.

The Gestapo didn't mind more beating, but when Ressler began fumbling for his sidearm, Gerhard came from behind and picked him up in a bear hug, pinning his arms. While all this was going on the handsome Gestapo man calmly set an army field telephone on the wooden table and began unrolling telephone wire attached to large serrated clips. He snapped the clips onto the hanging man's nipples and his testicles and ran the wire back to the phone.

Alexsi put his fingers to his ears before the Gestapo man began cranking the phone, because he knew how much of an electric jolt the magneto of a Field Telephone 33 could put out. He'd seen signalmen attach wires to the fingers of a sleeping man for a joke, and the victim nearly flew through the top of a tent. But this was no joke. The screams bounced off the brick walls.

Amidst all that, it took him some time to realize that Gerhard was shouting at him. Still trying to keep his grip on a still hysterical Ressler. Alexsi finally made out "Open the door, for Christ's sake!"

Alexsi did, and Gerhard practically threw Ressler through the open doorway. Alexsi closed the door, shutting the screams out. In the anteroom Gerhard was still trying to keep Ressler from charging back in. Alexsi noticed that the stenographer had knocked the earphones from her head onto the desk while she typed away at her machine. He could only imagine what all that screaming sounded like through a microphone.

"Go clean yourself up, old man," Gerhard was saying reasonably, while watching that pistol holster like a hawk.

"I'll be back!" Ressler raged. "The bastard will drink my spit like it was champagne, I promise you!" Practically weeping with rage, he stamped his feet until the guard opened the steel door to the hallway.

Breathing hard, Gerhard dropped into a chair and shook out a cigarette. "Thanks for all the help," he said acerbically, lighting up.

Alexsi held out both hands in his own defense. "I have to live in the same building with him. I can't go about manhandling SD captains."

Gerhard took a deep drag. "I see your point," he conceded. "You're quick on your feet, I'll give you that. Well, you ended up getting more of a reaction from Ressler than our prisoner, but thanks for the help anyway."

"If you don't need me anymore," said Alexsi. "I imagine Captain Ressler will be staying here."

"No, he won't," Gerhard said flatly. "You can't get emotional in this business. Anyway, we'll be running shifts on our friend in there day and night until he cracks. We don't get our hands on a Moscow illegal very often, and he has a lot to tell us."

"Good luck," Alexsi said.

Gerhard blew out smoke and peered at him through it. "You're not the typical lieutenant, I'll say. Usually they're nothing but questions."

"I'm an infantry officer, new to intelligence," Alexsi told him. "If it's my job, I ask plenty of questions because I'm trying to learn. But if it's not my job, like this, then I figure you'll tell me what I need to know."

"No, not the typical lieutenant at all," said Gerhard. "In all the excitement I forgot to have you tell me what you said to our friend in there."

Alexsi gave it back to him, word for word. The idea that he and the prisoner were the only ones who spoke Russian was laughable.

"Very good," said Gerhard. "And quite correct, also." He raised his eyes up to the guard. "Manfred will see you out. You can wait in your vehicle for Ressler. He'll come charging back in here soon, and I'll need to have a little talk with him."

Alexsi popped his heels and raised his right hand. *"Heil Hitler!"*

Still seated, Gerhard gave a weary little bob of the hand, to the stenographer's open disapproval. *"Heil Hitler!"*

37

RESSLER DIDN'T SAY A SINGLE WORD ON THE DRIVE BACK TO Abwehr headquarters. He just sat there hunched up in the corner of the backseat, glowering.

Mounting the grand stairway, from above came an echoing boom like the voice of God. "Shultz!"

What, again? Alexsi looked up. There was no mistaking that balding head with those outthrust ears extending over the railing. They all belonged to Colonel Hans Piekenbrock, chief of Abwehr I. The sight made Alexsi take the stairs much faster than usual. "Sir!"

Piekenbrock was not one of those officers who inspired terror; he was actually quite good-humored in that worldly upper-class German way that considered it vulgar to let the foibles of the world upset you unduly. Though he could be stern when he wished. He was tall enough to look down on nearly everyone, and even if he hadn't been he was aristocratic enough to do it anyway. "Where have you been, Shultz? People have been looking for you everywhere."

Alexsi just gestured helplessly down the stairs, where Captain Ressler was lagging behind.

Piekenbrock looked even farther down his nose. "Ah, Ressler." He was old army, and not inclined to accept the SS as anything approaching a military organization. "I realize we're all short-handed, but I can't have counterintelligence poaching my people."

Ressler finally made it to the top of the stairs, and popped his heels. "Apologies, sir. But we're finding it impossible to lay our hands on Russian speakers at short notice."

"Yes, yes," Piekenbrock said impatiently. And then he smiled. "Everyone loves lieutenants for odd jobs, because they can't protest. As it happens I don't have many lieutenants, and I have an urgent lieutenant job. Shultz, I need an officer with the proper security clearance to supervise the moving of Red Army files to Foreign Armies East at Maybach. Colonel Kinzel is briefing General Tippelskirch, and this constant messengering of files back and forth is making a real mess. So go down to Sergeant Dormer in records. He'll handle everything—you just make sure it's all correct. You'll move the entire cabinets in trucks, no mucking about. Just for the love of God make sure the receipts are filled out properly. If you can manage not to leave a trail of secret files scattered along the road to Zossen I'll be well pleased."

"As you order, Colonel," Alexsi replied formally.

"Sir, a moment," said Ressler.

Piekenbrock allowed himself to be led down the hallway. Alexsi waited at the head of the stairs, watching Ressler speaking urgently. Piekenbrock had his head cocked to one side, then he seemed to ask a very sharp question. Ressler shook his head. Another sharp question from Piekenbrock, and another shake of the head. Now a rapid-fire series of questions, and to each one negative shakes of the head. Then Piekenbrock was done and Ressler was summarily dismissed with a curt gesture.

Piekenbrock came back down the hallway with his rolling cavalryman's gait, and said, "Shultz, walk with me."

Alexsi fell in beside him.

"What does Ressler have against you?" Piekenbrock demanded.

"Sir, all I can think is that the captain is one of those policemen who believes that any German who speaks a foreign language is suspicious."

"Yes, policemen," Piekenbrock muttered with distaste. And then more pointed: "There's something else. What is it?"

"I'd prefer not to say, sir," Alexsi replied.

"I'd prefer you to answer," Piekenbrock said coldly.

"The captain invited me out on the town one evening," Alexsi said reluctantly. "Perhaps he thinks I would gossip about what happened."

"Well, what happened?" Piekenbrock demanded.

"I don't gossip, sir," Alexsi said flatly. "And certainly not about a fellow officer after duty hours. Not even if ordered, sir." Now that was pleasing. If you refused to talk you could always count on your audience to fill in the very worst they could think of, all on their own. And character assassination, done well, poisoned anything they tried to say about you later.

Piekenbrock folded his arms across his chest and stared down at him. "Quite right," he said finally. "That's how we felt in the old school, too. It's good to see a young officer with some sense." And then he was finished once again. "No more of Ressler and his errands, understand? Between his little jobs and my little jobs we'll never get you out on your mission. If you must, refer him to me."

Alexsi saluted. Not the Hitler salute—this was another traditionalist. "Yes, sir."

Not wearing a cap, Piekenbrock only nodded. "On your way, Shultz." And then he gifted him a cheerful smile. "Try not to foul this up."

MAYBACH WAS the code name everyone used for the army general staff field headquarters at Zossen, a little town about thirty-two kilometers south of Berlin. Tucked inside a much larger training ground that was used for artillery firing and protected by wire fence and a subtle but heavy guard force was what looked from a distance like a tiny village. Except that the twelve whitewashed

A-frame houses with shingle roofs were actually cleverly camouflaged solid concrete bunkers. The steeply pitched roofs were designed so that bombs would hopefully skip off them, and if that didn't work there were another two levels belowground under meters of concrete. There was also an underground communications facility, which controlled the entire German Army and all its conquests, called Zeppelin. All of it connected by tunnels.

On the other side of that little compound was a steam shovel and an excavator, busy digging down into the brown dirt and concealed by camouflage nets flung over the tops of the trees. Clearing out more space to be able to rule the rest of the world, Alexsi thought. What was interesting was that the rest of the world thought it all part of some merciless master plan, but to the German Army the speed of their conquests was more like an unexpected pleasant surprise. Not that they weren't drunk with victory and certain they were invincible now.

After Alexsi had his identification and orders checked three times at three different checkpoints, he and his four trucks backed up through the slender pine trees to the bunker/building they were directed to. The one housing Foreign Armies East. Close in, you could see that the windows were just boards attached to the walls with shutters on either side, and the chimneys actually ventilation towers. The door was solid steel, like a bank vault.

Sergeant Dormer, his old friend from the first day at Abwehr headquarters, was in the truck behind. The sergeant was the intelligent and efficient type who had made himself indispensable in the Abwehr records section and would have a very safe war among the files. All Alexsi had to do was stand there, look like he was in charge, and get the receipts signed. But he knew it wasn't going to be quite that easy when, before the truck had even stopped, there was a peevish-looking staff captain perched beside his door.

Alexsi stepped out, came to attention, and saluted. "Lieutenant Shultz, sir!"

"Captain Horn, Colonel Kinzel's adjutant. It's about time you got here." Without another word he plucked the thick portfolio from Alexsi's hands and examined it. "Well, let's make sure this is all right."

Alexsi calmed himself by imagining the look on the captain's face when a knife went into his guts. Sergeant Dormer had already established friendly relations with his opposite number in the bunker and had the soldiers they brought with them stack their rifles. He was waiting the order to begin. Alexsi said, "All right, Sergeant."

But Captain Horn held up a hand to stop the first pair of movers from entering the bunker. "You know these are going into a sensitive room. Do all these men have security clearance?"

This was the way of the German Army. They made sure all the fine captains were off commanding troops, and the pedantic shits were in staff jobs like this. Which was probably the way it ought to be, and probably the reason they defeated everyone in battle. But it didn't make it any easier when you were in a staff job and had to deal with the bastards. "They are all Abwehr I clerks, sir." He motioned for the first two soldiers to carry on.

"The inventory of files?" Captain Horn demanded.

"In the folder, sir," Alexsi replied.

"They'll have to be checked," said Horn.

"The cabinets are locked and sealed, sir," said Alexsi. "You need only see that the number is correct and the seals are intact."

"I'll decide what I need to do," Horn stated.

Alexsi snatched the portfolio back from him, and, ignoring the angry shock on the captain's face, flipped through the pages. "Then kindly sign here and here, sir, for the file inventory and the list of lock combinations."

Spitting mad now, Horn unscrewed his fountain pen and practically stabbed his signature onto the paper.

"Now they are yours to do what you like, sir," said Alexsi, removing the papers and handing the carbon copy to him.

Horn just gave him a look that promised vengeance at the first opportunity.

The soldiers rolled the cabinets down a hallway on the first floor, and into a large but crowded office space. Alexsi was expecting it to be damp and cold, but it was actually quite warm and comfortable inside all that concrete. Though stuffy. No way to properly air out a place like that. One wall had been cleared for the files. Alexsi just planted himself there while the cabinets came in over several trips. There were order of battle charts tacked to the walls, and a large-scale map of western Russia and the Ukraine, covered in clear acetate with colored grease pencil markings. He gave them careful attention while Captain Horn was busy trying out the combination locks on the file cabinets.

While he was doing that, the two sergeants just glanced at each other the way sergeants did around officers. Alexsi caught their eye and gave them back a shrug and a tip of the head toward the captain, and they both had to pretend to rub their faces to keep from smiling.

Soon the soldiers were finished but the captain wasn't. Alexsi told Sergeant Dormer, "Find the mess and get yourself and the men something to eat, or at least some coffee." His eyes fell back on the captain poking into the files. "I'll come find you. Whenever."

The Zossen sergeant gave Dormer the "good lieutenant" look, and they went out together.

Now Alexsi had reached his point of decision. Risk it? Or not? There was a good chance this was all a cleverly laid trap for him. After all, hadn't he watched the NKVD convince a group of university students to assassinate Stalin?

Finally he made up his mind, and said, "While you are busy here, sir, I will go and get Colonel Kinzel's signature for my receipt."

"I am his adjutant," Horn said, in the tone captains used for speaking to stupid lieutenants. "I sign everything here."

"I'm sorry, sir," said Alexsi. "But I have my orders from Colonel Piekenbrock. Colonel Kinzel's signature only."

Horn said, "Now look here—"

"Sorry, sir," Alexsi said flatly. "Orders."

As Alexsi had predicted, Horn was torn between the now-open
file cabinets and a clear desire not to let this annoying lieutenant
anywhere near the commanding officer alone. After a period of
indecision long enough to have the instructors shaking their heads
at officer training school, he snapped, "Up the stairs, end of the
hall."

"Thank you, sir," Alexsi said politely. He had intentionally
timed his arrival as close to the beginning of lunch as possible.
For staff soldiers the lunch hour was holy.

He climbed the stairs, and at the next level viewed the hall.
Totally deserted, and Alexsi didn't care for that one bit. If there
had been just one soldier passing by one look at his face would tell
him everything he needed to know.

His iron-studded boot soles rang loudly on the concrete, echoing down the hallway. It sounded like a horror film, as if there
were ghouls waiting at the end to throw a net over him. Or
Gestapo. It was everything he could do just to keep his legs moving and not dash back down the stairs to the warm safety of his
German identity.

Alexsi followed the placards on the doors. Finally he reached the
one that announced, in Gothic script: *Foreign Armies East, Lieutenant Colonel Eberhard Kinzel.*

Alexsi opened the door to an outer office that held two empty
desks. Not even a clerk on duty. They must have the main switchboard taking messages during lunch. One desk had Captain Horn's
name board on it. Alexsi looked it over, but there was nothing interesting. He left the door to the hallway open a few centimeters.
The inner office door read: *Lieutenant Colonel of Infantry Eberhard
Kinzel.* All the German intelligence officers wanted to remind
everyone they were real soldiers first. Unlike in the Soviet Union

there was no prestige in intelligence. Alexsi knocked. No answer. He carefully opened the door and peeked in. The office was deserted. Another moment of decision. Alexsi unbuckled the flap of the pistol holster on his belt. There would be no escape shooting his way out of this place with a Luger, but it was a better end than hanging from a meat hook.

He stepped inside. There was a large desk and an even larger map table covered with map sheets and files. Alexsi circled the desk, distracted for a moment by the photograph of a really stunning blonde. The colonel, it seemed, was quite the ladies' man. Following Yakushev's training to the letter, he made a complete circuit of the room first, taking in everything in sight and touching nothing. Then he flipped through the visible papers and files, taking great pains not to move them from their original positions. The procedures were how you did the job without being overcome by the thought of being tortured to death.

He had only just begun when he thought he heard the clang of boots on the stairway. Alexsi closed the file he had been reading and dashed for the door. He swung it shut as fast as he could before slowing down that last inch and gingerly closing the lock so it wouldn't make any noise. He dropped into the nearest chair as if he'd been shot, and had just crossed his legs when a lieutenant colonel stepped through the doorway, looking down at the knob in his hand as if it were out of uniform because it had been open.

His eyes fell on Alexsi and he demanded, "Who the devil are you?"

Alexsi stood to attention as if he'd been sitting there all day, and saluted. "Lieutenant Shultz, sir. Abwehr I."

Kinzel was pure Prussian officer, right down to the steel monocle screwed into his right eye. He had a round face but a narrow chin, and appeared to be one of those officers who always looked upset so his subordinates would always be running about trying to please him. He wore the Iron Cross First and Second Class from the Great War. Clearly that answer wasn't sufficient for him, so he growled, "Yes?"

"Delivering the Red Army files from Abwehr I, sir," Alexsi added.

"Finally," Kinzel exclaimed. And then, "Did you carry them here yourself? I saw no trucks."

"I sent my men off to eat lunch, sir."

"Very good. Always take care of your soldiers, Lieutenant. Now why are you here in my office? And where is Captain Horn, I wonder?"

"Captain Horn is downstairs checking the files, sir. Colonel Piekenbrock asked that while I had you sign for them I pass on his compliments and see if there was anything more you required." It was a centuries-old tradition for a messenger, having delivered his dispatches, to ask if there were any verbal communication between commanders that they did not want to commit to paper, so Alexsi was sure it wouldn't arouse any suspicions.

"More men, a bigger budget, and an OKH that doesn't question my every judgment," said Kinzel. "But since I know I won't be getting any of those things, my thanks to Colonel Piekenbrock. Now what must I sign? It seems I sign my life away every day."

"Just this, sir," Alexsi said, flipping open the portfolio and handing over his fountain pen.

Colonel Kinzel leaned over Captain Horn's desk to sign the receipt. "Anything else?"

"No, sir. Thank you, sir," Alexsi said, the very model of the earnest young lieutenant, who certainly could have had the adjutant sign but wanted to do everything by the book.

"Good day, Lieutenant."

"Good day, sir." Alexsi saluted, and the colonel returned it with a casual but correct hand to the cap brim. Then he broke the effect with a wide yawn that he covered with that same hand. Alexsi

imagined that an after-lunch nap was on the agenda in the colonel's office.

Shutting the door behind him, Alexsi paused and took a shaky
breath. His stomach felt like it was filled with whole walnuts.
That had been close. And to think he'd been tempted to bring one
of the Abwehr miniature cameras along, to definitely convince
the NKVD. Just imagine if he'd had the desk there all set up for
photography when he heard those footsteps. Or hadn't left the
door ajar so that he could hear them.

Walking to the mess Alexsi buttoned his greatcoat up against
the wind that was whipping the dirt from the construction piles
about like shrapnel. In little more than a month 1940 would be
over, with Germany on top of the world. And he had his own victory now. Since that first day at Abwehr and his interview with
Admiral Canaris he had been scrupulously careful not to ask a
single question or volunteer to do anything regarding the Soviet
Union. But he had also been certain that something like this was
bound to come up. There were only sixty-three officers assigned
to Abwehr foreign espionage at the Berlin headquarters—fewer
than were in the headquarters of a single German army corps.
Something else that Moscow hadn't believed when he told them.
But they'd believe this.

Alexsi recalled Yakushev's parting words on how a single spy
could change the course of history. Knowing how the Soviets
wrote theirs, he was sure they would make his mission sound in-
finitely more heroic than while moving furniture, he had walked
into an office, poked about a bit, and won the war. But even if
they kept it secret they would have to reward him all the same.
All he really wanted was to be left alone. But that was a lot to ask
for in the Soviet Union. You had to be a hero in order to get it.

38

1940 Berlin

ALEXSI BEGAN WITH A CLEAN SHEET OF PAPER. HE'D MAKE IT short and to the point.

CASE BARBAROSSA. THE GERMAN INVASION OF THE SOVIET UNION. PLANS TO BE SENT TO HITLER DECEMBER 1940. INVASION EARLY MAY 1941. ARMY GROUP NORTH, COMMANDER LEEB. 3 PANZER DIVISIONS, 3 MOTORIZED INFANTRY, 20 INFANTRY. ATTACKING FROM EAST PRUSSIA, MAIN EFFORT BALTIC STATES AND LENINGRAD. FINNISH ARMY WILL MAKE SUPPORTING ATTACKS TOWARD LENINGRAD AND WHITE SEA. ARMY GROUP CENTER, COMMANDER BOCK. 9 PANZER DIVISIONS, 5 MOTORIZED INFANTRY, 35 INFANTRY. ATTACKING FROM POLAND, MAIN EFFORT NORTH-SOUTH CONCENTRIC ATTACK MINSK, SMOLENSK, MOSCOW, DESTRUCTION RED ARMY WESTERN SOVIET UNION. ARMY GROUP SOUTH, COMMANDER RUNDSTEDT. 5 PANZER DIVISIONS, 4 MOTORIZED INFANTRY, 50 INFANTRY INCLUDING ROMANIAN, HUNGARIAN, ITALIAN. ATTACKING FROM VICINITY LUBLIN POLAND, HUNGARY, ROMANIA. MAIN EFFORT SOUTHEASTERN DRIVE TOWARD KIEV AND RIVER DNIEPER, DESTRUCTION RED ARMY SOUTHWESTERN SOVIET UNION. BARBAROSSA INITIAL OPERATIONAL GOAL CONQUEST OF EUROPEAN SOVIET UNION WEST OF LINE

FROM ARKHANGEL TO ASTRAKHAN, REFERRED TO IN PLANS
AS A-A LINE. PLANS WITNESSED PERSONALLY. DAVID.

That ought to do it. Moscow was getting the plans before Hitler himself—what more could they ask for? He opened his almanac and began enciphering the message.

39

ALEXSI WALKED HOME THE SAME ROUTE EVERY SINGLE DAY. Across the River Spree and cutting through the southern part of the forest park of the Tiergarten. He wasn't alone. Petrol rationing had left only the military and party big shots driving, and the streetcars were always packed to bursting. Everyone who could walked or rode their bicycle.

Yakushev said that a spy might feel more comfortable alone, but there was always greater safety in crowds. The tree-lined walk was as busy as a city street.

Alexsi didn't look directly at it, because there might be someone watching specifically to see who looked directly at it. But in his peripheral vision he noted the upside-down V scratched in chalk on the side rail of the park bench.

It was the signal to him that his *taynik* was loaded and ready. Moscow was sending him something via the dead letter box? Now? Alexsi felt like a deer who had suddenly come upon a large and delicious pile of apples in a forest clearing. Very inviting, thanks, but I'll pass.

He'd already gone through the checklist in his head. First he was nearly caught using his radio, and then a Russian spy was caught using his radio. Ressler shows up asking him to translate a Russian shopping list, as if the SD and Gestapo had no one who spoke Russian. And then let's go out on the town with the SD counterintelligence man who just wants to be friends, even though in the end all the idiot did was make *himself* drunk and foolish and probably get lashed and buggered for his trouble. Are you curious about this Russian spy, Shultz? Are you worried, asking a lot of questions? No. Shultz could care less. Shultz, please come down to Gestapo headquarters to speak some Russian to a prisoner. How stupid did they think he was? The Gestapo wanted the two of them face-to-face, to see if one recognized the other. Or for him to make some clumsy excuse to signal his guilt.

The proof was about to present itself. If he was just being a suspicious Russian, then fine. Moscow could order him to unload the damned dead letter box over the daily radio message.

Alexsi did what he would have anyway, Yakushev's voice in his head. *Do not succumb to routine. Complacency has killed more spies than carelessness.* He walked right past the path leading to the *taynik*.

And there they were. A man and a woman looking as though they were talking, but not looking at each other. If you followed Yakushev's rules and picked a spot for your dead letter box that was easily accessible and in a public place, but also where you would be totally hidden from view as you loaded or emptied it, you would always be safe. Because if the enemy ever discovered the box they would be forced to stack up their surveillance very close by in order to catch you. You would always bump into *someone* if you passed by and then doubled back.

Alexsi turned at the next intersection and there was a single Gestapo on a bench, reading a book like the student no one would ever take him for in his trench coat and fedora.

As he left the Tiergarten and crossed over onto Potsdamer Strasse, there were the two staff cars filled with uniformed Gestapo reinforcements carrying machine pistols. Easy to pick out wearing the SS uniform with the SD arm insignia, but no SS runes on the right collar. Just a plain black patch.

There was no other explanation. The Russian spy hanging up in Gestapo headquarters was the contact who passed along the mail from his *taynik*. And he'd cracked and given the Germans both the *taynik* and the load and unload signals. All praise to Yakushev that the man never knew who was on the other end of the dead letter box.

There was just one nagging question. Was it every officer in Berlin who spoke Russian, or just him? Should he run or should he stay?

It had to have been just suspicions. They never would have let him go to Zossen otherwise. Or they would have trapped him there.

Alexsi remembered Ressler trying to talk Colonel Piekenbrock out of sending him. Even though he hadn't heard a word, he knew what Piekenbrock was asking: What proof do you have? And Ressler having to admit: absolutely none. Now Piekenbrock, and therefore Admiral Canaris, would never believe a thing Ressler said about him.

It was incredible good luck his uncle had sent him into the army. If he'd been a civilian the Gestapo would be beating him senseless right now just out of suspicion. The SD could do whatever they wanted with an SS man. But the German Army, always standing on its privileges, would never let them touch one of their officers without firm proof. And they had nothing. Alexsi made up his mind. He would stay. Especially since the Abwehr was about to send him out of Berlin anyway. It was getting much too warm here.

Since he was going to remain a German, he couldn't breathe a word to Moscow about all this. The last thing he needed was for them to panic and order him back to Russia just as the German Army was about to crash over the border.

40

ALEXSI PUT HIS HEAD IN THE OFFICE DOOR AND BARKED OUT, "Captain Ressler!"

Ressler jumped in his chair. Gunnar the Alsatian went from fast asleep to up on his paws and wobbling about in confusion.

Alexsi wiped the smile off his face before the chair swiveled around.

Ressler looked over his shoulder and muttered, "Jesus."

"No, just me," Alexsi said, smiling again. "I hope I'm not intruding?"

"What do you want?" said Ressler.

"As you probably know, I'm leaving soon," said Alexsi, "and I wanted to treat you to lunch."

"That's not necessary," Ressler said.

"After all your kindness?" said Alexsi. "It's the least I can do. Please. I insist. It would be the comradely thing."

Ressler squinted slightly, as if that would reveal all ulterior motives. Finally he said, "Oh, very well."

"I'll come back and collect you," said Alexsi.

"What are you doing now?" Ressler inquired, ever the policeman.

"Just some radio practice."

And at that moment Alexsi watched Ressler's face transform itself into pure boyish longing. "I've always been fascinated by wireless," he said.

"You don't say," Alexsi replied.

"They don't let anyone into the signal section who isn't qualified. Mind if I tag along?"

"Not at all," Alexsi said, still smiling.

Down in the signal section he signed the post log for one of the
transmitter rooms reserved for training. "I'm going to do some
speed work training to Hamburg," Alexsi said to the duty sergeant. "Do you have a useless old message in code I can send without anyone getting upset?"

The sergeant pulled a paper flimsy off a pile impaled on a metal
spike. "Here you are, Lieutenant."

"Thanks," Alexsi said.

Ressler coughed.

"I've signed you in as an observer," Alexsi said.

"Finally got someone to let you sit in, eh, Captain?" The sergeant
said it with borderline insolence, confident in the impunity his
technical expertise gave him.

Ressler just glowered at him.

There were already two chairs in the booth, for an instructor
if needed. Ressler took one and shook a cigarette out of his pack.

"If you don't mind," said Alexsi. "Smoke isn't good for the elec-
tronics." Actually, he didn't want him stinking the place up. The
room reeked of stale tobacco anyway.

"Oh, of course," said Ressler, putting it away.

Alexsi switched on the transmitter and let it warm up.

"Tell me what each one does," Ressler demanded, eyeing the
wall of dials, switches, and needles with childlike delight.

"Here, you set the frequency," said Alexsi, pointing to the dial.
"Abwehr Hamburg is twenty-one meters. There, that's it."

While Ressler was ever so carefully dialing the number in,
Alexsi disconnected the power switch to the Morse key.

"Is that it?" Ressler asked anxiously.

"Close enough," said Alexsi. "We'll probably have to adjust it
once we start."

"All this marvelous technology," said Ressler. "Vacuum tubes and crystals and electric wires."

When he finally sat down, Alexsi put his hand on the key and tapped out *RESSLER LOVES TO BE BUGGERED IN HIS ASS*. Not even a twitch of recognition came across the captain's face as the key clicked away. He was the type who would find it impossible to keep his composure in the face of any insult, so he definitely could not read Morse code. This radio fascination wasn't an act after all, he marveled.

"What are you sending now?" Ressler asked.

"Just warming up the fingers."

Alexsi switched the power key back to on and began tapping out code. "Hamburg is call sign AOR. And I'm sending a series of V's until they come in." He tapped, and paused. In a moment faint dots and dashes came through the static of the speaker. Alexsi leaned forward, adjusted the tuning dial slightly, and kept sending. The Morse from Hamburg came in clearer now. "All right, we have each other." He tapped away. "Now I'm telling them in the clear that this is training, transmission speed practice, I'm sending a message that doesn't need to be decoded, and I'm sending it more than once."

Ressler nodded without looking at him, his face rapt at the sight of the bouncing power needles.

Hamburg acknowledged, and gave him GA for "go ahead." With the message paper clipped to the metal holder, Alexsi began sending rapid Morse. Except he wasn't sending the message in front of him. He was sending his own coded message about Operation Barbarossa, the invasion of the Soviet Union.

When he'd lost his radio and nearly been caught, Alexsi had sent an invisible writing letter to the NKVD postal box in Berlin, letting them know and telling them to listen for him sending practice messages to Abwehr Hamburg. Which they monitored as a matter of course. The Abwehr had him practicing wireless for his mission anyway, so it would be good cover, though very risky. Anyone looking into it closely might ask questions he would have a hard time answering.

Abwehr agents used a hand code since they couldn't very well carry the standard Enigma coding machine along with them. Their columnar transposition hand code was based on a keyword and sent letters in groups of five, so he also gave the Russians a simple letter substitution for the 0–9 numerals of his Soviet code. In any event he had memorized the message he was sending, because now there was no way in the world he would carry anything incriminating around on his person.

He sent the message, and AR to indicate the end. Then KA to begin and repeated it faster as if it was part of the exercise. "That's it," he said to Ressler.

"How do you do it so fast? I couldn't even make out the difference between the dots and the dashes."

"It's just a matter of practice. An experienced operator can even identify you from the way you tap out a message. They call it your fist."

"I've heard of that," said Ressler.

Actually, the Russians had taught him a few simple tricks to disguise his fist. You just had to send with a few specific quirks as a matter of routine, then be careful to transmit smooth and either fast or slow when you wanted to conceal yourself. "Now we'll see what Hamburg says about my speed."

The dots and dashes came over the speaker, and Alexsi translated them out loud. "They say that the speed of the first was well above the standard operator, and the second was first class."

"Well done," said Ressler.

"I hope that wasn't too boring for you."

"Not at all. Now his face was nothing but longing. "I've always wanted to train in wireless. But I never had the opportunity.

"Perhaps one day," Alexsi said. He signed off with Hamburg and powered down the transmitter. "You can have that cigarette now."

"Oh, right," said Ressler.

Alexsi signed out in the log, and gave the message flimsy back to the sergeant. Who stuck it back on the sent-message spike, to be forgotten. That was that.

"Now what about some lunch?" he said to Ressler.

41

1940 Berlin

THE NEW MAID WENT TO THE WINDOW TO CHECK THE BLACK-out curtains, even though the British bombers hadn't raided Berlin in four months. And then only one night when they barely even managed to hit the city. But predictably Hitler had flown into a rage, made one of his bloodthirsty public speeches, and the air force had been blitzing London ever since.

"Thank you, Elke," Hans Schultz said.

The way Elke looked at his uncle on her way out made Alexsi think he was fucking her. He just lay back in the padded leather club chair, stretched his legs out, and shook his head when his uncle held up a cigar. The rump steak had to have come from the black market—nearly an entire week's ration almost crowding the potatoes and winter cabbage right off the plate.

"Was your farewell dinner all right?" Hans Shultz asked gruffly.

"Delicious, thank you, Uncle."

"So, do you feel ready for this?"

"I do, Uncle," Alexsi said.

"Well, I know you have wits," Hans Shultz said. "Just make sure you keep them about you."

Alexsi grinned, knowing this was the German equivalent of a Russian weeping with emotion. Though you always had to watch the hands of a Russian weeping with emotion. For weapons. "I will, Uncle. There is something I wanted to talk to you about, though."

"So?"

"There is an SD captain in Abwehr counterintelligence. Not a bright fellow by any means, but a certain cunning. He seems quite suspicious of my Russian."

Hans Shultz was fully alert now. "How much trouble has this fellow made?"

"He has no proof, nothing but suspicions. He has no credibility within Abwehr, but he is energetic."

Hans Shultz produced a small leather-bound notebook and a silver mechanical pencil from his jacket pocket. "What is his name?"

"Ressler, Uncle. Hauptsturmführer Kurt Ressler."

"SD you say?"

"Yes, Uncle."

Hans Schultz jotted down a note. "This fellow probably needs to burn off all that extra energy hunting Jews in Poland."

Alexsi just nodded. That was that.

Echoing his own thoughts, Hans Shultz said, "It is probably better you are leaving Berlin." Now he coughed, as if he were embarrassed. "When you told me where you were headed, well . . ." He hesitated, and then, "I wonder if you would do *me* a service."

Ears prickling with suspicion, Alexsi still said, "Of course, Uncle." This was classic Hans. Even though you both knew you were obligated, he would still remind you that you owed him, however subtly.

Alexsi had mentioned that he would be leaving for Vienna and Switzerland. But nothing else. He wasn't about to risk any unintentional loose talk that might result in people whose acquaintance he didn't wish to make awaiting his arrival in Iran. After all, he couldn't be the only spy in Berlin.

Hans Shultz rose and unlocked a door in the wall cabinet, withdrawing a leather case. He sat it on the table in front of his nephew and resumed his seat by the fire. "For when you are in Zurich."

Alexsi made a "may I?" gesture, and his uncle nodded. He opened the case. It was filled with neatly banded stacks of high-denomination Reichsmarks. A tidy sum. Uncle had been doing deals for more than rump steaks. Well, the world ran on *blat*. If you had influence and you didn't present a bill for your services, then you were a fool. And Uncle Hans was no fool.

"The bank and account information is in the envelope, nephew. You will deposit these marks, but the account is in Swiss francs. The Swiss will give you no problems. There will be a fee for the currency conversion, of course. With the Swiss there is always a fee." He paused. "I assume you will be able to pass over the Reich borders without undue difficulty?"

Alexsi was still gazing down at the money. Because he was Abwehr there would be no German search at the Swiss border, and the Swiss were happy to let you bring in as much money as you wished as long as you were going to leave it there. "This will not be a problem, Uncle."

"Good. Good. I certainly appreciate it."

Alexsi opened the envelope. "It is a numbered account? No name?"

"Yes. Better to keep these things confidential."

Alexsi nodded. It was illegal to hold a foreign bank account. The Nazis didn't keep that airtight seal over every single aspect of your life the way the Soviets did, but they still liked their thumb on you and your money. A Swiss bank account, they felt, was a sign you didn't think the Third Reich was really going to last a thousand years after all.

He took the letter over to the fireplace and set it in the flames. "I will remember the bank information, Uncle. And the case will remain in an Abwehr safe until I leave for Switzerland."

"Of course. Very wise. Very wise, indeed. You know, nephew, I must tell you frankly that my own son was a great disappointment to me. I do not feel the same of you."

Alexsi was neither surprised nor overcome with emotion.

After all, he did everything the old man wanted. "Thank you, Uncle. That means a great deal to me. I will never be able to thank you properly for taking me into your home."

"No need for that. Just bring yourself back to it, safe." Hans Shultz was on his feet again, and gazing at the silver-framed photographs on the shelves of his cabinet. "When my father sent me off to war he told me he would have a mass said every week for my safe return. And unlike so many others I did return. But I know I was not the only soldier who had masses said for him, and the others died by the millions." Now he turned and faced his nephew. "It's pleasant to think of God as the driving force of our lives, isn't it? But I will tell you, my boy, God is not the driving force of our lives. Nature is. And nature is not kind."

42

ALEXSI WOKE EARLY THE NEXT MORNING AND TURNED ON HIS
radio. It must have been a fine day in the ionosphere, because the
Morse code from Moscow came in crystal clear.

The message was very short. Well, they wouldn't be effusive
in their congratulations, would they? Regardless of the magni-
tude of his information. That was all right. A simple well done
would be sufficient. He consulted his almanac and deciphered
the message. And it stared up from the paper at him, in block
letters.

YOU ARE CATEGORICALLY ORDERED TO CEASE
RELAYING BRITISH PROVOCATIONS.

Fuck all their mothers!

How in the devil could he, sitting in Berlin amongst a sea of
Germans, even know what a British provocation was?

Alexsi crumpled the paper up in his fist and tried to calm himself. He sat back, closed his eyes, and concentrated hard, trying to
reason out an explanation for this madness. No one in the NKVD
would have the courage to do this on their own. It had to mean
Stalin himself had decided there would be no German invasion,
and any intelligence to the contrary was just a British trick to
try to drag him into the war on their side. That was the party
line, and everyone was following it. Well, Alexsi thought, if that's

how it is, then good luck to you, Iosef. That's the last you'll hear of it from me.

This was probably going to be one of those very rare times when everyone would get exactly what they deserved.

PART III

Operation
Countenance

43

IT WAS A DISAPPOINTMENT. THE VAUNTED ORIENT EXPRESS was a casualty of war. The victorious German Mitropa rail line had replaced the conquered Belgian Wagons-Lits, and the luxury sleeping cars had gone the way of mundane sitting cars and couchettes. Bread and coffee for breakfast, and if you didn't care for the brief menu of soups and stews, you were free to go hungry. Alexsi just listened with amusement to the other passengers complain. They should try a Soviet prison train sometime.

It had been difficult leaving Zurich. A wonderful country, Switzerland—as long as you had money, which he did courtesy of the Abwehr. He'd learned many things there. The textile business from a Swiss company whose majority stockholder was German intelligence. The ins and outs of both Swiss banking and the financial affairs of Uncle Hans. And the perfect excuse for keeping away from the NKVD.

At least the journey from Zurich to Istanbul was incredibly fast. Only six days. The political situation in Yugoslavia made the shorter line through that country too dangerous for German trains. Hungary was all right, as long as you liked your food heavy and full of paprika, but Bulgaria in the wintertime made rural Russia look like Switzerland.

He recognized his contact immediately when the man boarded the Istanbul to Ankara train at Eskisehir. Still wearing a Russian suit, a mistake that made him stand out like a lighthouse beacon.

He dropped down next to Alexsi in the sitting car and rubbed his jaw morosely.

Alexsi set his book down on his lap and regarded him. "Feeling all right?" he asked politely in German.

"Terrible toothache," said Sergei from Moscow and that very first meeting in the park at Munich. "But I have a dentist appointment in Ankara."

"Make sure you go to one who uses the nitrous gas," Alexsi advised. "It's quite painless."

"Thank you," said Sergei. "Would you happen to know what time it is?"

Alexsi held up his wrist so his watch was visible.

"You've filled out," Sergei observed. "You look quite well, actually."

I'm not so hungry anymore, Alexsi thought. No more feeding dishes of sausages into my face, and mistaking bandsmen for policemen. He reached into his jacket pocket and took out a large cardboard packet of Turkish cigarettes. He handed it to Sergei. "Here, keep the pack." There was no one else within earshot, though everyone still had eyes.

Sergei opened it so only he could see. There was one cigarette and the rest of the space was filled with tightly packed onionskin. He removed a cigarette and lit it, casually slipping the packet into his pocket. One puff and he removed it from his mouth, staring at the burning cylinder between his fingers. "These will take some getting used to." And then, "You've done well."

"Really?" said Alexsi. "Listening to the radio gives the impression that everyone is unhappy with me."

"No one expects your information to be one hundred percent accurate all of the time," Sergei replied smoothly. "Your penetration of German intelligence has been beyond all our dreams for you. You give us gold. Never think this has not been noticed."

"You don't say. Were you aware that they threw me out of the

Soviet consulate in Zurich as a provocateur? I nearly had the Swiss police on me after the scene they made."

Sergei said, "Rest assured, the fools involved have been disciplined."

"I had to follow one of the neighbors," Alexsi said, using the Soviet slang for an intelligence officer, "and make him accept a message at knifepoint. A blade under his chin as I stuffed the paper into his pocket. Picture that."

"You must understand that these are troubled times," said Sergei. "The Organs are in a state of flux at the present."

Alexsi paused to translate that statement. Stalin was still more interested in shooting Russians than in being invaded by Germans. He was purging State Security as well as the party and the army. It was just like the French Revolution. Terror devouring itself. Well, Stalin had to keep killing off his band of murderers, didn't he? Before they woke up one day and decided to kill him. "You know the Germans are poised to take advantage of that," he said.

"Have no fear," Sergei replied. "We are ever on guard against our enemies."

Of course you are, Alexsi thought. Another Russian parrot, squawking out his slogans. Well, that was the last he'd mention it. "So how is my old master?"

"He sends his fraternal greetings and commends your work as a true Soviet fighter."

Alexsi leaned back in his seat. So Yakushev was purged, also. If he wasn't dead or in a camp somewhere, there would have been a message characteristic of him. "What of you?" he said to Sergei. "Moving up in the world?"

"We all serve the Soviet Union," Sergei said quietly.

"How true," Alexsi replied.

"How will you reach Iran?" Sergei asked, as if the conversation had gotten too hot for him.

"I'll try for a plane in Ankara," Alexsi said. "I don't relish a horseback trip through the mountains. Who knows what mood the Kurds are in."

"Why didn't you take a train through the Soviet Union directly to Teheran?"

"I went the way the Germans wanted me to," Alexsi lied. "The Swiss textile firm that is my cover also has business in Turkey."

"Your contact in Teheran will be Comrade Matushkin in the Soviet embassy," said Sergei. "Ostensibly a commercial attaché but one of us. A colonel. No one else will be read in to your mission."

A diplomat with immunity for a contact, Alexsi thought. If something went wrong the diplomat would only be expelled. While he would be hanged. "Tell him to be social. I'll be staying away from the embassy, but I'll make sure I run into him in town." The sight of his Berlin contact hanging like meat in the Gestapo cellar proved the risk of dealing with someone less careful than yourself.

Sergei nodded. "Your identifier is as follows. The person initiating the conversation will ask if you have met before. The other will ask if he has ever been to the Italian city of Florence. The reply will be no, but he has always wanted to see Michelangelo's famous statue of David."

"Simple enough," said Alexsi. "Any other orders?"

"Has your assignment from the Germans changed since you reported it?"

"No. Establish espionage networks and prepare for sabotage actions." Alexsi would never again mention invasion.

"Then merely keep us informed of those activities, taking care to identify fascist operatives and both pro- and anti-Soviet elements in Iran."

The conductor came walking through the car. "Ankara, one half hour." He said it in four different languages.

"I must get my luggage together," said Alexsi. "Anything else?"

"No," said Sergei. "Good luck."

"Good luck to *you*," Alexsi replied. Sergei would need it, if not from Stalin then definitely the German Army.

He went off to find the attendant of his sleeping couchette. So old Yakushev was gone. Well, the future belonged to the Sergeis of the world, who would diligently execute their orders to the letter no matter who gave them, or even if they happened to contradict those of the previous day. Alexsi's thoughts expressed themselves in Russian for the first time in a very long while. *Ugadat, ugodit, utselet.* Sniff out, suck up, survive.

44

SHE STRADDLED HIM, USING HER FEET CURLED AROUND HIS legs just below his knees to push herself up and down. At first deliciously slowly, and now more deliberate as she was approaching the finish. He'd shown her all the little movements she could make to increase her enjoyment, and she had embraced every one. Now her rocking was faster, and her eyes glassy. She was near.

"Go as fast as you need to, my love," Alexsi whispered in Farsi. Iranian men would never let their women make love in the dominant position.

She took him at his word, speeding up until that wonderful moist sound of their sweating skin slapping together sounded like a steam piston. Wrapped up in pleasure, it was that moment when it was as if he wasn't even there.

Her head thrust up toward the ceiling, and all her muscles tightened. Alexsi gathered her breasts in his hands, lightly rolling her rock-hard dark-brown nipples between his thumb and forefinger.

She grabbed his wrists and the cry tore loose from her throat. Not for the first time he was glad he had bought a house. Otherwise the neighbors would be impossible to deal with. With this going on he couldn't even keep a maid—he had to have a housekeeper come in.

She convulsed, and her cries continued lower now, and throatier. Alexsi didn't come. He didn't dare. Once these Iranian women got a taste of climax they couldn't get enough. She had already come once from his tongue, and this was her second atop him.

She collapsed on his chest, sliding her arms under his armpits to pull herself up and kiss him. Alexsi wrapped his arms around her. "Ah, my Zahra," he said tenderly.

"By God," she declared. "If women knew the Swiss made love like that, no man in your country would be safe."

"Will you tell them?" he asked playfully.

"No," she said, kissing him again. "There aren't enough Swiss to go around in Teheran. You'll be my little secret."

He hugged her, and she put her face in his neck and gave a little sigh of contentment. Muslim men were supposed to get up and wash right after sex, and women liked to be held. So there was another point of contention.

She was married to a general. In Iran if you fucked an unmarried girl and were found out, someone would be killed. Her, at least, and by her family. An honor killing—she had to die because they felt dishonored. And most likely you, too. There were none of what the Americans called shotgun weddings. Not with infidel foreigners. No, everyone ended up dead.

He nearly ran his hand through her hair, but she had expensive permanent curls in the Western style, and if he displaced them there would be trouble. So instead he traced the curve of her buttocks. She was perhaps ten years older than he, though that was uncertain. Alexsi had done many foolish and dangerous things, but asking a woman her age was not one of them.

He was still inside her, and still semihard. She shifted herself slightly to enjoy it. Most women were sensitive afterward, but this one had the private parts of a crocodile. "So what have you been up to?" she asked in that sleepy postclimax voice.

He always let her ask him first. They were such gossips. But then if all the women were allowed to do was sit in a room with other women, what did anyone expect? They were their own spy network, and had become his network. Their husbands were all looking to trade information for money and influence, and what wasn't outright lies was the fantasy of conspiracy that Muslims loved so much. And what was neither was simply incorrect. The women were rich, educated, and well connected, but still kept in a tight little box by Iranian men. They knew everything, and were frank about everything but their own plots and plans. "I'm worried about my business," he replied. "If the British invade like everyone says, then things won't settle down for months, if ever."

"They will invade," she said confidently. "The Russians from the north, and the British from the south. Any day now."

He playfully slapped her buttocks, and she groaned happily. She liked a friendly spanking, not too rough, to warm herself up. "That's not what I wanted to hear, Zahra."

She chuckled. "Well, that's what will happen. Within the week. The Shah has always been too sympathetic toward the Germans. The Allies gave him an ultimatum to expel the ones here, and he refused. The German Army might be smashing their way through Russia right now, but they won't get here fast enough to save him."

"Perhaps the Shah will make a deal instead, to keep them off?"

"Too late," she said. "Now that the British have put down the revolt in Iraq they'll move against him. They've always wanted our country anyway. Would you believe King Farouk of Egypt warned the Shah of the entire British plan?"

Unlike the NKVD, the Abwehr was effusive in their praise when he radioed them this stuff. It was easy. Six months in Teheran, and all he had to do was go into business. He was making money hand over fist, and the money took him into the highest social circles. The foreigners because he was a successful foreign businessman. The Iranians because he was a rich foreign businessman who actually spoke Farsi and wasn't one of the arrogant Englishmen they despised. Just as Yakushev had said: he was in a position where people couldn't wait to tell him things.

It wasn't all sex, though as always the Russians had been astute in their training. Men were concerned with how to get ahead today, while women worried about the future, and that of their children. So if Iranian men were not about to work toward that goal, their women would. A private boarding school in Switzerland. A loan of some money to speculate in gold. A word with a diplomat about a visa. A relative with textiles to sell. Alexsi was always ready to give them what they wanted. "Will the Shah fight?" he asked.

She only laughed at that. "He will order the army to. But no one will tell him that all the division commanders are negotiating the best deal for their surrender. The British will pay more. And they're afraid the Russians will kill them before they have a chance to put up the white flag. Or send them to Siberia if by some chance they survive. So of the four divisions in the north, there may be a race south to see who can reach the arms of the British first."

"How will so many troops make it down three roads?" Alexsi asked innocently.

"Their officers, my silly Swiss. They will get in their staff cars and have a road race between themselves, leaving their poor soldiers behind."

If the Iranian men heard this, their manhood would shrivel out of sight. But Alexsi knew this was far more realistic than them boasting they would crush the British if they dared invade.

She went on. "And I am sure the British agents have already made their golden promises to the three divisions in the south."

"I'll have to be quick to get as many of my goods as I can out before that happens," he said, talking like a good Swiss businessman.

"If you need help, darling, let me know."

She was already a silent investor in one of the fabric companies he bought from. Family money, and he was fairly sure her husband had no idea. Which was fine. Alexsi wanted as many people dedicated to his prosperity and survival as possible. He kissed her forehead. "Here I am worried about my business, and I haven't asked about you."

"You're so sweet. Kayvan is trying to arrange another marriage with some little girl. Instead of ever learning to use his member properly he'll just keep marrying virgins to save face."

Kayvan was her husband. Muslim men were permitted four wives. Which was just a recipe for chaos, as far as Alexsi was concerned. Life was hard enough as it was. "Idiot," he said.

"That's all right," she said into his neck. "At least I have my Swiss." And then she laughed.

"What?" Alexsi said.

"I was just thinking, the way the Germans are racing through Russia the British might have a shorter stay in Teheran than they think. Do the Germans compare to the Swiss in bed, I wonder?"

"Much rougher, I would guess," Alexsi said.

She laughed again, and pushed herself up so she could whisper in his ear. "I know the Swiss are famously neutral, my darling. Which is a wonderful thing in the midst of war. But you still speak German, and mistakes do happen. The Allies will round up all the Germans in Iran."

"My dear, both the British and Russians know the difference between a Swiss and a German."

"This may be so," she said. "But if need be, my people can get you across the border into Iraq. And then Turkey is only a short journey."

Even in the upper classes marriages were made as tribal alliances. She was a Lur of western Iran, and her husband a Bakhtiari. Both of the highest rank. "Unless Germany invades Switzerland also, my dear, I am perfectly safe."

"I pray to God this is so," she said. "Know you anything of the military arts?"

Alexsi was afraid that even if he acted calm she would notice his breathing. So he rose up in the bed, taking her along with him. "Every Swiss man must spend a time in my country's army, Zahra. Why do you ask such a thing?"

"It is good to know what there is to trade. If bargains need be made."

Oh, these women were something. They made their men look like simpletons. Alexsi warned himself to never underestimate them.

"Now may we do it again?" she asked sweetly.

45

1941 Teheran, Iran

IT WAS GREEN AND SHADED BEHIND THE WALLS OF THE TURK-
ish embassy. Just the antidote to the Teheran summer. Since Alexsi
was a good Westerner he had to wear a suit and tie in this heat,
like the rest of those fools. Even Iranians had to suffer since the
Shah had taken women out of the chador and put men into suits.

He watched the English and Americans smack the balls back
and forth across the tennis court, sweating like cheese in their
white flannels. Idiots.

A servant brought him a glass of ayran. The yogurt, water, and
salt over ice was the perfect Turkish invention for summer. Teheran was so dry his mouth always felt like dust.

Alexsi felt the approach, and turned before the hand came
down on his shoulder. "Excellency!"

He and Ambassador Davaz embraced by gripping each other's
biceps. "How are you, my friend?" the ambassador said, giving the
traditional Turkish greeting. He was short and built like a cannon-
ball.

"Fine, thank you," Alexsi replied in classical Turkish.

The ambassador made a sweeping gesture toward the more
austere man standing beside him. "Allow me to introduce my successor, Ambassador Ilhami Uzel. Ambassador Uzel, Mr. Walter
Berger. A most distinguished Swiss businessman. And a great friend
of Turkey."

"A rare privilege, Excellency," Alexsi said, shaking hands. "The friends of Turkey welcome you from their hearts. Your predecessor is as cherished by us as he is respected."

"The pleasure is mine," Ambassador Uzel replied.

Ambassador Davaz was smiling. "Now that I am leaving, I can afford to be undiplomatic for once," he told Ambassador Uzel quietly. "Herr Berger is my favorite European in Teheran. Not only has he the soul of a Turk, but does he not speak the most poetic Turkish?"

"Yes, most refreshing," Ambassador Uzel replied. "Do I detect perhaps a touch of an Azeri accent?"

"I have spent much time in the north on business, Excellency," Alexsi said.

"Regrettably, we must continue our interminable rounds," Ambassador Davaz said, gesturing over his shoulder at the embassy secretaries anxiously hovering behind them. "We will see you at the reception tonight?"

"Of course," Alexsi replied.

The ambassador embraced him again, tighter this time, and whispered in his ear, "Thank you for the wonderful farewell gifts."

"Poor things compared to your hospitality," Alexsi replied.

"My wife cried that in three years of shopping in Iran, she had not found carpet and silver so exquisite."

"And I am certain it was not for lack of trying," Alexsi said.

The ambassador laughed loudly and undiplomatically. His successor looked a bit pained at the breach of official dignity. They rumbled off with their entourage and Alexsi resumed his seat. At least his drink was still cold.

Just then he noticed the figure looking at him from the trees. About time. He waved, and of course the fellow hesitated. That Russian love of conspiracy. Alexsi waved again, more insistently. Finally the man gave up and walked around the tennis court to his table. Alexsi stood up one more time to shake hands. "Comrade Counselor, how good to see you." Now the language of the moment had switched to Russian.

The only thing certain about Colonel Evgeny Dmitrovich Matushkin was that that was not his real name. He was one of those keen-eyed, pitiless Russian falcons who resembled a commercial attaché as much as Alexsi did a Russian grandmother. Barely past thirty, but there were plenty of openings in Soviet intelligence these days.

Matushkin sat down and gave Alexsi the critical eye. "Your boldness will be your undoing, David."

"Let's look at it this way," Alexsi suggested. "Which looks more like a conspiracy? You and I walking alone among the trees, or sitting here having a drink at my table?" He caught the Iranian waiter's eye and held up his glass, gesturing toward Matushkin. The waiter smiled and bowed. Berger the Swiss tipped well. Now he waited to hear what was bothering Matushkin. Everything with them always began with a complaint. Always.

And Matushkin didn't disappoint. "David, we're not comfortable with what you're radioing Berlin."

"Everyone knows we're coming in," Alexsi said. "It's the worst-kept secret in Teheran. They even know that the British call it Operation Countenance."

Matushkin took a moment to digest that. He had to chew over everything he heard at least twenty times before swallowing. "But still."

"The Germans can't do a thing about it. And I have to maintain my credibility with them, don't I?"

A nod from Matushkin the only concession to that.

"There's hardly a stick of gelignite in northern Iran you don't know about," Alexsi pointed out. "You have every German radio, and with the radios go the networks. I've given you everything."

"Thank you, David. You may now restrain your natural impertinence."

"You're very welcome," Alexsi replied.

Matushkin chose to ignore his tone. "We have an assignment for you. Of the most vital importance."

Alexsi braced himself.

"It is imperative," said Matushkin, "that once the Red Army crosses the border any attempt by the Iranians to reinforce their units in the north be foiled."

"They won't resist," Alexsi said flatly. "A few soldiers who as usual won't know what's going on may fire a few shots, but there will be no organized resistance. Nothing is more certain, I assure you."

"We cannot count on it," said Matushkin. "You have tribal connections, yes?"

Now it was Alexsi's turn to nod. Unbelievable. The world's most perfect situation in Teheran, and they were going to send him out in the desert on some useless errand dreamed up by some military genius who knew nothing about Iran. No wonder the Germans were kicking their arses all over Russia.

"We require that you make contact with the Iranian nomads," said Matushkin, "and use them as the means of delaying any attempt by the Iranian Army to move their forces north to oppose us. Can you do this?"

"Look, if you're worried, throw the same amount of gold at the Iranian generals. You can always get it back later when they come begging you for protection. You'll never see it again if you give it to the tribes." No wonder wars lasted so long. People were too stupid.

"Can you do this?" Matushkin repeated, as if he hadn't heard a thing.

Alexsi wasn't about to surrender just yet. "The tribes are not an army. Whether you pay them or not, they'll fight only if they feel like it. And they have to feel there is some advantage in it for them."

"The arms they acquire in combat with the Iranian Army, perhaps?"

So they'd given it at least some thought. "If they think it will be easy enough."

"So it can be done," said Matushkin.

Alexsi sighed. If there was one thing a Russian learned at his mother's knee, it was to recognize the inevitable. "There are only a few good roads, and the terrain is not suited to flanking maneuvers. *If* the tribes will fight, any force can be delayed. Not stopped, but delayed." What he was really thinking was that if he played his cards right he could spend a few idle weeks enjoying the rough hospitality of the Lur, on Zahra's introduction, and then back to Teheran as if nothing had happened.

"Very good," said Matushkin. "Your connections are with the Lur, correct? The Shahsavan would not be so friendly, if by some chance they did remember you after all these years."

It was always like a little knife, the way they constantly pricked you. He'd always been afraid that if they ever found out there was one little secret he'd neglected to tell, he'd turn a street corner one day and find himself shot in the face. "You realize the Shah crushed the power of the tribes. If they get it back, and become accustomed to using their rifles for more than stealing sheep and raiding villages, they will be very difficult to deal with."

"That," Matushkin said, "is a problem for the British. Not us."

46

1941 Western Iran

THERE WAS NO WAY TO PUT OFF THE LUR ANY LONGER. THE news kept pouring into camp, with that near-telegraphic speed preliterate people passed information by word of mouth. The British had crossed the border from Khanaqin in Iraq. The Iranian defenders at the Paitak Pass, who should have been able to keep an army from advancing up that single road through the mountains, had run away in the dead of night. Kermanshah, the next city in the British line of march, had asked for a truce to negotiate a surrender, and there were scattered Iranian Army and police units in full flight toward Hamadan to the north.

Exactly what the Lur had been waiting to hear. Demoralized soldiers fleeing in panic were just their meat. And nothing Alexsi could do about it. Because that was tribal warfare. Even if the chiefs hadn't been enthusiastic, the tribesmen would have gone off hunting anyway. And then the chiefs would have lost both their face and their authority. So everyone was inexorably pulled along whether they liked it or not.

Which was how they'd wound up in the bare brown hills above the Hamadan road, at the very northern edge of the Lorestan range. Alexsi was actually much more concerned about their bumping into one of the rival Hamadani tribes than the Iranian Army.

They were lying in shallow scrapes half covered by sand under the broiling sun. At least the Lur were sensible enough to dress in light and roomy trousers and long-tailed jerkin shirts. And loosely wound cloth turbans. Everyone had their brown sleeveless capes tented over them, as much for shade as camouflage.

But the Lur did know their camouflage. Alexsi doubted whether anyone would be able to pick them out of the hillside from farther than twenty meters, and they would be long dead by then.

Now, as in any ambush, there was nothing to do but wait. One would have thought the tribesmen would be ill-suited to it, but as long as there was the prospect of fighting and loot, they would lie there for days without twitching a muscle. And nothing larger than a mouse could pass them without notice.

Alexsi dozed off. It would be fine with him if no one came along the road.

He thought he was dreaming when he heard that same low, muffled whistle the Shahsavan had used. But he snapped awake and saw six travelers on horseback hurrying down the road. Beside him Jafar Khan firmly whispered, "No," and the order passed down the line. In camp there might have been an hours-long argument that would only end in at least the threat of violence, but on a raid one and all would obey him without question.

Alexsi took a very short drink from the water bag he was using for a pillow, and went back to sleep.

He awoke again to the sound of excited muttering and vehicle engines. Now this was definitely something. He braced his binoculars on the water bag and focused on the hidden bend in the road in the far distance.

The vehicle sound had been deceptively loud echoing throughout the hills, and it took some time before the actual article appeared round the bend. Alexsi suppressed a groan once it emerged from the dust and haze. It was a Rolls-Royce armored car. Essentially, a four-wheel Rolls-Royce automobile sheathed in steel armor with a machine-gun turret. The Iranians had a few, but kept them in the armored car battalion of their only mechanized brigade. And if this was it, there would probably be Czech-built tanks with a 37mm cannon following close behind. If the Lur were foolish enough to open fire, the day would become both very noisy and very hazardous in short order.

Alexsi pondered his options. If he told Jafar Khan not to open fire the young chief most certainly would just to show that he was not to be ordered around by the foreigner. Better to wait and see what happened.

But the armored car was followed by trucks. Now that was lucky. Perhaps it was a supply convoy with an escort.

As the Rolls-Royce proceeded down the road, Alexsi was finally able to make out the details through the heat haze. Oh, no. The armored car was flying the British flag from its aerial. Before someone made a horrible mistake he passed the binoculars to Jafar Khan, hissing, "English!" The Iranian Army must have been running away so fast they'd disappeared down the road before the Lur had even gotten into position.

Jafar Khan gave him a look of surprise, then peered intently through the binoculars. He made a thoughtful clucking sound with his teeth.

Alexsi could feel him wavering his way into potential disaster. And decided it was time to come in with an argument a tribesman would understand. "If you thought the Shah hounded you, then make an enemy of the British. Your camps will be machine-gunned by planes, and you won't have a moment's rest."

Jafar Khan thought that over and nodded. To Alexsi's overwhelming relief. That would be all he needed. The Lur thought he was a German. He'd asked Zahra to tell them that, to protect his Swiss identity. She'd agreed, since the Germans had the fiercer military reputation and the tribesmen wouldn't know what a Swiss was in any case. German or Swiss, the British would dedicate themselves to hunting down the fellow who'd ambushed their column. And he doubted whether the Soviets would be terribly pleased about it. They certainly wouldn't tell the British it was their man who had done it. He'd never be able to go back to his fine life in Teheran, and he most definitely didn't want to spend the rest of the war out in the desert with the Lur.

Jafar Khan turned his head to give the order. And before he could open his mouth one of the Lur got excited and fired a shot from his rifle. Alexsi listened in dismay as the tribesmen on either side, probably thinking they had missed the command, opened fire also. Then he just dropped his head down on his water bag in utter despair as every Lur on the hillside started shooting.

The canvas tops of the British trucks flipped up and the soldiers inside fired back from behind the wooden sides. The armored car swung its turret around and the Vickers machine gun laced a long burst at the muzzle flashes on the hillside. The bullets kicked up a shower of dirt, stampeding a few of the more nervous Lur into flight.

"Now, Walters!" Jafar Khan shouted.

Of course he hadn't given the Lur a correct name, let alone one that anyone had heard before. Alexsi shook his head and bellowed back over the deafening sound of the rifle fire, "Too soon!"

The British were well disciplined. Rather than be stationary targets the Rolls-Royce sped down the road, the trucks following. The machine gun kept shooting, though, and found the range of the hillside. The tribesmen didn't like it one bit. A few more sprang up and dashed down the reverse slope for their horses.

Alexsi watched them. As far as he was concerned, having the whole enterprise degenerate into panicked flight would be the perfect solution.

"Walters!" Jafar Khan shouted.

"Not yet!" Alexsi shouted back.

And then Jafar Khan's pistol was pressing into his temple.

Alexsi was nearly overcome by the stupidity of the world. Absolutely no one would listen to reason. The armored car had almost reached the prominent dark-colored rock next to the road. The one he had marked out.

Alexsi grabbed Jafar Khan's wrist with his left hand and pushed the revolver forward. It fired across the hillside to no effect except to completely deafen him. With his right he pressed the telegraph wires onto the two terminals of the salvaged automobile battery. The wires sparked and leaped up in his hand.

A very long second of absolutely nothing. And then the road blew up in a huge black explosive cloud, the armored car appearing above it, sailing far into the air. It spun gracefully and fell back to earth, slamming onto its side in a tangle of wreckage.

The Lur actually stopped shooting to watch it. Then an exultant shout went up and they settled back down, pouring rapid fire into the convoy.

The smoke from the explosion blew away, revealing an enormous crater that completely blocked the road.

Alexsi could see the trucks hesitate. The ones at the very rear began to turn around. Then someone obviously gave an order, and the troops all poured out of the trucks and leaped into the cover of the drainage culvert that ran beside that part of the road. Indian Sikh soldiers in their khaki turbans. Alexsi admired their discipline. In a matter of a minute or two all the trucks were empty and the troops were under cover and steadily firing back.

Now, German troops would have plastered them with machine gun and mortar fire, pinning them down. And then attacked from the flanks, rolling them up with rifles and grenades. But the Lur had no mortars and machine guns, only rifles. And they were not infantry. A hand-to-hand knife fight was one thing, but not close combat against disciplined soldiers with rifles and bayonets.

The entire affair would have ended inconclusively because the British were not about to accommodate the tribesmen by either running away or surrendering. The Lur would have shot from the hillside until they ran low on ammunition and then slipped away as darkness fell. Or sooner if British reinforcements arrived.

And Alexsi would have been all for that. But Jafar Khan was shouting, "Walters!" again, and waving that old Webley revolver in a most threatening manner.

There was no way out of this. In resignation Alexsi picked up the second bundle of wires and pressed them to the battery. The entire length of the culvert blew up, throwing men and their arms and legs into the air like dolls.

The Lur stopped shooting again and watched in awe. Until Jafar Khan screamed and they all stood up and ran down the hillside toward the trucks.

Alexsi stayed there and packed up his things, leaving the salvaged battery in his scrape. He kicked sand on it for good measure. Too clever for his own good, as usual. He'd joined the Lur with a string of horses packing Russian gold and twenty-five-kilogram sacks of potassium chlorate from the textile trade. It was one of the Abwehr's favorite recipes for homemade explosives: potassium chlorate mixed with crude oil the Lur stole from the nearby Naft-i-Shah–Kermanshah pipeline. With a little sugar added. The mixture packed into a large cooking cauldron and buried in the road. Then when he saw the pile of small-diameter pipe the Lur had stolen from the oil rigs even though they had no earthly use for it, the brilliant inspiration of loading them with explosive and mining the culvert. Because he knew soldiers would instinctively leap into it for protection. Only sheer curiosity, combined with his vivid description of what would happen, had persuaded the Lur to overcome their aversion to digging. Yes, he was a genius.

From his boyhood with the Shahsavan he knew that the more Lur who were killed fighting the more they would blame him. And the more loot they gained the more they would love him.

His plans had all worked perfectly, and it was the worst possible thing that could have happened. He was ruined in Iran.

Alexsi trudged down the back side of the hill to find his horse. He glanced at his watch. About fifteen minutes to loot before the British outside the ambush area set up their mortars and stampeded the Lur into flight. And perhaps an hour or two before the aircraft came looking for them.

47

1941 Western Iran

THE CAMPFIRES WERE BURNING BRIGHT. AGAINST HIS ADVICE, of course. Alexsi had both ears cocked for the sound of aircraft engines. The tribesmen were babbling excitedly and showing off their British Enfield rifles. And handling Mills grenades with an insouciance that kept Alexsi's eyes fixed on available cover within diving range. A gleaming Bren machine gun sat in pride of place at their circle for everyone to admire.

Then the sheep came out entire, blackened from the oven pits, on an enormous hammered steel platter, splayed out on a bed of rice.

The speeches had all come before the feast, while they were waiting for the mutton to cook. When it came time to eat the Lur were eminently practical.

The sheep's scorched face was directly in front of Alexsi. Jafar Khan gestured extravagantly for him to go ahead. Alexsi politely demurred. Jafar Khan insisted again. Alexsi politely declined. Jafar Khan bowed his head and reached out and plucked both the sheep's eyes. He set them on his plate, and then transferred them to Alexsi's. Alexsi bowed back and popped one into his mouth. Even though it was quite good, the events of the day had killed his appetite. Nonetheless he chewed and smiled and then carefully set the other eye back on Jafar Khan's plate. Knowing everyone was waiting for him, he reached out with his right hand and tore some flesh off the sheep's cheek and scooped up a palmful of rice hot enough to raise blisters on his hand. Another nod and Jafar Khan served himself. Then you could practically hear the grunt of relief that the niceties had now been observed, and the other tribesmen in the circle around the platter began tearing off chunks of flesh and handfuls of rice. Pieces of fat were flying everywhere, and all you could hear were the sound of bones being cracked open for the marrow. They made a platoon of famished German infantrymen look like a party of delicate aristocrats.

They were still gorging when Alexsi rose under the pretext of relieving himself, really just to gain a moment's peace.

As he picked his way through the obstacle course of tent lines, a voice off to the side, in English, "Mr. Walters?"

Alexsi recognized it. "Hoessein?"

"May we speak?"

"I will follow you," Alexsi said. Whatever this might be about, he would not be the first to walk into it.

He followed Hoessein's dark form through the clusters of black tents. Outside the final ring, but not too far outside. There were sentries up in the rocks. Prudent camp raiders never forgot about being raided themselves.

Alexsi squatted down in the sand. Hoessein took a little walk around to make sure they were alone. Now Alexsi was definitely curious.

Hoessein squatted beside him and said in a low voice, "Do you remember the offer you made me?"

"Of course, my friend," Alexsi said. He had marked Hoessein from the start. A young man of about nineteen who, unusually, had been to school in Kermanshah. Very intelligent, but by no means a warrior in a culture that valued the manly arts. The Lur had no truck with an intelligent man who could not also shoot and ride better than the rest. The city Iranians would always consider him a tribal savage, while the Lur looked down upon Hoessein as at least half a contemptuous city man. Part of the tribe but always an outsider. The very type Alexsi had been taught to cultivate.

"Does your offer still stand?" Hoessein asked. "Because I have valuable information for you."

"Then I have money for you. Or whatever it is you might require."

Hoessein dropped his voice even lower. "They intend to sell you to the British. To make peace with them."

Alexsi merely nodded to himself in the darkness. It was shrewd. Almost shrewder than he'd given the Lur credit for. He was not one of the tribe. By giving him up they would be able to keep the British arms they had taken, or at least most after surrendering a token amount. And gain some gold. And not have to worry about British bombers flattening their camps. No one did betrayal while hosting you to a feast like the Iranians.

He said, "You bring me one good saddled horse, and three more bridled. Two full water skins, bread and fodder in the saddlebags. And I will give you one hundred British gold sovereigns. If you can be ready as the moon rises tonight."

"Cash on the nail?" said Hoessein.

Alexsi smiled at the expression. Jonathan Swift, as he recalled. "Cash on the nail."

Hoessein pointed in the near distance. "The little bowl in the rocks, outside the picket line. You know it?"

"I know it," Alexsi said.

"One hundred gold?"

"One hundred. You will need to get the stock outside the picket line."

"And you will need to get yourself outside the picket line," Hoessein retorted. "At the first rise of moon." And then he was gone.

IT WAS quite literally impossible to sneak out of a tent filled with sleeping tribesmen. Unless, of course, you put chloral hydrate into their warming nightcap pot of tea. The women bringing the tray in, and Alexsi jumping up and exclaiming, You have the best tea. The Lur saying proudly, Of course we do. Alexsi opening the lid and breathing the aroma in deeply, saying, I've never tasted its equal. Everyone watching him talking and gesturing animatedly, and missing the chloral hydrate bottle tucked away in his palm being poured in. The Lur added so much sugar to their tea that no one even noticed. Alexsi toasted their health and poured his out between crossed legs before rolling up in a blanket and waiting for the drug to take effect.

He pulled up a stake and slipped out underneath the back, leaving them snoring away or dead—considering what they had planned for him he didn't much care which. And once again carefully picked his way through the tent lines. It wouldn't do to be shaking anyone's tent at such a late hour.

The pickets were looking for danger in the other direction. But he'd marked out where they'd positioned themselves and slowly and quietly slipped through the rocks, taking the same route the horsemen did when they left camp to scout out the area. He guessed that was how Hoessein would bring the horses.

As he approached the rendezvous Alexsi heard the faint sound of whinnying. But no sense rushing in.

He climbed up a little higher and circled around very quietly. From his higher vantage point he could see Hoessein standing in the bowl with the horses. And in that first light of the moon he could also see a tribesman tucked into the rocks, with his rifle propped up on one and aimed down into the bowl. That would be Hoessein's brother Shapour.

Shrewd. The hero Hoessein shooting the foreigner trying to escape. Gain the gold and keep the horses. Which probably belonged to Shapour. And the finger of suspicion would never fall on him, unlike if Alexsi made a successful escape.

Alexsi set his shoulder bag and blanket roll gently on the ground. Then slipped his boots and stockings off and tucked them into the back of his belt for even quieter movement. He picked his way through the rocks a centimeter at a time. He saw the narrow sandy path Shapour had taken into his firing position and slipped down onto it for a silent approach. Feeling the ground ahead carefully with his toes before putting his full weight down, he advanced just one or two steps a minute.

Shapour was fidgeting. That was good—let him make his own noise. The moon was to Alexsi's front, so he knew he wouldn't cast a shadow. He came around a rock and was within two meters of Shapour.

You could come right up on a sleeping man. But an alert one, especially a tribesman, would usually sense something even if he heard nothing. Shapour tensed up and began to turn.

Alexsi took two long strides forward and smashed the stone in his hand into the side of Shapour's skull. As Shapour collapsed Alexsi pinned him against the rock with his weight, grabbing the rifle with his left hand to keep it from clattering down. With a firm grip on the rifle, he eased the body to the sand.

Once Shapour was settled Alexsi poked his head up. The rock hitting Shapour's head had sounded like an explosion to him, but Hoessein had heard nothing. He was still standing there with the horses.

Alexsi took Shapour's knife and ammunition bandoliers. He had his own Iranian Army–issued Czech Mauser carbine slung over his back.

More than one helper and Hoessein would be afraid they'd band together and kill *him* for the money, brother or not. Still, it paid to be careful. Alexsi put his boots back on and completed the full circle to satisfy himself. And retrieved his shoulder bag once he was finished.

He slipped down from the rocks onto the sandy bowl and let his boots scrape. Hoessein jumped and whirled about. He made the horses nervous, and they whinnied loudly.

"Sling your rifle," Alexsi said. His Belgian Browning pistol was in his hand, and cocked. "Are we not friends?"

Hoessein hesitated a moment, then put his Mauser up behind his back. "We are. Do you have the money?"

Alexsi let the pistol's hammer down gently, and tucked it back into his holster. He watched Hoessein relax. He didn't acknowledge the question. He just began checking the horses. They all had sacking tied over their hooves to muffle the sound of their movement. Very thorough. He felt them all over in the darkness. They weren't Thoroughbreds, but at least they weren't cripples. Bread and grain in the saddlebags. Water skins filled. Very good.

"The gold?" Hoessein demanded impatiently.

Alexsi could hear the tension come through in his voice. "Sewn inside my belt. Now you know why it's so wide."

Hoessein ran his hand extravagantly through his hair.

Alexsi smiled and just kept checking the horses. He'd moved around the string, putting his hands on each one, and now had made his way back around to the lead mare, whose bridle Hoessein was holding.

Hoessein ran his hand through his hair again. And again. Practically waving.

Now Alexsi was right beside him. "You look like a man who is expecting something to happen."

Hoessein turned toward him, fear on his face. Alexsi drove the brother's knife into his throat.

A gagging sound from Hoessein. Alexsi pushed him to the ground, pinning his head down. He yanked the blade from Hoessein's throat and plunged it into the gap in the skull behind his ear. Hoessein's body spasmed beneath him, and it was all over. Quicker than waiting for him to bleed out.

Alexsi left Shapour's knife in Hoessein's brain. Let the Lur puzzle over it when they found the two corpses.

The horses had barely stirred while all this had been going on. Perhaps they were used to knife play.

Alexsi took up the bridle and led the horses out to the trail through the far gap in the rocks. He'd walk them until they were well out of earshot of the camp, then take the sacking off their hooves. No sense becoming careless now.

48

1941 Western Iran

ALEXSI RUINED TWO HORSES REACHING THE HIGH PASSES OF the Zagros Mountains. He felt much worse about them than the people, regretfully cutting their throats so no one following would be able to use them once they recovered.

Now as the two remaining animals drank from a pool of water at the base of a rock wall, he steadied his binoculars on an outcropping and glassed the area he'd already passed through.

Exactly what he'd been afraid of. The Lur weren't about to let their prize slip through their fingers, or their dead—deservedly or not—go unavenged. They were doing exactly what he was, sacrificing horses to catch up with him.

They were just tiny dots in the distance. Alexsi did some quick calculations. Run or fight? There were four of them, with more horses than he.

Well, why not run *and* fight? Back up the trail there had been a gap in the rocks only wide enough for a single horse to walk through. This was not one of the well-traveled routes over the mountains to Iraq. Not a road but a path, made not by men with tools but worn down by animals over untold years. He'd listened to the Lur talking, asked a few innocent questions, and carefully marked it on his map. He'd been worried, but once you found it all you had to do was follow the signs other travelers had left. Unfortunately there were a few forks that dead-ended into abandoned campsites, which required backtracking. Which was why the Lur following him were a bit nearer than they would have been otherwise.

Alexsi let the horses keep drinking, retrieving his shoulder bag and walking back up the trail.

Careful to make as few of his own footprints as possible, he laid his cape on the sand and used his knife to dig two small but deep holes across the trail.

He had two short twenty-centimeter sections of pipe loaded with explosives. Leftovers from that unfortunate British ambush. He carefully placed them in the holes vertically.

He had no pipe threaders or caps, so he'd bent one end and carved wood stoppers that he could hammer into the other. He'd planned to use them as something like hand grenades in a pinch, but now they would serve as land mines.

Alexsi had no blasting caps left. But he did have a little wooden box in his kit filled with glass vials of sulfuric acid packed in cotton wool. He balanced two of the vials on the open metal edge of each pipe, then set the wood stopper lightly atop them. Sulfuric acid reacted very violently with potassium chlorate mixed with sugar and oil.

Alexsi ripped the front and back covers from one of his books. The poems of Yeats, which he had been reading out loud to himself to improve his English. Fine fellow, Yeats. The Irish were as good as the Persians, in poetry. Alexsi placed the covers very carefully atop the wooden stoppers to both shield them and give his apparatus a bit more surface area. With everything balanced precariously, he gingerly scattered sand to conceal his two land mines, ready to bolt at the faintest tinkle of broken glass. How ironic to come this far and blow himself up.

Finished, he stepped back and surveyed his work. The mines were hidden belowground but the area didn't look right. Too clean. Tribesmen didn't miss a thing while tracking, and they wouldn't miss this. He sat down and thought it over. He didn't have a spare horseshoe to put tracks across the top of the mine holes. And he certainly wouldn't walk his horses back over it.

He was very tired, and he couldn't think of anything. He picked up his cape with the leftover dirt from the holes, and used the edge to feather his footprints away as he backed up.

His horses were fully watered and enjoying the rest. Alexsi was about to tie his bag back on the saddle when he looked down and received an inspiration. He scooped up a fresh pile of horse shit in each hand and walked back down the trail, setting the turds very gently atop the two mines. After a little careful sculpting, they looked as if they'd fallen on their own.

This was even better. Either one of the Lur horses would step on them, or a tribesman would climb down to put a hand on the shit to determine how long ago it had been dropped. Either way the pressure would force down the book cover and wooden stopper, cracking the glass to release the acid. Alexsi brushed away his tracks again and cleaned his hands in the dregs of the pool.

Four hours later the faint echo of a bang rolled across the peaks. Well, it had actually worked. The Lur weren't used to booby traps. If that didn't spook the survivors and send them home, at least now they would be creeping down the trail, panicking at every pile of horse shit.

ALEXSI RODE for three days and three nights. The horses were close to staggering, and he was nearly blind from fatigue. He didn't notice a thing until the two Kurds stepped out from the rocks with rifles leveled.

Alexsi reined in. Trapped like a fool with his rifle slung across his back. Well, at least they hadn't shot him already. "As salamu alaykuma, friends," he said, greeting them in Farsi.

No response from the Kurds. Without waiting to see what might happen next, Alexsi rushed headlong into his sales proposal.

"I am German, escaping from the English. Guide me to Kirkuk and I will make you rich."

This was not what the Kurds were expecting to hear. "Speak words in German," the older, more grizzled one of the pair demanded.

"What do you wish me to say in German?" Alexsi said in German.

The older one thought that over. No discussion between them. The younger one just kept his finger curled around his rifle trigger.

The older one made another demand. "You have money?"

Alexsi knew it would be the vultures stripping his carcass if he admitted to that. "My countrymen in Kirkuk will pay you gold."

Alexsi watched the older one's eyes as he thought it over. No, he was going with the bird in the hand, and the rifle and two horses, rather than the uncertainty of a long trip to Kirkuk.

Then he surprised Alexsi by saying, "Is that gold?"

Pointing to the brass-cased compass dangling around Alexsi's neck.

Alexsi seized on the opportunity. "No, my friend. It is a brass compass. Very handy. Let me show you."

Before they could say anything, he swung down from the saddle. And with his back to them reached into the front of his cape and eased out his pistol.

As he touched ground and turned, he shot the nearest Kurd, the older one, square in the chest. The Kurd fired his rifle at the same time, and Alexsi literally felt the bullet fly by. The two shots were so close together they sounded like one report. As soon as he fired Alexsi jerked the reins, and his horse reared forward. The younger Kurd fired his rifle, hitting Alexsi's horse instead of him. The horse screamed and fell on its side, and Alexsi leaped back to keep from being pinned underneath. He landed flat on his ass while the young Kurd was frantically working his bolt to get another bullet into the chamber. Still sitting there in the dirt, Alexsi leveled the pistol and shot rapid fire. The Kurd was hit, but he still slammed the bolt home. Alexsi kept shooting. The Kurd finally dropped, and as he did he fired his rifle into the ground.

Alexsi sprang back up on his feet. And only then noticed that he was still squeezing the trigger even though his pistol was out of ammunition. Shaking, he removed the empty magazine and dug a fresh one out of his pocket. As he slammed the slide home the older Kurd was weakly trying to reach out for his rifle. Alexsi walked up and shot him in the head. The younger Kurd was already dead, but Alexsi put a bullet in his skull, too, for good measure.

His horse was on the ground, struggling to get up. A fine horse, too. Alexsi patted her gently and put the pistol to her head to end her misery.

He calmed his other horse and transferred the saddle to him. Then, holding his reins securely, followed the Kurds' footprints back to where they had tied their own two mounts. Well, one horse lost but two gained. There could have been a higher price for his carelessness. When the only way was a Wild West shoot-out, you knew you'd been particularly stupid.

Alexsi hunted around in his bag for the tin tube of Benzedrine. Unscrewing the cap, he shook two tablets out into his palm. The German soldier's friend. He'd wanted to be careful, but he needed them now. Finally heading downhill into Iraq, he'd been trying to find a good hiding place, perhaps with some scrub the horses could graze on, and sleep for a few hours. Now he'd have to worry about the Kurds' friends or relatives finding them and coming after him. Even if he covered the bodies with rock, the vultures would still smell death and circle.

The Benzedrine was beginning to work on him now. He tied the Kurds' horses to his and thought about what to do with his rifle. Considering the problems the Kurds had had with rapid fire in a tight spot, he decided to leave it slung across his back and keep his pistol in hand.

Another day and a night, and fifty hard kilometers, and he was at the end of his strength. At one point he'd been convinced it was snowing. And only after failing to feel any wetness realized it was a hallucination. He had to stop, Benzedrine or not. He led the horses off the trail and made a wide circle, so anyone following him would have to pass in front of him as they tracked, giving him time to run. He had intended to camouflage himself with his cape, but as soon as he hobbled the horses he collapsed onto the sand and was dead asleep.

It was dark when he awoke. He was freezing cold. Alexsi knew he was lucky not to be waking up to a knife at his throat. His head ached and his stomach was jumping about from the Benzedrine. No question of lighting a fire, so he walked to try to warm up, eating the last of his Lur bread. His water was ice, but he knew he had to drink. It was really only then that his mind cleared enough to remember the Kurds' saddles, which were still on their horses. He dumped them in the rocks after looting the bread and dried mutton and fodder.

Since he was awake now, Alexsi resolved to travel by night and sleep by day. He couldn't keep going the way he had. He would just blunder into another ambush. And sensible thieves didn't sit by trails at night when they could be sleeping, because travelers didn't ride at night.

The next evening he came up over a little rise, and the wide expanse of the Iraqi plain appeared below him in the moonlight. In the distance were the clustered lights of a good-sized town. Alexsi shot a compass bearing and read the number off the luminous dial. That had to be Kirkuk. After five days of the most brutal travel he had ever done. Perhaps another day and a half to get there. But Kirkuk was safety. With a Swiss passport in his pocket and gold sovereigns in his belt. A hotel and a banquet for him, treats for his horses.

From Kirkuk a slow and comfortable journey north to Mosul. Where the Trans-Baghdad railroad went all the way to Istanbul.

Alexsi finally allowed himself to think of the future rather than surviving the present. If he went back to Russia they would pin a medal on him for all his fine work and then throw him in front of the advancing German tanks. Neutral Turkey was a pleasant idea, but it was the playground of Soviet intelligence and he'd never survive long there without their leave. Switzerland was even more of a spy circus, not to mention smaller and harder to hide in. South America? The NKVD had killed Trotsky there, and he rather imagined himself as less of a challenge. Even if his ship wasn't sunk by a German U-boat first.

It was crazy enough to twist his stomach into a knot, but the safest place for him was probably Germany. At least *they* would be pleased about all the British soldiers he'd blown up.

PART IV

Operation
Long Jump

49

1943 Berlin, Germany

IT WASN'T HARD TO TELL YOU WERE BEING FOLLOWED IF THEY were in an automobile and you were on foot. It was a rainy morning, and as Alexsi stepped out of his uncle's house in the diplomatic quarter, there was that vehicle parked down the street. With three men wearing hats inside. Could they be any more obvious?

They shadowed him as he walked down Tiergarten toward Abwehr headquarters. Then finally the automobile raced up and squealed to a stop ahead of him, nearly running up over the curb. Two of the men wearing overcoats spilled out. The driver kept the engine running.

"Captain Walter Shultz," one of them said. No question, there.

All the Germans in the vicinity were like turtles yanking their heads back into their shells. Looking in every direction except his. They saw nothing.

"And you are?" Alexsi asked calmly.

The one who'd spoken reached into his open coat and pulled the watch chain from his waistcoat pocket. But no watch. Attached to the end of the chain was a Gestapo warrant disc. A simple stamped oval piece of steel that read secret state police and the agent's number. It was all the identification they were required to present.

"What's this all about?" Alexsi asked, still calmly.

"Come with us," the agent ordered.

Alexsi stood his ground and looked at them with an annoyed expression. Just long enough for them to get nervous. The second agent's gun hand began creeping into his coat.

Then Alexsi gave an exasperated sigh and got into the back of the automobile. One Gestapo man beside him and the other in the front seat next to the driver.

It was a short drive to Prinz-Albrecht-Strasse. Alexsi thought he really had no right to be upset. It had been a good run. He'd actually lasted much longer than he thought he would when he was a frightened teenager on the Munich Station platform.

He considered the cyanide capsule. Abwehr issue. He had never carried it in Iran, but back in Germany he'd sewn it into the sleeve of his uniform jacket. Raise his hand to scratch his nose, tear the seam open with his teeth, and it would be all over. He looked out the window at gray Berlin and thought about sunny Iran. And, for the first time in years, Azerbaijan.

But these Gestapo hadn't even searched him for weapons. Alexsi knew, eventually, there would come a situation he couldn't talk his way out of. But it wasn't absolutely clear that moment had arrived.

They drove through the same gate, to the same courtyard. Alexsi decided that if they began making their way through that ground floor to the interrogation rooms it would be time to think about cyanide.

They passed through the doors and inside. The guard at the desk glared at Alexsi in his army uniform. His escorts did not sign in. They stood there as the guard unlocked the iron door, as if they were expected.

There was that next iron door, just beyond the stairs. Alexsi felt his sleeve to be sure the cyanide capsule was still there. It was.

But the Gestapo nudged him up the stairs instead. Alexsi relaxed a bit. So it wasn't the cellars right away. He had at least a bit of room to maneuver.

They kept climbing.

And stopped at a floor with another guard behind a desk. The placard on the wall read: AMT VI, AUSLAND-SD.

Now Alexsi relaxed a bit more. SD Foreign Intelligence. Abwehr's rival. Not Amt IV, Gestapo.

His escorts sailed by the guard without even giving him a second glance.

Alexsi's boots tapped down the marble hallway. They halted before a large and richly carved wooden door. The placard on the wall to the right read, in Gothic script, *Oberführer-SS Walter Schellenberg. Chief, Amt VI*.

Inside an SS adjutant sat behind a desk, a major. He was on the telephone. He clapped a hand over the mouthpiece and said, "Captain Shultz?"

Alexsi popped his heels together and gave the Hitler salute. *"Heil Hitler!"*

The adjutant raised his hand in return, and to do that had to switch the phone in his hand and press it against his chest. *"Heil Hitler."* He gestured toward an open chair. "Kindly take a seat. General Schellenberg will see you momentarily." He gave the two Gestapo men a look. They nodded and went out the door.

The sun might not exactly be shining, but Alexsi no longer felt it was raining on him.

Schellenberg himself? That would be quite something. On the level of meeting Canaris for the first time. Deputy chief of the SD. Answered only to Reinhard Heydrich, who answered only to Himmler. And now Heydrich was dead, killed by Czech partisans. Remembering his time in Czechoslovakia, Alexsi thought, of course the assassins had to parachute in from London because they couldn't find any local Czechs willing to pick up a gun. Now Schellenberg answered only to Himmler, whose personal aide he had been. The Nazis' longtime dirty-tricks man. He'd made his reputation right after the war began when he lured a couple of British secret service men to a meeting in Holland, kidnapped them, and dragged them across the border to Germany. And unlike the

Communist hard case Alexsi had met in the basement here, the much more sensible Englishmen only had to be threatened with being hung from the ceiling before they coughed up every existing British network in Europe.

The phone buzzed. The adjutant picked it up and said, "At once, sir." He turned to Alexsi and said, "You will go in."

The office was bigger than Canaris's. And much better furnished. Alexsi came to attention in front of the desk, thrust out his right arm, and barked, *"Heil Hitler!"*

Walter Schellenberg was quite nearly as good-looking as a film star. Only in his early thirties, he was wearing his SS brigadier's uniform. With a gleaming smile he came around the enormous desk to shake Alexsi's hand.

Alexsi took that as a good sign. Schellenberg's desk was notorious. Supposedly armored in steel, with built-in automatic guns he could deploy at the touch of a button to wipe out anyone in front of it. True or not, it was the sort of Hollywood melodrama everyone expected from the SS.

"Captain Shultz," he exclaimed, pumping Alexsi's hand. "Come, sit."

Schellenberg grasped his elbow and led him over to the circle of sofa, coffee table, and padded chairs on the other side of the room.

Alexsi tensely took a seat. Unlike Heydrich, the Teutonic Nazi ideal, now in Nazi Valhalla, Schellenberg was dark and fine-featured.

"So, Shultz," he began. "For nearly two years now you've run the Near East Desk at Abwehr I here in Berlin, yes?"

"That is correct, General," Alexsi said slowly and cautiously.

"You have all the information on the area at your fingertips, so to speak?"

With Schellenberg theatrically waving two sets of fingertips at him, and it being more of a statement than a question, Alexsi only nodded.

"That isn't what I want to talk about." Schellenberg had dropped his voice to a confiding tone, as if he were imparting a secret. He leaned over the coffee table and picked up a thick file. Alexsi recognized it as his Iran report.

"I must say this reads like the finest adventure story," Schellenberg announced, slapping the pages enthusiastically. "I took it home and it kept me awake half the night. And I said to myself: I must meet this man."

Alexsi decided to take the risk. "I would have been pleased to present myself, General, at your convenience."

Schellenberg laughed appreciatively at that. "My boys gave you a start, eh? Let's just say I didn't wish to call the switchboard over at Abwehr headquarters and invite Captain Shultz over to Prinz-Albrecht-Strasse."

Alexsi nodded politely. No need to remind himself that this was a clever, slippery fellow. A lawyer, after all.

Abandoning that line of discussion, Schellenberg shook the report in front of Alexsi's eyes and tossed it back onto the table. "Do you know the key to what I read here, Shultz? Local knowledge. And an agent who not only knows how to keep his eyes open, but is creative enough to remember that he is a spy and not some news reporter." He threw himself back onto the sofa and spread his arms out on the cushions. "This is our problem. Other than yourself, our operations in Iran have come to naught. I tell you this confidentially, of course."

"Of course, General."

"My high-ranking people meet with pro-German princes in restaurants, like newsmen, and no wonder they are instantly scooped up by the British and Russians. While you are producing brilliant, timely information. Doing business with their wives and no one suspects you in the least."

Alexsi's face must have given him away on that, because Schellenberg laughed. "Oh, yes. We had information from other sources in Iran. Who had no idea you were one of us. This Swiss businessman who knows everyone, every woman of influence in Iran tells him everything. And is suspected only of being nefarious. The people who don't owe you money or favors are making money in business with you. Brilliant! Not to mention that your operations even return us a profit in foreign currency, which considering what our other agents cost is worth another promotion at least." Schellenberg's eyes were twinkling. "Tell me, Shultz, how are these Persian women?"

"Like champagne shaken in the bottle, sir," Alexsi told him. "Everything looks calm. But release the cork . . ." He made an eruptive motion with both hands.

Schellenberg delightedly slapped the back of the couch. "Fantastic! But more's the point, when the Allies roll in, as you informed us far in advance—well done, by the way—you don't stay there comfortably screwing your way across Teheran. You follow your orders and head out to the tribes like a good officer. And win yourself this." He pointed to the Iron Cross First Class pinned to Alexsi's left breast pocket. "It should have been a Knight's Cross, but unfortunately you had no German witnesses. But it was no trouble correlating the details of your report with our intercepts of British army wireless traffic in Iran. You stung them very badly."

Other than the fact that his heroic achievement was the result of a series of horrible mistakes, Alexsi had accurately recounted the details of both the ambush and his escape. His original thought that the Germans would be the only ones pleased turned out to be correct. A medal and promotion to captain as the reward for a fiasco. He'd been comfortably sitting behind a desk in Abwehr headquarters ever since.

"I have other people with the Iranian tribes," Schellenberg confided. "They take our gold and sit on their asses. And when the gold runs out sell us to the British. While virtually every casualty the British suffered in their walkover invasion was caused by you, personally. And you successfully escape. Why?"

Even if that wasn't a rhetorical question, Alexsi wasn't about to answer it.

"We have people who know how to shoot and blow things up, good soldiers, but they have no flair as agents," said Schellenberg. "We recruit people who speak the language, which is necessary, but they lack the resourcefulness of first-class agents. As soon as you joined the tribe you made sure you developed your sources, however treacherous they proved to be. You kept your eyes open and your ear to the ground, and so were able to get out in time."

"Unfortunately, as soon as I joined the Lur my radio fell under their control," Alexsi said. "Otherwise I might have been able to remain active."

"It would have been an empty gesture, I assure you," said Schellenberg. "It is the downfall of our operations." He leaned forward and struck his hand on the coffee table. "Lack of support! We have a few people doing brilliant work, amongst countless dross, but they wither on the vine for lack of support." He smiled across the coffee table. "I have forgotten my manners in my enthusiasm. May I offer you something? Coffee? Tea?"

"No, thank you, sir," Alexsi replied dutifully. Schellenberg had covered him in honey. Now, was he about to be eaten?

"As you wish," said Schellenberg. He unfolded a large-scale map of Iran and spread it across the coffee table. "Now, while I have you captive here, perhaps you would be so good as to answer a few questions I have about Iran?"

"Of course, General," Alexsi replied. As if he had any choice.

For nearly four hours Schellenberg interrogated him about Teheran, its geography, and finally the tribes and the border. At first Alexsi thought it was to try to trip him up on his story. But no. It became clear, despite his careful circumspection, that Schellenberg had something up his sleeve.

Finally the general refolded the map. "I think this is all I need for now. But I'll tell you what. Come see me tomorrow, at this same time." He offered up that honey smile. "I don't think I need to send a vehicle for you again, do I?"

"No, General," Alexsi replied.

"Thank you again, Shultz. Most enjoyable. Oh, and you will keep our meeting confidential, won't you? Especially from Abwehr."

It was perhaps the nicest death threat Alexsi had ever received. "Yes, sir."

They shook hands, and Alexsi saluted again. *"Heil Hitler!"*

"Heil Hitler," said Schellenberg. He waited until Alexsi was nearly to the door when he added, "Oh, Shultz?"

Alexsi turned about. "Yes, General?"

"That Swiss identity of yours. Is it still good?"

Alexsi doubted it. But with his connections another passport wouldn't be hard to find in Teheran, and he didn't want to close off any options. Berlin was far away from the war now, but who knew what another year might bring? So he let his Russian instinct for what people wanted to hear reply, "Yes, General."

And then once he was outside the office and walking down the corridor a free man, wondered just what he had done. Because if he knew nothing else, it was the difference between a briefing and an employment interview.

50

1943 Berlin

UNCLE HANS WAS DRINKING TOO MUCH. THE MAID MADE A point of telling him. Another new one. Elke was gone; presumably the love affair had ended badly. That's what happened when you fucked your employer, Alexsi thought. You either became the new wife, or the former maid.

She was right, at least. The after-dinner brandies were about twice the size they had been. After the surrender at Stalingrad everyone who knew what was going on had taken to drink. If the Russians lost a half million men in a single battle they could just grab the country by the heels and shake out half a million more. When Germany lost that many it was the beginning of the end. You could always tell how bad it was when the radio started bleating about new weapons and ultimate victory.

"I'm sorry I can't offer you a cigar, my boy," Hans said. "The good ones have grown scarce, and what's available isn't worth putting into your mouth."

"I will most likely be leaving soon, Uncle."

Hans took that news with more concern than Alexsi would have imagined. "Reassignment?" he asked. And then a pregnant pause. "The eastern front?"

"Another mission," Alexsi said.

"You can tell me nothing more?"

"I'm sorry."

Hans slumped down in his chair and made a bitter little laugh.

"Even if you were in Switzerland again, I have nothing to give you. And I doubt the Swiss are all that eager for Reichsmarks these days. They are a very practical people."

Alexsi said nothing. He watched his uncle in the firelight.

Hans Shultz drank off his brandy and refilled the snifter from the crystal decanter. Now he kept it on the table beside him so he would not have to get up. Another loosening of his old disciplines. "At least until the Allies invade France we will have good brandy."

Alexsi just sat there, and for some reason his uncle found it hard to bear this night. Hans Shultz seemed to retreat to his own sullen thoughts, until finally it erupted out of him. "I will need to send a message to Moscow."

Alexsi wasn't sure he'd heard that correctly. "I'm sorry, Uncle?"

"A message to Moscow. To offer my services."

Without a lifetime's experience in keeping his countenance, Alexsi most certainly would have lost it then. His first impulse was to begin shouting treason, but he dismissed that as cheaply theatrical. Instead he said quietly, "How will you do that, Uncle?"

Hans Shultz just looked at him as he would an idiot. "I will not. You will."

And then even quieter. "And how will I do it, Uncle?"

The entire brandy went down. "There is no reason to play the fool with me any longer. Because as you know, I myself am no fool."

Alexsi knew it was just an optical illusion, but Hans's eyes looked blood-red in the firelight. "I honestly have no idea what you're talking about."

Hans Shultz laughed that same bitter laugh again. " 'Honestly.' What a word!" He filled his glass again. "Do you think, can you even think, that when I begged and pleaded with the Communists to allow my nephew out of Russia, I thought for a moment, a single moment, that they would not send a trained intelligence officer?" Now the drunken glare was harsh. "Are you even my nephew?"

The same quiet, even tone. "Of course I am your nephew, Uncle. You have had too much to drink."

A defiant slug from the brandy snifter. "Not enough. Not by half. Don't play the comedian with me. You are a Russian spy. No one knows it better than I. I helped you, and now Moscow will have to reward me. Tell them I am at their service. Tell them, damn you!"

It was a very, very dangerous moment. And not just because the man was very drunk. A whole alternate universe yawned up before Alexsi, once cloudy but now as clear as day. And he regarded it in awe, perfect awe at the game everyone had been playing.

So all along Hans Shultz intended him as insurance in case Germany lost another world war. After all, the man had created a new legend from a dead German cousin even better than the NKVD could have. And at every step smoothed his way, easing him into the army and then Abwehr. Placing him in the perfect position to steal secrets. Running him like an intelligence officer himself. Even removing enemies like Ressler from his path. But now his life rested on a razor's edge. Yes, Hans was most likely looking to feather his nest with Moscow in case the Red Army turned what was left of the Third Reich into the German Soviet Socialist Republic. And, truthfully, they would want a man of his talents and lack of scruples. They would make use of him. He wouldn't be living half as well, but he would still be living better than everyone else.

But if Alexsi revealed himself, then he would be handing Hans a powerful card to play if he ever found himself in trouble with the Gestapo. Here, gentlemen, in exchange for my life I will give you a Soviet intelligence officer inside the Abwehr. Probably he had always been prepared to trade his Russian nephew away in case of emergency.

And, in the end, it was Comrade Yakushev standing by his shoulder who made up his mind. Alexsi could still hear the dead man's voice. *Unlike in melodramas, there is no moment when an agent can reveal or even allude to his true identity to anyone who is not already aware of it. It is inevitably fatal, and regardless of the circumstance there is always a way out if you keep your wits.*

So after all this, the time had come for Alexsi to play his own card. He stood up, in order to make his own German-style statement. "Uncle, out of my love, and my gratitude, and my loyalty to you I will consider that this conversation never took place." And then he added, "If you wish to offer your services to the Russians then I suggest you wait patiently until they arrive in Berlin."

He walked out. Out of the room. Out of the house. He thought he had acted the German officer prig well enough, but he still had to get out. And he couldn't go back. He would have to find some military quarters.

He snatched up his greatcoat and closed the door behind him. The night was overcast from rain. He needed to walk. He picked his way carefully down the blacked-out streets.

A man burst out of a doorway right on top of him. Alexsi almost pulled his knife before he realized it was an air raid warden. The man shouted, "Air-raid danger fifteen!" and hurried down the street, still shouting it at the top of his lungs. That meant a large enemy bomber raid was on the way.

A minute or two later the sirens went off all over Berlin. Alexsi didn't see how the British could bomb with such low visibility from the rain that afternoon, so he just kept walking.

Searchlights popped on, and the sky lit up. Then the antiaircraft guns on the Zoo flak tower in the Tiergarten opened up. They were shooting rapid fire and the sound was deafening. The time fuse shells began exploding above the clouds, and each cracking detonation silhouetted the cloud layer with a flash of light. Alexsi just stood and watched it. An amazing show.

Then, between the bursts of the flak, the sound of approaching airplane engines. They seemed very low. And in an instant all those sounds were canceled out by exploding bombs in the distance. Alexsi counted the time between the high explosive flashes and when the sound reached him to get an idea how far away they were.

A green flare a meter long crashed to earth a hundred meters down the street, bouncing end over end until it came to rest, hissing like a thousand snakes. It lit up the street like a hideous nightmare, and Alexsi realized instantly what it was. An aiming mark for the bombers above. He began to run.

He was directly in the line of what the Germans called the bomb carpet. The explosions drew closer and closer.

Alexsi ran with both palms clapped over his ears and his mouth open. The noise was deafening and the air pressure was terrible. The explosive shock waves had been slamming into him like his father's punches, but now they were like a beating with iron bars. The ground heaved under his feet, and he fell flat on his face. The detonations were bouncing him up and down on the pavement like a doll. Their force was such that there was no way he could get back up. A flash and a spray of fire two streets over as an incendiary bomb went off. The entire wall of a building fell down into the street in front of him. Another blast picked him up into the air and slammed him back onto the ground. The pressure made it feel like he couldn't get any air into his lungs. Every window on the street blew out. Alexsi wrapped his hands over his head and lay there under a rain of broken glass. When he felt it stop falling he poked his head up to the sight of the street carpeted in rubble. And the glass glittering in the red light of the fires on the horizon.

In the midst of the blasts a person ran by him on the street, on fire. Engulfed in flame and running. He thought he heard a woman screaming, "Murder!" In the din he didn't know if he had really heard it or it was only in his head.

Realizing it was death to stay there, he crawled to the nearest doorway. The door was blown off and he scrambled inside and down the pitch darkness of a hallway. The bombs were violently shaking the entire building, the walls swaying back and forth.

By some miracle he bumped into a stairway. He crawled down in search of safety. The building shook like it was about to fall apart.

After the first turn down he was able to grab the banister for support and get to his feet. Stumbling, one arm thrust in front of him to feel whatever might be there. He ran into an iron door that was locked, and pounded on it. He pounded and shouted. The door opened and hands pulled him in.

It was as black as the bottom of a well, but babies were screaming and women were crying. Alexsi actually found that sound a great relief. He was pulled in a little farther and the door slammed behind him. Someone uncovered a lantern and he could finally see. It was the building's air raid shelter, packed with people.

Someone asked the world's stupidest question. "How is it out there, Captain?"

"Bad," Alexsi managed to say. "Very bad."

He found a spot near the door and slumped down onto the floor. The brutal pounding continued, like an orchestra of kettle-drums this far underground.

Someone was poking his arm. A young boy beside him said, "What is that on you, Captain?"

"What do you mean?" Alexsi said.

The boy began brushing him off with his hand. "It's glass," he said. "You have glass all over you."

"Careful, don't cut yourself," Alexsi said automatically.

"Don't worry," said the boy. He had his Hitler Youth cap over his hand as he dutifully brushed away.

When he was done, there was a pile of powdered glass at Alexsi's feet. It glittered in the lantern light.

Alexsi remembered the street above carpeted in it, gleaming in the red firelight. The first thing he thought of was that the Germans were getting their payment for what they'd done to the Jews on the night of the broken glass.

After an hour the pounding subsided, and a debate began whether to go and take a look. That was interrupted by the pounding of a fist on the shelter door. They opened up and a fireman was standing there with his own battery torch.

"Everyone out," he ordered. "Winds are rising. There may be a firestorm."

When they stumbled into the street, the horizon was glowing red in three directions. They began walking toward where it seemed to be clear, carefully picking their way through the rubble. Alexsi took a little girl onto his shoulders and a toddler in his arms so the mother could carry her baby. As they walked, an eviscerated building would come crashing down, or a delayed-action bomb would explode the silence, and everyone would scream in terror.

Alexsi vowed that he would get out of Germany. No matter what Schellenberg had up his sleeve, he'd agree to it. He had to get out.

51

1943 Berlin

"GOOD, YOU MADE IT," SCHELLENBERG REMARKED CASUALLY as Alexsi came through the door. "Devil's own time getting through the streets. My adjutant must have bought it, poor fellow. Can't think of any other reason why he wouldn't be here."

No, you probably couldn't, Alexsi thought. He was still in his bombed-out uniform, and unshaven, though Schellenberg looked smart and perfectly pressed. He was bent over a map spread out on his enormous desk. In the same posture beside him was a major of the Armed SS, a burly giant in his forties who had to be close to two meters tall. He wore the sleeve band of the Das Reich division and a Knight's Cross around his neck. But the first thing you noticed about him was that deep scar across his left cheek. Considering himself something of an expert, Alexsi ruled out a knife or shrapnel wound. He had never been impressed by Germans with their fencing scars. Show him the fellow who gave you the scar, then he'd be impressed.

Schellenberg said, "Captain Walter Shultz—Major Otto Skorzeny."

So this was him, Alexsi thought as they shook hands. Skorzeny sizing him up the same. That Knight's Cross had come from leading the mission that plucked the Italian dictator Mussolini from captivity by his own people and brought him back to Hitler. Though Abwehr gossip said it was the crack Air Force Parachute

Training Battalion doing all the work, and Himmler making sure the SS man Skorzeny got all the credit. Nazi politics.

"I'll be straightforward with you," said Schellenberg. "I need a first-class agent to go into Iran and lay the groundwork for a military operation. I've made up my mind that you're the man. What do you say?"

Whenever they said they were being straightforward with you, you could count on the fact that they weren't. But Alexsi had made up his mind, too. "I'm your man, General."

Schellenberg gave him another dazzling smile. "Excellent! Well, now there's no more need for pussyfooting around. I can tell you what's up. And it's big, so we'd better sit down."

They settled themselves onto the soft and padded chairs. Alexsi waited patiently. He knew Schellenberg, like the rest of them, couldn't resist dramatics.

"We know it for a fact," Schellenberg began. "That the so-called Big Three—Stalin, Churchill, and Roosevelt—will be meeting together in Teheran between November 28 and December 1 of this year. This will be a golden opportunity that we will not let pass by. We will wipe them out." He made a cutting gesture with his hand. "It will set back the Allied military operations for years and give us some breathing room to deploy our new weapons. What do you think?"

Alexsi thought it was the craziest thing he'd ever heard in his life. Even worse than a bunch of Russian university students thinking they could kill Stalin. Never mind Churchill and Roosevelt. As long as those two stayed close to Stalin they'd be surrounded by an entire division of NKVD machine gunners. Especially in Teheran. But he was still Russian enough to recognize the party line when he heard it. So, like a good party man, what he said out loud was, "I agree, General. We would be failing in our duty otherwise."

"That's exactly what I wanted to hear," Schellenberg said exultantly. Skorzeny was just watching Alexsi intently. "This is the plan. Time is short, so we will parachute you into Iran. You will find safe houses in Teheran near the conference area, obtain vehicles, and prepare and mark a sizable parachute-landing zone. When the time is ripe Major Skorzeny's men—SS Special Unit for Special Assignments Friedenthal—will drop in to do the job. Afterward the force will fall back to the tribal areas and across the border to Turkey." He smiled over at Skorzeny. "Otto here made the Abruzzi jump to rescue Il Duce, and now he will make the long jump to eliminate the Big Three. Operation Long Jump. You will be their guide throughout. Your thoughts?"

Alexsi had no plans to verbalize his thoughts. But if everyone in the room was going to act like a lunatic then he might as well join in. "You recall our meeting yesterday, General? When we discussed the problems that both your people and I had with the tribes."

"Yes," Schellenberg said, frowning.

Oh, this was one who did not like to be thwarted in the least, Alexsi thought. "Well, if I may make a suggestion? Just south of Teheran on the Qom–Teheran road is a salt lake bed. The area all around it is perfectly flat. And will be as dry and hard-packed as concrete in the fall of the year. I could prepare some drums of fuel as runway lights, and even the largest aircraft could easily land and take off on it. A radio signal from me to hone in on. In this way the major's force could be extracted." Good luck with that. But no harm in being helpful.

"Local knowledge!" Schellenberg exclaimed, grasping Skorzeny by the arm. Something, Alexsi noted, the big man did not care for in the least. "This is why you must have local knowledge. Brilliant, Shultz. You solve a multitude of problems with a single inspiration. Wait. One moment." He grasped his chin, deep in thought.

Alexsi and Skorzeny waited patiently.

"I have it!" Schellenberg said finally. "You will kill Stalin and Churchill, as planned. But you will abduct Roosevelt and bring him to the Führer to negotiate America's exit from the war." He smiled triumphantly and eagerly searched out Alexsi's and Skorzeny's faces for their reaction.

In a way, keeping composure through all this was nearly as bad as weathering Uncle Hans's wanting him to get in touch with Moscow. If the Allies could only see how decisions were made in the Third Reich they'd piss themselves laughing. Then again, considering how Stalin had taken being told the Germans would invade, perhaps not. In any case Alexsi thought Schellenberg had been reading far too many adventure novels for his own good. Never mind his own Iran report. Perhaps the real reason the Nazis had thrown the famous psychiatrist Freud out of the country wasn't because he was Jewish, but to keep him from diagnosing them all as madmen. He turned to see how Skorzeny would handle it. Or whether he was as crazy as Schellenberg.

"If I can," Skorzeny said slowly, speaking his first words in Alexsi's presence. His voice was deep and raspy, just as you'd imagine from someone of his looks. "Kill, definitely. Capture if possible."

"Of course, of course," Schellenberg said, patting him on the knee. "Rest assured, the Reichsführer and I have no doubt of your success."

Alexsi was glad he wasn't the only one getting the screws. Here was Schellenberg beating Scarface Otto over the head with Himmler.

"You will immediately go into isolation." Schellenberg was speaking to Alexsi. "We cannot risk the slightest security breach. Spies are everywhere. Why, did you know that the Russians even had an agent who told them we would invade?"

That gave Alexsi a start that he was unable to disguise.

"Yes," said Schellenberg. "Some bastard named Sorge. Posed as a German journalist in Tokyo. Probably Russian all along. The Japs caught him."

Well, Schellenberg had mistaken whatever had passed across

his face for outrage. Alexsi wondered if you could eventually become immune to extreme shock. Based on his own experience the answer was no.

"So we can't be too careful," Schellenberg went on. "And you will need help. Someone to run your radio."

"I am a fully qualified wireless operator, General," Alexsi said quickly.

"Well, we feel a partner would be helpful," Schellenberg said insistently. "We have discovered to our cost that two men together are far too noticeable, so I will be gifting you a wife." He sat back again, as if expecting applause.

Alexsi said, "As you know, General, I had no trouble working alone before."

"Of course, of course. But in this case another pair of hands, so to speak, could make all the difference in the world. Unlike your last mission, the SD will make sure you are properly supported this time."

It required no great powers of perception to know when a general didn't wish to be argued with. The only reason they were kidnapping an army man from Abwehr was because they needed him. They would send some SD woman agent along to keep an eye on him and take credit for success along with Skorzeny.

"I tell you frankly that at this stage of the war it is nearly impossible to find the correct people with the requisite languages," Schellenberg said. "She will be your German-speaking Swiss wife. But have no fear—it would be unacceptable for a woman to outrank you." He went over to his desk, picked up the phone, and pressed a button. Alexsi could hear the intercom buzzing outside the room.

After an uneventful moment Schellenberg hung up the phone, only slightly abashed. "I forget I have no adjutant." He walked over to a side door, opened it, and said, "Come in, come in."

She was a brunette, not unattractive, hair pulled and pinned severely back behind her head and body concealed under an SS uniform. A first lieutenant, with the blitz arrowhead of the signal service on her left sleeve, and the brown piping of concentration camp guards circling her shoulder boards.

"Captain Walter Shultz," Schellenberg said formally. "Obersturmführer Erna Fuchs."

"Lieutenant," Alexsi said politely.

She snatched up his hand and pumped it briskly up from his collarbone to down below his belt. "I look forward to our mission, Captain!"

More thorn than rose, there. Alexsi wanted to tell her there was no need to shout. He only smiled instead.

All things considered, it really was fantastic luck. No doubt every SD agent who spoke Farsi had already been captured by the British and Russians in Iran. So, really, he was going back to Iran as a German agent thanks to his own efforts as a Soviet agent. Life was so strange. But at least he'd be out of Berlin. Even if he hadn't nearly been blown to pieces by British bombs, the writing was there on the wall for anyone to see. If the Western Allies didn't land in France this summer, it would definitely be the next. If the Russians didn't crack open the German front in the east this year, it would be next year for sure. And when it all fell apart the last thing he wanted was to be an intelligence officer in Berlin with both sides converging on the Nazi capital. The Germans would almost certainly decide that a captain with the Iron Cross who'd trained in the infantry needed to be killed by the Americans at the head of a battalion. Not for him, thanks.

52

1943 Over Iran

ALEXSI KNEW HE HAD BEEN DREAMING, BUT WHEN ROUGHLY shaken awake couldn't remember what of. Then he opened his eyes and couldn't see anything. After realizing he was now awake and not dreaming, and thinking himself blind, he finally remembered that he'd tied his scarf around his eyes to block the light through the flying goggles. He lifted them up with embarrassed relief and returned to the reality of the grimy, oily cabin of the Junkers Ju 290. At least asleep, with ears packed full of cotton and the leather flight helmet buckled down, he didn't have to endure the stink of petrol from the auxiliary tanks lashed down inside the cabin, those four deafening engines, or waiting for that rickety, shaking behemoth to either fall apart or catch fire in midair. There was something to be said for long train journeys.

Lieutenant Fuchs's lips were moving in front of him. Alexsi lifted the corner of his flight helmet and the sound flooded in.

"How can you sleep?" she demanded.

"It's better than staring out a window for eight hours," Alexsi shouted back. "Did you wake me up just to ask me that?"

"The navigator wants you."

Alexsi went hand over hand up to the front of the bucking aircraft. Even in his sheepskin coat it was freezing cold.

The navigator was bent over the map at his table. Alexsi tapped him on the shoulder.

The navigator pointed to the line of their route on his map.

From Vienna to Bulgaria, where they'd last touched down to top off their fuel tanks. Across Turkey and Iraq, and now to Iran. They were almost there. Alexsi wedged himself behind the navigator's chair to get a look out the observation window. The clear night sky revealed just the blackened expanse of the Iranian desert, the few cities of any size bare pinpricks of light. They corresponded perfectly to the map. Yes, that was Hamadan below. Alexsi tapped the city on the map, and nodded. The navigator nodded back. Alexsi was glad the fellow was thorough. These men of the Luftwaffe Test Formation special mission unit knew their business. Spending all their time flying behind enemy lines, they had better.

The Iranian desert was very big. Being dropped in the wrong spot could mean running out of water before you made it to somewhere people lived.

She was already donning her parachute. And her hands were shaking as she buckled the straps. Frightened nearly out of her skin, Alexsi thought. And why not? His knees had been knocking when he'd stepped off the train at Munich Station, years before. And no parachuting involved there. Once you had survived an Aida you would never sneer at a woman spy. But this was a wireless clerk who, when they called for volunteers, had put her hand up in a fever of National Socialist enthusiasm. No idea what she was getting into.

They were both wearing flight coveralls over civilian clothes. Alexsi reluctantly pulled off his coat and insulated boots and laced up the leather jump boots. Then the leather-covered sponge rubber kneepads.

He checked the RZ20 parachute carefully before throwing it across his back. Two straps that clipped around his legs at the groin, two more that buckled across his waist and chest.

German paratroopers who jumped into action wearing the RZ20 carried only a pistol, a knife, and perhaps a submachine gun due to the chute's peculiarities. All their other equipment was dropped separately in containers. Alexsi and Fuchs didn't have that option. She had insisted on carrying the radio, and the suitcase was strapped to her English rucksack. Alexsi had a rope wound around his, clipped to his waist belt. He'd go out with the pack in his arms and drop it once the chute opened.

One of the aircraft gunners came up and plugged his intercom wire into one of the cabin jacks. He opened the rearmost of the Junkers's double side cargo doors and even colder air blasted in. Alexsi pointed to the hatch and Fuchs shook her head violently. She wanted to go first. Suit yourself.

The plane began to gradually lose altitude. Fuchs clipped her braided rope parachute static line to the beam overhead and put a death grip on one of the exposed aluminum ribs just shy of the hatch. Alexsi clipped his to the same beam and stood behind her, holding the static line to keep himself steady in the bouncing aircraft. He glanced out the small side window and was fairly sure they were passing over Qom.

The gunner was talking to the cockpit over his throat microphone. He held up one finger. One minute. Fuchs was staring out at the black hole. Alexsi nudged her with his boot until she looked over and saw the signal.

Holding on to that metal rib for dear life, Fuchs skidded forward until she was right on the edge of the door. The gunner signaled stand by. Alexsi gave his static line a tug. With a German parachute you had to go out the door in a headlong dive. If you weren't horizontal when the chute opened you'd be flipped upside down and probably tangle in the lines.

The gunner signaled go. Fuchs just stood there, staring at the open hatch as if she didn't quite believe it. They were flying over 125 kilometers per hour, and a lot of ground was rushing past while she made up her mind. Alexsi wasn't about to fly back to Berlin because she froze up on him. He grabbed the overhead beam with one hand, swung himself forward, and kicked her out the door. Then he followed right behind, grasping his pack tight to his chest with both arms.

As he dove through the slipstream Alexsi had the impression that the forked tail of the Junkers was passing only millimeters over his head. Then he was falling through the night sky. As always it was eerily quiet. One parachute was the German way; if it didn't open it was an even faster ride down. It hadn't opened yet.

Then a bang, and the opening shock, hard enough to pop his eyeballs out, doubled him up so hard his knees nearly struck his face. Alexsi actually saw stars. They weren't real stars because the two thick riser lines were attached to the sides of the waist belt, sending you toward the ground leaning forward, facedown. There was no holding on to his pack through that impact, and the line now dangled between his feet. The weight on it told him the pack was still there.

There was a desert wind tonight, and it was rocking his parachute back and forth. Not good. You couldn't grab the lines on the RZ20 to steer yourself. All you could do was make a swimming motion so you were at least facing into the direction the wind was pushing you. Which made kneepads a necessity.

Now the parachute was oscillating wildly. Alexsi was afraid the canopy might collapse before he reached the ground. He was watching the horizon to try to gain some clue before it surprised him. He put his feet together and bent his knees. At least he'd know when his pack touched ground first.

Just then the wind pushed him back, swung him forward, and instead of making the standard German parachutists' forward landing roll he smashed face-first into the side of a large sand dune.

He might have blacked out for a few seconds. It was the sort of thing you never knew until someone told you. But the next thing he realized was the still-inflated parachute yanking him out of the dune and dragging him down and over the ground.

He couldn't reach the lines to collapse the chute, and there were too many buckles to undo. Alexsi felt for the special snap pocket on the right leg of his flight suit and grabbed ahold of the German parachutist gravity knife. The blade slid out of the handle as he pulled it from the pocket, and he pressed the thumb lever to lock it into place. He rolled sideways to grab one of the risers. He got ahold of it and slashed away with the knife. He was still being dragged. The line gave way. He rolled to the other side and slashed wildly at that line, trying hard not to cut his left hand off. A tearing sound, and his forward progress stopped as the canopy sailed along without him.

Alexsi just lay on the ground for a while, spitting out sand. He felt his face, and was pleasantly surprised to find that his nose was neither broken nor bleeding, and all his teeth were intact. He gingerly moved everything. No broken bones, though a grim foreboding of how he'd feel the next morning. He seemed to be in reasonable condition, and tentatively stood up. A little wobbly, but it could have been much worse.

Alexsi laboriously unbuckled the parachute harness and stripped off the flying coveralls. It was about three-quarter moonlight, and he could see the parachute canopy, finally deflated, in a pile on the ground about forty meters away. Alexsi pulled the entrenching tool from his pack and began digging a hole. The loose sand was easy going. He tossed in the coveralls, kneepads, helmet, parachute, and harness, covering them over and smoothing out the sand.

Finally he slung the rucksack onto his shoulders and climbed to the top of the nearest dune to see if he could get his bearings.

Nothing but dunes. And no sign of Lieutenant Fuchs. A German woman who spoke no Farsi, out in the Iranian desert? If she didn't turn up she'd better hope she was found by the British. Otherwise it was either death from thirst or after rape by Iranians.

Alexsi took a long piss off the top of the dune and then pulled out his map and compass. A light suddenly shone off to his left. He dropped down flat on the dune. The light disappeared, then shone again. This wasn't good. He'd either dropped right on top of someone, or someone had gotten there awfully quickly. He reached inside his coat for his pistol.

Alexsi cocked the Browning 9mm and waited patiently. The light popped into view again, closer this time. An instant later the wind shifted and he could hear the faint sound of someone shouting, "Shultz! Shultz!"

Fuchs. Wandering around the desert with her battery torch on, shouting at the top of her lungs. She would be shooting off signal flares next.

Alexsi had always been uncomfortably unsure whether the Soviets would own up to him if he were captured by the British. Depending upon which way the wind happened to be blowing in Moscow that day, the bastards might just sit back and let him be shot as a German spy.

He pondered his options and decided that she was so inept it was no danger having her along.

Fuchs was walking between the dunes, of course where she could see nothing. Battery torch in one hand, Luger in the other. Still bellowing, "Shultz!" Though now her voice had a fine edge of hysteria to it.

Alexsi wasn't about to spring out at her. Not with a gun in her hand. From atop the dune he said, in between all the shouting, "Careful with that pistol."

The sound of his voice made Fuchs leap in alarm, and she accidentally fired the Luger into the side of the dune.

Alexsi just shook his head. Other than setting off some TNT, that was about as much noise as one could make in a night

Fuchs practically slumped over with relief. "My God."

Alexsi said, "Why not put that pistol back in your holster before you make any more noise? And for heaven's sake shut off that torch."

Shamefaced, she did as she was told. "Where were you?"

"Looking for you. Except without trying to alert everyone within two kilometers."

"Christ, it's cold," she exclaimed, rubbing her arms with her hands.

"It's the desert," Alexsi said. "Did you bury your parachute?"

A defiant "Of course."

"All right," said Alexsi. "Then let's get up to that hill over there so we can find our bearings."

"There's a road in that direction," she said, pointing.

"Yes, I saw it while I was coming down. That's the Qom–Teheran road."

"Well why don't we take it?"

"Because assuming we don't flag down a British patrol, anyone we meet with an automobile will drive us right to the nearest British garrison to sell for cash."

Chastened silence from the lieutenant.

"We'll get our bearings and then walk to Qom," said Alexsi. "It will be no more than twenty kilometers. We'll make it before daylight."

"Why not Teheran?"

"Teheran is full of British, American, and Russian soldiers. And they're all looking for German spies. Qom is a Shia Muslim holy city, pilgrims and religious students coming and going all the time. We can lie low there until the time is right."

"Why didn't you mention this during our preparations?" she demanded.

"Because then someone who didn't know all that would tell me to do it differently. I'm the Iran expert, remember?"

Silence in response.

Actually, Alexsi didn't want to go charging right into Teheran only to find out that his Swiss identity *was* blown, and the British were still looking for Berger the German spy. Better to hide out in Qom and carefully dip a toe into that water first.

As he went to put his pack on, Fuchs caught his arm. There were headlights far off in the distance. And the headlights were following the exact route they had walked.

"Who do you think it is?" Fuchs asked anxiously.

Alexsi just shook his head in the darkness. Seriously? "A British patrol, of course. No one else would be *driving* around in the Iranian desert at night."

"Why couldn't it be criminals?" Fuchs demanded.

The fear in her voice was apparent. "Criminals wouldn't have their lights on," Alexsi explained patiently. "They would be worried about British patrols."

"How do you think they found us?"

"I'm sure it had nothing to do with torches, shouting, and pistol shots," Alexsi replied. "See for yourself how far light travels in the desert at night."

As if in response Fuchs pulled out her Luger.

"Let me see your pistol for a moment," Alexsi said.

Her gaze fixated on the light in the distance, she handed it over.

Alexsi made sure the safety was on and tucked it into his jacket pocket.

"What are you doing?" Fuchs demanded. "Give it back."

"We're not shooting them," Alexsi said patiently. "If they don't turn up the whole British Army will be out looking for them. If they're found shot they'll also find our buried parachutes, and there will be a nationwide manhunt for two German spies." He thought for a moment. "Give me your torch."

Fuchs handed over the battery torch.

"Just relax and don't do anything foolish," Alexsi advised. He leaned over her back and cut off a piece of the sacking that padded their radio. He wrapped the sacking around the lens of the torch and clicked it on. The light shone dimly through the fabric.

"What are you doing?" Fuchs demanded, close to panic.

"Bringing them up here," Alexsi replied. He placed the torch on the ground so it shone toward the advancing headlights. They had been weaving slightly, but now were headed directly toward them. And much faster. As it approached he could see that it was one of those strange-looking American Willys vehicles they called a Jeep. "All right," he said. "Now let's head down the back side over here." Fuchs followed him like a puppy.

The Jeep stopped at the base of the hill, the headlights shining on the pair of footprints in the loose soil that headed straight up. Two men got out, both wearing the distinctive pie plate helmets of the British Army. One pulled out a revolver; the other reached back into the Jeep for a rifle. To which he attached a long bayonet. They conferred quietly for a moment, then, well spread out, advanced up the hill on either side of the tracks, weapons at the ready.

On the edge of the hill, two dark shapes rose up from the rocky ground they had blended into. One figure circled quickly around the base of the hill, the other following.

Alexsi gently set his rucksack into the back of the Jeep and slid behind the wheel. The engine had been left running. The simplest tricks always worked the best. As soon as Fuchs was seated Alexsi let out the clutch and pushed the accelerator pedal to the floor. The Jeep bucked backward and stalled out. Two muzzle flashes exploded from the top of the hill, and the bullets cracked overhead. The dashboard was practically empty. Alexsi twisted a lever switch. Nothing happened and he twisted it back. A bullet snapped past his side and shot the side mirror off.

"Get it started," Fuchs screamed.

Alexsi couldn't see the floor, and was feeling around with his feet near the pedals. Over the gunfire he shouted, "Do you see a starter button?"

Fuchs dove underneath the dash, and Alexsi could see her thrashing around. She must have hit something because the engine turned over. Alexsi pumped the accelerator and he began with the shift lever down this time. The Jeep lurched forward.

Alexsi swung it around and gave it more petrol. The forward gears ended at three, so that didn't take long. Another bullet thumped into the bed right behind him. With the accelerator to the floor, Alexsi finally had time to push down the plunger that turned off the lights. In darkness the bullets were still coming, but not as close now.

It wasn't a racer, but they were moving. Alexsi looked over. Fuchs was still on the floorboard, practically tucked under the dash. Alexsi shouted, "Don't worry, we're out of range."

An instant later a bullet struck the windscreen right where her head would have been. "I stand corrected," Alexsi said.

Fuchs was now sitting upright, staring at the bullet hole and gripping the sides of her seat with both hands.

"At least now we don't have to walk," Alexsi shouted.

She turned and gave him a look that was half terror and half fury. "We're in the same boat as if we killed them. They'll find this thing and find us."

Alexsi had to laugh out loud, both at her and for the sheer joy of being alive. It carried over the sound of the motor, the wind rushing over the open vehicle, and the now faint crackle of gunshots that still continued obstinately in the distance. "Don't worry. They'll think they were tricked by Iranian thieves. We'll leave this on a street I know. By noon there won't be so much as a bolt left."

He settled down and concentrated on the desert ahead. It would be shameful to run into something and then have to start walking all over again.

53

ALEXSI TWISTED THE KEY IN THE LOCK AND CHARGED INTO the hotel room. The suitcase he'd bought for her was open and the contents carefully unpacked. For heaven's sake, they were spying, not on holiday. He burst into the bath. Erna was in the tub, and the shock of his unexpected arrival had her nearly launching up into the ceiling in a roiling surge of water.

"What are you doing?" she demanded, half up and half out, instinctively covering her breasts with one arm. And they were very nice.

"Get dressed quickly," Alexsi ordered. "We have to get out of here."

"What is it?" she said, fear making her voice rise.

"Quickly," Alexsi repeated.

Back out in the room he tore open the drawers of the bureau and there was everything neatly folded and in order like a good German. He flung everything into the case and snapped it shut. And staged it, his unopened case, and the one containing their radio next to the door.

She came out of the bathroom, buttoning her blouse with one hand and brandishing her Luger in the other.

"Put that damned gun away," Alexsi snapped, "and get your shoes on. We're about to receive a visit from the British Army."

"How do you know?" she said, voice shaking, struggling into her footwear, a missed puff of soap dangling under one ear.

"Always tip the staff generously." He had the door open and their two suitcases in hand. The one containing the radio was hers. "Quickly, quickly."

She put on her jacket, tucked the Luger away in her purse, and picked up the radio case.

Alexsi was already moving down the hallway. They reached the back stairs and went down fast. She turned toward the exit, but it was a small hotel and Alexsi already knew they kept the back door locked to keep the guests from departing with bills in arrears. He was holding the staff door for her.

The few employees were elsewhere in the middle of the day. There wasn't even a laundry—they must send the sheets out. Or not at all. Down the dingy hall and there was the service exit. Alexsi opened it just a crack and checked for surprises. No, the alley was empty. "Come along," he said.

At the end of the alley he poked one eye around the corner. Another British Jeep was sitting in front of the hotel entrance, a single soldier in khaki smoking and paying no attention at all.

Alexsi exited the alley and headed in the opposite direction. As it happened an empty horse-drawn cab was heading down the street toward the hotel to check for fares. Alexsi hailed it and the driver swung the cab around.

He got their bags and Erna aboard and pointed the driver down the street. "They got around to checking hotels a little faster than I thought," he said in a low voice, in German.

Erna opened her compact, but at the moment her face was perspiring beyond the repair of powder. Her hand was shaking badly. "Where will we go?"

"Not to worry. That's what I was doing out. I engaged us a house."

54

ALEXSI SAID, IN RUSSIAN, "GREETINGS, COMRADE COMMERCIAL Counselor."

Evgeny Dmitrovich Matushkin spun about quickly. No mean trick in the labyrinthine warren of the Teheran Grand Bazaar, crowded with shoppers and sellers. It was an easy place to follow without being seen, and perhaps he had been careless. Perhaps fatally so. He had to look Alexsi over for a moment, then he relaxed. And, now relaxed, he shook his head, bemused. "You never cease to surprise, David."

"Will you join me for a coffee?" Alexsi inquired.

"That would be pleasant." A pause. "At least I hope it will be."

"I will do my best to make it so," Alexsi said.

A short walk to a coffee shop. A table in the corner and two cups. Matushkin tasted his tentatively, winced at the strength, and added a great deal of sugar. "The last we heard, you were in Berlin."

"I parachuted in four days ago."

Matushkin was one of those who took it as a professional requirement never to look surprised. "Why did we not hear of this?"

Alexsi sighed. Nice to know Matushkin hadn't changed. Always a complaint to start with. "Because the Germans had me in isolation."

"What is your mission?" Matushkin demanded.

"To assassinate Stalin, Churchill, and Roosevelt."

Matushkin had been taking a sip of coffee. He coughed and clapped his napkin to his face to keep from spitting it out. "What did you say?"

"Do I really need to repeat myself?"

"And you are saying the Germans put you in charge of this plot?"

"I'm here to lay the groundwork." Alexsi handed over a packet of British Player's cigarettes. "Here, have one."

Matushkin shook out the one cigarette and lit it, briefly glancing down at the wad of paper folded up inside before the pack went into his pocket. "Brief me on the broad details now."

"I am based out of Qom. I am to rent one house near the conference site for the attack, and another farther out for assembly purposes. Also purchase vehicles. The Germans drop in Otto Skorzeny and his band of SS parachutists. You know, the fellow who snatched Mussolini? I drive them to the house in Teheran. From there they launch an attack to kill the Big Three. Schellenberg and the SD are in charge of this. They plucked me from the Abwehr because I speak Farsi and know Iran. I was pleased to volunteer."

Matushkin had been listening with his mouth slightly ajar. Then he gave Alexsi a suspicious look. "They will not use the SS already in the country?"

"What are you talking about?" Alexsi said sharply. "What SS already in the country?"

"The sabotage teams," said Matushkin, as if now he didn't know what Alexsi was talking about.

Alexsi was at sea for a moment; then he finally realized what Matushkin meant. "You mean from Operation François?" Another of Skorzeny's plots. Dropping SS sabotage teams to the pro-German Qashqai tribe. Or at least the antigovernment Qashqai tribe, which made them ostensibly pro-German. The SS teams were to blow up the roads and trains the British and Americans were using to ship supplies to Russia. They'd gone in this summer.

Skorzeny doing the planning, but taking care not to jump into Iran himself. "I radioed Moscow all the information while I was in Berlin. Are you telling me you didn't get them?"

"We did," Matushkin said defensively. "Only one team is still at large."

Alexsi sensed there was something he wasn't being told. "Schellenberg gave me the distinct impression that he considered them all lost. Due to lack of support." The Luftwaffe transport fleet couldn't spare any aircraft—they were too busy evacuating generals from the debacle in Tunisia and dropping supplies to encircled units in Russia. The Qashqai took the gold, and guns, and the weapons training, and then when they didn't get any more they turned the Germans over to the British. "This one team must have been more careful with their money."

Matushkin seemed not to want to talk about that anymore. "And they are truly serious about this harebrained scheme? They think we will not take the proper precautions to safeguard the greatest man in the world?"

Of course he was talking about Stalin, not the other two. Alexsi nodded. "I jumped in with a woman SS lieutenant. She speaks nothing but German, and could not find her own ass even with the help of her makeup mirror."

Matushkin laughed loudly. "David, I have missed you. You are frequently infuriating but always amusing. I was worried when you went missing before. But like the proverbial bad penny, you always turn up."

"Do we really want to speak of that unholy mess?" said Alexsi.

"No," Matushkin said definitively. "Your previous mission here was regrettable. But orders are orders."

"Of course."

"Moscow will have to be told at once," said Matushkin. "There are decisions which must be taken at the highest level."

"The British are nipping at my heels," Alexsi said.

"I am confident you will ensure they do not find you," said Matushkin.

As Alexsi suspected, he was on his own. As always. The British would want to know why they should forget about two German spies, and the Russians would never tell them they had an agent inside Abwehr. "Give me your telephone number at the embassy. I will call every day."

Matushkin wrote it on a piece of paper. Alexsi only looked at it and nodded.

"Call at nine thirty in the morning," said Matushkin. "I will only tell you when, so we agree now that this place will be the location." He looked down at his cup. "Though next time I will have something other than coffee."

55

1943 Qom, Iran

"WHERE HAVE YOU BEEN?" LIEUTENANT FUCHS SNAPPED.

Alexsi had to force himself not to roll his eyes. So this was what being married was like. "I told you, my dear. Teheran."

"These prayer calls are driving me mad," she complained, as the neighborhood muezzin called the faithful to Asr, the afternoon prayer, at the top of his lungs. "Just listen to this screeching."

The house had an Iranian leaseholder. Alexsi had the clock running in his head. Time for the neighborhood to know of them, time for the neighborhood to begin gossiping, time for them to move. "It's only five times a day," he said. "They do make sure you're an early riser, though."

"It's not funny," she said, resuming her pacing of the room. Then she turned back on him. "Do you know how many Jews are here?"

So she had been exploring the city while he was gone. He'd already known that she was one of Hitler's fanatical handmaidens. It didn't matter which country, Russia or Germany, they both seemed to be full of people who fervently believed that it would be a perfect world as soon as whoever they hated was dead: capitalists, Trotskyites, Jews.

Iran was full of refugees from all over Europe. Unlike the West, the Iranians didn't make a fuss about letting them in. As far as the Jews, they had all disappeared from Berlin this year. And from the stories people told about what was going on in the east, you didn't need much imagination to guess their fate. Considering that brown piping on her shoulder boards, Erna probably knew better than he. Alexsi was with Uncle Hans on this. The night of broken glass was all the warning necessary for anyone the Germans hated not to loiter. He'd never understood the pull of home and hearth, the love of the familiar and the terror at the unknown. And probably wouldn't have sympathized even if he did. The murderers were always out there, wearing red stars or grinning silver skulls on their caps. Waiting for their evil prince to come and unleash them. So if they wanted your blood you ran—even if all you had was your nightshirt. But he just said, "No, I don't."

"They're everywhere. Something needs to be done," she muttered.

She had definitely not taken to being a spy behind enemy lines. But this was more than her usual nerves. "Erna, what's wrong?"

She said, "Did you get the trucks?"

"I'll have the last one in a day or two," Alexsi replied, peering at her face. Actually, he'd only bought one truck, so she could radio Berlin. The Germans had given him a thousand British pounds, and no sense dipping too deeply into capital. Matushkin would hemorrhage to hear him talk like that. "Why?"

"You need to hurry up."

Oh, do I? But before he said anything Alexsi noticed the message paper on the table next to their radio. The suitcase was open with the Morse key and earphones on the table. "Erna, what's going on?" He really didn't need to know what she was sending. The NKVD had their crystal frequency and code. They were reading everything.

"There's a change in plans," she said. "They're going to drop a six-man communications group, before they drop the main body."

Alexsi was instantly suspicious. "When?"

"In two days."

"Why would they do that?" Alexsi demanded. "With time so

short? Two separate parachute drops? Am I the only one who thinks that's risky?"

She only shrugged.

"Did something happen to make them distrustful?" Alexsi demanded. He was reading her face, and what he saw there made him drive on relentlessly. "You remembered to add the control sign, didn't you?" This was a unique word or a few letters. Like him signing "David" at the end of his Russian messages. Leaving out the control sign was saying you'd been captured by the enemy and they were making you transmit under their control.

"Of course," she said.

Neither her words nor her face convinced him. "You forgot and left it out of one of your messages, didn't you?" Alexsi said. "So now Berlin isn't entirely sure we're still free. That's why they're sending a few people in with their own radios, before they commit Skorzeny."

"I don't have to listen to this!" she shouted, storming into the bedroom and slamming the door.

Now Alexsi let his eyes roll. Just another complication. He hoped Matushkin didn't kick up a fuss about it. Imagine. She might have blown the entire operation on her own, without any help from him at all.

But he was left with a nagging feeling that something else was going on. The table couldn't be seen from the bedroom keyhole, he'd made sure of that. He checked the open radio, and it was set on the correct frequency. He flipped through the stack of paper she was using to compose and code messages. All blank. He checked the first sheet for subtle indentations. If she had set her message down upon the pile of paper, rather than a single sheet on the hard table, it would be possible to rub with a pencil and bring up the writing. No, it was perfectly clean.

He walked around the kitchen, thinking it over. Perhaps some tea? He put his hand on the stove. Then knelt down and opened the firebox. Paper ash. Burning her messages. A section of

scorched paper was sitting there, intact. Sloppy. Ever so deli-
cately, Alexsi picked it up and placed it atop the stove. It didn't
crumble, but clearly it wanted to.

He took a kitchen match from the can on the shelf. And gently
tilted the burned paper on the stove until it was vertical. Back on
his knees, and eye to eye with the paper, Alexsi struck the match
and held it behind the paper. The flame illuminated the brown
scorched paper, and then consumed it.

All he could make out were four words in German. Alexsi
swept the new ashes into his hand and tossed them back into the
firebox. OUTCOME WITH SECOND VARIANT. Second variant? A part of the plan they weren't sharing with him? Because he
was army, and they were all SS? Or some other reason?

Then he had to laugh out loud. Here he was acting like a German spy instead of a Russian one. The Russians had the message,
which probably explained the second variant. Why should he
worry? He was in Iran, and the British weren't bombing him. Whatever it was, it was the NKVD's problem now.

He glanced back at the closed door. No sex tonight.

56

1943 Teheran, Iran

"I DON'T UNDERSTAND WHY YOU WANTED ME TO ACTUALLY rent the house right next to the vehicle gate of your security zone," Alexsi said. "I could have just radioed the Germans that I had it without going to all the trouble."

Matushkin was drinking tea this time. "There may be other German agents confirming your movements. Better that your preparations for them be real."

Alexsi was an old farm boy. He knew shit when someone was shoveling it onto his boots. But he also knew to drop it. "By the way, the security fence was very clever." The NKVD had erected a fence four and a half meters high of bright purple cloth completely encircling all of Teheran around the embassy. A fast and cheap way of sealing the area off. No one could see through it to make a sniper shot. It didn't matter that it was cloth—the entire ring would be constantly patrolled by NKVD sentries with automatic weapons. And no one could set foot inside without being cleared. There were probably smaller circles—stricter security zones—within that. He'd seen antiaircraft guns being towed into place. "If I was still in the fabric trade here I could have gotten you the best price."

Matushkin groaned. "Enough. Please."

"Very well. Don't forget I also got the second house, south of the bazaar." The Germans wanted an intermediate one to stage their force at, to keep from attracting attention to the one close by. He used it himself when he didn't care to drive back to Qom. Erna was the only woman he'd ever met who became more difficult to deal with the more he fucked her. "They both cost a bit of money."

"We're not concerned with that," Matushkin said. And then, as if to clarify, "As long as you're spending German money."

"Of course." And they called *them* capitalists.

"The decision has been made to allow this fascist communications team to land. Then we will take them and allow them to send a message that their mission is compromised."

"You don't intend to capture Skorzeny and his entire force?" Alexsi said, surprised. Then why have him get the house?

"No."

"It seems a missed opportunity."

"Make no mistake, we would love them in our hands," said Matushkin. "But we cannot take the slightest risk with the life of Comrade Stalin."

"Your choice," said Alexsi.

"Do not be disappointed," said Matushkin. "Your fine work in exposing this plot has not gone unnoticed. It also has had an unexpected benefit."

"Oh?" Alexsi said.

"The embassy of the United States is on the outskirts of the city," said Matushkin. "As you know, the British embassy is quite literally across the street from our own. With the exposure of this fascist plot to liquidate the great leaders, it has become necessary for the American president Roosevelt and his staff to be housed in the Soviet embassy for the duration of the conference. For reasons of security, The Americans have agreed."

"I see," said Alexsi. "And while they are there you will be listening to all their private conversations and reading their secret papers."

Matushkin took a bite of his *kolouche* cookie, then wiped a bit of the fig filling from his mouth. "Such is the nature of diplomacy."

Alexsi said, "Now what of this second variant?"

"Nothing to concern yourself with," said Matushkin.

"You don't say?"

"We are not concerned," Matushkin said, more firmly this time. "So you should not concern yourself."

Alexsi nodded submissively. But whenever Russians made veiled threats, there was always something to be concerned about. Both German and Russian, every side he was supposed to be on seemed to be keeping secrets from him.

57

1943 Qom, Iran

THERE WAS A HORSE TIED OUT FRONT WHEN HE RETURNED.
Alexsi was fairly certain Erna hadn't gone out shopping and purchased a horse.

At first he thought of turning about and never coming back. If
it had been an automobile he would have. But a horse? Curious,
he parked his little Fiat 1500 well away and circled the neighborhood on foot. He greeted the neighbors and carefully examined
their faces.

No, there was no surveillance other than the Russians who
had been watching ever since he made contact with Matushkin.
And if there had been any other surveillance, those Russian professionals would have been long gone.

Still. Alexsi came around to the back of the house and drew
his pistol as soon as he was out of sight of the neighbors. He
slipped in the rear door, carefully moving the chair he always
kept propped up there to fall over and make noise.

As soon as he was inside he heard a male voice talking to Erna.
Of course he stopped and listened. Just chitchat. But the man's
voice was so familiar. He couldn't believe it.

Alexsi walked in with the pistol leveled, and they both jumped
up like they'd been caught stealing.

"Don't shoot!" Erna cried out. "It's all right!"

Standing next to her with his hands up was Hauptsturmführer
Kurt Ressler of the SD. In what would have passed for Iranian

tribal costume if he hadn't had his hair slicked back like a German.

In spite of himself, Alexsi just had to laugh. But the pistol stayed leveled. "What the hell are you doing here?"

Ressler managed to get out, "I'm to contact you."

Lieutenant Fuchs said, "Walter—"

Alexsi said, "How did you get here?"

"I rode," said Ressler.

"I know that," Alexsi said impatiently. "I saw your horse. I meant Iran."

"I've been here for some time."

It was impossible that he was working on his own. The British would have had him inside a week. Alexsi thought quickly. It had to be that one remaining SS sabotage team, the one Matushkin said they hadn't caught yet. But the fact that they were still free meant that Ressler could not possibly be in command.

Alexsi snapped the safety back on his pistol and holstered it behind his back. This was one of those nearly unbelievable coincidences that life sometimes threw your way. "Sit down," he said pleasantly. "I see you finally managed to become operational." And escape from wherever Uncle Hans put you.

"You know each other?" Erna said.

Alexsi could tell from her tone that she was lying. Ressler had already told her. "Oh, we knew each other well in Berlin. But I can't seem to recall any mention of you in my mission briefing."

"I received a signal from Berlin," said Ressler. "*I* will be meeting the advance party when they jump in."

"Says who?" Alexsi demanded. They had both retaken their seats. He was still standing.

Erna got up and handed him the decoded message.

Alexsi read it over. Yes, it was for them. New orders. Not making any sense, but . . . Actually, now that he thought about it, better for him. "Fine. You can take one of the trucks I've already purchased."

Ressler seemed surprised not to be arguing about it. "No, I've already made arrangements."

"Oh?" Alexsi said pleasantly. "Do you need petrol?"

"I've come up with a better idea," Ressler said proudly.

"Is it a secret?" Alexsi inquired.

"I've bought seven camels," Ressler said.

"You what?" said Alexsi, not quite believing his ears.

"Camels," said Ressler.

That stopped Alexsi in his tracks while he absorbed the news. "You're taking camels. You went out and bought camels?"

"Of course."

Of course. He could just imagine the flea-bitten monsters Ressler would have picked up at market. "I can't help it. I have to ask. Why camels?"

Now Ressler was the one talking to the fool. "To remain secret, of course. Men on camels will blend in."

Yes, how could he have been so stupid? They would look exactly like seven Germans on camels. "So you intend to ride camels to the dropping zone, and then on to Teheran? Sixty kilometers?"

"Of course."

"One more stupid question, if you please. Have you ever ridden a camel?"

Ressler gave him a contemptuous look. "When I bought them."

"Excellent. Now, will you bring the party to the house I prepared in Teheran, or somewhere else?"

"The house in Teheran," said Ressler.

"Would you like the address? Directions, perhaps?" Alexsi inquired.

"I already gave them to him," Erna broke in. "Along with radioing Berlin," she added. Until then she'd prudently stayed out of the ring while punches were being thrown.

"Yes, the lieutenant has briefed me well," said Ressler.

"No more questions, then," said Alexsi. "Anything else I can help you with?"

"I have it all in hand," said Ressler, smirking.

"When will you be leaving?"

"Almost immediately."

Yes, it would definitely take some time on camel. "Some food before you go? A drink perhaps? I'm sure it's been dry with the Qashqai."

"What do you know about the tribes?" Ressler demanded.

"Probably more than you," Alexsi said pleasantly. "Unless you've picked up Farsi to go with your schoolboy French."

"I have a few words," Ressler said defensively.

"I'm sure you do," Alexsi said, prodding openly now. "Still a captain? I'm one myself now."

"Yes, I heard." Ressler forcing himself to be pleasant now. "Perhaps a drink."

"Vodka?" said Alexsi. He'd gotten it for Erna. The only thing keeping her nerves in check.

"*Russian* vodka?" With the kind of suspicious emphasis on the word that only a former counterintelligence man could achieve.

"We're much nearer to vodka right now than schnapps," Alexsi observed. A nod to Erna. She got up and fetched it, handing them three glasses.

"I thought you didn't drink," said Ressler.

"I'm still the same," said Alexsi. "But I'll have a sip to wish you good luck before I leave."

"You're leaving?" said Ressler.

Alexsi glanced at his watch. "I have to meet a man about another truck in a half hour."

"You don't say," said Ressler.

"Yes, I do," said Alexsi. "They don't grow on trees in this country, you know. I assumed you knew that, since you're not driving one. Though your horse looks quite even tempered," he added quickly.

Ressler just glowered at him.

Alexsi stared back. It wasn't Berlin. They were on his ground, now.

Lieutenant Fuchs came up off her chair and held up her glass to them. *"Prost,"* she said quickly, with that woman's instinct for impending conflict.

Alexsi would have paid admission to watch Ressler mastering the basics of camel handling. Not to mention what was going to happen out in the desert. At night. With a whole string of the filthy beasts. And six SS signalers who had most assuredly never ridden a camel in their life. Forget about the Russians. Ressler and the signalers might never be seen again due solely to their own volition.

Instead of *"prost,"* as they touched glasses he said, *"Tschuss."* The German word seemed more correct. This wasn't Until I see you again. This was good-bye.

58

1943 Qom, Iran

ALEXSI WALKED DOWN THE STREET TO MR. EBRAHIMI, THE grocer. Who had a telephone.

"Ah, my dear Swiss friend!" Mr. Ebrahimi announced.

Alexsi smiled. The neighborhood grocer knew everything about everyone. Everyone shopped there. He delivered food to their homes. He gave them credit. A fine intelligence source, if he had cared about Qom. Which he didn't. He just needed the telephone. They shook hands, because Mr. Ebrahimi thought that was what you did with a European. "Peace and health," he said in Farsi.

"Peace and health," Mr. Ebrahimi said, returning the Salam. "You will have coffee with me?"

"As soon as I impose on your generosity for a brief but important telephone call," Alexsi said.

"Regard it as yours," Mr. Ebrahimi said, gesturing toward the old wooden wall phone behind the counter where he settled the bills.

Alexsi slipped through the shoppers to get back there. The counter with its glass displays ringed the store, the walls of shelves behind it. Mr. Ebrahimi's sons were pulling goods off the shelves for the male customers, his daughters for the women. Because it was Qom and not Teheran.

Alexsi plucked the earpiece from the cradle and turned the magneto crank to ring the local exchange. He had to do it five times before the operator woke up. He gave him Matushkin's number. Everywhere in the world the telephone operators were women. Except the Middle East. And Russian embassies. And in all cases they were about as efficient as you'd expect men to be in that job.

The embassy switchboard finally tracked Matushkin down, and he picked up. Alexsi spoke in Russian to confound the vast majority of those listening on the line. Plus the fact that he had to shout through the mouthpiece to make himself heard. He made a quick but cryptic explanation. "Yes, that's right. On his way now. Him, and the six new arrivals I assume you've heard about from *everyone*. Yes, camels. I know, I know. You need to take that into account, so just blocking roads may do you no good. Yes, if worse comes to worst, at the assembly house. But knowing this fellow the way I do, the end result may be all of them lost in the desert forever. Yes, I am heading to the house myself, just in case they make it there. You will have people in the area to back me up, if needed? I know who is coming in today—don't tell me you don't have enough men. I know you have as many as you need. Yes, I am aware that I am being impertinent again. Very well. I will be driving north soon." Alexsi hung the earpiece back on its hook.

"No problems, I hope," Mr. Ebrahimi said.

Alexsi put some money in his hand that Ebrahimi tried to give back. Not very convincingly, but for the sake of form. Alexsi closed the grocer's fingers around the bills, and they disappeared into Mr. Ebrahimi's pocket. "You know how it is in business, my friend. Always something." Churchill was flying in today after having met Roosevelt first in Cairo. Either that or Stalin already being in Teheran had set Matushkin into a dither.

"Shall we have our coffee now?" Mr. Ebrahimi asked.

Alexsi was sorely tempted. Especially since Mr. Ebrahimi's wife made a wonderful sherbet that went perfectly with her coffee. But he wanted to get to Teheran well before dark. The British checkpoints on the road made the drive twice as long.

And between the British soldiers and now the NKVD special troops out hunting German parachutists, that was too many jittery trigger fingers to suit him. At least he wouldn't be waiting out there in the desert in the middle of the cross fire. "I would enjoy nothing else, my friend. But urgent business calls me away. I promise you, another time."

"God protect you," Mr. Ebrahimi said.

59

STANDING BEFORE HIS FIAT, ALEXSI PATTED HIS POCKETS. Where the devil were his keys? Another search, a bit more frantic this time, and then he realized: he had left the keys on the table.

Damn it. He'd almost been grateful to Ressler before, because he'd gotten him out of the house without Erna's usual withering interrogation on where he was going. Well, there was nothing else to do about it.

Alexsi went in through the front door, without any preliminaries. But the sitting room was empty. Walking through the kitchen, there were no keys on the table where he usually dropped them. This was crazy.

He heard the voices through the open kitchen window, and quickly dropped down out of sight. Ressler and Erna were in the back.

"He's always out," she was saying. "Mostly in Teheran. I think that's why he got the house here in Qom, contrary to orders. He leaves me here, refuses to bring me along, and never says what he is doing. And you know Teheran is full of British and Russians."

"Is that why you left the control signal out of your messages?" said Ressler.

"Yes," she said. "I was suspicious of him."

Alexsi's mouth fell open in outrage. The lying bitch. She'd fucked up and was now trying to put the blame on him. And

Ressler the perfect audience for it. That's what he got for not shooting her out in the desert.

"I haven't been sure about sending a signal about him to Berlin," she said.

"Do it," said Ressler. "By all means."

Alexsi quietly slipped back into the sitting room, pulled the frequency crystals from the radio, and crushed them underfoot.

Back in the kitchen he heard Erna say, "Was I correct not to tell him about the second variant?"

"Yes," said Ressler. "If the main drop doesn't take place, for any reason, we will carry on regardless. It's fine, now. I've been waiting for years to deal with that traitor."

That was enough. Alexsi drew his pistol and stepped through the kitchen door. They were both startled. Ressler was quicker getting to his gun than Alexsi would have given him credit for, but then Alexsi already had his ready.

He'd learned to keep shooting until his opponent went down, and Ressler took quite a few shots. In fact Alexsi thought the thirteen-round magazine might run out before Ressler hit the ground, and it gave Erna time to dash around the corner.

Ressler was on his back. His eyes were open in surprise, and his mouth was moving soundlessly. As he ran by, Alexsi put a bullet between his eyes. At least he knew who had done it to him.

By the time he got around the corner Erna was just disappearing around the next one. Alexsi sprinted hard, but he already knew she was light on her feet. And what happened to Ressler wasn't giving her reason to run any slower.

In another of those coincidences that were doing their best to madden him this day, the street she'd picked to run down was exactly the one where he'd parked his Fiat earlier. And now he knew where his keys had gone, because when he turned that corner she was just climbing into the automobile.

Alexsi fired two quick shots at her, and then the magazine ran out. By the time he got a fresh one into the pistol she had roared off.

All the shooting had aroused the neighborhood, so he was totally blown. As he was tucking the Browning out of sight, two
of the Russians who had been watching them came running up,
their own Tokarev pistols out.

"After her!" Alexsi shouted in Russian. "She knows about us,
and she's headed for Teheran. You have to tell Matushkin: there's
another German team. That's the second variant—he'll understand. They're prepared to attack, and they may already be in the
city."

"What of the other fascist?" One of the NKVD demanded.

"Dead," Alexsi replied.

He had to give them credit; they didn't dawdle. An instant later
they were off in their own automobile. Alexsi hoped they had a
radio.

He ran back to the house and grabbed the keys to the other
vehicle parked in the back. A Citroën P45 truck. He wouldn't be
catching even a Fiat in that, but it would get him to Teheran.

60

THE OLD FRENCH TRUCK WHEEZED AND COUGHED AND bounced as it transitioned from the sand-swept and rutted Qom road to the paved streets of Teheran. There were still more automobiles on the streets than horse-drawn carriages. And now, coming in to the southern edges of the city, just shy of the bazaar, soldiers in the uniforms of many countries. Or, in the case of the British, soldiers of one country in many uniforms.

Past the railway station the rickety wooden homes of the outlying poor transitioned to sturdier brick and better streets. Alexsi had chosen this house away from the busier center of the city, with its noisy street-level shops.

Someone was there. He'd been careful to leave the window curtains open. Now they were all shut tight. Could Erna have reached it and managed to get inside, with the Russians on her tail?

Alexsi drove right by and kept going. He stopped the truck at the first place he knew would have a telephone, a pharmacy. It was all old dark wood and glass cabinets filled with bottles. Old-fashioned scales on the counter. You could practically smell the dust.

"I must use your telephone," he barked as he charged inside.

The pharmacist was an old, gray man who looked as if he might die at any moment. He sputtered under the attack. "I . . . you cannot . . . I have orders coming in . . ."

Alexsi literally threw money at him and took sole possession of the candlestick telephone.

The Soviet embassy switchboard finally picked up. The usual suspicious voices, as if only an enemy of the state would dare to call them. Matushkin wasn't available. And of course the operator wouldn't dare to connect him with any NKVD. It was the Soviet embassy, after all. The neighbors didn't exist. This had to be a provocation to smoke out their identities. Alexsi blustered and threatened, but it did no good. He slammed the earpiece down on the hook and dashed outside.

He left the truck there, trotting down the street and making up a plan on the fly. Of course he had marked out an escape route from every house he ever set foot in. And for this one it would be his way inside.

There was a low wall in the back, where horses had once been tied. All good Iranian houses had walls, as protection from that uncertain world outside. Alexsi climbed up and walked along it until it turned and traveled near the side of the house. Then he was up a trellis attached to the outside wall, which took him up to the second floor. From his days as a thief he'd learned to always go in an upper story. They were never as well locked or guarded as the ground floor. Hanging on to the trellis, he swung over and slipped his knife into the jam of the nearest window. A twist of the wrist and it slid up enough for him to get his fingers under and open it all the way, very slowly and quietly.

Getting a firm grip on the window frame and pushing off from the trellis, Alexsi dangled for a moment in midair before pulling himself through the window. He walked himself in on his hands until all the way inside.

He crouched there, reaching all the way to the back of his waistband to unholster the Browning. He waited carefully, just listening. If you were patient a house eventually gave up the secret of who was inside. Minutes passed. Nothing.

Carefully, to keep the floor from creaking, Alexsi passed

through the room and out into the upstairs hall. He held the pistol cocked and at the ready. It would be a hard day if anyone suddenly appeared behind him, so he checked all the upstairs rooms first. Nothing, though someone had been using the bath. More than one man. Women always left their telltale traces, and never towels on the floor.

Now the dicey part. Down the stairs. Because if anyone was there, and they had heard him, that's where their weapons would be aimed, waiting for him to show himself.

Alexsi resolved not to make it any easier for them to shoot him. He mounted the wooden banister and slid down it side-saddle, just like he used to do at the orphanage when the staff wasn't about. He leaped off just before reaching the bottom and landed in a crouch, arm extended, pistol presented. No one took a shot at him.

He saw something strange in the living room, but he was too wary to go directly to it. Instead he slid around corners, checking the rest of the ground floor first. Even, in his caution, throwing open closets and cabinets. No one there. But the bit of food he'd laid in the pantry was eaten, the sink filled with plates. What in the hell?

Now that he was sure he was alone, back to the living room. And sitting in the middle of the floor was exactly what he thought it was at first sight. A Waffenhalter. A beveled cylindrical container, one and a half meters long, that German paratroops used to air-drop their weapons. A parachute pack on one end, empty on this one, and a corrugated metal shock absorber on the other. Painted in sand camouflage, it sat open on the floor in the midst of the detritus of war. A lot of open and empty sixty-four-round fiber boxes of 9mm ammunition for the MP 40 machine pistol. Hand grenade cases. Blasting cap and safety fuse boxes. A discarded test lamp for a field exploder. And empty wooden crates he had never seen before. They were sitting open, with a rack inside for two of some kind of munitions. But what?

Alexsi flipped the cover over. Stenciled on the front was RMun 4322. Rocket Munition 4322? What the fuck was that? 43 . . . 43 had to be a new weapon, this year? What was new? Agitated, he tried to calm himself and search his memory. Holy fuck! The curse in Russian slipped right through his lips. RPzB 43. Racketen-panzerbüchse 43. Rocket Tank Rifle 43. The brand-new German copy of the American bazooka. It fired an antitank grenade up to a hundred meters.

An automobile pulled up outside. Alexsi rushed to the window. It was an American automobile, but painted in their dull green military color. The two men who stepped out, though, were unmistakably Russians in civilian clothes. Not the pair from Qom, but definitely NKVD.

Alexsi yanked the door open before they reached it, careful to keep his gun hand hidden behind it.

The two Russians went for their own pistols.

"Stop!" Alexsi said in Russian. "Take it easy. I'm David."

The two Russians relaxed. "We're from Matushkin," the leader said.

"Quickly, come in," Alexsi said insistently.

He practically dragged them through the door and over to the Waffenhalter. "You know about the SS sabotage team that's still at large?" he said.

The Russians didn't seem excited at all. "We know," said the leader.

"Well, can't you see?" Alexsi said, practically shouting now. "They were here. They have machine pistols, probably a machine gun, and definitely a new rocket launcher that can blow up a tank at a hundred meters. This is the second variant of the assassination plot."

"We know of this," the leader said calmly.

Alexsi was nearly beside himself now. "You know? Do you know that if they're not here, they're in the house right next to the vehicle gate of the security zone with their grenade launcher?

And they're not fucking here! If you don't have a radio you need to get to a telephone and warn them."

"Don't worry about it," the leader said.

"Don't worry!" Alexsi shouted. "Are you mad? They'll kill the Big Three."

"I said don't worry," the leader repeated, as calm as any man who ever lived. "Comrade Stalin and Roosevelt are safe in our embassy."

"But Churchill is flying in today!" Alexsi bellowed, as if sheer volume would pound some sense into their heads. "He'll be driving in from the airport—" Then suddenly he stopped dead. The entire savage reality of it suddenly became clear to him, and he almost choked on the words. "You knew all about it. You've watched them. You're going to let the Germans kill Churchill, and then eliminate them."

The two Russians glanced at each other. And then the leader said, "Don't concern yourself with things that don't concern you."

It had been a long time since Alexsi had been spoken to in such pure Russian. *Ugadat, ugodit, utselet.* Sniff out, suck up, survive. In an instant he changed his entire posture to one of perfect Russian submission. "Of course, Comrade," he said humbly.

The two NKVD men relaxed.

Alexsi raised his pistol and shot them both.

61

AS SOON AS HE WAS CERTAIN THE TWO NKVD MEN WERE DEAD Alexsi began rooting through the packaging and the Waffenhalter to see if there was anything he could make use of.

He had no choice now. No one knew better than he how the NKVD worked. If he hadn't been made a party to their plot, and he clearly hadn't, then he was already marked for liquidation as soon as it was over.

In the German debris were a few scattered rounds of 9mm ammunition that topped up his pistol magazine. In the bottom of the Waffenhalter a canvas bag with four one-kilogram slabs of TNT. Evidently unneeded and discarded. But no blasting caps or fuse. They might as well be bricks with nothing to set them off. What the hell, maybe something would turn up. He slung the strap of the bag over his shoulder.

A closed metal hand grenade case was sitting next to the open and empty ones. Inside, neatly racked end to end, were three Stiel-handgranate 24. The German wooden-handled stick grenade, what their enemies called the potato masher. Out of the original eight in the case. Alexsi snatched one up and unscrewed the handle from the explosive charge to get a look at the detonator. It was not the zero-delay booby trap that would blow up in your hand. They must have had enough grenades and discarded these as superfluous.

He jammed the grenade handles into his belt and went out the door at a run.

The NKVD automobile was an American Chevrolet 1500 series. American military lend-lease. The Russians hadn't even bothered spraying over the paint. He'd been hoping there were weapons in the vehicle, but no luck there.

Alexsi started the engine and pulled out into the road. He raced through the gears, and upon reaching the end stamped the throttle pedal down to the floor. All his luck had abandoned him. He'd been hoping that another idea, any other idea in fact, would present itself rather than driving at full speed toward a house full of German assassins, in the midst of trigger-happy Allied soldiers. Unfortunately, he could see no other option.

Alexsi clamped his hands on the wheel and flew through the Teheran intersections without a pause, as if his was the only vehicle on the road. The meter on the dashboard read 80, which he would have known was miles not kilometers even if the American engine hadn't been protesting so vehemently.

Taking a turn at full speed against an intersection full of automobiles, he ran over an Iranian traffic policeman's shade umbrella planted in the middle of the street. The poor man dove out of the way for his life. The Chevrolet tires screeched through the turn and Alexsi went up over the sidewalk to get around the stopped traffic blocking his path. That was the one point in his journey where he downshifted.

He sent a horse drawing a carriage stampeding in panic, only the carriage overturning stopping the animal's flight. At the next intersection he rammed another automobile out of his path in a crunch of metal.

He was drawing near now. He plucked one of the grenades from his belt and stuck the metal cap at the end of the handle into his mouth to unscrew it. The cap off, he shook out the porcelain bead on its cord and jammed the head of the grenade into the crevice of the seat beside him.

Both sides of traffic were stopped up ahead, the road packed solid with automobiles. Alexsi swerved onto the sidewalk, pedestrians running for their lives. He could see the house now, that house he'd rented next to the gate of that goddamned Russian cloth fence. And he could see the window on the upper floor thrust open wide enough to shoot a fucking rocket through.

His chaotic arrival was certainly no surprise. The two Russian military policemen halting the traffic emptied their pistols at him as he blew by. But they had helpfully left the intersection completely empty. As he cut the steering wheel, Alexsi's eyes caught the vehicle gate up ahead, the small caravan of automobiles stopped before it, and a famous portly figure casually standing beside one sedan smoking a cigar.

No choice now. Alexsi aimed the Chevrolet directly at the house. He grabbed the grenade from the seat, slipped the porcelain bead through the fingers of his left hand, and yanked hard to activate the friction fuse.

As the Chevrolet sped across the intersection, Alexsi opened the driver door, leaned out with only his left hand gripping the steering wheel keeping him in the vehicle, and hurled the grenade at the open window of the house's upper floor. The windscreen glass exploded from a hail of gunfire and if he had been behind the wheel, he would have been killed. He could feel bullets flying all about. All he had time to do was dive back into the car across the length of the seat.

The Chevrolet crashed into the side of the house. The impact lifted Alexsi up and slammed him into the dashboard and then down onto the floor. It knocked the air from his lungs, and him senseless for a moment. He thought he heard an explosion, but whether it was the grenade or the car hitting the house he couldn't be sure.

Alexsi bounced up, a stabbing pain in his side making it hurt to draw breath and crawled through the open hole where the windscreen had been. Scrambling over the hood and into the house. The Chevrolet was half inside and half out. Slipping over scattered bricks and wood, air filled with dust that had not yet settled, Alexsi stumbled across the living room. A burst of machine-pistol fire from the top of the stairs said that there were definitely Germans alive up there. Alexsi jerked out his pistol and fired a few shots in that general direction, just to keep them from rushing down.

Two long machine-pistol bursts, fired from upstairs down through the floor, stitched bullets through the ceiling at him and blew plaster all over. Alexsi rolled away from the line of the burst, and a stick grenade sailed down the stairs, struck the wall, and bounced into the room.

At least he knew the house. He dove into the next room, frantically yanking one of his own grenades from his belt.

The German grenade exploded with a deafening noise and a jarring blast. Alexsi knew the drill: they'd be following the shock action of their grenade to charge down the stairs and shoot him. He bounced to his feet, yanked the lanyard to activate his grenade, and dashed back into the room, filled with a thick smog of high explosive smoke.

One thousand.

But though he couldn't see, he knew where the top of the stairs was. Alexsi fired his pistol left-handed at the top of the stairs, wildly and inaccurately, but it was just to drive them back.

Two thousand.

The grenade fuse had burned enough that they wouldn't be able to pick it up and throw it back at him. He hurled it at the top of the stairs, not directly to give them a shot at him, but at an angle to bounce it off the wall and into the upstairs hallway. He was ready to run in case he'd missed but it exploded upstairs.

Deafened by the two blasts, he couldn't hear any sound of feet above. Which would have been helpful. No matter. He didn't have much more time. With only him and his pistol against automatic weapons he would either be killed by the Germans upstairs or the Russians coming through the door at any moment.

What to do? Still a little groggy from the grenade blasts he lurched back and forth on his feet, as if torn in indecision between running and fighting. He only had one grenade and one more pistol magazine, and there would probably be another grenade coming down the stairs at him any second. This time the Germans would learn from their mistake and follow it up faster.

It was only that back and forth movement that made him realize he still had the bag of TNT slapping against his back. He'd never taken it off when he'd first jumped into the car.

Alexsi yanked the strap off his neck, jammed his last grenade into the bag head-down, and wound the strap around the bag tightly to press the TNT slabs against the grenade. He unscrewed the grenade cap, grabbed the porcelain bead, took a deep breath, yanked it up, and ran.

One thousand.

His path took him right across the front of the stairs. As he darted past it a burst of machine-pistol fire came down at him, just an instant too late.

Two thousand.

Into the kitchen. Without breaking stride he snatched up a chair, holding it in front of him like the lance of a medieval knight.

Three thousand.

Alexsi dove. The chair punched through the glass of the kitchen window and he followed it out through the opening. He landed hard, an electric jolt of pain shooting up through both elbows. He pushed himself up, to keep running.

Four thousand.

The house blew up.

There wasn't enough explosive in the bag to blow the house to pieces, but when TNT changes from a solid into a high-velocity gas in less than the blink of an eye, the cutting force of that gas searches out the weakness in any structure. The windows all blew out and the wood and glass became projectiles on their own.

The roof raised up and partially fell back in. The rest of the force of the explosion was contained within the house. The entire city block shook like there was an earthquake.

The shock wave sucked the air from Alexsi's lungs yet again. The force of it slammed him back down onto the ground. As soon as it passed it was an unconscious act, a survival instinct that had him blindly crawling on all fours in search of safety as pieces of the house fell all around him.

Only by finally looking down did he see that he was out in the middle of the next street. The entire area was a curtain of smoke from the explosion. Alexsi realized it was perfect camouflage, and probably the only thing keeping him from being shot right then. He stumbled across the street and went to the nearest door he could see. He tried it and it was locked. Alexsi reared back and kicked it in. His mind was moving so slowly. He felt in his jacket pocket. No, his pistol was long gone, somewhere along the line. But he still had his knife. His lucky Russian folding knife tucked away in the pocket he'd sewn into his underwear long before they'd boarded the Junkers aircraft for Iran.

"Hello?" he called out in Farsi. No answer. There was a chair next to the door where you could sit and remove your shoes. He jammed it under the doorknob.

Up the stairs, cautiously, with knife drawn. No one home. Probably everyone in the neighborhood had left to visit relatives rather than be stopped and searched by soldiers every time they ventured outside.

At the top of the stairway there was a ladder leading up to a door in the flat roof. Alexsi cautiously poked his head out. There were a few chairs set up out there. With no yard the roof was where you took the air in good weather.

He crawled across the roof to avoid exposing himself, and lifted one eye up and over the edge. He saw the purple cloth of the Russian security fence and soldiers running down the street from that direction. Brownish-green uniforms that had to be Russian. An occasional fast patter of automatic gunfire. There was always some jumpy idiot shooting at shadows. But confusion was good.

The houses on the street were in a row together, so there was a line of roof stretched out before him for at least two hundred meters. And he'd always loved roofs. Alexsi began slowly crawling down the line in the direction of the security fence. He took his time.

Peeking up over the next-to-last roof, Alexsi saw a Russian soldier up there leaning out over the edge, watching the show on the streets below.

Alexsi ran a practiced eye over the Russian sentry. Then he glanced at his watch and stretched out on the roof, making himself comfortable. It would be dark in a few hours. And that Russian looked about his size.

62

1943 Teheran, Iran

THE GUARD AT THE BRITISH EMBASSY HAD CHANGED OVER AT midnight, and now it was three o'clock in the morning. The private clumped down the path that ran along the inside of the stone wall surrounding the embassy. To his right the woods of the embassy park began. His wool battle dress jacket was just a bit too light for a November evening in Teheran, so he walked fast to keep warm. His breath steamed up the cold air. His rifle was slung over his shoulder. He was dying for a cigarette, but he knew if he lit one the bastard sergeant of the guard would catch him for sure. He reached the end of his section of the wall and faced about. And found himself looking down the barrel of a Russian submachine gun.

"Not a sound, please," Alexsi said in heavily accented English.

The private gulped.

"I mean you no harm," Alexsi said. "If you understand me, please nod your head."

The private nodded.

"I will need you to take me to a senior British intelligence officer," Alexsi said. "It is very important. Do you understand?"

The private nodded again.

"Good," Alexsi said. "You should have this." He handed the private the PPSh submachine gun.

The private took it. He looked at the submachine gun in his hand. Then he looked at Alexsi. Then he screamed, "Sergeant of the Guard!"

63

1943 Teheran, Iran

ALEXSI WAS STILL WEARING HIS PURLOINED RUSSIAN UNIFORM, though the buttons that ran halfway down the shirt tunic were open, exposing the elasticated bandage binding up his broken ribs. Sticking plasters covered the glass cuts all over his face and neck. He sat with his hands folded calmly upon his lap, and through his clothing he could feel the hard outline of his lucky folding knife. The British were no better at searching you than anyone else.

A British officer wearing colonel's insignia sat opposite him, with a pad full of notes. They had been at it for quite some time.

The knob turned and the door opened. And the great man walked in with absolutely no fanfare. He was smoking a cigar and wearing that same ridiculous one-piece collared jumpsuit he'd had on before, with a cloth belt loosely buckled over his girth, two big breast pockets, and a zipper down the front.

Alexsi stood at attention.

Winston Churchill swung the cigar out of his mouth with a sweep of the hand. That famous voice rumbled out. "They tell me I owe you my life, young man. Give me your hand."

With the British colonel watching him like a wary guard dog, Alexsi leaned over the table and shook Churchill's hand.

Churchill released him, and with a gesture that was pure noblesse oblige bid him to sit down. And took the colonel's chair for himself without a word.

Alexsi caught the aroma of the cigar. Cuban. Romeo y Julieta, Uncle Hans's favorite, too.

"Your story has been related to me," Churchill said, his famous lisp even more noticeable at close range. "Quite remarkable. If you don't mind, I have a few questions of my own."

"Your servant, sir." Alexsi hoped that was the right English, since it came from books.

In any case, it made Churchill's eyes twinkle with delight. Then they turned serious. "I am told you are a native Russian, is that correct? A Russian intelligence officer."

"Yes, sir."

"And that for seven years you have been posing as German. Eventually joining their army and becoming a German intelligence officer?"

"Yes, sir."

"Remarkable. Most remarkable."

Churchill sounded almost wistful at the thought of such an adventure. Alexsi wondered if he would have to disillusion the man by telling him he'd been dragged into the entire affair against his will. Blackmailed and threatened at every turn.

Serious again, Churchill said, "My question is this. As a Russian intelligence officer, was it possible that some lower-level official hatched this scheme without Stalin knowing of it?"

"No, sir," Alexsi replied instantly. "Out of the question. No one in the Soviet Union would dare such a thing. No one. Not even Beria. This had to be approved by Stalin personally. There is nothing more certain."

Churchill nodded gravely and drew on his cigar. He seemed lost in thought. And then, "I realize that only one man knows the answer to this question. But perhaps you can offer me some insight into why Stalin would do such a thing."

"You mean plot your death, sir?"

"That is correct."

"I can only guess."

"Please indulge me."

"You are an old-line anti-Bolshevik, sir. A dedicated foe of Communism since the time of the Revolution. If Stalin believes in nothing else, it is annihilating his enemies when the time is ripe."

Churchill didn't miss his hesitation. "And?"

"The Germans foolishly sneer at them. I do not know what the Russians think. But anyone with eyes can see that the Americans will be a great power after the war. Perhaps, sir, just as he was easily able to persuade them to reside in the Soviet embassy where the NKVD will be recording all their private conversations and reading their secret documents, Stalin feels that the Americans would be more easily persuaded in all things without you standing beside them."

Now Churchill was rumbling with outrage. "And he would accept this monstrous risk?"

"Not much of a risk, sir. All the NKVD did was stand back and let the SS assassination team they had been observing all along take position in the house I obtained for them but never intended to be used. I am told the Soviets delayed you at the vehicle gate demanding proper identification? For a period of some time before I arrived? As if they had no idea who you were?"

Churchill nodded.

"They knew that a man such as yourself would never carry an identification card in his pocket. So you have an overzealous Russian private soldier delaying the prime minister of Great Britain over the proper identification required to enter a gate. Just stupidly following his orders to the letter. Anyone who knows soldiers would laugh. And I'm sure you laughed, sir, as you waited for someone in authority to come and straighten it out."

His face fixed into that famous bulldog glower, Churchill nodded again.

"So all the Soviets have to do is make you a stationary target, sir, long enough for the Germans to take a clear shot. Stalin would not care in the least if they mowed down a score of Russian soldiers in the attempt. If the Germans succeed, all the Russians at the gate, and everyone who received the order to delay you, would be shot for criminal incompetence. The Germans who killed you would of course all die. Molotov would attend your funeral with an exquisite wreath of flowers, and most likely weep with emotion. They would perhaps name a street in Moscow in your honor. But if the Germans fail, heroic Russian soldiers gain the credit for saving the British prime minister. It was embarrassingly close, so everyone agrees to keep it secret from the world. And all the Russians along the line of the order will be shot just the same and silenced forever. Stalin takes his chance, and it costs him nothing. You are still his ally today, from necessity, and you will never love him in any case. This is how the man does his work, sir. He does not have to be this subtle in Russia."

Churchill concentrated on his cigar again. "And his work in Russia is as evil as I imagine?"

"There are more in camps than live now in your nation, sir. Unless they have been driven out to die in front of the German guns. Not including countless numbers shot out of hand in dark cellars all over the Soviet Union."

Churchill nodded, as if that was the answer he had been expecting. "One final question. Make no mistake, young man. I am deeply grateful to you for saving my life. But I am curious why you went to such extraordinary lengths to do so."

Alexsi knew this was a man of vast experience. He would not accept being told that it was someone risking his life because it was the right thing to do. His instinct told him to tell the truth. "Sir, when I was in Berlin I informed Stalin when and how the Germans would invade the Soviet Union. I am sure there were other warnings."

"I also informed him," Churchill interjected.

"Yes, sir. He ignored them all. Eventually, every Russian who gave him this intelligence will have to die. Stalin will never let it be known that he sat back and allowed Hitler to invade and nearly conquer the Soviet Union. He cannot."

Churchill went back to dreaming over his cigar.

Very much like Uncle Hans used to. Alexsi thought it was a fine way to make everyone wait while you thought things over. "And as I said before, sir. Sooner or later, every Russian with knowledge of this plot against you, even the very highest, will be liquidated."

"And a man of your abilities could not manage to disappear without a trace?" Churchill inquired.

"I chose not to, sir," Alexsi replied, boiling anger locked up behind his impassible Russian face. He'd saved the old bastard's life. He didn't expect them to kiss him like a Russian, but did he have to go down on his knees to beg the British Empire for refuge? Fine, he'd do it if he had to.

Churchill exhaled a puff of Cuban smoke. "You're quite an extraordinary fellow, aren't you?"

It did not come out as a compliment. Alexsi did not expect anyone to understand his story. All he said was "There is an old Russian saying, sir, that if you live among wolves you must act like a wolf."

A brief flicker of enjoyment crossed Churchill's face, as if he had been expecting another response and liked this one better. Now he rose, and Alexsi and the colonel rose along with him. He put out his hand to shake once more. "Thank you again, young man. We have high hopes for someone of your talents. Colonel—"

An undisguised warning glance from the colonel cut the prime minister off before he gave a name.

"Very well," Churchill said, with barely disguised petulance at being corrected. "The colonel here will discuss these things with you."

"Sir," Alexsi said, confused. High hopes?

They remained standing until Churchill left the room. As the door closed they both sat down.

The colonel rushed to light a cigarette. "The prime minister thinks cigarettes are unhealthy. Ten cigars a day, and they're unhealthy."

"High hopes?" Alexsi said.

The colonel waved out his match. "The German woman you were with crashed her car into a bridge on the outskirts of Teheran. Dead."

Alexsi nodded. No accident, there. The NKVD being thorough. "High hopes?" he repeated.

The colonel drew on his cigarette. "Having you with us is the most splendid opportunity. We intend to play you back into Germany as our agent. We've already begun negotiations through the Swiss to exchange you for a British intelligence officer in German captivity."

Alexsi only nodded. The Englishman smiled, thinking he was in accord. But for Alexsi it was more along the lines of, Yes, that was exactly what I should have expected.

This was what happened when you were foolish enough to tell the truth.

64

1943 Teheran, Iran

THE BRITISH ARMY CHOSE ITS MILITARY POLICE BY SIZE, LIKE their Guards regiments. Except the Guards were chosen by height to appear uniform during ceremonies. The MPs for overall intimidation. The two that were walking side by side took up the entire width of the embassy hallway. Perfectly creased olive battle dress. Gleaming black ammunition boots. White gaiters. White Sam Browne pistol belts. And the military police red covers atop their General Service caps. Incongruously, one carried a covered food tray. The lance corporal was carrying the tray. The sergeant was carrying nothing.

"Don't reckon it," said the lance. "A nice fry up. Egg and b, toast and tea. Treat him nice, they say. Breakfast in bed. But keep him locked up?"

"You don't have to reckon it," the sergeant said, in the way of sergeants in any army. "You just have to take the bloke his bloody breakfast."

"Some kind o' spy, in't he?" the lance said persistently. "Gave Reg Smythe a turn on guard duty, I hear. Pops up right out of the grass, inside the walls mind you, nary a sight nor sound, and put a Tommy gun to his face. Holding talks with Winston himself."

"You lot'll talk your way into glasshouse," the sergeant grumbled. "And you know what happens to redcaps who get locked up."

They stopped in front of the door.

"Hold up," the sergeant said. He made sure he had the key ready in his left hand. And unsnapped the flap of his pistol holster, exposing the butt of the Enfield revolver.

The lance just gave him a look that asked if all that drama was necessary.

The sergeant pounded his fist on the door. "Breakfast, sir."

They both leaned forward slightly, but there was no answer.

The sergeant shrugged and put the key in the lock.

"Suppose he ain't decent," the lance said with a snigger.

"Comedian," the sergeant said. He turned the key and swung the door open.

The room was empty. Alexsi Ivanovich Smirnov was gone.

"Fuck me!" the lance exclaimed.

"There go me fuckin' stripes," the sergeant said mournfully.

Author's Note

Since these are the days of fictional memoirs and nonfiction novels, I feel I should mention that this story is a work of fiction. But as it deals with the history of the twentieth century, perhaps a few final words are in order.

Operation Long Jump is mostly unknown in Western histories. It only achieved any notoriety in the Soviet Union, where it has long been a popular subject of both Soviet and then Russian history and fiction.

The historical record is clear on one point: that Stalin informed Churchill and Roosevelt of a Nazi plot to attack the Teheran Conference. As a precaution the Americans agreed to house their delegation in the Soviet embassy. British intelligence always maintained that they could find no corroborating evidence of any kind, even from their Ultra code-breaking program, which successfully read high-level German communications. They regarded Long Jump as classic Soviet disinformation with the aim of gaining access to the American negotiating positions at Teheran. But their secret archives on the period are still closed.

It is true that most Soviet/Russian accounts of Long Jump are highly contradictory and more reminiscent of their flamboyant wartime propaganda than anything else. Whenever an intelligence agency offers up a public account of its deeds, it should always be regarded, at best, as a tiny kernel of truth bundled up in lies in the service of an agenda. Though the NKVD/KGB intelligence archives opened briefly during the Yeltsin regime in the

1990s, they shut closed again and show no sign of ever becoming public.

Otto Skorzeny was tried as a war criminal, acquitted, and then escaped from American custody in 1948. He fled first to France, then Austria, and eventually settled in Spain. He remained an unrepentant Nazi who helped former SS men escape to South America and sold his military services to, among others, the Spanish fascist government, Argentina, and Egypt. It was rumored that he traded the Israeli intelligence service Mossad information on his clients in order to remain alive. He died of cancer in 1975. Skorzeny always insisted that Operation Long Jump never took place, and that the Soviets used his name in order to make their fictional account more plausible. However, he never denied Operation François, the 1943 SS plan for sabotage in Iran.

Abwehr chief Admiral Wilhelm Canaris was deeply involved in the resistance movement against Adolf Hitler, and after the failed assassination attempt against Hitler in 1944 he was imprisoned and all Abwehr intelligence operations were turned over to General Walter Schellenberg of the SD. Canaris went to the gallows, barefoot and naked, at Flossenbürg Concentration Camp shortly before Germany surrendered in 1945.

Despite being Heinrich Himmler's right-hand man, Walter Schellenberg was a clever enough lawyer to never leave his signature on the record of any major war crimes. As the war ended he was in Sweden unsuccessfully attempting to negotiate a separate peace with the British and Americans on Himmler's behalf. He was captured by the British in Denmark, testified against other Nazis during the Nuremberg trials, and was himself sentenced to six years' imprisonment. He was released in 1951 on grounds of ill health and died of cancer in Turin, Italy, in 1952. Penniless. The French fashion designer Coco Chanel, who was most likely his agent and probably his lover, paid his funeral expenses.

Joseph Stalin died in 1953, as he was preparing to initiate another round of purges. He either suffered a stroke or was secretly administered the tasteless rat poison warfarin by his lieutenants, who took to heart the fate of their predecessors during the previous purges. An autopsy report that surfaced after the fall of the Soviet Union, genuine or not, indicated severe intestinal bleeding that would be inconsistent with a stroke. In any case, his guards were under strict orders not to disturb his sleep, so he lay in extremis for an entire day until the deputy commandant of his residence worked up enough nerve to enter his bedroom. He died four days later.

By all accounts the Teheran Conference of 1943 proceeded uneventfully. There were a number of fires in the city, at least one serious, as there are in any city on any given day.